Lost to Heaven

Book 2

MONICA'S TRIALS

DA Cassidy

This book is dedicated to those who have influenced my belief that truth cannot be fabricated. Instead, it exists without explanation and requires no defense.

Acknowledgements

Venturing into the written word as an artistic expression has been a learning experience that has taught me a great deal, about writing and about life. I would like to thank those who have encouraged this endeavor, since I would never have been able to complete this volume without their support. I would also like to acknowledge some great thinkers and writers that I have either quoted or gained insight from their writings. A few in particular,

Plato (The Republic)

Aristotle (Nicomachean ethics)

Giovanni Pico della Mirandola (Oration on the Dignity of Man)

St Paul (Letters)

William Shakespeare (Numerous references)

John Donne (A Valediction: Forbidding Mourning)

Matt Haig (loosely adapted quote about hangovers).

Thank you all!

Table of Contents

1

After the Fall

Ehndale stood frozen as he watched Thurmond walk away with Monica, the timid companion who had single-handedly ruined his plans. Undeterred, Ehndale contemplated what to do next and considered the methods he would need to employ to coerce and corrupt Thurmond's emancipator.

Kate and Thomas led the small group of friends away from Ehndale and out of the terminal, with Monica and Thurmond following closely behind. They all exuded an unmistakable sense of relief, but Monica was still wary of Ehndale, whom she assumed would be more than a bit irritated with their having ruined his plans. Monica glanced back toward him to see a wicked smile on his face and turned her eyes quickly forward with a shiver like something cold had been poured down her back. Thurmond felt her shutter and hugged her tightly to relay his gratitude for her having saved him from himself, as she had always done.

Looking back at Thurmond, Thomas motioned towards Ehndale with his head.

"Wonder what he's going to do now?"

"Don't know, don't care!" Thurmond replied emphatically.

"I don't know that he's finished with his mischief...." Kate added, "...seems to me a man like that doesn't take no for an answer. I fear we haven't heard the last of him."

Monica still felt the effects of Ehndale's devious smile, and Kate's prognostication didn't help. She hugged Thurmond's arm tighter to get his attention, then looked up at him and changed the topic.

"I wonder where Bradley is?"

"Probably doing some errand for his 'Master'...." Thomas quipped sarcastically.

"That's not fair...." Thurmond replied, "... Brad's had a rough go of it with Becky's passing and all. I think he deserves a little compassion, even if he's been a jerk recently."

"Thurmond's right...." Kate said in support, "...Brad was instrumental in helping us find Thurmond."

"Yeah, only after we threatened him...." Thomas responded.

"We didn't threaten him, Thom...." Kate corrected, "...we reasoned with him, and he understood...."

Kate motioned with her thumb over her shoulder without looking back and continued, "...That man back there warped Brad's sense of right and wrong. Brad needed to be reminded of the kind of man his friend Thurmond was and what was best for him. Brad wasn't thinking straight, Thom...."

Thurmond became curious and asked, "What did you say to Brad to make him want to help?"

Kate replied without hesitation.

"That he isn't motivated by the same things as you...."

Even though it hadn't happened, Thurmond's likely departure had taken its toll on Monica. It was evident in her manner and appearance; she was pale and looked ill. When they reached Thomas' patrol car, Kate took Monica's arm and helped her into the rear seat, where Monica promptly curled up against the car door and closed her eyes. Thomas hopped into the driver's seat alongside Kate while Thurmond got into the back seat beside Monica. Believing Monica was falling asleep, Thurmond carefully reached across her to check that she had locked her door. Monica was awake but did not want to betray the appearance of her falling asleep, so she kept her eyes shut and remained motionless.

Although the anxiety Monica had felt about Thurmond's association with Ehndale was relieved, her mind raced with thoughts of the transgressions Vikki had relayed about Thurmond's behavior during their time apart. Monica loved him and knew that if their relationship was ever going to survive, it was essential that she forgave him for all his misdoings, but it was difficult to let her pain and resentment go. Monica considered her parents and the dedication they had to each other. She wondered if they had ever needed to forgive each other for some indiscretion or hurtful act, intentional or otherwise, and couldn't recall anything other than how happy they were in each other's company. They never seemed to have had anything between them that could have tested their relationship, which made Monica envious. She was doubtful that she would ever be capable of achieving the same.

As they made their way home, Monica struggled to keep from bursting into tears. She knew that would precipitate well-intentioned attempts to console her and that consolation may come at the expense of an admission that she was unprepared to make. After consideration, Monica decided she needed time to heal and think. Now that she knew Thurmond was safe, she needed to take a break from him.

~

Bradley lay in bed staring out a familiar window as a warm glow appeared along the horizon. He had slept only a few hours and was feeling the effects of having spent the previous evening drinking excessively before saturating his system with coffee once he got home.

With a sudden rush of urgency, Brad jumped out of bed and ran to the bathroom. While there, thoughts of the previous evening began to replay in his mind.

Brad recalled standing in the parking lot outside Cây Phẩm's after a rather large man had escorted him out the door. He remembered wondering about the consequences he was sure to experience for having helped Thurmond's friends find him and his trepidation about returning to the cottage at Ehndale's estate, where he'd been staying. Brad was relieved that, even in his stupor, he still had enough sense to return to his old house to spend the night because he knew no one would think of looking for him there. Brad hadn't been back to that old house since Becky's death, and although it was a complete mess, it made him feel safe.

After relieving his urgency, Brad returned to bed and resumed the position he had been lying in for hours. The sun peeked over the horizon and began burning the morning mist away. Its rays moved slowly across the ceiling in a subtle glow before bursting into brilliant rays that announced the new day. The brightness hurt Bradley's eyes and made him squint as they washed down the wall beside his bed. He shut his eyes, and his thoughts shifted to what he imagined must have been a frightening confrontation between his friends and Ehndale at the airport.

Bradley knew Ehndale would squash whatever attempt Thomas, Kate, and Monica made to keep Thurmond from leaving. Ehndale's response would be calculated and terrible in its ferocity. Bradley was terrified of the repercussions from Ehndale for having been complicit in his friend's attempt to dissuade Thurmond from leaving. He knew Ehndale would figure out that he had helped his friends, and he wondered about the wisdom of doing so. His anxiety about the confrontation prevented him from going back to sleep, so he rolled out of bed and made something to eat as he considered what he would do next.

~

The phone cried out and jolted Vikki from a pleasant slumber. She had spent the previous day celebrating the acquisition of the Foundry and was exhausted. The last of her party guests had departed only a few hours earlier, and she had intended to spend the next day in bed.

When she picked up the phone, a voice bellowed on the other end.

"Good morning, my dear,"

"Ehndale? Is that you?"

Devoid of emotion, Ehndale replied, "Why yes, darling, it is."

Then after a brief pause, Ehndale continued, "I'm afraid I have a bit of bad news."

Vikki's mind suddenly cleared. She believed she knew what he would say next, which made her quiver slightly. Ehndale continued:

"Seems Mr. Joseph has reconsidered his decision to embrace the opportunity of a lifetime and has abandoned the plan and missed his plane."

Vikki knew Ehndale was trying to accuse her of being complicit, but she remained stoic and replied, "That is bad news."

"Curious how his former friends could have managed to figure out when and where Mr. Joseph would be departing all on their own? They seemed like such a 'cuddy' lot, don't you think?"

Although she knew she was partially responsible for Thurmond's friends tracking him down, she was in no mood to hear Ehndale scold her for doing so. She considered admitting everything to him and dealing with the repercussions but thought better of that strategy and decided to deny involvement and replied.

"It is, isn't it, curious that is?"

Ehndale had hidden his true temperament until Vikki's snide reply and was having difficulty remaining unemotional.

"Very curious indeed. You see, I have a sneaking suspicion your friends were counseled by someone who knew the details of Mr. Joseph's departure, which is most unfortunate, for Mr. Joseph, that is."

"Most unfortunate," Vikki replied.

Growing impatient, Ehndale continued.

"I wonder if you thought Bradley might have spilled the beans. He isn't all that bright and may have misunderstood me when I told him not to tell anybody. Perhaps he thought I was referring to the weather or something? What do you think, V?"

"Perhaps," she offered tersely.

"Ah, that must be it then…." Ehndale said sarcastically, "I'll have to talk with him about the importance of following instructions. Can't have people in my employ that cannot follow instructions, can we V?"

"Certainly not…" Vikki agreed.

Ehndale ended the call cordially but abruptly. Vikki knew she had made him furious, but she didn't care. He tried to bully her, and she did not wish to be bullied.

Vikki had thought about Thurmond a great deal recently and concluded that the only reason he had agreed to Ehndale's plan was that he felt he was responsible for the horrific crash, a falsehood Ehndale promoted, which she found reprehensible. All she did was allow Thurmond's friends to tell him the truth and let him decide what he wanted to do with his life.

The fact that Thurmond decided to abandon Ehndale's plan was nobody's fault. It was Thurmond's decision to make, not Ehndale's. Besides, Thurmond, now being available, made her rethink her plans for the Foundry.

Her acquisition of and intentions for the Foundry had experienced severe local protests that had developed out of Kate and Monica's loosely organized opposition, which Vikki knew was out of concern for the town and not meant to be directed towards her personally. Although Vikki wished it had been different, she understood and respected Kate and Monica's concerns, but malicious rumors began circulating about her intentions for the Foundry. These rumors propagated a belief that the townspeople considered potentially catastrophic. The most damaging rumor was that she intended to close the company after stripping it of all its assets, leaving the town with nothing while lining her own pockets. This accusation was a scenario unsubstantiated by her actions. Still, it was entirely plausible that since Vikki had done this type of thing multiple times before, she may be considering doing it to Smithworks, but that all changed when Thurmond re-entered the picture.

With Thurmond, everything was different. She saw potential where there was none. He could undoubtedly run the operation and would make an excellent Chairman. He knew everything about the day-to-day operations of the Foundry. He knew all the clients, and they all liked him. He had also become a celebrity because of his role in the trial. Vikki knew she could use that to leverage a considerable marketing plan, which would help promote the company expansion she was considering. She knew the company's running was inefficient, but she could make it much more profitable with Thurmond's help. She wasn't going to let Ehndale make her feel guilty about taking advantage of Thurmond becoming available. They both knew he was an asset. She was doing business the best way she knew how and had Ehndale been in her shoes, he would have done the same; after all, it wasn't personal; it was just business.

2

Commencement

Bradley had no plan other than to stay alone at home for as long as he could to remain hidden from Ehndale. He avoided all contact and went to great lengths to ensure that the old house still appeared vacant, as it had been since Becky's passing. He drew the shades and used no lights of any sort, and under no circumstances did he ever venture outside. He rationed his food by being frugal in its consumption and made frequent use of the stockpile of alcohol that Becky had stored in their basement, which he drew upon to curb his appetite for both food and companionship.

When his provisions were finally exhausted, Bradley had to decide whether to procure some food or drink himself to death, which turned out to be more difficult than he could have ever imagined. After weighing the options, Bradley believed that if he went out early enough in the morning, he could avoid people who knew him, so he set his alarm to go off before dawn and slowly drank himself to sleep.

The following day, Bradley awoke with a splitting headache, dragged himself out of bed, and washed down a handful of aspirin with tap water. He then put on some old clothes he had carefully selected the night before to help him hide his identity. On his way out the door, Bradley grabbed an old hat and some sunglasses to help further that attempt to disguise himself. When he left the old house, he was careful not to make any noise and did not turn on his headlights until he was out of the driveway and well on his way.

As dawn broke in town, it revealed a noticeable lack of activity which initially surprised Bradley, but he laughed at himself when he realized that it was a Saturday, which meant he had managed to lose track of the days. When he arrived at his destination, Bradley was disappointed that he would not be shopping alone. A handful of vehicles were parked in a tight group directly in front of Chauncey's market, so he quickly pulled around the side of the building and parked behind a dumpster. In his haste, he failed to see Kate's car amongst the vehicles parked out front.

Bradley skulked through the market in a manner that gave the impression that he was intentionally trying to avoid people but was immediately spotted by Kate's son Hunter, who had borrowed his Mom's car to pick up a few things. Hunter had always felt guilty about the car accident with Bradley's wife, and although everyone had told him he was not to blame for what had happened to her afterward, he had always felt partially responsible.

At the time of Mrs. Ballard's funeral, Hunter was in the hospital recovering from his injuries and never had the opportunity to express his condolences to Mr. Ballard. He wondered if this was the opportunity he had been hoping for and decided it was as good a time as any. He patiently waited for the right moment to approach Mr. Ballard, and when Bradley stopped at the end of an aisle and removed his sunglasses, Hunter quietly advanced in his direction.

Straining to read the label of an item he had taken off the shelf, Bradley was utterly unaware that Hunter was approaching. He softly read the ingredients on the label aloud, and when Hunter had drawn close enough to hear, he stopped and politely said,

"Good morning, Mr. Ballard...".

Bradley was alarmed that he had been discovered but was relieved that it was not Ehndale's voice he had heard. Without redirecting his attention from what he was doing, Bradley placed the item he had been holding back on the shelf and, without looking at who was addressing him, replied, "Good morning...".

Hunter had not considered how to begin to express his condolences for the loss of Mrs. Ballard and was unsure where to start. To keep the conversation going, he asked how Bradley was doing, and without consideration to whom he was saying it, Bradley replied with the first thing that came to mind and answered, "Killing me!"

Bradley then looked up to see whom he was addressing, and a sinking feeling came over him when he saw it was Hunter. Unsure of why Mr. Ballard said what he did, Hunter assumed it to be an attempt at humor, managed a weak smile, and replied, "Good one, Mr. Ballard."

Neither of them knew what to say next, and a short awkward silence ensued. After a few moments, Hunter decided it was probably best to abandon his attempt at reconciliation and said, "It was nice to see you, Mr. Ballard. I just wanted to say hello. Take care of yourself now and have a nice day."

Hunter left the store considering some rumors he had heard about Bradley and wondered if any of them were true. At the same time, Bradley tried to rationalize his distasteful response, but the more he thought about it, the more ashamed he became.

Bradley hastily filled his cart with groceries and quietly left the market. As he loaded everything into his car, he thought about Hunter, Becky, and the events of that horrible evening. Bradley remembered just leaving them both there and was ashamed that they could have both died that night. As he drove home, Bradley wondered if the kid harbored any resentment.

Surprised at how easily his remorse returned, Bradley questioned his accountability for the car accident once again and the aftermath that led to Becky's suicide. He remembered how easily Ehndale had reasoned away the guilt and had convinced him of his innocence.

'Circumstances affect the outcome and should be considered when assigning blame…' he recalled Ehndale saying, '…It stands to reason that when one is forced to make a hasty decision, which, once rendered, causes injury or harm, neither the victim nor the perpetrator can be held accountable if the circumstances are beyond their control. That is the very definition of FATE, my dear boy, which is thankfully in the hands of those more deserving of wielding that power than oneself! Wouldn't you agree?"

Ehndale had a talent for obfuscating things using an enigmatic logic that contradicted obvious facts. This tendency enabled him to make people question themselves, even when they were confident in their beliefs and unwavering in their convictions. He was also very fond of using analogies to make his point and had used one in this case that had stuck with Bradley, so he adopted it to relieve himself of his anxiety about what had happened to his wife.

It was simple in its premise and, therefore, quickly recalled. Ehndale reasoned that it was difficult to assign blame even if it was easy to assume guilt and continued.

'You cannot blame water for carrying a boat over a waterfall because somebody was incapable of tying a proper cleat hitch. On whom does the fault lie in that scenario? The person who could not tie the hitch, or the person asking them to tie it. It certainly isn't the boat's fault, and one could also argue that it's not the fault of the person who requested the knot to be tied, especially if they had no idea that the person they requested to perform the task was not capable of doing so. It may not even be the fault of the person who could not tie the knot properly, especially if they were instructed to follow directions without question or delay. How could you blame them if they were required to do something they were not qualified for or capable of doing, especially if they were denied the ability to question that decision by conveying that they were incapable?"

Bradley turned off the main road and headed home down a lengthy side street as he thought about his conversation with Ehndale.

'Therefore, it stands to reason that unless the rope or cleat were defective, the 'circumstances' would be the only thing that could logically be blamed, not the individuals involved.'

Bradley remembered asking Ehndale whether he was more like the person requesting the knot to be tied or the person tying the knot, to which Ehndale had replied, 'Neither would be responsible, so why would it matter which you were, my dear boy? You see, the accident and your wife's unfortunate demise were the results of many things, none of which could be said to have been primarily responsible.'

Then as more of an admission than a question, Bradley had asked, "What if I fell asleep while I was driving?'

'And what of the other driver?' Ehndale immediately replied, '…was he distracted or distraught? Perhaps he was asleep at the wheel. And Rebecca? Is she above culpability? If she had been more providential and curtailed her excessive drinking, she would probably have been more attentive and recognized that you were tired and needed relief or assistance. One could argue that she was the one who was ultimately responsible for the accident!"

Bradley didn't understand how Becky could be responsible, so Ehndale explained, "Your reluctance to admit your poor wife's role in the accident is unwarranted. She had as much responsibility to ensure your safe passage as you did hers, and she was negligent in that regard.'

Ehndale laughed when Bradley reminded him that Becky was dead drunk and sleeping when the accident occurred. Ehndale explained, 'Over-imbibing does not exonerate her from responsibility, my dear boy. You were the one acting responsibly, and you were the one who took it upon yourself to care for her. She put herself in such a state to be unable to make any decisions independently. You recognized the need for her to go home, and she declined to accept any responsibility for her own care, never mind yours. You took risks while she abandoned her obligations, making her responsible for the incident."

Ehndale's logic confused Bradley, but it made sense somehow. Ehndale continued, 'Your concern for her is admirable, my dear boy, but her selfish reliance on you may have been the actual cause of the accident. Why should you be punished for being concerned? Why should you suffer the consequences of her irresponsible and selfish behavior? You did not tell her to get drunk. She was responsible for her actions. She would not have done it without assuming she could rely on your help, which is selfish. So, you see, responsibility for the entire affair needs to be focused on where it truly belongs! That is why I counseled you to put her behind the wheel and leave. You were probably just as tired as she was, if not more so, but you were the one who took it upon yourself to make the sacrifice and agree to drive her home.'

Ehndale's explanation did not reconcile Bradley's remorse for his wife's suicide. Bradley suggested that his leaving her behind the wheel made her feel responsible for the accident, which made her suicidal.

Bradley remembered Ehndale becoming annoyed at this confession.

'That's an entirely different issue and entirely untrue!' Ehndale surmised, 'While unfortunate, her demise can hardly be considered your fault. The argument that somebody should be to blame for her suicide presupposes that someone or something other than her own fear was to blame, which was simply not the case! My dear boy, the poor wretch was solely responsible for her demise. Had she waited to find out what had happened to the young man, she would have known that he was okay and never would have considered taking her own life.'

Ehndale's words rattled around in Bradley's brain until his head hurt. Although the logic seemed plausible at the time, it confused him. So, to avoid making mistakes during the trial, Bradley did precisely what Ehndale told him, and everything came out exactly as Ehndale had predicted.

'Don't worry, my good man....' Ehndale had said, '...everything will be fine. There may be the matter of a ticket or a fine, but it will all blow over after that. Just like it never happened....'

Bradley arrived home and parked his car in the driveway of his house. As he unloaded the groceries, Bradley wondered how different things could have been had he not listened to Ehndale.

~

Thurmond had not considered returning to his old job and began looking for a new one when Vikki approached him with an offer of a new position at the foundry that would give him 'the authority befitting someone of his abilities,' as she put it. Monica confirmed that Vikki had joined the foundry board, which made Thurmond seriously consider her offer.

To convince Thurmond to join her, Vikki mentioned that she had arranged an interview with the same board of directors who had unceremoniously fired him during the trial. She further explained that the meeting agenda was to discuss responsibilities at the foundry and invited him to join her. Thurmond was not ready to formally accept her offer, but he agreed to come to listen to what those bastards had to say.

When word spread amongst the employees that Thurmond Joseph was returning to the foundry, they lined up in the parking lot outside the main entrance to thank him for what he had done to help save the company. When Thurmond arrived at the foundry, he was greeted with a surprisingly warm welcome from his friends and former colleagues. A jubilant young attendant named Ben had been dutifully awaiting Thurmond's arrival and became excited when Thurmond entered the main lobby.

"Good day, Mr. Joseph. My name is Ben. I have been given the honor of welcoming you back to the foundry!"

The young attendant scurried beside Thurmond as he made his way through the lobby and continued, '…We are pleased that you are considering returning to work with us, Mr. Joseph. The whole place is 'abuzz' with excitement over the prospect. You are a hero around here, and I wouldn't be surprised if people began asking you for your autograph!"

Thurmond was amused by the young attendant's enthusiasm and joked about signing a foundry brochure Ben held in his hand.

"Oh, would you?" Ben asked, "…I was hoping I could get your autograph, but I wasn't sure how to ask."

Ben handed Thurmond the brochure as he continued, "It means a lot to me that you would think of offering Mr. Joseph! Thank you ever so much! When Nora finds out, she'll be awfully jealous."

"I'll sign one for her too!" Thurmond jokingly replied as he handed Ben back the autographed brochure.

Thurmond then looked back at all the employees still watching him from the parking lot through the lobby glass wall and remarked, "Can't figure out what all the fuss is about."

"Fuss?" Ben exclaimed, "…How can you be so modest, Mr. Joseph? You saved the foundry, possibly even the town!"

"I don't know about all that…." Thurmond modestly replied.

"Nonsense, Mr. Joseph! Everyone here thinks you were called in to be offered a top job. Maybe run the company or something! I would not be surprised if they didn't make you the Chairman of the Board!"

Thurmond was thoroughly entertained by the excitable attendant and smiled as he continued to the boardroom. Ben followed alongside, continuing to shower Thurmond with praise.

"There's a wager, you know?" Ben exclaimed, "… People are betting on what position you will be offered. Golly, Mr. Joseph, and to think we knew you when, and now you will be the 'Big Cheese' around here. How exciting!"

Thurmond wasn't sure what Ben was talking about, but he would be wholly satisfied if they offered him back his old job. After all, how could they expect the company to survive if they let Howie run things? He would undoubtedly make a mess of it if he hadn't already.

Ben then joyfully escorted Thurmond to the executive floor as Thurmond marveled at the extensive renovations around him and wondered what else had changed since he'd been away.

~

Vikki had requested that every board member attend Thurmond's interview and insisted they arrive early to ensure that none of them would be late. As each arrived, Vikki instructed them to leave an open seat at the far end of the table for Thurmond. When everyone was accounted for, Vikki returned to the hall and patiently waited for Thurmond.

When Thurmond finally arrived, Vikki promptly dismissed Ben before kissing Thurmond as she thanked him for agreeing to come. She escorted Thurmond into the crowded room and invited him to sit in the only open seat at the table. Vikki then positioned herself at the table's head and stood beside the board chairman, who was seated there. She waited for Thurmond to settle in, then cleared her throat to get everyone's attention and said, "I believe you all know Mr. Joseph?"

Thurmond looked around the table at the executives he had come to despise and fought to restrain his urge to make them fully aware of his profound gratitude for their decision to terminate him for simply carrying out his responsibilities. He was surprised that they allowed Vikki to control the meeting and quietly listened to her introduce everyone. When Vikki had finished, she invited the board chairman to take over the interview and smiled at Thurmond as she sat in an oversized chair away from the table in the corner of the room.

"The reason we have asked you here today, Mr. Joseph," the Chairman began, "...is to offer you a job at the foundry...."

The pernicious executive then made excuses for his decision to fire Thurmond and qualified that decision as 'in the company's best interest.'

The Chairman explained that, after much consideration and debate, the board had decided to bring Thurmond back, qualifying that decision again as being 'in the company's best interest.'

Thurmond laughed at the Chairman's retraction and was about to ask if they were ever going to make up their minds when Howie's uncle (the chief financial officer) remarked, "No hard feelings, Mr. Joseph...."

Thurmond thought for a second and sarcastically replied, "No sir, no hard feelings, but I can't help but wonder how this will work. I mean, who's to say that in a month, you won't decide to fire me again, in the company's best interest, of course."

Vikki had been sitting quietly in her chair, allowing things to proceed without her input, but when Thurmond made his snarky remark, she stood and approached the table to clarify. This was the moment Vikki had been waiting for, and she began by addressing Thurmond.

"You see, Thurmond, my vision for the foundry is expansion, and I see your position here as integral to that development."

"Expansion?" Thurmond chaffed.

"Yes, Thurmond, expansion!" Vikki confirmed as she walked around the table behind the company officers who did not necessarily agree with her vision. Vikki continued, "I see the present foundry offerings to be limited and want you to help me expand operations with new facilities. Not necessarily here at Smithworks, but potentially abroad, to take advantage of attractive wage structures overseas, like in Taiwan perhaps. Possibly under a new corporate brand name like CMC Enterprises, the shell corporation I created to protect the company during the court proceedings.

"Taiwan?!" Thurmond exclaimed.

"Yes, Thurmond, Taiwan," she repeated.

Thurmond pointed to the executives at the table and asked, "... and these gents here don't have any issues with that?"

"Nope..." Vikki replied, then continued, "You see, Thurmond, I have assumed a controlling interest in the company, and as a result, I now own the foundry. You could say that I am the 'Chairman of the Board.'"

"You mean these fellas here work for you?"

"Yes, Thurmond, they do," Vikki said with a smile.

Thurmond was astonished. He looked around the table at the affectatious executives, who suddenly began clearing their throats and shifting in their chairs to hide their embarrassment. After a brief pause, Thurmond replied, "If you can get these gents here to do what you want, and you're willing to listen to what I have to say about how things are done around here, then yes, I accept!" Thurmond shouted, then continued, "I'll accept a position here if it requires my reporting directly to you and no one else. If you can do that, then I'm in."

As Thurmond was speaking, Vikki continued circling the table, smiling at the executives who were insulted by the fact that they had let this woman take their company and embarrassed by Thurmond's delight in her power over them.

Thurmond pushed his chair away from the table and stood as Vikki approached him. She extended her hand and said, "I think I can arrange that."

"Deal!" Thurmond shouted as he happily and heartily shook the hand of his new employer.

3

Celebration

Thurmond was excited about the recent developments at the foundry and drove home, imagining how different things would be there for him now. With the authority Vikki had promised him, his decisions would no longer be subject to the whims of the bumbling executives, who had no idea how to run the foundry. He knew that meant increased productivity, a better working environment, and a more profitable operation. He also thoroughly enjoyed the irony that those executives who had seen fit to fire him would now be accountable to him.

Ecstatic about the prospects, Thurmond could not wait to tell Monica and called her as soon as he got home. Monica had been anxiously awaiting news of his interview and instantly knew it was Thurmond when her phone rang. Monica expected it would go well but mentally prepared herself to console him if it hadn't. She picked up the phone, but before she uttered a word, Thurmond shouted, "You're not going to believe what just happened!".

Monica thought his excitement was a good sign and laughed. She replied, "Hi, Thurmond."

"What are you doing right now, Mona?" Thurmond gasped, "…I mean, at this very moment?"

"I was just getting some supper ready; why?"

"Forget that!" he said emphatically, "… we're going out, you and me! There's lots to tell you, but the main thing is we have good reason to celebrate! You would not believe how wonderful things have turned out, and it's all because of you!"

Thurmond seemed out of breath. His words fumbled over each other as if he was trying to speak before he thought of what to say. Monica was flattered that he attributed his good fortune to her, but she didn't believe she had done anything to deserve it and said, "I don't know, Thurm...."

"Nonsense, Mona. There's no reason we can't go out. You can put supper away for tomorrow...."

"That's not exactly what I meant..." she said sheepishly.

It suddenly dawned on Thurmond that Mona was being humble about her part in his fantastic news and replied, "You saved me from making a horrible mistake, and now everything is turning out better than I ever dreamed. I'm probably happier than I have ever been, and I want to share that with you. I want to take you to dinner tonight to thank you properly for everything!"

Monica knew trying to dissuade Thurmond from believing that she had anything to do with his good fortune was pointless, so she focused on his impetuous invitation to dinner and replied, "Tonight, Thurm?" That's short notice, and I don't know why we shouldn't wait. After all, I just finished making supper...."

Thurmond wasn't interested in hearing about the supper Mona had prepared for herself and said: "Of course, tonight! Just stick whatever you prepared in the oven and put on something fancy. I'll be right over!"

Monica had hoped that Thurmond would be pleased with how things had gone at his interview, but his excitement was more pronounced than she could've imagined.

Thurmond had hung up the phone before Monica could reply, so she knew he was already on his way over. With no time to waste, she put a lid on the stew pot, turned off the burners, and then ran upstairs to quickly get ready.

Monica was proud of Thurmond for having had the courage to face the people who had humiliated him during the trial and wanted to make sure she looked good for him. She rifled through her wardrobe and tried on several dresses until she selected one with a boldly colored floral pattern that she knew Thurmond liked. She slipped the dress over her head and adjusted it as she studied herself in the mirror, then, satisfied with her appearance, grabbed a pair of platformed sandals, and threw a cashmere wrap over her shoulders to complete her outfit. She sat briefly at her vanity to select a few pieces of costume jewelry while she quickly applied some makeup, then grabbed a brush and a clip for her hair and skipped down the stairs like a schoolgirl.

Monica stopped in front of the large mirror in her front hallway and quickly looked at herself before furiously brushing her hair. When she heard someone pull into the driveway, she knew it was Thurmond. She gathered her hair in a bun behind her head and fastened it with the rhinestone clip she had selected. With one last glance at herself in the mirror, she tucked her purse under her arm and hurried out to meet him.

Thurmond had stepped out of his truck and was on his way to meet Monica when she burst through the front door and came bounding off the porch. He had always considered her pretty but was surprised when he saw how beautiful she looked.

"WOW!" he exclaimed, which confirmed that she had made the right choices.

Monica loosened her grip on her purse and slowed her approach. Thurmond stood waiting and offered her his arm, which she took as he escorted her to his truck. He was speechless until he opened the door for her.

"Mona, you look beautiful! I mean it!"

Monica thanked him for the compliment as she settled into her seat, then glanced up at him and quipped: "You don't look so bad yourself."

Monica tucked her dress under her thigh as Thurmond hurriedly closed her door. He rushed around to the driver's side of the truck and jumped in, anxious to continue their conversation.

"I had to put on a suit for the meeting with the board, don't you know…" he said as he put the vehicle into gear, "…besides, I knew I was gonna get some good news, and I wanted to be ready to take you out for dinner and drinks after."

"You did not!?" Monica insisted.

"Did not what, Mona?" Thurmond coyly replied.

Monica thought he was being cute and repeated her assertion in more detail to play along.

"You may have suspected that you would get good news, but you certainly didn't expect that I'd be able to go out with you afterward."

"Yes, I did…." Thurmond assured her, "…think about it? Why would they call me back after they fired me? I couldn't possibly be getting into more trouble. I didn't work for them anymore. Plus, I knew you would want to drop what you were doing and go out with me. Why wouldn't you? I'm a big cheese now."

Monica was pleased to see Thurmond happy and laughed at his giddiness. As they drove off, she began to ask simple questions about the interview to pass the time and satisfy her curiosity. After a short while, she became curious as to where they were going.

"Where are we going for dinner, Thurm? I don't believe you mentioned it."

Thurmond had wanted it to be a surprise, but since neither of them had ever been to the restaurant he had in mind, he decided it didn't matter if Monica knew.

"Fluke," he replied, "It's a bit of a drive, but from what I've heard, it's well worth it."

Monica wondered what Thurmond considered a bit of a drive and fully expected that she would not like his answer, but she wanted to know and asked anyway.

"How much of a drive would that be, Thurm?"

"Not much more than an hour, maybe two…." Thurmond replied as he began to accelerate, "…kinda depends on how fast I drive!"

Monica laughed and said, "An hour, maybe two? Don't you think that's a little out of the way, Thurm?"

"Maybe, Mona, but it's well worth it. I mean, it's not every day that you get to celebrate the opportunity of a lifetime! Besides, it's on the shore, and it's gonna be a beautiful evening. What better way to spend it than to have a fantastic dinner, at a fantastic restaurant, with a fantastic person to celebrate some fantastic news!"

Monica agreed that their celebration should be memorable, but she was not prepared to sit in a truck for a couple of hours.

"Would you consider something just as fancy but perhaps a little closer to home?"

"I don't mind driving if that's the issue…." Thurmond offered.

"It's not that, Thurm, not exactly. It's just sitting in a truck for that long. I'm really not prepared for it. We can go there some other time, maybe even stay for a few days; make a weekend trip out of it."

Thurmond was disappointed, but a vacation on the shore with Monica sounded appealing, so rather than argue, he focused on celebrating his good fortune with her and decided that any place would do.

"If that's what you want, Mona…" he replied, trying not to sound too disappointed, "…Did you have any place in mind?"

"I did…" Monica began, "…Vikki had mentioned a place called 'Tulaisy' that I think might be nice. She said it's top-notch, and I don't think it's that far from here."

Thurmond's playfulness dissipated when he heard the name 'Tulaisy' because he knew it was one of Ehndale's favorite restaurants. It also reminded Thurmond of his indiscretions during his time away from Monica, which he desperately wanted to forget. Monica sensed his hesitation and believed it might be out of concern for the expense.

"My treat, Thurm. You can't expect to pay for a dinner in your honor, now, can you?"

"That's very kind, Mona, but I wouldn't hear of it!"

Thurmond wanted desperately to change her mind, but he couldn't think of anything short of a confession that would do it. He had no interest in running into Ehndale or explaining his apprehension to Monica and quickly suggested an option.

"If we're going to stay closer to home, why don't we eat at Cây Phẩm? We both know it, and it's less expensive."

Thurmond's suggestion made Monica suspicious because she knew he loathed that place. She wondered about Thurmond's sudden concern over the distance and the cost when he had intended to drive for hours and had already offered to pay for dinner. Monica had been looking for an excuse to go to Tulaisy ever since Vikki had told her about it, but now she wanted to find out why Thurmond didn't want to go. She sensed he wanted to avoid Tulaisy; for some reason, he refused to share, which intrigued her. She smiled at him and spoke.

"Really, Thurmond? You're the one that wants to celebrate at someplace fancy. We can eat at Cây Phẩm anytime. Cây Phẩm is fine if you like simple dinners I can make at home, but I want this to be special. Something we never get to do. Someplace we never get to go."

Thurmond considered telling Monica they may run into Ehndale, but he wasn't sure where that would lead. He also knew that once Mona had made up her mind, it was pointless to dissuade her, so he resigned himself to the unwelcome fact that they were on their way to Tulaisy. He altered their course and said, "OK, Mona. I guess we're going to Tulaisy if that's what you want?"

"It'll be wonderful, Thurm. You'll see...." Monica assured him, then asked, "...Do you know how to get there?"

"Never been there myself, but I know it's just past Pottersville...." Thurmond responded as his mind began to imagine their running into Ehndale and what that might include.

Monica thought he hadn't answered her question and asked again, "...so you're sure you know where it is?"

Thurmond replied, "Thomas mentioned he had gone there with Vikki several times and said it's not hard to find. He said there are lots of signs."

"OK, Thurmond!" Monica replied, "…as long as you think you can get there."

Thurmond found Monica's repeating of her question incredibly annoying, even condescending in the way she had phrased it. As if she was treating him like a child being asked to be truthful, and without thinking about how it might sound, he snapped back.

"I CAN GET THERE!"

Thurmond's response was surprisingly defensive, which stoked Monica's curiosity about what was going on inside his head. Rather than push for an explanation and risk losing the opportunity to find out the truth, she sat silently, believing that she would find out what was going on soon enough.

Thurmond realized his gruff response might elicit questions from Monica, possibly about things he had no desire to discuss, so he changed both his tone and the subject after a brief silence.

"Did Vikki happen to mention what's on their menu, Mona? I was looking forward to some seafood."

"I don't know Thurm…" she replied, "…all kinds of things I'd imagine."

"I guess it doesn't matter…." Thurmond said affably, "…I mean, if Vikki eats there, it all must be good. She has excellent taste!"

While Monica appreciated Thurmond's effort to soften his tone, his comment about Vikki made her oddly resentful. Something about his confidence in that woman made Monica jealous, and she wondered if Thurmond had made similar comments about her opinions on other things. After their brief exchange about the menu, they spent the remainder of the drive in silence.

~

The valet helped Monica out of the truck, took the keys from Thurmond, and disappeared into the evening as the couple stood silently admiring the restaurant's exquisite setting. Monica took Thurmond's arm and lightly tugged it to encourage him to walk with her under a beautiful Porte-cochere projecting from the building's entrance.

Thurmond had been busy considering what would come next and was slightly distracted, which Monica took to suggest his reaction to the restaurant's splendor. When they reached the door, Thurmond unintentionally ignored the doorman's pleasant greeting, which Monica quickly rectified with a gracious smile and a whisper to Thurmond that he was being impolite.

The elegant illumination inside the restaurant revealed tufted leather banquettes, burgundy lacquer walls, chocolate-colored lounge chairs, and a floor-to-ceiling wine display behind a long bar. Everything was just as Monica had imagined, except how intimate the expansive restaurant felt, which she considered an attractive feature.

The couple stopped in front of the maitre'd station and explained how they had come for a spontaneous celebration and did not have time to make a reservation. The maitre'd smiled politely at Monica and replied.

"It is the restaurant's policy, Madame, to make reservations. I am sorry, but it is impossible to dine with us without one."

Thurmond was relieved to hear the news but was careful not to show his relief. Monica, however, was undeterred and persisted.

"Can you make an exception? We have come a long way to celebrate our good fortune here."

The young maitre'd brought Monica's attention to the number of people dining and said, "Madame, one cannot question the wisdom of your desire to have your celebration here with us, and I wish I could make an exception in your case, but as you can see, we are busy, so without a reservation, it just simply is not possible. Pardonnez-Moi madame et monsieur."

Monica was tremendously disappointed but resigned to the situation and politely thanked the young maître d, who quickly flitted away to greet the other patrons. Thurmond saw the disappointment on Mona's face and became annoyed with what he considered the smug maître d's lack of empathy. Forgetting his reasons for not wanting to stay, Thurmond quickly surveyed the restaurant to see if he recognized someone he might have met through his brief association with Ehndale. He hoped to solicit their assistance to help salvage their celebration plans and alleviate Monica's disappointment. After a few moments, Monica heard a woman's voice coming from behind them that seemed to be addressing her.

"I thought that was you?"

Monica turned to see who was addressing them and saw a beautiful woman approaching whom she did not recognize. She prepared to apologize for not remembering who the woman was, but the strange woman walked directly past her. Monica suddenly realized the woman was addressing Thurmond.

"TJ, darling!" the woman exclaimed, "How are you? I was just thinking about you!"

Thurmond blushed instantly when he recognized the beautiful woman as Adisa, the seductive indiscretion he had been introduced to at one of Ehndale's soirees. Bewildered, Thurmond stood still as Adisa walked straight up to him and passionately kissed him without concern for Monica, who realized that this woman must have been someone Thurmond had been with when they were apart.

Embarrassed, Monica didn't know how to react and decided to remain silent.

The strange woman quickly summoned the young maitre'd, who hurriedly excused himself from the patrons he had been chatting with to scamper back to his station.

"Harold…" Adisa gasped, "Don't you recognize Mr. Joseph? He is terrific friends with Mr. Ehndale! I'm surprised at you!"

"I beg your forgiveness…" the maitre'd sheepishly replied as he quickly ran his finger down the reservation list.

"Don't worry, Harold…." Adisa offered, "… I'm dining alone this evening. TJ can sit with me."

Adisa noticed Thurmond looking at Monica and added, "…your friend can come too, TJ, if she would like to join us for dinner?"

Monica didn't like how this strange woman clung to Thurmond's arm and thought she would rather leave than spend another second with her. Monica replied as courteously as she could.

"We sincerely appreciate your offer Miss, but we are out to celebrate something personal between us and would rather do it alone. Thank you for your generous offer just the same, but we can find another establishment to celebrate."

Adisa gently released Thurmond's arm and stepped back to look at the couple together. "I see…" she replied with a sinister grin "…is it something involving a choice between blue and pink? Will there be champagne? I love champagne!"

Monica became annoyed with the woman's insinuations and said, "I don't believe that we've been formally introduced. My name is Monica, Thurmond's fiancé, and we are here to celebrate our engagement!"

Thurmond's jaw dropped as Adisa giggled before she excused herself and flitted away. Not knowing why she had said what she did, Monica took a deep breath in anticipation of an unwelcome reaction from Thurmond, but he was flabbergasted and said nothing. Amid the confusion, the maitre'd stated that he might have a cancellation and would be able to fit them in.

"That won't be necessary…." Monica said graciously, "…but thank you anyway."

Thurmond stared speechless at Monica, who calmly took his arm and led him slowly out of the restaurant to the valet station, where their vehicle was quickly retrieved. Monica directed Thurmond to sit in the passenger's seat while she got behind the wheel and began driving to the restaurant by the shore.

4

Proposal

The drive to the shore seemed endless as Monica considered what she would say regarding her shocking announcement about their engagement. Thankfully, Thurmond had dozed off, but she knew that only delayed the inevitable. She gripped the wheel tightly in nervous anticipation of a series of awkward questions and took advantage of his drowsiness to consider what she would say and, more importantly, what it would mean.

By the time they arrived, it had gotten quite late, and Thurmond had fallen fast asleep. The restaurant was dark and appeared closed, but several vehicles remained parked alongside the expansive wood building. Monica pulled off the road into the parking lot, and the sound of shells crushing beneath the truck's tires awakened Thurmond from his deep slumber.

After such a long drive, Monica was not interested in returning home and recommended they look for a place to stay for the evening. Thurmond looked out his window and, noticing a few people gathered on a rear deck overlooking the water, suggested that even if the restaurant were closed, the bar was likely still open, and they should at least stop in for a few drinks. Monica was hesitant but agreed.

They saw a young man methodically flipping chairs atop empty tables in a large but unoccupied dining area when they entered the restaurant. The room's rear wall was mostly glass, which afforded a panoramic view over the deck to the ocean. Off to one side was an impressive bar that extended almost the entire length of that wall. A row of high cushioned stools was positioned uniformly along the front of the bar, temporarily occupied at its far end by a few customers who had come in from the rear deck to order some drinks.

Thurmond stepped to the bar and plopped onto a stool as Monica silently sat beside him. Thurmond anxiously watched the lone bartender attend to his other customers as Monica waited for the uncomfortable questions she knew would be coming from Thurmond. The bartender finished what he was doing and slowly walked over to them. When he greeted them, they both told him they were tired, thirsty, and hungry.

"I can help you with the thirsty part…" the bartender quipped, "…but we have no rooms here, and the kitchen closed almost an hour ago. I do have some bar snacks, though. Would you like some to tide you over?"

"You're very kind…." Monica replied, "… we'd also have a couple of sparkling waters to start and two highballs, please."

"Any preference for the highballs?" the bartender asked as he filled a bowl with a mix of nuts and pretzels.

"We're not particular…." Monica replied, "…you choose."

"Very good…" the bartender responded as he placed the bowl of snacks in front of the weary couple.

Thurmond immediately grabbed a handful from the bowl and stuffed it into his mouth while Monica took a single pretzel and continued, "We've driven a long way and could use a place to stay for the evening. Do you know of a place that could accommodate us this late?"

"Óstán Drew," the bartender quickly suggested, "… it's an Irish Inn, and it's always open. Make a left at the grocery store's stoplight, and it's half a block down on your left. They're friendly and accommodating, and I know they have rooms available…" the bartender said as he leaned forward and continued with a wink "… don't tell anyone, but I know that because I stopped in for a pint on my way to work earlier."

The bartender reached into a cooler beneath the bar and withdrew two bottles of sparkling water. He deftly removed the caps with a church key he had pulled from his rear pocket, and as he was about to place the bottles on the bar top, Monica grabbed one from his hand and immediately drank half the contents. The bartender laughed and handed the second bottle to Thurmond, then pulled two chilled glasses from a bin beside the cooler and filled them with ice.

Without looking up, the bartender continued, "If you're going to be here tomorrow night, I can make dinner reservations for you now. Óstán Drew serves good ale and humor, but their food takes some getting used to."

Monica found the attractive bartender a welcome distraction from the predicament she found herself in with Thurmond and unknowingly stared at him. He was charming, handsome, and uncomplicated; best of all, she owed him nothing. Although she was not in the habit of thinking such things, she was exhausted and had abandoned her usual caution without any concern of reprisal or reproach from Thurmond.

Conversely, Thurmond seemed to have shaken off his fatigue and attentively watched Monica. He didn't appear perturbed by Monica's interest in the handsome bartender. Still, when Monica realized that Thurmond had been watching her, she became embarrassed and quickly picked up a menu to redirect her attention. Thurmond washed down his mouthful of snacks and asked.

"Are you going to tell me what just happened back there? We never talked about anything like that before, and I don't know what it means?"

Monica understood his confusion and knew she had drastically overreacted. She wanted to avoid talking about what had happened at Tulaisy, but she knew Thurmond deserved some answers. Monica placed the menu on the bar as Thurmond took a long swig of water before turning to face her and repeating his question.

"Don't misunderstand me, Mona. I'm happy about it if it means what I think it means, but I don't want to assume anything, which is why I need to know."

Monica had always believed she would marry Thurmond, but she also knew there were no guarantees. She imagined that Thurmond would come up with some slightly childish but adorable way of proposing to her, but she had always imagined the proposal would come from him. She never dreamt it would happen this way, but something about that woman they'd met at Tulaisy infuriated her. Her insinuation about Monica's being pregnant was disturbing, and not knowing what was between Thurmond and her was unsettling.

"Well, Mona? Are we going to talk about it," Thurmond asked, "…or would you rather we leave it alone for now?"

"Can we discuss it later, Thurm?" Monica asked quietly, "I'm tired, and I want us to celebrate your success at work. Can we wait until tomorrow to discuss it and enjoy tonight for what it is?"

"Of course, Mona. Whatever you want…." Thurmond replied.

The bartender placed their highballs in front of them, and Monica immediately lifted her glass. She sipped her drink and nodded at the bartender to let him know she approved, then lifted it towards Thurmond and proposed a toast.

"To prudence and perseverance!" she remarked, "…may you always have the wisdom to allow one to help you achieve the other!"

When she finished her toast, she clinked her glass into Thurmond's and finished it in one gulp.

"Why do I get the feeling you've done this before?" Thurmond remarked light-heartedly. Monica laughed before replying.

"That's likely because I have…" she quipped.

"When?" Thurmond asked incredulously.

"Do you think I never go out, Thurm?" Monica asked, "…that I have no exposure to anything but the bowling alley and Kate's?"

"What's wrong with the bowling alley and Kate's?" Thurmond asked, feigning bewilderment.

"Nothing…" Monica replied, "…but there's more to life than burgers, pizza, coffee, and beer."

"There is?" Thurmond asked jokingly.

Monica knew he was kidding and laughed, which made her feel good. The heaviness of her anxiety waned as they enjoyed each other's company until they had finished several rounds of drinks. When they agreed it was time to retire for the evening, they thanked the bartender for his hospitality, paid their bar tab, and left the restaurant for the Irish Inn.

Thurmond was happy and had forgotten all about Monica's shocking announcement. Still, the memory of the kiss Thurmond had received from that woman flashed in Monica's mind and made her wonder what she would say when Thurmond brought up her announcement of their engagement.

When they retired to their separate rooms for the evening, Monica called Fr. Elias to schedule an appointment for when they returned to discuss her doubts and fears regarding Thurmond's indiscretions and the couple's possible future together. She had no interest in mentioning it to Thurmond, as she considered it part of her marriage preparation now that that possibility was on the table.

~

Monica awoke early the next morning and slipped a note under Thurmond's door to let him know she was going for a walk along the beach. She had insisted that they stay in separate rooms to ensure no misunderstandings about what was intended by her shocking announcement the previous evening.

The waterfront was a short walk from the Inn through town, which Monica enjoyed taking alone. When she arrived at the town beach, she found a modest boardwalk on the far side of the parking lot that provided a path up and over the dunes and down to the beach. Monica enjoyed the sound of the ocean, and with her shoes in her hand, she stepped off the boardwalk and slowly approached the surf.

Her dress billowed in the morning's gentle breeze, and a mist blown from the ocean's cresting waves began to sprinkle her face with saltwater. The sand made a curious noise against the soles of her feet, which sounded like fine sandpaper running gently over a wood board, which surprised and delighted her.

The morning light was still dim, but Monica could make out the silhouette of a young man jogging along the beach towards her and two women chatting with dogs playing at their feet. She also noticed a couple engaged in an embrace further down the beach, which made her think of Thurmond and the previous evening's events.

'What am I going to do?' she wondered, '…Thurmond deserves an answer, and I don't know what to tell him.'

Lost in her thoughts, Monica wandered along the water's edge and only realized that Thurmond had come down to join her when she heard him calling her name. She stopped and turned to see him jogging down the beach towards her. He was wearing the same clothes he had worn the previous evening, which made her laugh when she realized that she was as well.

"Penny, for your thoughts…." Thurmond said as he stepped up beside her and clumsily removed his shoes.

"Good morning Thurm. How did you sleep?"

"Very well, thank you, and you?"

"Well enough…" she replied, "…but not as good as I should have hoped."

Thurmond wasn't sure what she meant by that but decided to leave it alone. He walked beside her, put his hand around her waist, and pulled her closer to kiss her, but Monica felt a sudden need for space. Thurmond immediately noticed her awkward body language and desisted in his attempt to kiss her.

"Anything wrong, Mona?"

"Nothing and everything, Thurmond…" she replied as she reached out to take his hand.

Monica led him along the surf in complete silence as she watched the waves wash over her feet. Thurmond collected his thoughts as they walked. There was much to talk about, but Thurmond didn't know where or how to begin. After what seemed like an eternity, he broke the silence.

"I get it, Mona…" he began, "…I understand that last night at Tulaisy was probably an uncomfortable moment for you. I mean, Adisa probably deserved to be reprimanded…."

Monica stopped abruptly and let go of Thurmond's hand. She turned to face him and looked deeply into his eyes and asked.

"Then why didn't you reprimand her, Thurm?"

Thurmond could think of nothing to say in his defense except that he was sorry. Monica put her hand on his cheek to let him know she wasn't angry.

"What happened when that man coerced you into doing things you would never have done is none of my business, Thurm. What you did or did not do while we were apart is up to you to divulge when and if you ever feel the need to do so."

Thurmond began to feel ashamed and feared what Monica would say next. He braced himself for what he believed would be a verbal thrashing, but Monica surprised him.

"…I love you, Thurm, and I always will. You're a good, decent man, and I need to come to grips with the fact that there is a void in our relationship that may never be filled. That's my burden, not yours."

Thurmond remembered how empty he felt at the airport when Monica relayed that Vikki had told her everything. He didn't know what that meant precisely, and he couldn't ask, so he wasn't sure of the extent of what she knew. He had hoped that certain indiscretions had not been conveyed, but even if they hadn't, he felt ashamed just the same.

"I'm so sorry, Mona. I can never apologize enough for everything I did, but I was certain my life was over, and I had no hope of ever returning to my old life. You must understand that I gave up and felt like I was being controlled like a marionette with Ehndale pulling strings."

Thurmond felt himself beginning to cry but immediately got control of his emotions, wiped his eyes quickly, and continued.

"I will tell you whatever you want to know, Mona, so we can put this all behind us. I'd rather you know everything than keep secrets between us. I hope you will truly find it in your heart to forgive me, but if you cannot get past it, so be it. I only want you to be happy and wish you could be happy with me."

Monica took Thurmond's hand and replied, "I understand, Thurm...."

Monica hadn't given Thurmond the answer he sought, which made him worry, but he didn't know what else to say. He looked into her eyes and let the first thought that popped into his head come out of his mouth.

"I want you to know, Mona, that I am only truly happy when I'm with you. You make me want to be a better man."

Monica smiled and replied:

"I will never ask you to fill in the blanks, Thurm, unless you feel the need to do that yourself. I would rather put all that nonsense behind us and start anew like nothing ever happened."

Monica could see the relief on Thurmond's face as she spoke but wondered if she truly meant everything she was saying. She was trying to make peace, potentially even at the expense of her own happiness. She felt the need to relieve Thurmond of the burden he carried but had doubts about being with him and was experiencing emotions she had never experienced before. Monica kissed him to reassure him but was still as unsure of herself as she had ever been.

~

Because of how infrequently they visited the shore and how far they were from home, Thurmond and Monica agreed to spend the entire day there together that next day, so after their walk along the beach, they purchased some new clothes in town and ventured to see what else they could find.

They ate lunch at a quaint beachfront seafood shack on a local pier, then took a long stroll through town. Monica noticed a library on their walk and intended to spend a little time there. Thurmond thought he might sneak off to a local jewelry store he had seen to look at some engagement rings while she was there. However, their plans changed when they stopped at a local candy factory they had found for what turned out to be a prolonged visit to sample some saltwater taffy and ice cream.

The two had such a wonderful day together that when they returned to the restaurant they had been to the night before for dinner, Monica didn't notice the handsome bartender until he made a point to welcome them back. The service was swift, and the food was delicious, just as the bartender had told them it would be. However, even though there was no mention of Tulaisy nor the conversation they had on the beach that morning, it had been on both their minds all day and a silent tension was mounting.

Uncertain about how she would approach her conversation with Fr. Elias, Monica spent a great deal of time on the ride home that evening pretending to be asleep so she could think about what she'd confess to the priest. She carefully considered what she would say, but she had no idea how it would go.

~

Monica wore a simple crocheted shawl over a modest but elegant dress and pinned her hair under an ivory cloche hat. She stepped onto the second empire rectory's rickety wooden porch and rang the bell beside the double front door. She waited a few minutes for an answer and became instantly anxious when she heard some latches being undone inside. One of the doors leaves opened a crack, and her mind went completely blank.

When Fr. Elias saw it was Monica, he became ecstatic. She was one of his most faithful parishioners and a delightful person besides. He threw open the door and proclaimed.

"Good morning, my dear! I was so looking forward to meeting with you. Please do come in!"

Not knowing what else to say, Monica politely asked, "Is this still a good time, Father? I can come back when you're not busy."

"Nonsense!" the priest excitedly replied, "I've been expecting you! Please, do come in!"

Monica fumbled through her thoughts to recall what she had wanted to say, but nothing came to mind. She had hoped that he would ask her to come back later, but when he didn't, she politely thanked him and stepped inside.

The exuberant priest closed the front door and locked it before leading Monica through the rectory. She followed close behind, looking from side to side into the rooms to confirm they were indeed alone. The long, creaky corridor squeezed past an old stair and ended at the rear of the rectory, where she found herself in a large kitchen filled with the smell of some delicious treats.

"Linda has made us a little something to enjoy while we visit, my dear…" the priest remarked, "…Please help yourself!" He then held his prodigious belly with both hands and continued, "…Linda is an exquisite chef, and we are truly blessed to have her here with us."

Monica was extraordinarily nervous and not hungry, but she wanted to be polite. She took a few pastries she had no intention of eating and placed them on a paper plate she held in one hand with a napkin. The priest then handed her a small cup of juice, which someone had already poured out for them, then filled his plate with so many treats that he had to hold them with his other hand to keep them from falling off the sides. As he carefully balanced his goodies, Fr. Elias pinched his fingers around the lip of a cup of juice and led Monica into an adjacent parlor that she assumed was his office.

The room was illuminated by three slender stained-glass windows filled with mosaics portraying biblical scenes and several small lamps scattered about the room sitting on any available flat surface. Bookcases covered the better part of two walls and were filled with papers, knick-knacks, and books of every size and shape. Framed photographs of religious figures and copies of historic iconography covered the remaining wall space. A large wooden desk, littered with paper organized haphazardly into piles, stood near a corner of the room, and behind it was an old leather chair on a swivel with two antique leather armchairs in front.

Fr. Elias put his plate and cup on the desk beside one of the piles of paper and slipped one of the cookies into his mouth. He then held his hand in the armchair's direction to invite Monica to sit.

Once seated, Monica nervously nibbled on one of the pastries before taking a small sip of her juice to wash it down as she thought about what she would say. She then carefully placed the plate and the drink on a table beside her chair and began.

"I'm not sure how to start this conversation, Father, but I know I need to talk with someone."

"Of course, my dear…" the priest replied earnestly, "…just pretend I'm not here and allow yourself to think out loud."

"I guess I'd call it a conflict of conscience, Father. I mean, I feel one thing but think another…."

"Please, call me Eli…" the priest interrupted as he took a sip of juice to wash down the pastry he had just hastily eaten, "…I prefer Eli because it's less formal and easier to say, don't you?"

Monica smiled at his attempt to make her feel more at ease and replied, "Yes, thank you, Fr. Eli…".

"Very good! Now, please continue…."

Her nervousness began to wane, which helped her explain how she had 'accidentally' proposed in a fit of jealous anxiety. Monica explained that although she loved Thurmond, she had doubts about the viability of their relationship. She was careful not to mention particulars about his 'indiscretions,' believing that was something

Thurmond needed to take care of for himself. Still, she explained how a slight doubt in her mind had become a substantial concern about whether Thurmond was indeed the one for her.

Fr. Eli sat quietly eating his pastries, listening to her 'confession.' He rested his elbows on the desk and pressed the palms of his hands against his forehead. He looked down as he listened to Mona explain her hesitation to commit to marriage. The priest remembered the advice he had given to another penitent, which he now assumed to be Thurmond, who had shed tears of remorse for his sins, which Fr. Elias believed to be genuine and heartfelt.

He wanted to help her with some insight into what he assumed to be Thurmond's frame of mind, but because of the sanctity of the confessional, he couldn't reveal anything, even though it would likely help her. He waited for an opportunity to interject, and when Monica paused, he offered his advice.

"I understand your frustration, my dear. It can be very confusing when it comes to love because you're not thinking with your head but with your heart, which is much more generous than trustworthy. I will tell you that the simplest, but by no means the easiest, way to find your way through the tribulations of love is to learn how to truly forgive. That's the key! Forgiveness and patience because, as human beings, we are afflicted with the propensity to commit the same transgressions again and again, even when we are truly sorry for having committed them. It's a condition that exists in all people."

Monica appreciated the priest's words but found no consolation in them. The idea that '...we are afflicted with the propensity to continue to commit the same transgressions again and again...' was a sobering thought that made her wonder if she could continue to forgive Thurmond for his transgressions if he continued to repeat them.

After a rather lengthy dissertation from the well-intentioned priest, they scheduled another time to continue their conversation. Monica thanked him for talking with her and left the rectory feeling like she hadn't accomplished anything.

5

Retribution

As was his routine, Thurmond left early to pick Emerson up on his way to work in the morning. On the drive to his friend's trailer, he thought about the incredible developments at the foundry and the bizarre interactions he'd had with Monica recently, which made him wonder what could possibly be next for him.

Thurmond tried focusing on his new position at the foundry, but the specter of a contentious relationship with Monica was a significant distraction. He desperately wanted to know what she was thinking, but he knew giving her space until she was ready to talk about their future together was probably the best course of action. That way, she would not feel pressured, but staying away from her wouldn't be easy.

To alleviate the anxiety caused by his daunting speculations about Monica, he decided to dive into his work and spend as much time as possible with his best friend, Emerson. He just wasn't sure how much he should share about what was going on with Monica.

~

From the moment that Kate had been made aware of Thurmond's promotion, she had wanted to congratulate him but hadn't seen him since receiving the news. When Emerson burst into the Diner, Kate immediately rushed out behind him and saw Thurmond pulling away from the curb. She ran after him as fast as she could and managed to get his attention by tapping on the rear quarter panel of his truck. Thurmond looked in his side view mirror to see what had caused the noise and saw Kate. He stopped his vehicle, rolled down his window, and said, "Morning, Kate! What can I do you for?"

"Morning, Thurm. I was wondering if you'd like some coffee and pie on the house?!"

Thurmond had wanted to start his day at the foundry sorting through some personnel decisions with Vikki, but she wasn't likely to be there for a while, and Kate's offer made him feel important. Consequently, he flashed a confident smile and graciously accepted Kate's invitation.

"Perfect!" she replied, "… I'll see you inside!"

Thurmond parked his truck and leisurely walked into the Diner, where other customers unexpectedly greeted him with tremendous applause. He instinctively turned around to see if someone behind him was worthy of such a reception, and the Diner collectively burst into laughter.

Thurmond was embarrassed and didn't know how to react, so he looked around until he spotted Kate setting an empty table for him. As he made his way towards her, people began congratulating him for saving the foundry and told him they appreciated the sacrifices he had made to do so. When Thurmond had come close enough to hear her, Kate said, "Here you go, Mr. Chairman…."

"Thanks, Kate, but I'm not sure what all the fuss is about. Is this your doing?"

"Nope!" Kate replied, "…people just wanted to show their appreciation, is all, and I thought I'd join them."

As Thurmond sat down, Kate poured him a cup of coffee and pushed an enormous slice of pie in front of him.

"Your favorite, Thurm," Kate said proudly, "…Strawberry rhubarb! Mabel made it special, just for you!"

"Please thank her for me…." Thurmond replied as he picked up a fork.

While pointing towards the register, Kate said, "You can thank her yourself! She's right over there."

Mable was chatting with Midge, who nudged her when she noticed Kate pointing at them. When Thurmond caught sight of her, he held up his fork and yelled, "Thank you kindly!"

"My pleasure!" Mabel returned, smiling.

Thurmond told Kate he thought people were making too much of a fuss, but she assured him it was all well-deserved and left him to enjoy his breakfast.

Thurmond thought the pie was delicious and devoured it. When he had finished, he looked up and noticed Mable staring at him. He smiled at her in appreciation, then stood to leave but was immediately approached by several people who wanted to shake his hand. Kate heard the mild commotion and stopped what she was doing to rush back to Thurmond's table. When she got there, she cleared his table and said, "That didn't take long. I hope it was to your liking?"

"It was great, Kate, thank you! I couldn't have asked for a better way to start my day."

"My pleasure, Thurm. I just wanted to let you know how much everyone appreciated your sacrifices!"

Kate left him and returned to her duties in the kitchen as Thurmond shook hands with dozens of people who had lined up to thank him on his way out the door.

~

Thurmond was unaware that Vikki had planned for him to be received at work that morning, so he saw no reason not to take his time to get there. Besides stopping at Kate's, he also spent some time at the front guard booth casually chatting with Clarence, the amiable security officer whose company Thurmond had always enjoyed.

Meanwhile, Ben, the ambitious and dutiful attendant, had been assigned the honor of greeting the company's newest executive and had been patiently waiting for Thurmond in the front plaza for more than an hour. When Ben finally spotted Thurmond's truck, he waved him into a parking spot reserved for him directly in front of the main entrance. Ben then ran to the lobby door, used his body to prop it open, and waited for Thurmond.

"Morning Ben." Thurmond bellowed as he approached.

"Good morning, sir!" Ben returned, ecstatic that Mr. Joseph would remember his name.

Thurmond then briskly walked through the open door and crossed the main lobby towards the employee lounge, where he had begun his workday every morning for as long as he could remember. Ben hurried to catch up to him and redirected Thurmond towards his new executive office. As they made their way, Ben briefed Thurmond on his schedule for the day until they reached the executive elevator lobby.

Trying to ignore the excitable young man's effusive blathering, Thurmond stared at his reflection in the elevator doors, lost in his thoughts about Monica and his new role at the company. When the doors finally opened, Thurmond was surprised to see a man he didn't recognize standing inside the elevator cab wearing a dark suit with a cap and gloves. Before Thurmond thought to ask who the man in the elevator was, the man offered.

"Good morning Mr. Joseph and congratulations!"

Thurmond had no idea what to say in reply, so he thanked the man and stepped into the elevator cab.

"Executive level, please, Michael, if you don't mind…." Ben said proudly.

"Certainly, sir…" the attendant replied before closing the elevator doors.

After only a few seconds, a slight jolt signaled that they had reached their desired destination, and the elevator doors opened to reveal something Thurmond hadn't expected.

The previously painted walls were now covered in stained raised wood paneling, and marble tiles replaced the old wood flooring. Where there had been dingy surface-mounted light fixtures were beautiful chandeliers that sparkled in beveled mirrors that flanked exquisite portraits of company VIPs. Beneath each portrait was a handsome table with lavish floral arrangements and a crystal bowl filled with jellybeans.

As they walked down the hall towards Thurmond's new office, the loquacious attendant continued to dispense information while Thurmond studied the portraits on the walls. One painting of a former mentor caught Thurmond's attention, making him stop. Ben was slightly in front of Thurmond and didn't notice that he wasn't still with him, and he continued talking as he walked alone down the hall.

Thurmond smiled and nodded at the portrait as if he was greeting the man in person, then grabbed a handful of jellybeans and stuffed them into his mouth. He winked at the picture and jogged down the hall to catch up to Ben. When they reached the end of the hall, they entered an expansive room through a tall door with a brass plaque with Thurmond's name etched on it.

"Wow, Mr. Joseph…" Ben exclaimed, "… I've been in this room before, but it has always been a mess. They must have fixed it up just for you! It looks fantastic!"

Thurmond was impressed as well and could appreciate the young man's excitement.

"Thanks, Ben, it's something alright!" Thurmond replied while looking around the room and continued, "…if there's nothing else, I'd like to explore the place for a bit, so I know where to find everything."

"Certainly, Mr. Joseph…" Ben replied, "…just let me know if you need anything else, sir."

Ben then rattled off the last few bits of information about a secretary and Thurmond's schedule and closed the door behind him as he left.

Thurmond was finally alone and slowly scanned the room. He spotted a large wooden desk in front of several tall arched-top windows and slowly made his way over to it. As he stepped behind the desk, he ran his hands over the two beautiful leather chairs in front of it and flopped into a third leather swivel chair behind it. He repositioned himself to have a clear view out the windows of the town's hills beyond the vast parking lot. After a few minutes of admiring the landscape, he turned his attention back to his new office decor and took note of everything.

An elegant crown molding ran along the ceiling and wrapped around everything that touched it, including window valances and various floor-to-ceiling bookcases scattered throughout the room. The shelved bookcases were filled with books Vikki had selected for him. Other bookcases featured beautiful granite countertops, which separated the cabinets above from the drawers below. A grand fireplace with a large mantle and a mirror above occupied another wall. The final wall had a colossal tapestry hung above a long antique credenza with a mysterious door beside it.

Once Thurmond had finished surveying the room, he turned his attention to the enormous mahogany desk he was sitting behind and began looking through the drawers when a knock came at the door. He quickly closed the drawers and fumbled to his feet like a child caught sneaking into something until he remembered that it was his office. He cleared his throat and replied, "Come in…."

The door opened wide enough for a plump middle-aged woman to peek her head through. Thurmond assumed it to be the secretary Ben had mentioned and waved her in. The woman timidly stepped into the room and said.

"I hope I'm not bothering you, Mr. Joseph?" she began, "I'm Sheila, your new secretary, and I just had a few things I wanted to go through with you if you had a little time?"

Thurmond had had his fill with instructions from Ben and was not interested in hearing any more at the moment. He politely asked her to come back after he had a few minutes to settle in, and the woman promptly left the room and closed the door behind her.

Once she had gone, Thurmond continued exploring his new office and casually walked around the room. He opened and closed some cabinets and drawers to see if they contained anything. He glanced at books' titles and wondered if there was any purpose or meaning to their selection. He made his way to the front of the fireplace and thought about how nice it would be to have a cozy fire at his workplace instead of a furnace.

Looking back at the tapestry hanging on the opposite wall, Thurmond slowly ran his hand across the top of the mantel, and his attention shifted to the door beside the long antique credenza. Wondering what was behind it, Thurmond made his way to the door and was surprised when he opened it to find a private bath equipped with a shower and a sauna, which made him laugh at the notion of the former executives sweating for relaxation while he was on the shop floor sweating to earn his paycheck.

While laughing about the irony of it, he heard another faint knock at the door.

"I'll be right there…." Thurmond bellowed as he quickly left the bathroom.

When he stepped back into his office, Thurmond saw Vikki sitting behind his desk with her hands folded behind her head and her feet up.

"So…how does it feel?" she asked with a smile.

When Thurmond didn't immediately respond, Vikki continued.

"Makes you wonder why you labored all those years down in the muck and the mire when you should have been up here enjoying all this!"

Vikki flung her arms apart and spun around in Thurmond's chair. Thurmond motioned back toward the private bathroom he had just discovered and replied.

"I always wondered what they did all day. Now I know...."

Vikki laughed, walked around behind the chair she had been sitting in, and pointed it toward Thurmond.

"Here you go, Mr. Joseph. I believe this is your chair?"

Thurmond walked behind the desk, fell into the chair, and softly said, "Never imagined I'd be sitting here...."

"Nonsense!" Vikki shouted back, "... That's your failing, Thurmond! No faith in yourself."

Thurmond looked confused, and Vikki continued.

"You have done everything that needed to be done to deserve it. It would have helped if you recognized it long ago, but what you should be wondering is why? Why did it take all these years? Why did you toil without the slightest expectation that you would be rewarded with a position you deserved!?"

"Yeah, I guess...." Thurmond replied.

"No guessing involved, Thurmond! The truth is they kept it from you because they were afraid. Afraid of being found out."

"I don't understand...." Thurmond replied, and Vikki continued.

"Many people in positions of authority find themselves there for reasons other than their being worthy of it. When that happens, and it happens a lot more than you think, they tend to hide in rooms like these, hoping nothing will come across their desk that would test them. The simple truth is that they're scared. They don't want their weaknesses or incompetence exposed for all to see. I believe Abraham Lincoln said, 'Better to remain silent and thought the fool than to open your mouth and remove all doubt.' A mantra which many of these figures preach to their protégés so they can be safe too, just like them."

"I guess that explains a lot...." Thurmond replied.

Vikki wanted to be sure that Thurmond would follow 'the lesson' she was giving him, speaking calmly and clearly. As she spoke, she walked over to a cabinet that Thurmond hadn't explored and opened the doors to reveal a liquor cabinet filled with various pewter tumblers, crystal glasses, and decanters arranged neatly on beveled glass shelves with a black marble countertop beneath, complete with a sink and a water tap.

Vikki reached under the counter into a freezer and pulled out a few ice cubes, which she dropped into two crystal glasses. She then poured equal amounts of an amber liquid from a decanter into both and continued without hesitation.

"When a capable person comes along, these powerful people feel threatened and become afraid. They realize that if they don't control these 'upstarts,' they risk being exposed as the incompetent cowards they are, which could ruin everything. Unchecked, it could challenge their authority, intentionally or not, and consequently, destroy the security they've built up around themselves while they hide in these luxurious offices."

Thurmond accepted the drink Vikki offered him and intently listened as she continued.

"…and the way they control competent people like you, Thurmond, is they promote you into positions that maximize your potential for their benefit, not yours. They keep you happy by throwing you a bone occasionally to make you feel like they appreciate your hard work, like small salary increases or a bonus. Perhaps they will give you an extra day off or allow you to leave early or come in late. They throw parties to build morale and invite you to participate in company functions where they give you false praise and give you cheap awards to make you feel good about yourself."

Vikki took a long sip from her glass and continued.

"Your 'Gallery of Achievement' or 'Employee of the Year' are perfect examples. They make you feel appreciated when they actually despise you because you know more than them. Because you threaten their security and, most importantly, they know they need you. That's the worst part, Thurmond. They hate you because they need you, which eats them up."

As she paced about the room, Vikki described Thurmond's entire experience at the foundry, shocking him that it had all been by design.

"Those bastards!" was all Thurmond could think of saying, which made Vikki laugh. She continued.

"Yes, Thurmond, those bastards, but the fact is, if you are persistent, if you can wrestle through the punishments they dish out when they feel they have to keep you in line, you will have the last laugh. It never fails."

"How do you figure?" Thurmond asked, and Vikki calmly replied.

"Well, Thurmond, you see, these people have a 'shelf-life,' which means their power can expire, and there isn't anything they can do about it when it does. Either they become infirm from all those years of being afraid and give up their power because it costs them their health, or they slip up and do something stupid, exposing their insecurities and making them weak and vulnerable. Like what they did with me."

Vikki looked straight at Thurmond and smiled slyly when she mentioned herself in her 'lesson.' She finished the drink in her glass and walked back to the bar.

As she poured herself another drink, she asked Thurmond if he wanted a refill, but Thurmond hadn't touched his drink; he was utterly engrossed in what she was saying.

Vikki put the stopper on top of the crystal decanter, closed the cabinet doors, and sat beside the fireplace. Staring into the fireplace, she took a long slow drink and finished her 'lesson' by saying.

"You've won, Thurmond. You waited them out. You stood up to them, and they lost their power as a consequence, and because I took advantage of an opportunity, I exposed their incompetence. As a result, their power is now mine. Mine to do with as I so choose, and I choose to share it with you. Not because I'm altruistic necessarily, although I'd like to think I have that tendency, but because I know your worth. I know what you mean to this place, and I know you can make this place better, more efficient, and more profitable. All this ultimately makes me more powerful and wealthy. It also makes you more powerful and wealthy because you benefit directly from your hard work. And the best part is that you get to do what you do best, what you love to do. What you were born to do."

Thurmond leaned back in his chair and finished his drink in a single gulp. He couldn't believe how clear it all seemed. Vikki's explanation suddenly washed away the resentment and trepidation he had felt all these years. Besides giving him an opportunity that he had never dreamed possible, Vikki also permitted him to be happy.

As she put her feet up on an ottoman and lit a cigar, Vikki said, "Now, Mr. Chairman, what will we do with all these damn executives?"

6

Indignation

Along with several of his fellow officers, Thomas arrived at the library in a police van filled with boxes of books collected as part of a massive effort to expand the library's offerings. They were greeted by Monica and some other library staff members, who were all amazed at the number of books that had been collected. Monica directed Thomas to park around the back, so they had access to a large storage room, referred to as 'The Archives.'

"I can't tell you how much we appreciate your help with this…." Monica told Thomas as they began unloading the van. "…The kids are going to be so excited!"

"It's the least we can do, Mona…." Thomas replied as he stopped to wipe the sweat from his face.

Thomas and his fellow officers had been loading the van since sunrise and packed it to its capacity with thousands of books organized neatly in cardboard boxes. After emptying about half the van, some large pitchers of lemonade were brought out and distributed to everyone in small paper cups. As they took a break to enjoy the refreshment, Thomas asked Monica if she had seen Thurmond lately.

"I believe he's been busy at the Foundry." Monica replied, "Why do you ask?"

Thomas took a long drink of lemonade and wiped the remaining sweat off his brow.

"I've been begging Vikki to take a break so we can get away for a few days…" he said, "…but she keeps telling me she's extremely busy at the Foundry. I was wondering if it was the same with Thurmond?"

"From what I can tell, she's telling the truth…." Monica said reassuringly, "I don't know what they're busy doing, but I know that Thurmond is taking it very seriously. I haven't seen him since he took me to the shore to celebrate his promotion."

"That sounds nice!" Thomas said smiling, "…I wish I could convince Vikki to spend some time at the shore. I know she has a lot to do, but I wish she would give herself a break and take some time off to relax."

The mention of the shore reminded Monica of her trip with Thurmond and her conversations with Fr. Elias. As her mind began to wander, Monica replied.

"Thurmond needs to do what Thurmond needs to do. His preoccupation with that place gives me time to do what I want to do. So, you see, it all works out for the best."

Thomas was confused by Monica's curious response, so to lighten the mood, he attempted to be funny and asked, "What if there is nothing to do?"

Without realizing how callous her response would sound, Monica said the first thing that came to mind.

"Then there's nothing to do!"

Thomas noticed a change in Monica's demeanor and decided to drop the subject. He replied, "Very good then. I guess I'll get back to it. Thanks for the lemonade!"

Thomas finished his drink, crumpled his cup, and threw it into a nearby trash can before he picked up the box of books he had been carrying and disappeared into the 'Archives.'

~

Vikki knew she needed to remove many of the former executives and hire their replacements; after all, keeping the fools around who had made a mess of things was bad for business. She saw no reason for the delay and intended to eliminate them as quickly as possible, but she also knew her expansion initiative required hiring additional staff.

These actions were likely to be perceived as a drastic move, so she wanted to be cautious about how she introduced that notion. She considered arranging a press conference to explain her intentions but decided against it because she knew detractors would twist her words to incite opposition to her leadership, no matter what was said. Most importantly, she needed Thurmond to be on board and would not say anything to anyone until she had figured out all the details and discussed them at length with him.

After investigating viable options, Vikki concluded that Taipei offered the most attractive prospect for the Foundry expansion, but it was unlikely that Thurmond could have ever imagined it that way. She had mentioned the idea of expansion to Thurmond before but had not been specific about the details. She decided to proceed with the notion that they would be expanding but would not relay exactly where that expansion would be until after Thurmond had settled into his new position and new employees were in place. Regardless, the fact remained that they needed to hire new staff. The only question was, how many?

With that in mind, Vikki wondered whether it would be more prudent to limit the new positions they were looking to fill to the vacancies created by the removal of the incompetent executives or include the staffing they would need for the expansion. Overstaffing the current Foundry would allow her to reassign and relocate employees familiar with the operation to Taipei. Still, if that were too bold a move, she could hire people locally in Taipei to run the new plant when the time came. Both scenarios would require training employees, so after careful consideration, Vikki decided to focus on the home plant for the time being and not worry about Taipei until after the plant's construction had been completed and the Foundry operations were underway. That would give her time to figure out how to introduce her plans to Thurmond. Hopefully, he will be amenable to the idea.

The most pressing need now was to remove the deadwood and hire competent individuals who could help Vikki with her ambition to make the Foundry more profitable. Accordingly, she assigned Thurmond to conduct all the interviews, as no one else would be better suited to determine what was required.

~

Although confident that her intentions for the Foundry would eventually be understood, Vikki was still concerned that firing all the high-level executives at once could send the wrong signal to the townspeople. She developed a strategy where they would downplay and expedite the change in leadership while flooding the papers with job vacancy announcements to reinforce the company's intention to expand. That way, people could see the process moving forward.

To that end, Vikki instructed Thurmond to process both the hiring and firing interviews simultaneously, allocating as much time as he needed to interview each prospective candidate, but as little time as was required to remove the existing executives. She told him that it was vital that he conduct all the exit interviews as quickly and as quietly as humanly possible.

Vikki knew Thurmond would relish the opportunity to fire the executives who had treated him so poorly and explained the importance of being judicious. She advised him to remain measured in his approach to what she anticipated to be heated exchanges and asked him to respond without emotion to their outrage, which Thurmond worried he might not be able to do, though he said he would try.

Thurmond knew the exit interviews would be easy, given the people he would be firing, but he considered hiring candidates more complex. Firing someone required only the knowledge of what the person had or had not done, but hiring involved evaluating what the person could do.

Being as familiar as he was with many of the applicants, Thurmond could tell their resumes had been greatly exaggerated and anticipated the same from external applications. This fact made evaluating aptitude and competency a lengthy process, which Thurmond thought would take him too long, so he delegated the responsibility of screening the applicants to his secretary Sheila, who became flustered with the proliferation of applications and was quickly overwhelmed.

On several occasions, Sheila did not compare the vacancy applicants with the exit interviewees and scheduled vacancy interviews for several recently terminated executives who had reapplied for lesser positions with the company. One such former executive angrily stormed out of Thurmond's office when he was unceremoniously informed that there was no place for him at the company in any capacity.

When Sheila realized what had happened, she was upset that she had neglected to screen the applicants properly and apologized profusely. Thurmond laughed and said, "No harm done, Sheila. I know it's a confusing process. Why don't we look at today's list and see if we can pick these guys out to save us all a headache?"

Sheila was relieved. She handed Thurmond the clipboard she had been using to keep track of the applicants, and as Thurmond scoured the list, he heard a familiar voice coming from down the hall. He looked up and saw Howie talking to the former executive who had just left his office, and neither of them looked happy. When the angry executive disappeared into the elevator, Howie turned towards Thurmond and began marching towards him down the hall.

"Fancy seeing you here, Howie," Thurmond began. "I should think after our last conversation that you would have had enough of this place."

"I know what you're thinking, and I have something to say...." Howard began.

"Do you know?" Thurmond asked condescendingly.

"Yes. I do!" Howard trumpeted in reply.

Thurmond found Howard's attitude amusing. He smiled and said, "By all means, enlighten me."

Thurmond began at the top of the power structure to expedite the firing process and worked his way down. He terminated all the uppermost level executives without exception but considered some of the lower-level executives who had been actively engaged in the company's operation not as useless and therefore worthy of some consideration. However, Howie was one of those lower-level executives who were not vital to the company and had been scheduled by Thurmond to be dismissed.

Sheila sat at her desk, trying to mind her own business, but she couldn't help but overhear the muffled sound of intense arguing between the two men. When Howard stormed out of Thurmond's office, Sheila anticipated she had made another blunder and was prepared to apologize for making another mistake. Still, Thurmond came out of his office with a smile.

"That cheeky bastard!" Thurmond said as he laughed.

"I'm so sorry, sir....' Sheila said apologetically, "...it won't happen again. I'll cross him off the list and review the remaining candidates with you before I schedule anything."

"Not to worry, Sheila...." Thurmond sprightly replied, "...you can bring the list into my office, and we can review the remaining applicants, but first, I wanted you to set up an interview with Mr. Mallory for the next available time slot."

Sheila scheduled Howie's appointment for the following afternoon and notified him immediately. When he received the news, Howie was confident that he had made an impression on Thurmond and could convince him to give him his old job back. Possibly even get a promotion if Thurmond could get past his own bias.

The following day, Howie arrived promptly, strode confidently up to Sheila's desk, and announced.

"Shirley, I have come to see Thurmond! Tell him I'm waiting."

Sheila had known Howard Mallory for years, but Howie had always considered her too lowly and unworthy of his attention, so it was no surprise that he did not remember her name. She knew Mr. Joseph's low opinion of the man, which seemed to be shared by many others at the Foundry, so rather than feeling insulted, she was amused by his behavior.

Suppressing her urge to laugh at his bluster, Sheila pointed at a group of comfortable-looking chairs nearby and said, "Have a seat, Mr. Mallory. I'll let Mr. Joseph know you're here…."

Sheila disappeared into Thurmond's office, reappeared moments later, and settled behind her desk. She shuffled through a stack of papers, pulled out Howard's application, and offered it to him, saying, "You can go in now. He's ready for you…."

Howard stood abruptly, strode towards her desk, grabbed the papers from her hand, and said, "Thank you, Shirley…."

Sheila smiled but said nothing.

Howie burst into Thurmond's office and closed the doors behind him without turning around. After a brief silence, Sheila could hear shouting from inside the office, which didn't surprise her since previous interviews with other former executives had been heated, but this was slightly different as Mr. Joseph was also yelling.

"You know why you're here, Howie…." Thurmond began, "… based on your evaluations and our staffing requirements, it seems there is no longer a need for your services here."

"I know what you're doing, Thurmond. Retribution, pure and simple! I have been a foreman here for more than a decade and have earned the respect of the workers…."

"Is that so?" Thurmond asked, "… it's interesting you should say that because, as part of our evaluation process, we allowed employees to come to your defense, and you know what, not one of them did!"

"Get over yourself!" Howie said mockingly, "If you think for one second that anyone will stand for your prejudicial behavior, you have another thing coming!'

"The truth is, Howie, that your uncle protected you from being exposed as a dead weight around here, and he's no longer here. So, with that being the case, I'd like to know what leverage you think you have. Beyond that, what exactly do you think you can do that would be considered productive!"

Howie staunchly argued his position for half an hour and concluded that nothing he could say would sway Thurmond's bias. Discouraged, he replied.

"I can do whatever you need; I just want to keep my job."

"Splendid!" Thurmond returned, "… I'll come up with something worthy of your experience and expertise! Something to keep you busy?"

Howie knew what that meant and stormed out of Thurmond's office, muttering to himself, with Thurmond following slowly behind. Thurmond stopped at Sheila's desk, watching Howie stomp down the corridor like a spoiled child.

As Howie waited in front of the elevators, he looked back at them with disdain and suddenly disappeared into the elevator cab. Thurmond leaned on Sheila's desk with both hands and said, "I want you to prepare the paperwork for that bastard to start working in the mail room next week."

~

Howie had not considered the repercussions of pushing all his chips in against Thurmond during the trial. He was sure his uncle had taken all the necessary steps to protect the Foundry's interest, including his job, but the recent events proved otherwise. Thurmond had become the hero and now had all the power. The power to change every aspect of the Foundry and, along with it, the ability to change people's lives like his.

After accepting his menial job, Howie made a habit of drinking, typically in excess, at the local bar that was a popular place for many other employees whom Howie often recognized but seldom interacted with. Drinking in the cramped and darkened pub room had become a daily ritual for Howie. He arrived early every afternoon and would guzzle several pints of beer as fast as he could. The bartender only tolerated Howie's belligerent behavior because he left exorbitant tips, which Howie used to compensate for what he recognized to be his offensive manner.

One particular afternoon, Howard assumed his usual stool in the middle of the bar and guzzled one beer after another. The barroom was typically quite dark, but that afternoon, the daylight streamed through the front window and danced between the bottles and glasses, neatly arranged in rows on glass shelves mounted to an enormous mirror built into the barback. The glimmering light caught Howie's attention, and as he tried to see where it was coming from, he caught a glimpse of his reflection, which Howie watched go further and further out of focus as he continued to drink.

"Here ya go, Hughie…." the bartender said as he pushed yet another pint in front of his customer.

"I TOLD YOU, IT'S HOWIE, NOT HUGHIE…." Howard shouted as he grabbed his beer. "… you'd think you could at least get that straight, seeing as I've been spending all my time here lately."

"Apologies…" the bartender replied, as he restrained his inclination to throw his belligerent customer out of the bar.

"It's been a really rough week…." Howie remarked after taking a drink of his beer.

"So, you said…" the bartender cooly replied as he wiped the bar top with his towel to clean up the beer that spilled from Howie's mug.

"You don't understand…." Howie shot back as he took a gulp and continued, "…A really tough week. Like the worst week anyone could ever imagine!!"

The bartender could tell that his inebriated customer wanted to discuss his lousy fortune, so to increase the amount of his tip, he obliged and asked.

"How's that? How has it been tough?"

'Well, first off, I got 'The Boot.'" Howard began, '...' Let go.' 'Canned.' 'Dismissed'..."

As he used every synonym he could think of to replace the word 'fired,' Howie waved his glass around demonstratively, spilling most of his beer on the bar top, himself, and the floor.

"That is a bit of bad luck, but I know you'll be back on your feet in no time..." the bartender replied, "...right as rain. I'd bet on it. You'll see."

"Will I?" Howard asked indignantly, "... How do you know? Are you psychic or something? What does that mean anyway, 'right as rain'? Does it mean that I'm all wet? I don't even know what that means. I'll bet you don't either!"

Howard's tone did not amuse the bartender, and although he considered playing 'psychologist' to be part of the job, he was losing patience.

When Howie tried to take a drink from his glass, he was surprised to find that his beer was all but gone. He wiped his mouth on his sleeve and said.

"Don't be stingy on the suds, pal. When I ask for a beer, I expect a full mug! Hit it again!!"

Howie stared at the bartender, who said nothing as he grabbed Howard's empty pint glass, and, rather than replacing it with a new clean frosted one as he had been doing, he placed the same one under the tap and began to draw another draught. Once full, he set the pint glass in front of Howard and spoke.

"You don't have to get snippy with me, 'Howie.' I meant to say that these kinds of things usually have a way of working themselves out. I'm not a mind reader or a psychic, but I have been around the block a few times and know when something is really bad, not just emotionally bad."

"Emotionally bad?" Howard replied, beginning to slur his words slightly.

"Yeah, emotionally bad…" the bartender repeated in a tone that clearly indicated his growing annoyance with 'Howie.'

The bartender was about to ask Howard to leave when Eddie and Stan burst through the front door. Streams of blinding sunlight flooded the darkened pub room.

The two men had arms around each other and were obviously in good spirits. They laughed as they made their way to the bar, and Eddie raised his hand to get the bartender's attention. Stan looked down the length of the bar and noticed Howie sitting alone, staring blankly into a pint of beer. He elbowed Eddie to draw his attention to Howie, and Eddie shouted, "Fancy meeting you here, Howie!"

Howard looked at himself in the mirror and tried to determine if he was hallucinating. He turned towards the two men and said, "Just trying to find my bearings, boys…."

As Howard spoke, he stood up to get out of his seat but lost his balance, fell back into his stool, and began laughing. Stan realized his former boss was in bad shape and said, "Stay there, Howie. We'll come over."

Howard settled back into his stool and stared straight into his pint of beer. Eddie and Stan sat on two stools beside him as the bartender came over to take their order.

"Two bourbons Ted, neat…." Eddie began, "…and another beer for our friend here…."

"Very good, Eddie, but your friend here has had quite enough. I was going to ask him to leave before you guys came in…."

Eddie laughed as Ted poured the two men their drinks. Howie leaned towards Eddie and whispered, "Is he talking about me?"

"Yes…" Eddie returned disparagingly, "…I believe he is."

"Don't kick him when he's down, Eddie," Stan replied. "… can't you see he's drunk!"

"C'mon, Stan…" Eddie said without regard to Howie sitting beside him, "… I know he's drunk! But he's been busting our chops for as long as I can remember, and now the tables have turned. I can say anything I want!"

Ted placed the two bourbons in front of his customers.

"What's right is right, fellas…" Ted replied" … I mean, I have just as much a reason to throw this guy out on his keister as anybody, but just because you can, don't mean you should. The man's a mess. Let him be."

~

Howard awoke the following morning with a terrible hangover. With his head pounding, he vaguely recalled the previous afternoon and could not remember anything about the evening, including how he'd gotten home.

Stumbling out onto the balcony of his apartment, Howie lit up a cigarette, which managed to ease his nausea a bit. When he'd finished, he went back inside, drank a large glass of water, and collapsed on the couch. He picked up a newspaper that lay on the coffee table next to him and read the headline:

'Federal Trade Commission to decide on Smithworks merger.'

Howard wondered if the merger meant expansion and continued reading the entire article. When he'd finished, he realized the merger might represent an opportunity.

It was apparent his future under Thurmond at Smithworks looked bleak. Remaining there would mean begging Thurmond for a chance to prove himself, which didn't seem to be an option. However, if the expansion meant a new location, he could transfer there and explore other opportunities because of his experience.

Howard determined that he needed to clean up his act if he was going to change his fortunes. He tossed the newspaper on the table and dragged himself into the shower, imagining how things could be different.

7

Exposition

The article about the Federal Trade Commission's impending ruling on the Smithworks merger fueled gossip about what was next for the Foundry. Reports began to spread about Smithworks firing company executives, which made some people wonder if the new ownership wasn't in the process of dismantling the company. Thurmond Joseph's appointment as the company's latest executive had been considered a good thing, but rumors suggested he may have betrayed their trust for personal gain.

Thurmond detested being depicted as the 'bad guy' and met with Vikki to be reassured that none of the rumors were true. Vikki knew that anything perceived as a threat to the Foundry would be considered undesirable, but she had been waiting for the right moment to explain her intentions to Thurmond in detail. Now that the 'old guard' had been removed, she was ready to reveal her plan without the worry of meddling.

Vikki explained that she understood how Smithworks had served as the backbone of the community for generations and how it had become a brand representing an important place in the town's history. But she suggested that the company's reputation had been tarnished by the cronyism exhibited by the previous executives and suggested their ineptitude had been responsible for the company's decline. She emphasized that their incompetent actions after the horrific plane crash precipitated the Van Der Staar lawsuit, which damaged the company name irreparably.

"The company's operation needed to improve," Vikki began, "...so we fired the old executives, started hiring new employees, and are planning to expand operations. The company needs a new vision, Thurmond. A vision that portrays a commitment to quality. That commitment requires new leadership, which you and I represent."

"I understand…" Thurmond replied as he pondered what Vikki was saying.

"The company needs to change, Thurmond…." Vikki reassured him, "… it can never be what it was. It must be something new, and in my opinion, that requires a new name. A name that would project the company's commitment to its customers and community."

"Everything you're saying makes sense, Vikki, but changing the name? That I don't understand."

"I was getting to that…." Vikki replied, then continued.

"You see, Thurmond when a hero becomes a victim, people lose hope. They feel unsafe and insecure. When the fools who ran this place didn't laugh at the suit filed against them by Van Der Staar, that image, that rock, that security people had relied upon came into question. It developed doubts which turned into fear. It was palpable. Didn't you feel it?"

"Yes, I think everybody did." Thurmond agreed.

"Well…" Vikki continued, "…what I have in mind is a new hero, born of the old hero. The offspring of 'the fallen,' as it were. The heir to the throne; bigger, stronger, brighter, and more secure! I want to quell people's fears and give them something to make them proud again. Make them feel secure again. Make them feel like they are a part of something bigger than themselves, and I want them to be proud of being involved in creating it. I want them to feel like they are involved in saving their community. Something that is theirs, not their fathers, or their father's fathers, or their fathers before them."

"I understand, but how will a name achieve that, and how do you deal with people's questions about our intentions?"

Thurmond remained concerned about perceptions, but Vikki had convinced him that her intentions were in the town's interest, which made him feel more at ease.

"It's not just the name Thurmond!" Vikki excitedly exclaimed, "That's just the beginning! We will transform the place from a dingy old facility into a shiny new jewel! Like we did for the executive level. We'll give her a face-lift! We'll make her the envy of her competition! We'll make her shiny and new! State-of-the-art! We'll increase her capacity, her efficiency, her reputation, and we'll give her a brother!"

"A brother?" Thurmond asked, again a little confused by Vikki's explanation.

"Yes, Thurmond, a brother. A sibling operation. We'll expand, build another facility, and perhaps expand our production to include additional products and services."

"Why would you do that? Things have been fine with one facility and what we produce there."

"Have we been doing just fine, Thurmond?" Vikki asked, "…if that were so, then how could a silly lawsuit almost close the place down? How could a company doing so well be so vulnerable? No, I say it wasn't doing well at all. If it were doing that well, I wouldn't have been interested in buying the place, and it wouldn't have made any business sense."

Vikki explained that during the trial, most of Smithworks' vital assets had been transferred, under the guise of being sold, to a company she created called CMC Enterprises. The idea was to protect the company's assets from being liquidated if the trial did not turn out in their favor. She explained that she had carefully organized it so that the companies were distinctly different enterprises that just happened to operate in the same trade, which was why they would need approval from the Federal Trade Commission to merge.

"It's simple, Thurmond. The company assets needed to be protected in case something went wrong. I arranged it to protect the company regardless of the trial's outcome. Smithworks would close if we lost, but the new company would have all the assets and could keep going. If we won, which I was certain we would, we would merge the two companies into a single entity, then leverage that to expand."

"It's all Greek to me…." Thurmond returned, "…but I believe you know what you're doing, so I'll let it go at that. As long as the Foundry is safe."

Vikki laughed and said, "Not to worry, Thurmond, I have everything under control."

"Glad to hear it…." Thurmond replied.

Thurmond thought the lesson was over and started out of her office, but Vikki continued.

"There were a couple of things involving identifying personnel for the expansion initiative that I needed you to handle for me, Thurmond…."

"Whatever you need, Vikki, just let Sheila know, and she'll set it all up."

"Sounds good!" Vikki replied, "… I'd spare you the trouble, but you're the one who knows the production and operation. I imagine you would be infinitely more qualified to staff up than anyone. Certainly, more capable than me."

"Don't sell yourself short…." Thurmond said as he opened the door to continue his exit, "…for someone who knows as little as you do about foundries, you've done a pretty good job so far."

Vikki's ideas represented a complete departure from Thurmond's thinking about the Foundry, but she was very persuasive. He believed he would consider anything she proposed if she could make him understand it.

~

It was a bright and beautiful Saturday morning. Dew had begun to evaporate into a mist that rose gently as the sun sparkled in the water droplets collected on the monkey grass surrounding the house.

Thurmond had told Vikki he needed a break and said he would not be coming to work that Saturday. Consequently, Thurmond hadn't planned on getting out of bed until he had to prepare for the resumption of his weekly BBQ with his friend Emerson, but the surprising sound of a vehicle pulling into his driveway had awakened him, and the slamming of the screen door finished the job.

When Thurmond came downstairs to find out who had come over so early, he was excited to see Monica, but before he could say anything, she demonstratively slapped a newspaper down on his kitchen table in front of her and demanded answers.

"Is it true, Thurmond?" Monica asked as she pointed to an article that denounced the new executives for their intention to shutter the Foundry, "…have you agreed to this?!"

"Of course not, Mona…." Thurmond returned, "…they make it sound so terrible."

"It is terrible, Thurmond!" Monica replied in a tone Thurmond hadn't been accustomed to hearing from her.

"They make it sound like we're shutting the place down when we're doing the exact opposite."

"Explain!" Monica demanded in a manner that portrayed an elevated level of annoyance.

"I want you to explain what they're talking about, Thurmond! I want you to tell me what you and that woman have been doing!"

Thurmond was happy to see Monica, but she hadn't been the same since their trip to Tulaisy's. She was aloof, impatient, and demanding, and Thurmond felt responsible for all of it. He tried to assuage her concerns, but the more he explained, the more upset she became. As he explained, she marched over to the pantry before heading to the fridge as she assembled the required particulars to make some coffee. Thurmond did not stop explaining; "…you have to understand, Mona, it's not what it seems…" but Monica interrupted him by saying.

"Lord knows what you've been up to with her, Thurmond, but I don't like it! You spend endless hours with her at that place, and although you had done that before, you were usually not this happy because of it. I mean, what have you been doing with that woman?"

Thurmond was at a loss for words. It was one thing to accuse him of being unscrupulous with the Foundry, but now she seemed to be implying that he was engaged in an affair with Vikki. He became agitated but restrained his reaction and in as polite a manner as he was capable, he replied.

"Nothing is going on between us, Monica. I wish you wouldn't say that. We have been trying to figure out how to change the perception and operation of the Foundry."

"Change? What do you mean by change?"

Thurmond suddenly realized that Monica had come over for a fight, and there was Nothing he could do to dissuade her from it. He was going to have to engage with her whether he wanted to or not, so he reciprocated.

"Those clowns running the place had made a hash of it. The more I learn about what they did, the more I wonder how we kept it running."

Thurmond pulled out two coffee mugs, a sugar bowl, and a milk bottle and placed them on the counter next to the coffee pot. Monica had taken her seat at the table after spouting her outrage, and Thurmond continued:

"If people are so stupid and narrow-minded as to trust the grumblings of some disgruntled former executives that were summarily dismissed, then fine, let them believe what they want to believe. The truth is they screwed it up and deserved to be fired, if not worse!"

Monica did not immediately reply, so Thurmond sat across from her, rested both arms on the table, and clasped his hands, awaiting her response while never once taking his eyes off her, but her response never came.

Monica felt intimidated and fumbled with her thoughts to find the right words to express her concerns. Still, she had blown her opportunity at a civil discourse when she began the conversation by attacking and accusing Thurmond. She was confused and angry. Unsure and insecure. She wanted to take back the words she had shot at him in anger, but that was no longer possible.

They sat there in silence until the coffee finished brewing. Then Monica rose from the table and poured the coffee into only one cup. She carefully placed the mug on the table before Thurmond and left without saying another word.

~

Once Vikki had convinced Thurmond of her plan's wisdom, it immediately gained traction, and everything proceeded at an alarming pace. The newspaper's characterization of Thurmond's support of the company's activities portrayed him as a Judas, which angered people and made them question his motivations. He had tried to dissuade his friends of the notion that this was a betrayal, but he had lost the hope that anyone would believe him without Monica's support. Consequently, he focused on the assigned duties and worked diligently to prepare for the company's evolution. He was convinced he was doing the right thing and felt obligated to prove it to his friends by ensuring success. His only solace during this lonely time was the humble friendship offered without condition by his lone supporter, Emerson, who was due to arrive shortly, so Thurmond finished his cup of coffee and began preparing for his friend's arrival.

~

Thurmond was happy to spend time away from the troubling thoughts and was out back, packing the cooler with beer and ice, when he heard the rear screen door slam shut, signaling that his friend Emerson had arrived.

"Howdy, Thurm! Beautiful mornin', ain't it?" Emerson said in salutation.

Thurmond stopped what he was doing and greeted his friend with a handshake and a beer.

"Puts a grin on yer face like a gift!" Thurmond said in imitation of what his friend would say every time he came to visit.

Thurmond offered his friend a bottle opener and laughed as Emerson pulled a pipe wrench from his overalls' side pocket and clumsily used it to remove his bottle cap. Emerson sucked the foam that spilled from the bottle he had been jostling around, and the two men clinked their bottles together.

"Like a gift!" Em repeated, "Makes ya happy to be alive!"

"Agreed!" Thurmond returned.

The two men took a long drink of their beer, and Thurmond asked, "Thought you didn't much like drinking in the morning, Em?"

"If you have to, you have to…" he said matter-of-factly, which made Thurmond laugh.

"Saturdays are made for relaxing, Em. It wouldn't be Saturday without a cold beer before noon."

"Heard that!" Emerson replied before guzzling his beer and grabbing another for his friend and himself.

Emerson had heard all the rumors and knew that Thurmond was having a tough time. He had also overheard Monica telling Kate how unhappy she was with the amount of time Thurmond had spent at the Foundry and with his new boss Vikki, but Emerson didn't believe it to be anything more than just a hard-working man working hard.

"So, how goes the battle?" asked Em.

"Same old same old," returned Thurmond, "…just working with the new boss on her plans for the Foundry. It's interesting, but it has taken up too much of my time to tell you the truth."

"I guess so, Thurm…." Emerson replied, "… haven't seen hide nor hair of ya in a while. I know you've been busy with it, which is why I was surprised when you asked me over, not that I mind. Heck, cain't think of anythin' I'd rather do than plow the froth off a couple with my best friend! It's the highlight of my week!"

"Me too, Em. I've just been trying to learn what it takes to run the business, but it hurts my head to think about everything you gotta do. Vikki's been teaching me, but there's a lot to learn."

Emerson wanted to be careful not to stir the pot, so he thought about what he was going to say for a moment, then said, "Peoples been talkin', I know you know, but I don't think they's getting it straight. Herb thinks you're fixin' to shut the place down, but I know that ain't the truth."

"It's not…." Thurmond replied, trying to remain calm, "…and not that it's any of his business, but Vikki's got big plans for the place that will make people wish they had been a little more understanding. They'll learn it was all being done in their best interest."

"Believe that Thurm. I know you. Ain't nothin' but kindness in yer heart, far as I'm concerned. I told Herb as much, but people are gonna believe what they want to believe."

"True enough, unfortunately…." Thurmond replied, thankful for his friend's kind words.

"You know what, Em, why don't we stop all the talk about work and start charring some meat? I'm getting mighty hungry, and the coals are probably ready by now. Why don't you grab the pack of burgers and some buns from the kitchen while I stoke the coals?"

"Sounds like a plan…." Emerson replied as he put his beer down on the cooler and disappeared back into the house.

When Emerson entered the kitchen, he noticed the newspaper Monica had left on the table and saw a headline that read, "FTC approves Smithworks Merger."

Emerson removed a box of burger patties from the freezer, grabbed a package of hamburger buns from the top of the refrigerator, and placed them all on the table. He picked up the newspaper to read a bit of the article. It read:

"With the announcement of the trade commission approval, it appears imminent that the shell corporation known as 'CMC enterprises' will absorb Smithworks, Inc. in the largest takeover in town history.

Experts agree the possibility exists that the stalwart company, richly steeped in town history, could be shuttered after its assets are liquidated, and the entire operation moved to a new location, under a different name."

The article was no different from the rumors Emerson had heard at the Diner. It was all hat and no cattle. Hyperbole intended to stir up trouble so they could scare people and sell newspapers. Phrases like *'experts agree'* and *'the possibility exists'* were speculation and, therefore, not worth the paper it was printed on. Emerson knew whatever Thurmond was up to, and it wasn't what the article suggested.

Emerson tossed the paper in the trash can, tucked the buns under his arm, picked up the box of frozen meat patties, and then headed back out to enjoy some burgers and beers with his friend.

8

Subterfuge

Once Vikki received the official approval for the merger, she went to see Kate, told her she wanted to celebrate the good news, and asked her to cater the party. Kate was honored but concerned about handling such a large party. Vikki solicited Thomas's assistance to help convince Kate to accept the job. After days of discussing the details, Kate finally agreed. Elaborate preparations for the celebration began, and news of it spread like wildfire until everyone had become aware of it, including Bradley and Ehndale, who were both interested in attending, but for entirely different reasons.

Bradley had spent much effort concealing himself from Ehndale for fear of reprisals for interference in his affairs and had become very lonely as a result. Accordingly, he desperately wanted to re-assimilate but knew that attending the party would expose him. After considering the consequences, Bradley decided that the time had come for him to take a chance. Ehndale, on the other hand, was very curious about the Foundry's activities and sought revenge against all those he held responsible for his failure to corrupt Thurmond. He wanted to wreak vengeance, and Bradley was not the only one he had on his mind.

Since the unfortunate incident at the airport, Monica had become Ehndale's primary target, believing retribution against her was essential. Vikki had taken advantage of Thurmond's sudden availability and quickly made Thurmond part of Foundry leadership, which he would have also done. However, this new position would put tremendous demands on Thurmond's time and undoubtedly keep him away from Monica, which could impact their relationship. This separation could also allow Ehndale to engage with Monica without Thurmond's interference and enable him to push them even further apart. Once he isolated Monica, he would have ample opportunity to realize his revenge.

~

Ehndale followed Monica's activities and the workings of the Foundry very closely and was waiting for an opportunity to initiate his plan. He needed information about the Foundry that was not readily available and knew he couldn't rely on his protégé to provide it since, on several occasions, Vikki had defied him in deference to her new 'friends.' He believed she might also consider his interest in the Foundry suspicious since he had advised her against investing in it. Hence, he began scheduling meetings with former Foundry executives to find out what he could get from them. Possibly even solicit their assistance in covertly gathering information about the Foundry.

During one of these afternoon meetings, Ehndale met with a pompous former Foundry CFO named Elliott. He was accompanied by a decidedly cross younger man who neither spoke to nor seemed interested in anyone other than his uncle. Ehndale shook the hand of the former executive and remarked, "So nice to see you again, Elliott! Shame about the Foundry. Terrible business that. I'd imagine you didn't see that one coming, hey?"

Ehndale's comment was intended to humiliate Elliott while pretending to commiserate with him, which Ehndale found amusing. The former CFO wasn't sure how to take his host's comments and had no idea how to respond other than to agree. Ehndale abhorred the man's guilelessness. Although he intended to continue gathering what he could from him, the man's naivete immediately disqualified him from assisting Ehndale in any covert attempt at gathering information about the Foundry.

Ehndale noticed the younger man standing behind Elliott as they spoke and wondered why he hadn't been introduced. He gestured toward him and asked, "Whom do we have here?"

The younger man had no interest in talking to anybody and had only agreed to accompany Elliot because of the promise of an open bar, which was the only thing that had appealed to him. He had been waiting for Elliot to finish talking to the host so they could get a drink and was surprised when Elliot stepped aside to introduce him.

"This is my nephew, Howard Mallory."

With his hand behind his nephew's back, the CFO applied a little pressure to urge Howard to step forward and greet the party host. Howie extended his hand and reluctantly said, "Nice to meet you…."

"Pleasures all mine!" Ehndale returned.

As he squeezed Howie's hand, Ehndale's grip made Howard wince, which did not escape his uncle's notice. Concerned about the host's opinion of his nephew, Elliott continued with Howie's introduction, "Howard is the only former executive I know of that managed to retain a position at the Foundry since the layoffs."

"Is that so?" Ehndale said, "…good show, young man. Bully for you!"

Howard had no interest in recounting his embarrassing experience and grew impatient, which made Ehndale wonder if this angry little man could help him gather information. He was upset about his situation at the Foundry and was sure to have access to files at the company.

"And what is it you do at the foundry, if I may be so bold as to ask?"

"I used to be a manager…." Howard retorted, "…but I was demoted when the company ownership changed hands."

Howard was embarrassed at the admission, but Ehndale reassured him that what had happened to him was honorable.

"You persevered, my good man! Faced adversity and accepted the challenge!"

Ehndale saw an opportunity to coerce Howard into becoming a spy and continued complimenting him for his courage. As Ehndale lauded him with compliments, Howard began to feel worthy, which put him in a vulnerable position that Ehndale planned to exploit.

"So, if by taking a 'demotion,' as you called it, you feel the position you have accepted is beneath you, which I can tell is probably true, then I imagine you believe you have the tenacity to achieve more. Is that a safe assumption? Do you have even higher aspirations?" Ehndale asked.

"If you're asking me if I want more..." Howie replied, "...my answer is yes, I want more! I deserve more after everything I've done for them."

Ehndale had solicited the assistance of a thousand 'Howards' in the past and was very familiar with his sort. They were angry, unwelcome, and unfriendly. They are disposable because no one would miss them. No one cared. Their peers did not like them, and they garnered no support or empathy from others when lousy luck came their way. They were selfish, vacuous, and vapid—empty vessels existing only in their immediate presence and not in the context of time. Easily forgotten and hard to recall, Howard was the perfect person to help gather information, but Ehndale needed to be detached. He needed distance between him and this empty shell he hoped could provide him with valuable information he would use towards his ends.

Ehndale gave Elliott his card and told the former CFO to follow up with him later that week. He assured him he would help secure a position worthy of him at some other prestigious company. He also requested that Howard stick around so they could discuss some ideas Ehndale had on how Howard could make a little extra money. Ehndale assured Elliott he would have Howard brought home, so he didn't have to wait around for him. Elliott agreed, and after he had gone, Ehndale took Howard into the mansion's library to discuss business.

~

Although no one had physically moved the machines, the shell corporation's assets were finally reunited on paper with the bricks and mortar of the old Smithworks plant. With that, the company merger was officially complete.

Vikki commissioned a branding campaign for the new company. She requested that Thurmond accompany her to a presentation given by the marketing company she had hired to do the job. The marketing group was commissioned to develop a unique identity and presented multiple options. Vikki identified with the choice to brand the new company as 'C-Inc,' which she planned to substitute phonetically for the word 'Sync' in a marketing campaign to imply 'synchronous' operations of the various plants Vikki intended to open and operate around the globe.

The 'rebirth' of the company, as Vikki called it, included a major renovation campaign that Vikki had initiated to modernize the appearance and operation of the Foundry. This 'rebirth' was scheduled for completion by the day of the massive celebration.

Brightly painted steel canopies and re-pointed brick facades were only the beginning. They replaced roofs along with windows and doors. Insulated Glass was introduced, and much of the plant's interiors were stripped to the framing and replaced with modern, high-performance materials. The bathrooms were state-of-the-art like the employee lounges, and break rooms now included full kitchens and entertainment areas. Structural steel and mechanical distribution systems were exposed, painted, and treated like sculptural objects throughout the plant. Landscaping was also introduced in abundance, and outdoor plazas were expanded and adorned with many plantings, benches, light fixtures, decorative grating, paving, and artwork.

Thurmond had seen fit to engage in business development during the renovations and reached out to old and new customers to establish better relationships. The largest of their former clients, Van Der Staar, was pleased that Thurmond was now running the show and agreed to renegotiate their canceled contracts with C-Inc. Thurmond regularly invited executives from these companies to the Foundry to give them a tour of the facility's upgrades. Thurmond also invited everyone to join them for their company's inaugural celebration, which was accepted by all that had been asked, without exception.

~

The town was abuzz with anticipation as the day had arrived for the grand celebration at C-Inc. Lampposts and buildings were adorned with flags and banners that advertised the company's great celebration, and Vikki couldn't have been more delighted. Company employees were encouraged to invite their friends and family, which they did in abundance, to the point where it seemed the entire town would be there. Dignitaries arrived with their guests in droves until the town seemed to be bursting at the seams.

Children played in grass courtyards scattered between buildings throughout the facility as Gargantuan circus tents equipped with furnishings and air conditioning were erected in the expansive parking lot. Security guards were strategically positioned to direct vehicles and pedestrians to designated locations to keep traffic flowing smoothly. At the same time, Vikki greeted guests in the beautifully renovated main lobby. Nora organized people interested in a tour into groups that were subsequently escorted around the facility.

Meanwhile, Kate had been busy making the catering preparations and solicited Thomas and Thurmond to help her with the logistics of delivering the food. Kate had also stationed her son Hunter at the Foundry's dining facility, which was used as a support station to accept and store the deliveries because it wasn't large enough for the grand venue. Monica volunteered to manage the support staff hired to assist with the final preparation and distribution of the food and drink. Everything was running like clockwork, but Thurmond was beside himself with anxiety.

"Relax, Thurmond…" Thomas told his jittery friend, "…everything is going along just fine. I can handle the rest of the deliveries if you're worried about Mona or Vikki. Go ahead and enjoy yourself! All this is for you as much as anybody.!"

"Are you sure?"

"Yeah, I'm sure! Go ahead. I'll be fine. We're almost done here anyway."

"Thanks…" Thurmond replied as he made a mad dash for the tent where Monica had been stationed before running to the main lobby to help Vikki greet some of his customers.

~

Bradley had parked his vehicle on the side of the road leading to the foundry parking lot, far enough away from the main gate to keep him from being recognized by anyone he knew. He remained parked there for some time, staring off at the enormous circus tents in the distance, trying to decide whether he was brave enough to go to the celebration and risk being discovered. For hours a continuous stream of cars had been queuing up at the main gate, which eventually lined up past Bradley's car. Clarence was operating the guard booth at the front gate and greeting guests as he checked their invitations. He had also been keeping track of the queue to determine if he needed assistance to help speed things up and had noticed Bradley's car parked on the side of the road for some time. Although he was curious, the lengthening line of cars occupied so much of his attention that he eventually forgot about it.

Music spilled out into the darkening countryside as lampposts began to flick on across the parking lot. Most of the guests who had planned on attending the celebration had already arrived, and the queuing of cars subsided enough to make Bradley's car conspicuous again, which meant Bradley had to decide or risk being discovered. The celebration was an opportunity for him to make amends with his friends. He was sure he would have a good time, but his fear of Ehndale's reprisals proved too great to endure, so he decided to head home, and he left, disappointed at himself and angry at Ehndale.

~

Howard had been meeting with Ehndale to iron out details of an arrangement they had made between them and arrived late enough not to have to queue up to gain entry. Ehndale told him to be inconspicuous, so he intended to pretend to be a dawdling entertainer. When he arrived, Clarence no longer operated the guard booth, so he quickly drove through the open entry gate and past a shuttle-bus station set up on the parking lot's perimeter, which had been transporting people to and from the main event.

He spotted what appeared to be a tour bus for the band and parked beside it since it was next to some double doors that had direct access to the shop floor. He looked around to ensure he hadn't been seen and entered the building using the keys he had just been issued as a new employee.

Once inside, Howard made his way to Thurmond's office and rifled through some filing cabinets looking for files with specific headings that had anything to do with investors. He had only been there for a few minutes when he heard someone coming, so he grabbed an armful of folders indiscriminately, ran back out of the building to his car, and left.

~

"Our arrangement, my good man, was for you to provide me with intelligence about the company's financial operation. Instead, you bring me personnel files and party preparations."

Howard was not interested in being criticized by Ehndale for having made a simple mistake and became increasingly indignant as he enjoyed a drink beside the fireplace in Ehndale's library.

"If you were unclear as to the purpose of the enterprise, you should have requested clarification, my good man."

Ehndale walked to the fireplace and calmly tossed a handful of the folders Howard had given him into the fire. Howard remained still and said nothing as he watched the folders ignite.

"Have you nothing to say?" Ehndale quietly demanded.

Howard never lifted his head or altered the focus of his gaze. He watched as the folders curled and began to burn and replied.

"All I can say is you're welcome."

"Welcome?" Ehndale said laughing, "…pray to tell, welcome for what?"

"For breaking into the CEO's office. For gathering information, you could have never gotten otherwise. For taking a chance at being caught and for possibly losing my job. For any number of things. You're welcome…." Howard repeated.

"I hardly see the reason for praise, my dear fellow, when what I hired you to do remains undone."

Ehndale walked over to a lectern with a large book placed on it. Silk tassels that appeared to be stitched into the book's binding dangled from the pages. Ehndale used the tassels to turn the pages in bunches and slowly ran his finger down the pages filled with names.

"Am I going to get paid or what?" Howard demanded before standing and helping himself to another drink.

Ehndale stopped his finger on a page with a blank space on it he had reserved for Howie and replied.

"Ah, yes. You will be paid as soon as you complete the task I hired you to perform, my good man."

"Ok…" Howard replied, "…but I want more money. I'm taking all the risks here, and I think it's worth more than what you're paying me."

There it was, as he anticipated, greed. Ehndale understood greed. It was simple and obvious.

"Very well, my good man. I will pay you more, but first, I want a few other things."

Had Howard not been so impressed with himself, he would have noticed the sinister tone in Ehndale's voice, but turning failure into a more profitable enterprise was an accomplishment of which Howard was incredibly proud. This pride shrouded everything, which Howard would eventually come to regret.

9

Expansion

Vikki's ultimate decision to invest in the Foundry had been determined in large part by the feasibility of its capacity to expand operations. When discussing her plans for the Foundry with Thurmond, she made no secret of her intention to take advantage of this. Her past actions gave credence to the ominous rumors propagated by the newspapers about her intentions to shutter the company; however, to Thurmond's relief, the success of the recent celebration effectively obliterated that notion.

Heralded afterward by those same newspapers as a fabulous affair, this successful presentation of the company's resurgence re-established its distinguished reputation in the marketplace and the community. Vikki's speech outlining her intentions for C-Inc during the celebration confirmed her commitment to the company's success. However, the talk of expansion came as a bit of a surprise to most people, but it attracted their attention as she laid out her plans.

"The beautification program you see all around you here at C-Inc. is the beginning of an aggressive strategy we plan to implement here at the Foundry. Our next step is to expand production by introducing new components and increasing the company's offerings, attracting new clients, bolstering sales, expanding profits, and creating new jobs! To handle this growth, we need to expand our physical presence. Accordingly, we will hire more employees and construct new facilities to establish our position as the leader in the marketplace!"

The crowd's reaction was distinctly supportive, and her speech was frequently interrupted by outbursts of applause. She used that momentum to describe new policies being adopted to gain the support of her employees and the townspeople. She continued, "We will extend investment initiatives to the local business community, offering assistance in the form of money and company resources to help strengthen the local economy! We are also happy to announce that we will be sponsoring on-the-job training for employees interested in career advancement. We will also provide incentives for those who voluntarily transfer to our new locations to help us grow the operation. As vital contributors to the ultimate success of this endeavor, these volunteers would gain experience in an exciting new marketplace and will be handsomely rewarded for doing so!"

News spread quickly and gained tremendous support from clients, employees, and townspeople. It also attracted investors, whose funding Vikki planned to use to limit the company's financial risks. A few of these investors knew about her targeting Asia for physical expansion, which initially made her suspicious until she realized that the region's lower production costs made it an obvious choice to any seasoned investor. Vikki agreed to consider their proposals but only with their assurances that she would retain control of the company, regardless of the outcome.

Another interesting stipulation in every potential investor's proposal was that Thurmond Joseph must run the operation in Asia, which Vikki knew was the best course of action. When she presented the idea to Thurmond, he agreed that someone from the home plant familiar with the operation should be on the ground in Asia to protect the company's interests. Still, he wasn't interested in being that someone. Determined to convince him to accept it, Vikki explained that the investors' interest in his stewardship was because of his knowledge of the operation, personnel, and equipment.

To ease his anxiety, Vikki told Thurmond that her intention had always been to hire locals in Asia. Still, until they could find a qualified local candidate, the operation couldn't happen without someone with his expertise, so she asked him to consider a temporary assignment to help her get things up and running.

Thurmond worried that if they couldn't find the right person to replace him, it could mean that he would have to remain in Asia indefinitely, which was not an option, no matter how remote that possibility may have been in Vikki's mind. He explained his reservation was the amount of time he would have to spend there and that he wouldn't even consider going unless a date was established for his return as part of the official schedule.

Vikki agreed to limit Thurmond's time in Asia and included a milestone clause in every one of the equity partners' contracts. Thurmond said he needed a few days to think about it before accepting the assignment and immediately made plans to spend time with Monica. Thurmond needed her perspective since she always made difficult decisions easy for him, which he knew he desperately needed.

~

Since seeing the article in the newspaper, Howard had been considering how the company's expansion could benefit him. Still, given the lengths Ehndale was willing to go to gather information about it, he suggested there were other ways a handsome profit could be made.

As his greed grew, Howard began leveraging the information he stole from the Foundry and negotiated for more money each time. The information Howard was stealing was crucial to Ehndale generating interest in investment from his associates and securing his position of influence over them.

Although this development amused Ehndale, it was annoying that he found himself in a position where this could happen. He reluctantly agreed to Howard's demands and decided to deal with the greedy insect once the financial agreements with the Foundry were finalized.

~

Bradley was disappointed with his decision to skip the celebration and retreated to his old house, but he had grown tired of drinking alone. He began venturing out to places that precluded the possibility of running into Ehndale, and day after day, he drank himself into a stupor at some random bar.

One afternoon Bradley stumbled into a bar where he met a young woman with whom he attempted to become familiar. She refused his advances, but he remained undeterred and persisted until the bartender noticed the look of fear on the woman's face. When Bradley lifted one arm to put it around the young woman, the bartender shouted, "If you don't keep your hands to yourself, I'm gonna have to ask you to leave…."

"Why don't you mind your own business!" Bradley garbled in reply, "…I was getting to know the little lady, and I'd like to think I was making a bit of progress until you opened your mouth, so back off…."

The young woman pushed Bradley, and he stumbled into another man sitting a couple of stools away, spilling the man's beer all over himself. That man was Howie, who had just finished collecting his 'pay' from Ehndale for delivering some files.

"Get off me, you idiot!" Howie shouted out as he wiped the beer off his shirt and pants.

Steadying himself against the bar, Bradley tried to apologize, "Easy now, fella. I think you're mistaken about my intentions."

"Screw your intentions!" Howard replied, "…you spilled beer all over me, you moron!"

Howard's response shifted Bradley's focus away from the young woman long enough to allow her to extricate herself and leave the bar without Bradley noticing.

"Easy now, fella…." Bradley repeated as he leaned on the bar and fell into the stool the young woman had just vacated, "…I believe what we have here is a simple misunderstanding…."

"What makes you think I have any interest in talking to you? Get away from me!"

The bartender knew both men were intoxicated and watched them with some interest. They were in no danger of hurting each other, as neither seemed the type, so he anticipated a loud but harmless scuffle, after which they would probably need to be thrown out.

Expecting a big tip from Howie, the bartender was going to let the two men work it out on their own, but when their arguing began to bother other customers, he decided to intervene before it went too far.

"Ok, gentlemen. Why don't we calm down? How about I buy you both a drink on the house?"

"Splendid idea, my good man!" As he reached for his empty glass, Bradley remarked, "…Splendid indeed!"

Ehndale was the only person Howard had ever heard use that phrase, and he became curious as to why this drunk had just said it and asked, "What did you just say?"

"Say what?" Bradley replied as he handed the bartender his empty glass.

"'Splendid my good man'…." Howard repeated, "…splendid indeed…'. Nobody ever says things like that except that jerk, Ehndork! He says that nonsense all the time!"

Howard had just come from a meeting with Ehndale and was furious that he had declined to pay some extra money Howard believed he deserved for the files he had just retrieved.

Bradley's face began to grow pale.

"Ehndork?" he repeated, "…you don't mean 'Ehndale,' do you?"

"Yeah, Ehndale, Ehndork, whatever… you don't know him, do you? He's an arrogant jerk!"

Bradley suddenly felt lightheaded. He closed his eyes, crossed his arms on the bar, then rested his head against them as Howie continued complaining.

"He'll be sorry...." Howard shouted, "... I'll make his life miserable! He'll wish he'd never met me! I'll make him pay! He'll be sorry he crossed me! Mark my words."

Bradley was shocked at how Howard spoke of Ehndale and wondered if he was aware of how powerful Ehndale was and how vicious he could be. Why wasn't Howie afraid of what Ehndale would do to him if he ever heard him talk like that?

Howard's insulting Ehndale was sobering, and Bradley suddenly felt the urge to return home. He changed his mind about the free beer and thanked the bartender, telling him he had had enough. Reaching into his pocket, Bradley pulled out some cash, left it on the bar top, and then got off his stool to go.

As he was leaving, he leaned into Howie and whispered, "I'd be cautious if I were you, friend. If you knew that man as I do, you wouldn't be talking like that. It would serve you well to steer clear of him. He's trouble!"

"Nonsense..." Howie shot back as he wiped his mouth with his sleeve. "Full of hot air is all he is. Nothing I haven't dealt with before. I'm going to make him pay whether he wants to or not. You'll see. Make no mistake about that. He's gonna pay me!"

~

Monica had been attending regular sessions with Fr. Elias to help her deal with her concerns about the future of her relationship with Thurmond. When Thurmond approached her about the possibility of his going to Asia, she was unsure how she felt about him leaving. Objectively she knew that it made sense for him to travel there to set things up, but that meant he would be away for extended periods, possibly forever, and she wasn't sure how she felt about that.

As Thurmond explained his thoughts and fears, Monica knew she couldn't counsel him and listened to him, hoping he would come to his own conclusion, but it didn't work. Her advice had always been based on love, but she had doubts about their future, so she didn't trust herself to give him any advice. She found herself thinking more about their relationship than Thurmond's dilemma and didn't consider what it meant to him but what it meant to her.

The night at Tulaisy, Monica met a strange woman from a life Thurmond had embraced after abandoning his life with her. However temporary, that departure created doubt in her mind about committing to a relationship with him. It made her question her feelings about his leaving for Asia. If she advised him to go, was it because it was the best thing for him or for her? Would she recommend he go because she didn't want him to be around? Did she want him to go as a test of his commitment to her? Of her devotion to him? Did she trust him? Did she trust herself? Did she care? Did it matter?

~

Vikki had given Thurmond the luxury of taking whatever time he needed to be comfortable with his decision. Still, Thurmond knew his delay was beginning to cause concern amongst the investors. Vikki did not push or harass him, but local production had already started cranking up to meet demand, and he was beginning to feel pressure to answer.

The marketing campaign was in full swing, and the ad agency was looking for that big splash to keep its momentum. They wanted to release news about the company's expansion, but Vikki held them off. She explained that what happened next depended on whether Mr. Joseph was involved.

At a regularly scheduled board meeting, an executive who represented the primary equity partner for the Asian expansion initiative made an announcement that surprised everyone; Thurmond most of all.

"We are pleased and excited to announce that Asian operations are now finalizing the details for the organization of an exploratory committee on the ground in Taipei...."

Thurmond disliked sitting in on these board meetings because he found them tedious, but this announcement got his attention. Thurmond was unsure whether it was because he hadn't been included in the deliberations or because he was worried that he hadn't been selected.

"Does that mean that a decision has been made on a project manager?" Thurmond blurted out, "…has someone been selected to head up the Asian committee over there?"

"Yessir!" answered the exuberant executive, "…by golly, we have!"

Vikki had hoped to discuss this matter with Thurmond in private before it was announced to the board, but now that it was out in the open, she needed to address it immediately. She calmly rose from her chair and walked around behind the board members seated at the enormous table.

"Thank you for sharing this exciting news, Mr. Jacobs, but you may be a bit premature…" she began pleasantly. "As you may or may not be aware, statutory company regulations require this type of development to be qualified by distributing an executive summary outlining the details. All board members must review that summary and agree on its contents before making any announcements."

Vikki studied the board members' faces and was particularly interested in Randall Jacobs's reaction. He seemed a bit perturbed by her comments, so even though she wanted to squelch Thurmond's fears, she needed to appease the equity partners that Randall represented. She continued, "While I can appreciate the excitement this bit of news can bring, this topic will need to be rescheduled for discussion at the next board meeting after the executive summary has been distributed to the board for review as required by the statute, which I'm certain you can appreciate, Randall."

Randall Jacobs nodded in appreciation, but Thurmond looked at Vikki in astonishment. To him, she seemed unemotional about the bomb that had just dropped, which he couldn't understand.

Vikki noticed the look on Thurmond's face and suggested the board reconvene after lunch. As the executives broke out into small groups, independent conversations began to fill the room as the board members gathered in bunches.

"I'm sorry, Thurmond, I've meant to tell you...." Vikki began as she took his arm and walked him out of the room and into the executive lounge across the lobby from the board room, "...Randall was very excited and should have restrained his enthusiasm."

Thurmond was confused and wasn't sure where to start with his questions. He took a seat on one of the club chairs in the lounge as Vikki closed the door behind them.

"So, you knew about this?" Thurmond asked calmly but concernedly, "What exactly does it mean?"

Vikki replied, "We have engaged a group in Taipei to assist with the expansion. Our schedule was beginning to slip, and we had time commitments with the equity partners that caused some concern— there is nothing to worry about, Thurmond. Everything is under control and can be undone at a moment's notice, depending on what we determine to be the best course of action. We just needed to get some traction over there, and the optics of the delay were not sitting well with the money people. They're still waiting for my final review and approval of the conditions. I had to agree to let them engage someone to keep them happy. Randall was just excited, that's all. He wanted to say something to sound important, and he shouldn't have said anything. It doesn't mean anything other than they have some action going on over there that they can get excited about."

Thurmond was relieved they hadn't shut him out of the process but knew he was the only person to blame. Without any clear indication from Monica about her feelings, he couldn't decide what he should do. Thurmond had become frustrated with her equivocation but realized he was waiting for her permission and knew the decision was his to make, not hers. He couldn't wait any longer.

Anxious and in need of some assurances from Vikki before he agreed to anything, Thurmond replied, "Promise me that I won't get stuck over there, and I can come back whenever I want! Promise me you won't let them trick you into agreeing to anything without talking to me first!"

"I promise, Thurmond," Vikki said sincerely.

"Ok, then I'll go…." Thurmond replied, "…but I'll need to look at that agreement with the people in Taipei before I let them do anything."

"Of course, Thurmond…." Vikki delightedly replied, "…I was going to suggest that myself."

"…and I want you to tell them that I don't want anyone to make any decisions about the project manager over there. I want to pick them myself."

They both stood, and Vikki shook Thurmond's hand firmly.

"I couldn't see this happening any other way Thurmond. I think I speak for the entire team when I say we're all very excited! Let's go back and tell the board you've accepted the position. That you're ready to hit the ground running over there. I'll make all the arrangements. Just tell me how long you'll need to prepare before you leave."

10

Instigation

Monica's uncertainty about the future of her relationship with Thurmond persisted, and except for a few brief interactions, she steered clear of him while she tried to figure it out. She continued scheduling sessions with her pastor, Fr. Elias, hoping it would help resolve her dilemma, but the priest left her with more questions than answers. His tendency to equivocate frustrated her, and she considered canceling their sessions. Upon reflection, however, the conciliatory priest had helped identify the source of her anxiety, so she tolerated his annoying tendencies and continued meeting with him, hoping for some resolution.

When Thurmond told Monica he had accepted the position in Asia, she was sad but not surprised. She knew his leaving would strain their relationship, but when he sought her advice, Monica told him what she considered the truth, that he was the obvious choice. That comment reassured Thurmond that he was making the right decision, but Monica still wondered about his real motivations for leaving and her own for letting him go.

Nervous about his new assignment and excited about the opportunity, Thurmond was ready to leave in short order. While he was confident of his feelings for Monica, he was confused by her misgivings and tried to convince himself that her reservations about their future together would soon pass. He hoped that his time away could benefit them both because it would give each other space to consider what was important. Thurmond remembered a cliche about how absence makes the heart grow fonder and hoped this would prove true.

~

Thurmond received some fanfare when he arrived in Taipei but was soon left to his own devices. He was concerned that there might be some opposition to his presence there, so he focused on becoming accustomed to his new environment and identifying those he could trust.

His unfamiliarity with the language, the business community, and the local culture proved daunting. Fortunately, the language of commerce was English, so although he had trouble understanding anything written or spoken in the local language, he benefited from multiple associates who could translate.

These issues exacerbated his sense of isolation, so he frequently requested that Vikki send an associate from the home plant to assist him or make the trip herself. Vikki was sympathetic but explained that new orders had been coming in at a furious pace, creating pressure to keep the Foundry production up to satisfy the growing demand. As a result, she told him that he needed to rely on his team there in Taipei to help him while she addressed these concerns at home.

Thurmond was happy to hear how well things were going and wished he had not accepted his assignment. He asked if he could return for a quick visit to help her at home, but Vikki told him one of the reasons for the increased demand was the expectation of the new facility in Taipei.

Vikki knew Thurmond was eager to help, but she also knew he was homesick. She had to ensure that things continued progressing in Taipei but agreed to bring him back for a quick visit once he got things started over there and identified a competent person locally that they could trust to manage the project in his absence. Thurmond appreciated her consideration and immediately began fast-tracking his project and searching for an assistant to help facilitate his trip home.

~

Vikki expected that Thurmond's absence would create some lag in production, but she wasn't prepared for such a pronounced increase in demand. This development indicated the need for someone capable of managing production at home in Thurmond's absence. She did not have the expertise or time to take on that added responsibility, so she looked internally for a temporary replacement. She told Sheila to prepare a vacancy announcement and circulate it immediately. Gossip soon spread around the Foundry, generating tremendous interest, and they were quickly flooded with applications.

When Howard became aware, he convinced himself that he deserved the position more than anyone, especially since he had spent the last few years as Thurmond's immediate supervisor. Seeing this as an opportunity to regain his previously enjoyed authority, Howard immediately submitted his application.

Sheila was soon overwhelmed, and the process started to get out of hand. Anxious to fill the vacancy quickly, Vikki helped Sheila sift through all the applications, selected a handful of the most viable candidates, and then immediately summoned them to Thurmond's office for an interview.

Vikki believed that since it was only a temporary internal reassignment, giving candidates any advance notice was unnecessary, so she had Sheila summon them individually over the intercom during their shifts. As a result, no one knew who had been selected until their name had been called. Howie listened intently for his name, wondering if Vikki would lock him out as Thurmond had done but was relieved when Sheila called out his name. Confident that he would be offered the position, Howard immediately reported to Thurmond's office.

Sheila saw Howard approaching and picked up her phone to announce his arrival. When he strode to her desk, she told him to have a seat and handed him his application. Howard rolled it up and stuffed it in his rear pocket as he impatiently took his seat. After a short wait, Sheila's phone rang to notify her that they were ready to see Howard, and she told him he could go in. Howard proudly stood as he pulled his application from his rear pocket and strutted past Sheila's desk muttering to himself, 'About time.'

He saw Vikki sitting behind Thurmond's desk with a recording secretary beside her when he entered the office. He found the secretary's presence unusual but chalked it up to Vikki's peculiar personality and confidently took his seat in front of the large desk.

"Thank you for coming in today."

"You're welcome," Howard replied as he unfurled his wrinkled application and settled into his seat.

"Well then…" Vikki began, "…I understand that by now, everyone is aware of the obvious need for a temporary replacement for Thurmond while he's away heading up our expansion initiative in Taipei."

"That's the word," Howard replied smugly.

Vikki was astonished by the man's conceit and continued with a smile.

"Well, this meeting is not about that position. Not directly, anyway."

Howard became annoyed and asked, "What does that mean exactly, not directly?"

"Yes, well… in reviewing the internal personnel files to find someone with the background and qualifications to fill the vacancy created by Mr. Joseph's temporary reassignment, it has come to our attention that some files have been tampered with. After looking into the matter, it seems only a handful of people had access, and you happen to be one of them."

"How do you figure?" Howard shot back indignantly, "…I don't have anything to do with personnel…."

"You had access and had been seen several times entering and exiting from Mr. Joseph's office…."

Howard began to sweat. He felt like a criminal being interrogated, and he didn't like it one bit. He rolled up his application and began squeezing it with both hands.

"Seen?" Howie replied, "…seen by whom?"

"By our camera Mr. Mallory. We just wanted to know what you were doing in Mr. Joseph's office?"

Howard knew he was caught red-handed and couldn't think of a single lie quick enough to give himself an alibi or plausible excuse. He shoved his application back in his rear pocket as Vikki continued.

"The files in Mr. Joseph's office are confidential and, as such, are privileged information. They are sensitive and essential to the successful operation of this company."

"You said they were personnel files?" Howard replied, "…how are personnel files essential to the successful operation of this company? I mean, what could be essential about that?"

"We are engaged in the most profound expansion in the company's history and have contractual arrangements with equity partners that hold us to a very stringent non-disclosure clause in our partnership agreements. Any breach of confidentiality or the appearance of it has distinct and profound consequences, which we do not intend to become exposed to."

Howard remained silent, and Vikki continued.

"I don't imagine you had any reason to be personally interested in those files, which leads me to believe you were acting on someone else's behalf. If this is the case, I want to know who and why? Providing this information will go a long way toward how we decide to move forward from here."

Howie panicked and could think of only one way to avoid prosecution; he had to tell the truth and reveal that Ehndale had put him up to it. Howard didn't particularly care for the man, and he certainly wasn't going to take the fall for him. Besides, the money he had been paid for his trouble was a pittance, which made him feel exposing Mr. Ehndale was justifiable. Howie was sure Ehndale would be upset, but he needed to extricate himself and told Vikki everything he knew.

Vikki was shocked to learn that Ehndale had been behind the covert activities, and she rigorously questioned Howie. She listened to the descriptions of the information Ehndale had requested Howard to retrieve and tried to understand its reasoning. When she learned it wasn't the personnel files Ehndale was interested in but the due process info that Howie had collected for the Taipei project, she couldn't understand. He couldn't possibly be interested in local ordinances or construction agreements. It had to be the financial considerations that interested him, but why? Was he trying to gain leverage for negotiating equity partnership agreements? If so, then why hadn't he been part of the negotiations? Why hide as a silent partner in an equity contract? What possible advantage could he gain by being a third party? Was he hedging his bets because he didn't want to invest himself? Was he afraid her expansion effort could fail, and if so, why would he think that?

Vikki had many questions she intended to ask Ehndale, but at the moment, she had to deal with Howie. She began reciting snippets from the company handbook about acting on behalf of the company's interest and engaging in activities that compromise the integrity of the company, its officers, or its files and concluded her dissertation.

"…Company policy is very straightforward and clear as to the remedies for these types of infractions, which is immediate termination and possible prosecution, which we are willing to defer, given your willingness to divulge information as to the reasons why you had been engaged in this illegal and unacceptable behavior."

"Termination?" Howard repeated, not believing how different this meeting had gone from how he had anticipated. "You mean I'm fired?"

"Yes, Mr. Mallory, that's exactly what that means. You have until the end of the day today to clear out whatever you have in your workstation. We will deliver your final check to your home within a week of dismissal, effective as of today's close of business. Thank you. You can go now."

Howard was shocked and insulted. He had never been the recipient of reprimands and punishment; he had always been its administrator. He wanted to shout his displeasure at Vikki and lash out with verbal barbs, but he knew she was too stupid to take any of them to heart, which effectively made it a useless endeavor. The recording secretary was busily writing everything down, and Howie wanted to leave some final words that would become his legacy.

"You'll be sorry..." he began, "... you've made a terrible mistake, but I no longer have to worry about that, now do I? You'll have to muddle through the process of watching this dumpster fire of a company slowly extinguish while you pretend to be making improvements. You can't fix a decrepit leviathan with spit, polish, and a new coat of paint. Since before the lawsuit, this place has been dying, and you put the person in charge responsible for almost closing it down! How stupid can you be? You deserve what you get. I'm glad to be rid of this place, and I have more important things I should be doing!"

"Well then, I shouldn't want to keep you from doing them...." Vikki returned, "...Good day, Mr. Mallory."

Howard wanted to scream and jumped up out of his chair. He pulled his application from his rear pocket and threw it in Vikki's direction as she left the room. He stood there fuming while the secretary carefully finished recording everything that had been said.

Now that she knew the truth, Howie believed it wouldn't take long before Vikki confronted Ehndale and revealed his betrayal. Ehndale would undoubtedly be upset and come looking for him.

Suddenly, Howie remembered Bradley's warning in the bar and became concerned about the consequences, so he spent what was left of his money in the local bar blaming the world for being unfair. He drowned his sorrows in his beer and confided openly to the friendly bartender about all his misfortunes.

~

Vikki invited Ehndale to dinner to get him to reveal that he had hired Howie to steal confidential information, and she wanted to know why. Ehndale was furious but politely tempered his reaction.

"I had learned of your intention to expand operations in Asia, my dear, and thought it was brilliant! You should be flattered."

"Not that it hasn't since become public knowledge…." Vikki replied, "…but I was wondering when and from whom you learned of my plans?"

As he waved to the waiter to bring him another drink, Ehndale remarked, "You should know that my efforts are always intended to assist my associates in their endeavors while benefiting myself from their good fortune….'

"Of course," Vikki replied, and Ehndale continued, "Yes, I learned of your company's intentions and immediately saw its potential."

Vikki wanted to get to the truth, so she asked again, "From whom did you hear of this, if I may be so bold as to ask?"

Just then, the waiter returned with Ehndale's drink. Ehndale took a deliberate sip before smiling at the waiter to show his approval. When the waiter had gone, Ehndale snidely replied, "Am I being interrogated, my dear?"

Vikki knew he was being evasive, but she wouldn't let Ehndale intimidate her.

"As you know…." Vikki explained, "…there are confidentiality obligations to maintain, and any breach is of serious concern. Your knowledge of my intention to expand in the Asian marketplace is a breach, and I intend to ascertain the source. So, I need to know how you came by this information?"

Ehndale knew his protege would be persistent, so he smiled and replied, "From a dear friend who attended your celebration. By the way, I was insulted that I was not invited."

Vikki was amused by Ehndale's redirection, a trick he had taught her when she was still relatively young. She laughed and said, "My apologies, but there was no way I could have known of your interest. I would have invited you to the festivities if you had mentioned it. I'd even have given you all the information you desired about my plans for the expansion. You didn't have to employ anyone to steal it. I would have gladly shared it with you."

"If you must know…." Ehndale began, "…the truth is I find my involvement can become onerous. Cumbersome, if you will."

Vikki was well-versed in Ehndale's ability to twist the truth and was very interested in how Ehndale would justify his actions. His response was a clever one, but she wanted him to continue and replied, "You'll have to explain. I'm not sure I understand how that exonerates you from your actions."

"You see, my dear, people are attracted to anything I find interesting, which can impede progress. Once I lose anonymity by disclosing my intentions, I lose the ability to act swiftly. I surmised you would be under pressure from any investor to act quickly, and I wanted to respect that, so I remained silent. I hired Mr. Mallory to gather information to help me determine the best way to assist you with your endeavor without being discovered. When I read of your intentions, I discussed the possibilities with trustworthy equity sources and advised them to invest. So, you see, I only had your best interest at heart. Hiring that fool to assist me in this endeavor was a mistake. For that, I am sorry, but I was acting on your behalf."

Ehndale's explanation was plausible, but Vikki didn't believe him. He acted like she should thank him for hiring someone to spy on her, which did not make her happy.

Vikki was still suspicious of his intentions and wondered how to deal with him. She decided that the wisest course of action would be to make him think she had accepted his explanation. She could find out later what he was up to, but for now, she had the answers she needed.

"Thank you, Ehndale...." Vikki replied as she waved to the waiter to bring her check, "...as always, I am in your debt and ever grateful for your consideration."

"Don't mention it, my dear...." Ehndale replied, "...what else is a shepherd good for but to look after his flock. Your success is always my intention, my dear. I'm so glad I could help and am looking forward to a profitable partnership in your latest flash of brilliance. Well done, my dear, well done!"

~

Ehndale was not in the habit of apologizing and never intended to have another conversation with Vikki about this business again. He was furious that he had been embarrassed, and to ensure it never happened again, somebody needed to be made an example of, and that somebody was Howie.

He conceived of a plan to invite the hapless clod to an intimate evening with a few other select guests and reward him rather than admonish him for his betrayal. Ehndale would instruct the other guests to make Howie feel special and offer him compensation for his troubles in the form of a luxurious vacation. The smug and self-righteous little man would believe he deserved it, which is precisely what Ehndale wanted, and he enjoyed the irony.

It was a trap sprung by pride and avarice. Howie would be utterly unaware that he was being set up. He would relish luxury's attention and benefits while willfully participating in his own demise. Ehndale intended to deal with the fool in a manner befitting his egregious transgressions and immediately instructed Balaam to make all the necessary arrangements.

~

A few days later, Ehndale reached out in a way Howie did not expect. An exquisite invitation was delivered by messenger inviting Howie to a party at Ehndale's house that following weekend.

Howie couldn't decide whether it was a good thing or a mistake to accept Ehndale's invitation and found he had three options; ignore the invitation and get on with his life, go to the party and see what would happen, or run away and start his life anew somewhere else. Since there was nothing of value left for him at the Foundry anymore, Howie was leaning towards the third option.

To make up his mind, Howie decided to visit a local bar and solicit the advice of a bartender he'd come to know named Ted, who had a reputation for being patient. However, Ted had grown weary of Howie's incessant whining and did not want to be responsible for helping him decide. Instead, he didn't recommend any option and advised Howie to look on the bright side, which Howard found somewhat amusing.

Drinking one beer after another, Howard weighed his options with the affable bartender.

"I can't go on the way things are…." Howie confessed, "…I hate being in the mailroom. It's insulting."

"I can definitely see that…." Ted agreed.

"Plus, I don't have the extra money from 'Ehndork' anymore," Howie mumbled through his beer.

"I wouldn't imagine so." Ted agreed.

"But there's a lot to be said for starting over. I mean, the possibilities are endless! I could be an engineer or an architect or something!"

Ted smiled and replied, "Anything is possible…."

"Right!" Howie affirmed and continued, "However, if I go to this stupid party, I could find out what he has to say; I mean, how bad could it be? It's not like he's going to kill me or anything."

"No. Probably not…" Ted agreed.

"He'll probably yell at me or give me some stupid job to embarrass me...' Howie continued, "...he could even be proud of me for standing up to that witch, Vikki! I'm sure he knows how difficult and demanding she is. Maybe he'll ask me to do something to get back at her for finding out about him. Maybe he'll take her company away from her and put me in charge!"

"That's it...." Ted replied jokingly, "... he'll probably buy the company and make you president!"

"Why not?" Howie insisted, "...I mean, I know how to run the place, and it's not rocket science or anything. I mean, if Thurmond can do it, how hard could it be?"

~

Howie eventually accepted Ehndale's invitation and bragged openly at the bar to portray his confidence and satisfy his conceit, even though his fear of reprisal continued to fester. To disguise his fear, Howie made disparaging remarks about Ehndale, which managed to exhaust people's patience, until they challenged Howie's boastfulness by suggesting he may not have even accepted the invitation.

Howie resented this accusation and fiercely proclaimed it to be false. Now, more than ever, he was determined to go to Ehndale's party, if for nothing else, to prove people's insinuations untrue.

11

Chimera

On the day of Ehndale's party, Howie sweat so profusely that his shirt stuck to his skin. Bradley's warning about Ehndale had filled his head with dreadful possibilities, which Howie tried to convince himself didn't concern him. This mounting apprehension made him seriously question the wisdom of his decision, but once arriving at Ehndale's estate, his pride prevented him from leaving. Ignoring the urge to flee, Howie passed through the open gates and drove slowly down the private road, wondering what to expect.

Ehndale had instructed Balaam to greet his guests as they arrived, so the dutiful servant stationed himself at the foot of the monumental stone steps that spilled out from the main entrance. When Howard entered the courtyard, he saw Balaam waving at him, so he gathered his nerve and began driving toward him. When Howie had reached the curious summoner, a uniformed valet suddenly appeared and opened Howie's door. Howie stepped out of his car, exchanged places with the valet, handed him his keys, and then watched his car disappear behind the house.

Howie found himself standing alone with the peculiar little man he hadn't met before and wasn't sure what to do. They stood there looking at each other silently until Balaam languidly remarked, "Mr. Ehndale is expecting you on the Veranda, sir. Shall I show you around?"

Howie nodded in agreement and followed Balaam as he hobbled up the enormous steps, through the front door, and down the main hall, where everything seemed new. He tried to control his fear as they walked through the house, but Howie imagined himself as a prisoner being led to his sentencing.

When conducting his business with Ehndale, Howie had only been in a few rooms. Ehndale had told him to use the kitchen door to gain entry, so when they passed by it, Howie immediately knew where he was. Realizing his mouth was dry, Howie asked for something to drink. Balaam told him to wait in the hall while he fetched him some water, which Howie swallowed in a single gulp.

When they reached the back of the house, a glass wall revealed a patio and an expansive yard where other guests wandered outside. A server carrying a tray of champagne suddenly emerged from an unseen pantry and offered one to Howard. Howie handed the server his empty glass, grabbed a champagne flute, and began drinking it as quickly as possible. The curious little man then excused himself and disappeared with the server, leaving Howie with no idea what would happen next.

Howard grabbed champagne flutes from other servers as they passed by and guzzled them rapidly. He continued doing so until the alcohol started to take effect, making him feel more at ease. After a short while, Howie stepped onto the stone patio and began walking toward a balustrade stretching across the rear of the Veranda.

There was a generous central stair flanked by two short stone piers topped with iron lanterns, and as the daylight began to fade, the light that emanated from the lanterns drew Howie's attention to a couple that had just come up the stairs. Howard didn't consider their appearance particularly unusual until he looked around and noticed that all the guests looked like models from some fashion magazine. Handsome, gorgeous, exquisitely dressed, chatting, drinking, laughing; it was all so perfect that it seemed almost surreal.

He decided to wander down to the lawn but stopped short when he heard a voice bellowing after him and turned to see it was Ehndale addressing him.

"There you are my boy!" Ehndale shouted, "…I was beginning to wonder if you were coming! I was just about to send someone to fetch you!"

Howard didn't know how to respond, so he blurted out the first thing that popped into his head and said, "Welcome…."

Ehndale wore an elegant frock coat, a gambler plantation hat, and a handsome pair of cowboy boots. He held a champagne flute and wore a big smile on his face. A beautiful woman adorned in a colorfully embroidered silk tunic came up from behind Ehndale and slipped her hand around his waist.

"I'm glad you could make it, my dear boy…." Ehndale said as he looked beside him at the woman now in his embrace, "…Come then, meet Layla! My delight and my vexation!"

"You're terrible…" the woman replied in a decidedly heavy accent, kissing Ehndale before stepping forward to greet Howard.

"Enchanté…" she said as she tenderly took Howard's hand, then suddenly jerked him in against her body and wrapped her arm around his waist to keep him from pulling away. She pressed up against him so he could feel the curves of her body and then began kissing him passionately.

Ehndale laughed and said, "Insatiable and insufferable! Now you know why I say she is my vexation!"

Without ever taking her eyes off Howie, Layla suddenly released him from her grip and slowly backed toward Ehndale. When she returned to his side, she slipped her hand around Ehndale's waist and laughed delightfully. Ehndale kissed her and said, "I'll deal with you later, my dear…" then he slapped her on the buttocks and sent her away.

Howard felt strangely aroused by the entire experience but said nothing. He stared at the woman as she flitted away laughing, trying to figure out what had just happened. Ehndale noticed Howie lasciviously leering at her and remarked, "Lovely creature that! I should think you believe she likes you, but in all honesty, my good man, she does that to everybody. It's her way of saying hello!"

"I didn't mind it one bit!" Howie returned, "...I wish more people were like that."

Ehndale smiled and replied, "...one should only hope, if they were, that they would all be as attractive as my darling Layla. Otherwise, it would be more of a nuisance than a pleasure. Wouldn't you agree?"

Howard suddenly wondered why he was there as he thought about how to respond. His experience thus far gave him the impression that Ehndale was not mad at him, and although he was relieved, he couldn't figure out why. The confused look on Howard's face made Ehndale realize an explanation was probably in order.

"My dear boy..." he began, "...as you may or may not be aware, I have been able to negotiate some rather favorable contracts in the form of investments in the foundry's operation recently. These were due, in no small part, to the information you gathered for me, and I wanted to be sure to thank you properly."

Ehndale waved his hand, and a server immediately appeared with a tray of champagne flutes filled to the brim, and they each grabbed one. Ehndale threw his arm around Howard and led him down the central stairs to the lawn. As they walked across large stones arranged in a meandering path through the magnificently maintained property, Ehndale explained why Howie was there and, more importantly, why all these other people were there.

"I have arranged this little soiree in honor of our success and gathered some close friends to help us celebrate."

"I thought you were mad at me...." Howard declared, not thinking that he should probably have refrained from reminding Ehndale about his recent foul-ups.

"We'll not talk of missteps tonight, my dear boy...." Ehndale insisted, "... One cannot win wars without losing some battles. Tonight, we will celebrate the victories!"

Howard was relieved and began allowing his pride to influence his reason. His fear began to evaporate and was replaced instead with a growing conceit. He had always believed that Ehndale should have appreciated his efforts and Ehndale's statement warranted this belief.

Unknown to Howie, Ehndale had demanded his other guests congratulate Howie, the guest of honor, as a condition of their acceptance of his invitation. This condition was executed without exception, and every guest congratulated Howie, thanking him profusely for assisting their host with his recent investments.

After introducing Howard to more people than he could remember, Ehndale excused himself, but not before asking an exceedingly polite gentleman named 'Ganneau' to ensure that the guest of honor had a good time before leaving. Howard appreciated the offer but was more interested in making some young woman's acquaintance and preferred to mingle alone. He believed Ganneau's presence would hinder him in this effort because of his fabulously handsome appearance, but he couldn't say no, so Howie was stuck with this escort wherever he went.

Howie's aversion to being chaperoned was evident, so Ganneau began initiating conversations with guests he thought may interest him. One attractive young woman was introduced as an artist, and as they spoke, Ganneau mentioned a Paris exhibit, with which they both seemed somewhat familiar. This exhibit sparked a considerable discussion with the young woman and was, therefore, something of interest to Howie.

"I'm sure you know of the fabulous art exhibit Ehndale is sponsoring in Paris next month?" the young woman asked.

"No, unfortunately, I'm not...." Howard replied awkwardly.

"Well, I'm sure it was an oversight...." Ganneau offered, "...you absolutely must come! Ehndale has a Chateau in Provence, where we stay whenever we visit Paris. It's a stunning estate in an incredible setting. I'm sure he was planning on inviting you. Perhaps you don't remember?"

"No, actually, he hasn't invited me...." Howard returned impolitely, "...I think I would have remembered that."

The young woman laughed and told Howard he should come anyway; "...there are so many people there, no one would know! You should come! It's fun!"

"Well..." Howard stammered, not knowing what he should say, "...given my relationship with Ehndale, I'm not sure it would be appropriate for me to go. I mean, I'm his gofer, a messenger, and I can't imagine many messengers get invited to something that swanky."

"Nonsense! You're much more than that!" Ganneau exclaimed, "...Mr. Ehndale will confirm it! I'm sure he had just forgotten...."

Ganneau began scanning the lawn for Ehndale, and Howard replied.

"Don't bother. It's fine. I'm sure our host has more important things to do than confirm I'm invited to his stupid party in Paris."

Howie's disappointment was pronounced and indignant. The young woman suddenly lost interest and politely excused herself, disappointing Howard. He became noticeably reflective as he couldn't understand how all these beautiful people could celebrate him and then easily cast him aside. In truth, they had made him feel inadequate and out of place. The guests seemed to be living glorious lives, which depressed him when he considered how pathetic his had become. Ganneau noticed the sudden shift in Howard's demeanor and quickly tried to remedy it.

"I don't see a drink...." Ganneau remarked as he looked at Howard's empty hands, "...let me get you one. Is champagne OK, or would you rather have something more potent?"

Howard didn't respond, but Ganneau was undeterred. He promised to return swiftly and ran off to fetch Howard a drink, leaving him alone with his thoughts. As he waited for his obnoxiously happy and handsome escort, Howard considered how he had expected admonishment from Ehndale but was instead showered with accolades. He believed he deserved to be celebrated for his efforts on Ehndale's behalf, but he anticipated compensation in the form of payment, not praise. Congratulations were not what he wanted, and although he knew it was meant to make him feel appreciated, Howard did not enjoy it. He received praise from people he didn't know, people who didn't know him, and people who all seemed to know each other, which made him feel disconnected and resentful of what he considered insincerity. They were extolling his achievements like an assignment, not an honest acknowledgment. It cost these people nothing to praise him, yet they all had so much more they could give him.

Howard wanted to leave, but he knew he couldn't without thanking Ehndale for whatever that was worth. He decided to have one last drink, which he would finish while waiting for Ehndale to say his goodbyes. When Ganneau returned, he was accompanied by Layla and another young woman Howard hadn't met yet. This other woman was shorter than most and had dark hair arranged in a stunning box braid.

"Nice to see you again, darling…." Layla joked, "…I hope Ganny is showing you a good time here."

Being slightly sarcastic about the amount of attention he had been getting from the insufferably accommodating Ganneau, Howard returned, "Seems like more than I deserve…."

"Don't be silly…." Ganneau replied as he handed Howard his drink.

"This is 'Neema'…" Layla announced as she directed Howard's attention toward the beautiful woman beside her, "…she saw you walking around and wanted to be introduced."

Howard was sure that Layla had invented the story about the woman's interest in meeting him. Still, he was enthralled by her appearance, so he accepted the introduction to occupy himself with someone he didn't mind looking at while he waited for Ehndale.

Neema stepped forward, offered her hand, and said, "Pleasure…."

Howard leered at her as he gently took her hand and replied, "Pleasures all mine!"

Ganneau and Layla noticed his pronounced interest and left the two alone as they politely excused themselves. Howard became so infatuated with Neema's company that he forgot about Ehndale. He also lost track of time and the considerable amount of alcohol he was consuming. The two spent the next few hours drinking, talking, and flirting until they lost any inhibition they would have had otherwise. They became so familiar that they began touching and rubbing against one another, which excited Howard tremendously. When Neema suggested that they go for a walk, Howie quickly accepted. He took her hand as they strolled away from the manor house, and when they had gone far enough away so as not to be heard by anyone, Neema suggested they find a place more suitable for a little more privacy. He excitedly agreed, and she led him to the cottage where Bradley had previously taken residence.

~

Howard couldn't precisely recall what had happened the previous evening but awoke the following day to find he was still at the cottage. He was disappointed that Neema wasn't there, but he was elated that she had apparently spent at least a portion of the night with him. Besides the massive amounts of alcohol he knew he had consumed, Howie vaguely remembered sharing several different drugs with Neema, including something she had suggested would help him perform.

An urgent need to use the bathroom suddenly overcame him, so Howie fought his massive headache and rolled out of bed to take care of it. While in the bath, he found some aspirin, so when he'd finished, he returned to the kitchen and poured himself several glasses of water to wash down the aspirin and satiate his pronounced thirst.

His rough condition made him want to crawl back into bed, but he wasn't sure he was even supposed to be there, so he collected his clothing instead. As he gathered his things, he heard a knock at the door and couldn't think of anyone who knew he was there but Neema. He looked out the window and was disappointed when he saw the obnoxiously pleasant Ganneau smiling up at him.

"Bonjour, mon ami!" Ganneau shouted, "...gorgeous day this, no? You must come and enjoy it!"

Howard was not in the mood and wanted to ignore the invitation but changed his mind when Ganneau continued.

"Mr. Ehndale asked me to come to fetch you for breakfast. He had something important he wanted to talk to you about."

Howard was unsure of how Ehndale could know he was there, but it didn't matter as he was in no condition to try and figure it out.

"I'll be right down..." he shouted back, then proceeded to get dressed as he returned to the bathroom to freshen up.

Howard splashed water on his face, combed his fingers through his hair, and then wiped his teeth with his finger. He gathered up the last of his things and gargled with a soda he had found in the refrigerator to mask what he assumed to be his hellacious breath and jogged down the stairs to meet Ganneau.

Ganneau escorted him to the rear patio, where several tables had been set up for some guests who had spent the evening at the estate. A wait staff supplied a steady stream of Mimosas and Bloody Mary's, and a few side tables were resplendent with various fruits, crepes, waffles, cakes, coffee, tea, ice water, and juice.

Howard was not in the mood to chit-chat with anyone, so he immediately poured himself a large cup of coffee, grabbed a few treats, and sat alone with Ganneau.

Ehndale joined his guests within a few minutes and greeted everyone individually before sitting beside Howard. "I must apologize, my dear boy. It has been brought to my attention that I have inadvertently forgotten to invite you to the Paris opening."

"No worries..." Howard replied, "...your party last night was quite enough."

"Nonsense!" Ehndale returned. "I've sponsored this event for years, and every year they select an artist for an exclusive opening, with complimentary admission to all of my guests. I'm sure they have your name! I must have forgotten to relay that information to you. I suppose I assumed you already knew. My apologies, my good man."

Howard did not know what to say and began eating a piece of cake to give himself a moment to think. He was not welcome at the foundry and was about to look for a job, so the prospect of visiting Paris was incredibly appealing. Still, he thought he'd rather skip it if it were like his experience with the beautiful people at the previous night's affair.

"You simply must come!" Ganneau said excitedly, "…the pre-party is fabulous and makes last night seem like a bore. Besides, Neema will be there…."

Neema's presence was certainly welcome news, and entirely changed Howard's opinion.

"If you insist, I guess I could go."

"Of course, you will go…." Ganneau replied, "…everything is arranged! You have nothing to do but enjoy yourself. The Chateau is breathtaking, and the grounds are spectacular! You're going to love it!"

Ehndale's guests filtered out as the wait staff began clearing the tables. Howard thought of Neema as he listened to Ganneau's Paris tales until they were the only ones that remained other than Ehndale. Once the servers had cleared the tables, Ehndale dismissed them and asked Ganneau for a moment alone with Howard. Ganneau immediately excused himself, and Ehndale suggested they continue their chat inside. Howie agreed, and the two men left the Veranda and went to Ehndale's library.

~

The library was alight with a small fire that Ehndale had Balaam prepare to make the dimly lit room cozy. Ehndale invited Howie to sit in one of two oversized club chairs before the fireplace. Ehndale tugged gently on a chord beside the mantle and asked Howard if he wanted a drink. He then settled into the chair beside his guest and pulled a smoking pipe and a pouch of tobacco from his side pocket, which he placed on the table between them.

They were both quietly watching the fire when Balaam arrived and quickly took their drink orders before leaving to fetch them. Howie continued staring into the fireplace as Ehndale rose from his seat and walked over to a lectern with a large leather book. Using the long silk tassels that dangled from the book Ehndale turned the pages in bunches until he found the page he wanted. He shifted one of the tassels to mark the page and slowly ran his finger down the list of names until he found the space he had reserved for Howie. He covered the other names with parchment paper, placed a fountain pen on the book, and returned to his seat.

Balaam returned with their drinks, which he carefully set on the table between them. He stoked the fire gently and threw on another log before promptly leaving the room. Ehndale lifted his glass to toast Howie, and each took a quick drink. Ehndale then stuffed his pipe with tobacco and lit it with a few quick draws. As the room began to fill with the pleasant aroma of Cavendish tobacco, Ehndale leaned back in his chair and spoke.

"I have important things in mind for you, my good man! Things that people only dream of but rarely realize. I see potential in you and plan to introduce you to members of my inner circle, an honor only a select few can claim."

Ehndale's compliments made Howard feel important, something he had not felt the night before, despite everyone's praise. Ehndale continued.

"To be granted this honor, you must confirm your commitment with a solemn allegiance that extends beyond death. Every inner circle member has agreed to this and embraced the opportunity."

It all sounded terrific, but Howie was confused about the meaning of allegiance beyond death. Howard believed Ehndale was a bit eccentric, and his comment made him sound crazy, but the prospect of becoming a member of his elite group was enticing, so he asked.

"What do I have to do then?"

Ehndale motioned towards the lectern with his pipe and said, "You'll have to sign a contract, my dear boy, to guarantee a life of luxury and pleasure. A life without hardship, failure, or pain!"

Howard couldn't understand what this lunatic was talking about, but the more he spoke, the crazier he sounded.

"That all sounds great…." Howard returned, "…but what exactly is this allegiance…and what is beyond death supposed to mean?"

Ehndale paused to take a short draw from his pipe and released the smoke slowly. He picked up his glass and took a small drink.

"It means that after enjoying everything this earthly life has to offer, you agree to give me control of your immortal soul, to do with as I wish."

Something in Ehndale's tone made the lunacy of his claim sound sincere, but Howard didn't believe in any afterlife and began laughing out loud. Ehndale smiled and continued.

"Once that's done, my dear boy, you will enjoy all the benefits of membership in my inner circle, including the annual Paris opening and the Chateau party in Provence. You'll love it there. Ganneau was not exaggerating! It's breathtaking!"

Howard wasn't concerned about a soul he didn't believe existed, which meant Ehndale's offer cost him nothing! Excited about his prospects and enamored with the idea of spending time in Paris with Neema, he finished his drink and replied.

"Where do I sign?"

12

Fatal Error

Howard was excited about his trip but was disappointed with his travel arrangements. Despite his protests, Ehndale had assigned Ganneau to accompany him under the ridiculous pretense of ensuring his safety, so he was forced to travel with this obnoxiously attentive companion for his entire journey.

When they arrived at the airport in Toulon, they were met by an escort who immediately whisked them away to Ehndale's Chateau in a limousine. As they drove towards their destination, Howard marveled at the profound beauty surrounding him and wondered how people could come to own such stunning estates. His enjoyment of the countryside was eventually interrupted when he noticed that they had begun to slow down. The limousine turned off from the main road and drove towards two pillars that marked an estate entrance. Ganneau pointed to a bronze placard mounted to one of the pillars and said, "Voilà! Le Château de Bartholomé!" Howard did not speak French, but he understood that they had arrived at their destination.

Tiny pebbles crunched beneath the vehicle's weight as they drove toward a magnificent building high on a hill. The entrance drive stretched almost a mile and was lined on both sides with towering Cypress trees trimmed to a point. As Howard looked through the slender Cypress trees, he saw rows of grapevines on one side with olive trees in an open field beyond, and on the other side of the road were straight lines of purple lavender, rolling gently into the distance.

After passing several smaller structures, the road emptied into a walled courtyard immediately in front of the building that Howard had seen from a distance. Ehndale's house staff had seen the car coming up the drive and had assembled to greet the arriving guests in the courtyard. When they came to a halt, Ganneau quickly jumped out of the vehicle and directed the staff to retrieve their luggage while Howard gazed at everything he saw. Ganneau laughed at his new friend and said, "Magnifique, n'est-ce pas?"

The porters retrieved their luggage and carried it toward the main entrance across the courtyard. Ganneau gently pat Howard on the back to suggest they should follow, and the two men began walking behind as Howard continued to admire the building.

The principal structure was a magnificent building that stood several stories tall. Its central volume generally appeared square and had large round towers in each corner, capped with finials on pointed roofs that looked like witches' hats. The uppermost level was tucked away behind a series of slender dormers arranged uniformly across steeply pitched slate roofs. The building also featured many prodigious chimneys, one of which drooled white smoke with a delightful aroma that swept through the courtyard on a gentle breeze.

"They're preparing something for us to eat...." Ganneau explained, "Smells delicious, doesn't it?"

Howard was hungry and agreed, but he hadn't realized how tired he was until they had started up the entrance steps. Thinking he'd rather take a nap than sit at a table eating, he asked if he could grab something to eat from the kitchen to bring to his room. Ganneau replied, "Everything is at your disposal, my friend! You can do whatever you want!"

Ganneau informed the porters of their intentions and turned to Howard, saying, "Je suis affamée! Suis-moi!"

The confused look on Howard's face made Ganneau realize that he had continued speaking French, so with a laugh, he promptly translated, "Let's grab something to eat, my friend! I know the way to the kitchen! Come with me!"

Howard followed Ganneau as he navigated through the expansive house. When they reached the kitchen, they found a small staff scurrying around, busily preparing trays of delicious-smelling food. Howard quickly stuffed some croissants into his pocket as Ganneau exchanged pleasantries with the kitchen staff.

They selected a few treats from a tray on the service counter, which they hastily ate as they made their way to the second-floor lobby, where their porters had been patiently waiting for them. Ganneau spoke to the porters briefly and followed behind them with Howard as they were shown to their rooms. When they stopped outside a room numbered 16, the porter carrying Howard's luggage turned to him and said, "Votre Chambre monsieur."

"This is your room, my friend." Ganneau translated, "I'm just down the hall in 18 if you need anything."

As the porter placed Howard's luggage inside his room, Ganneau continued, "Mr. Ehndale has not arrived, but your lady friend and a few other guests should be here anytime!"

Howard assumed Ganneau was referring to Neema and was excited to hear that she would be arriving soon, but he needed to get some rest and hoped it wouldn't be for a few hours.

As Howard marveled at his accommodations, Ganneau followed him into the room and said, "Make yourself comfortable and get some rest! You're going to need it! We're going to Collobrières later this afternoon for the 'Fetes de la Chataignes.' It's an annual chestnut festival, and everyone loves it! It's a lot of fun!"

Ganneau then bid his friend farewell and promptly left with his porter.

Howard closed the door and placed his suitcase beside a dresser that flanked a canopied bed in the corner of the room. A freestanding claw-foot tub was situated in the opposite corner, which seemed odd to Howard that it would be out in the open, but then again, it was all new to him, and everything was strange.

Standing motionless, Howard studied the room, which he thought could be the most magnificent he had ever seen.

One wall was occupied entirely with built-in bookcases filled with books, artwork, and delicate knick-knacks. An elegant chandelier in the center of the room twinkled with sunlight pouring through enormous windows, which occupied most of an opposing wall. The deep-set windows were framed by large trim casings and curtain valances, which stretched from low built-in window seats to a coffered ceiling above, with tiny paintings occupying the scant space between.

A grand fireplace with an immense mantel framed by elaborate trim-work that rose gracefully to the coffered ceiling above was on an adjacent wall. Beside the fireplace was a door that led to what Howard imagined to be a bathroom, which he was suddenly acutely aware of the urgent need to use. He rushed to open the door and was surprised by a comely chambermaid who had just finished cleaning the room. She smiled at Howard and said, "Excusez-moi, s'il vous plaît".

It just keeps getting better! Howard thought to himself as he leered at the pretty young girl while she gathered her things and left.

Howard was exhausted and laid in bed, but a series of servants came to fit out his room for his stay and foiled his attempt to get some rest. Howard grew impatient and impolitely relayed his annoyance, but his complaints only confused and amused the attendants as none seemed to speak English. When he finally found himself alone and undisturbed, he fell asleep but was soon rudely awakened by another unwelcome knock at his door. Angered by the staff's persistence, he yelled, "GO AWAY! I DON'T NEED ANY MORE TOWELS!"

He threw his covers over his head and rolled onto his side, hoping he had rid himself of the annoying servants' interruptions. When he heard the door open and close, he threw off his covers to admonish the staff for disturbing him and was surprised to see Neema smiling at him. She removed her sunglasses and said, "I don't have any towels."

As she approached him, Howard leered at her lasciviously. She wore wispy linen pants, a felt fedora hat, and a translucent white t-shirt that left little to the imagination. She hung the rose-colored sunglasses between her breasts on the deep V-neck of her t-shirt and gently leaned in to kiss him on both cheeks. Aroused by her appearance, Howard pulled her over and passionately kissed her. Neema laughed and rolled off him to sit beside him on the edge of the bed.

Howard knew he would never get any rest, so he got out of bed, walked around to the bureau, and threw open his luggage to unpack. As he removed his clothing from the suitcase and placed it in the bureau, Neema began describing the details of her trip and asked, "Are you going to the Chestnut Festival with me this afternoon?"

"I don't know…" he replied, "… I'm pretty tired."

"The Festival is one of the highlights of our trip, love." She coyly said, "…you simply must come. Who else will chaperon me?"

Neema rose from the bed, walked up behind Howard, wrapped her arms around him, and pressed tightly against his body. He turned around to kiss her and replied, "Of course, I will, babe! I wouldn't miss it for the world!"

~

Over a dozen other guests joined Howard and Neema at the Fetes de la Chataignes festival in Collobrières. Howard and Neema were accompanied by Ganneau and another couple they had come to know rather well. They traveled separately in small groups in a series of exquisite cars Ehndale had put at their disposal while staying at the Chateau.

They found the streets crowded with vendors selling chestnut-derived treats when they arrived. There were roasted chestnuts, candied chestnuts, chestnut biscuits, pies, cakes, preserves, pastes, and some chestnut beer and local wine to wash it all down. Howard found the entire experience incredibly weird, but he enjoyed his time with Neema and believed it was something he would never forget.

After spending the whole afternoon there, Ganneau suspected his companions would appreciate having something other than chestnuts and suggested they return to the estate in time to enjoy a proper supper. They all agreed and piled into their car for the drive back to the Chateau, and when they arrived, Ganneau pointed at a chimney spewing white smoke barely visible against the darkening sky and announced, "I can almost taste the Duck Cassoulet!"

Howard had leaned over and was sleeping on Neema's lap as she stroked her fingers through his hair. When he heard Ganneau's comment, he opened his eyes, looked up at Neema, and said, "I'll fall asleep in my food if I don't lie down before I eat!"

Everyone found Howard's comment ridiculously entertaining and laughed as they left the car to return to their rooms so they could wash off the smell of chestnuts and dress for dinner. Neema walked into the Chateau with her arm around Howard's waist and quietly informed him that she had decided to stay with him. Howard was thrilled and suggested they skip dinner for some time alone together, and neither was seen again until the following day at breakfast.

~

Ganneau was pleased that Howard had enjoyed his time alone with Neema but maintained that to enjoy his Provence experience fully, Howard should also spend time with the other guests. Neema encouraged him to heed Ganneau's advice, and after breakfast, Howard accompanied Neema, Ganneau, and a few other guests on a full-day excursion to Arles and the Pont du Gard.

That evening the couple dressed for dinner and joined the other guests for a marvelous meal prepared by the estate executive chef. As Howard listened to people's stories about their trip to Arles and the Chestnut Festival, he suddenly wondered about everyone's association with Ehndale but learned nothing from what was said.

When they had finished dinner, Howard was informed that it was customary for guests to gather after dinner in the Chateau's grand ballroom for music and dancing until very late in the evening. Howard preferred spending his evening alone in his room with Neema, but when she confirmed that she intended to participate, Howard decided to join her.

As the evening wore on, people began breaking into smaller, more intimate groups and ventured about the Chateau to continue their partying until dawn. Howard discovered that these groups would find a place where they could be alone to indulge in behavior Howard had previously thought deviant.

The next few days went much the same, with lavish excursions during the day followed by an exceptional dinner with decadent revelry afterward. On each subsequent evening, Howard became more accepting of the other guests' behavior, which was very different from anything he had previously been accustomed to or even aware of.

~

Ehndale planned to arrive at his Chateau a few days after his guests had been without him. When the time had come for him to join them, he boarded his private jet and flew to Toulon, where he was greeted by a limousine that took him to his Chateau in Provence's countryside.

Before Ehndale's arrival, Howard had begun engaging in behavior he would never have considered. Drugs and alcohol were rampant, and sex was free-spirited and wanton. Neema had helped him abandon his preconceptions of acceptable behavior and encouraged him to embrace this new lifestyle as part of the life he would enjoy while in Ehndale's employ.

When Ehndale arrived, there was much celebration, and his guests lavished him with praise and gratitude. However, Howard had not yet gotten out of bed and was noticeably absent from the reception, which did not escape Ehndale's attention.

After greeting his guests, Ehndale pulled Ganneau aside and asked, "Where's the young lad Howard?"

"He's still sleeping…." Ganneau replied, "… he's been enjoying the company of Neema, who's taken more than a modest affinity for him these last few days."

"Excellent!" Ehndale exclaimed.

Awakened by the commotion, Howard was surprised to find himself alone. He took account of the 'injuries' he had sustained due to some intimate shenanigans he had participated in the previous evening with Neema, amongst others. With a splitting headache and an insatiable thirst, he slowly rolled out of bed, dressed, came downstairs, and went directly to the kitchen. Once there, he drank an entire pint of juice and then grabbed a croissant on his way to the veranda, where his insufferable escort immediately spotted him.

"Here he is!" Ganneau announced as Howard stepped out into the blinding sunlight of that midmorning. Insinuating the lateness of his arrival, Ehndale jokingly said, "Après-midi monsieur!"

Everyone laughed, but Howard had no idea that he had been made the butt of a joke. Ehndale continued, "I should think you have become accustomed to the fashion with which one approaches their time here in Provence, my good man!"

Howard had no idea what Ehndale meant and walked around the table to sit in a chair that Ehndale had asked his guests to make available for him. When he was seated, Ehndale continued.

"…and, if I am to understand Ganneau correctly, you have solicited the assistance of one of my female guests to help you. Yes?"

Howard assumed he was referring to Neema and nodded in agreement as he helped himself to some of the treats on the table before him.

"Outstanding!" Ehndale exclaimed, "…I knew you would be a quick study."

Ehndale's guests then told him about their excursions to local festivals and towns. When they had finished, Ehndale announced that he had arranged a special visit to a local winery for his guests, including grape stomping and a horseback tour of the winery's expansive vineyard.

Excited by the announcement, many guests left to prepare for the excursion, but Howard remained. He had never ridden a horse before and was not particularly interested in learning. Ganneau recognized his friend's reluctance and encouraged him by saying, "You will simply love it! The vineyards are spectacular, and the feeling of the mighty beast between your legs is beyond description!"

Much to Howard's disappointment, Neema told him she had made other plans and would not join them. Still, at the insistence of his insufferable companion Ganneau, Howard eventually agreed and spent the day riding through and drinking up the vineyard in the French countryside with Ehndale, Ganneau, and some other guests.

Ehndale knew the lifestyle Howard had been experiencing in Provence drastically differed from anything he had ever known. However, he was ecstatic that he seemed to have become accustomed to life there at the Chateau after only a few days. He was also pleased that, by all accounts, Howard seemed to be easily influenced by Neema, which perfectly suited his plan.

When they returned from the vineyard, Howard settled back into his room, where he found Neema anxiously waiting for him. After a brief but passionate interlude, the couple joined the other guests for dinner and danced in the great room.

That evening the festivities were more extravagant than they had been at any point during Howard's stay there. An assortment of dignitaries joined Ehndale in a jubilant atmosphere to celebrate his return to Provence. After a few hours, Neema suggested to Howard that they join a few other guests in the crypt for a 'special celebration.' Having already achieved a prodigious level of intoxication, Howie happily agreed and accompanied the incredibly effusive Neema and several other couples to the confines of the crypt beneath the main hall, where they could hear the muffled tones of the revelry above.

When they reached the crypt, a few couples accompanying them separated into corners of the chamber for some semblance of privacy, but when they spontaneously engaged in intimate acts, everyone there was close enough to be considered partners in an atmosphere of collective intimacy.

Neema took Howard by the hand to join a few others sitting on the floor around a low-lying table, where they shared drugs of every sort. The candles' flicker on the table enhanced the hallucinogenic impact, and after a short while, people's faces began to melt along with the wax onto the table before them. Neema left the group to join others who were stripping off each other's clothing indiscriminately. Howard became aroused and quickly joined in.

Some guests began inflicting pain to heighten their experience and used hot wax, ropes, and clamps to hurt and humiliate each other. Some wore masks, collars, and corsets and role-played positions of dominance and subjugation. They burned each other with candles and cigarettes and performed perverse acts that would have normally shocked Howard. Still, Neema had introduced him to pain and humiliation, so Howard embraced it as part of his experience with her.

Howard was initially agreeable to the bizarre experience, but it soon escalated into a frenzy. When it began to feel dangerous, Howard looked to Neema for reassurance, but she was gone, and he found himself alone amongst strangers that derived pleasure from inflicting pain. Stripped naked and bound with heavy ropes to a column, Howard felt incredibly vulnerable. He couldn't extricate himself and realized he was in trouble, but he could do nothing about it. He began calling out for Neema when a woman wearing a spiked leather collar, mask, stiletto heels, and nothing else stuffed a rag into his mouth and whipped him furiously. Frightened and alone, Howard began to cry and scream muffled screams through the gag that his tormentor had stuffed into his mouth.

~

Ehndale had asked Ganneau to join him for a drink away from the other guests so they could chat and retired to the balcony overlooking the ballroom on the second level of the Chateau. He placed his glass on the table between their two chairs and took a long drag of the Cavendish tobacco he had stuffed into his pipe.

Ganneau wondered if Ehndale could hear the faint but distinct sound of someone screaming above the constant noise emanating from the party downstairs. These muffled screams wisped through the air like the smoke from Ehndale's pipe and then disappeared as quickly. He looked at Ehndale as if to ask what that sound could be, and Ehndale suggested with a smile that it was nothing as he began to lecture his dutiful associate on the benefits, pitfalls, and responsibilities of power.

"Having the misfortune of being born into a world one did not choose to live in or be part of, is a universal experience. A common condition we all share. In this instance, there is nothing to justify one's existence. Therefore, the very nature of a man is to be consumed with personal affairs, which have the well-being of the individual first and foremost, as it should be. Without concern for the self, there can be no self-preservation, development, or accomplishment."

Ganneau took a drink from his glass and nodded to confirm his understanding. Ehndale took another drag off his pipe before placing it in the ashtray on the side table where he had put his glass and continued:

"Ambition, however, is not a matter of self-preservation but a pursuit of becoming greater than oneself...."

Ehndale shifted forward in his chair and stared straight into Ganneau's eyes, and continued:

"Ambition, if not tempered, can grow to an enormous degree, which is not necessarily an undesirable result or pursuit. There is a laudable desire to seek power. It is a just and noble cause, but there is also an obligation that comes with the opportunities afforded to those fortunate few who possess it."

Ganneau struggled to understand but nodded in acknowledgment so as not to interrupt Ehndale's discourse. Ehndale paused to take a drink, then continued, "Make no mistake, though, that when the indulgence of a man's ambition is confined to the breath of one's own selfish desires, it only disgusts those it oppresses, contrary to the entire enterprise. Understand that this appetite is not, in and of itself, an inherently bad thing. Still, before one covets wealth and attempts to utilize its power, it is essential to know how to use it or risk losing it to another's appetite for it."

As the sound of screaming became less pronounced, Ehndale smiled at Ganneau, tapped out what remained in his pipe and put it back in his pocket, then concluded.

"Ambitious men who find themselves in possession of power, whether by circumstance, luck or effort, ought to be wary of others who are accustomed to it and know how to get it; otherwise, they risk becoming casualties of their own ambition."

Ehndale rose from his chair, finished his drink, and said, "Bonne Nuit mon bon ami ! I will see you in the morning."

13

Nature and Dignity

A story appeared in the local newspaper about the tragic death of a local resident. The story's circumstances piqued the editor's interest, so it was placed on a side column of the front page instead of in the obituaries, where it would have ordinarily been. People who read it were intrigued, and the news of Mr. Mallory's demise began to spread.

This pronounced interest prompted the editor to publish a continuing series of articles elaborating on the more sensational aspects of the accident. One such development was the involvement of the French judicial police, who initiated an investigation to rule out any possibility of foul play. An autopsy was performed as part of the investigation, and the paper published a copy of the coroner's official report, which they had somehow managed to acquire.

That report concluded that although Mr. Mallory had sustained many physical injuries, his system had toxic narcotics levels, suggesting that a drug overdose was the most likely cause of death. The report also stated that Mr. Mallory's physical injuries were consistent with those typically suffered during sadomasochistic rituals. This convinced the investigators that the deceased had overindulged while partying and nothing more. As a result, no charges were ever filed, and the case was dismissed.

With the conclusion of the investigation, interest in the story waned, and the newspaper dropped the story. People considered

Howard Mallory nothing more than an unfortunate reprobate who had probably gotten what he deserved. He became the butt of people's jokes, until his memory gradually faded away.

~

Thurmond came home from Taipei on a scheduled rotation and learned of Howard's death from Emerson on a morning commute. As the men drove, Emerson relayed the newspaper's account of Howie's demise, which Thurmond considered a disturbing and terrible tale. Thurmond believed it was a fate nobody should have had to endure, not even Howie, a man he despised. Emerson didn't usually have any opinions on such things, but he believed the newspaper's accounts of the incident did not relay the whole truth and suggested a possible cover-up. Emerson argued his conspiracy theories well after people had lost interest and was mocked by his friends for his trouble.

When they arrived at Kate's, Emerson invited Thurmond to join him for coffee. Thurmond had always considered the invitation a respectful gesture for being given a ride and typically declined. However, he was keenly interested in finishing their conversation that morning and not in a hurry, so he graciously accepted his friend's invitation.

Kate's Diner had always been a source of scuttlebutt, and, for a short while, it was rampant with talk of the circumstances of Howard's death. Although the story was horrific, there was little sympathy for the man, and people eventually grew weary of discussing the matter. Emerson told Thurmond it was no longer a popular topic and suggested they sit alone at a table to keep their conversation private. Thurmond agreed, and the two men sat alone at a table to continue their discussion.

Emerson's friends wondered why he hadn't sat with them and tried to eavesdrop on his conversation with Thurmond. When they thought they heard Emerson repeating his ridiculous conspiracy theories about Howard's demise, they felt obliged to offer their opinions, which Thurmond tolerated because Emerson didn't seem to mind.

The conversation gradually spread beyond the two tables until it grew loud enough to be heard throughout the Diner. People turned their attention to it, listened intently, and interjected by shouting when they felt they had something to contribute.

Thurmond considered Howard an insufferable putz and had no affinity for the man, but he still found people's judgment of him shocking. Even those Thurmond knew to be Howie's friends denied affiliation with him because they feared they would be considered deviants by association. This betrayal angered Thurmond to the point where he unintentionally defended Howard's character until his voice became quite loud.

That morning Eddie and Stan had come to Kate's and overheard Thurmond's defense of Howard from across the Diner. They initially thought Thurmond was joking, so they laughed until they realized he was serious. Eddie was the more outspoken of the two and couldn't contain his urge to say something, and blurted out, "I can't believe what I'm hearing, Thurm. You don't even like him! The man harassed you for no good reason, and you defend him? I don't get it! I think you'd be happy he's gone; after all, he's been hard on you since his uncle hired him to be your boss!"

There was truth in what Eddie was saying. Thurmond did not like Howard, and there were many things about Howard that Thurmond found loathsome. Still, no one deserved to be ridiculed without seriously considering the facts, which Emerson had convinced Thurmond might not be what had been reported in the newspapers.

Howard's death was disgusting and undignified. He was accused of engaging in perversions most people could never have imagined. People had come to consider Howard a self-serving, perverted drug addict, which they believed was pointless to defend. Yet, aspects of the story didn't make sense, so Thurmond remained unconvinced that what had happened to Howard was entirely accidental. Emerson presented a few of these viewpoints, but none other than Thurmond felt those arguments had any validity. Thurmond felt obliged to defend Emerson's position and said what he felt had to be said. Thurmond began, "I agree with your account of the man's actions towards me, Eddie. Heck, I agree with most people's opinion of him. He was a jerk!"

"Then why Thurm?" Stan asked, "...why would you defend him? He never treated anybody with respect and didn't care about anyone but himself."

Thurmond thought for a moment about what he was going to say. He wanted to be sincere, which meant he had to portray Howie for what he was, a mean, selfish twit. Still, he wanted to be clear in his belief in a person's dignity, which he believed everyone deserved, even an insufferable fool like Howie. He took a deep breath and began.

"It's hard to admit, but even Howard deserves respect. He could have been a decent person at some point in his life. At least he had that potential. Everybody does. He must have had a mother who loved him, whom he loved back. He must have had moments where he elevated himself by doing things to help people, even if it was the unintended consequence of helping himself. Someone could have benefited from his actions. There must have been something admirable about him, even though none of us have ever seen it. Some hint of virtue? Some random act of charity?"

"Charity?" Eddie scoffed, "... can't think of a word more, unlike Howie, than 'charity.' He was selfish, greedy, and prideful. He only cared about himself!"

People listened intently to the conversation and muffled their laughter out of respect for Thurmond. Thurmond was not offended and continued.

"Seriously, Eddie, I mean it. Everyone wants to be loved, even Howie. Everyone wants to matter to someone, but when we make mistakes, we defend ourselves and let our pride bury that innocent desire, that simple joy. We act like it doesn't matter, but it does."

Memories of his youth began to run through Thurmond's mind as he searched for examples to prove his point. He continued.

"I'm sure it's not a stretch to assume you did something or said something you shouldn't have when you were a kid, Eddie. Maybe you felt justified. Like you had to get back at someone for being unfair or mean, or perhaps they cheated you somehow. Whatever the case, you knew it was wrong once you did it, but you allowed your pride to defend your actions. The problem with that is it allows destructive emotions to creep in, like remorse, regret, or even self-loathing for behaving in a way you know to be wrong or terrible. But once you've done it, you're invested in it because of your pride, and it comes to represent who you are, to others, and to yourself."

Thurmond was surprised at himself for carrying on the way he did, but his thoughts were clear, and he wanted to get it out before he forgot them. He continued.

"Admitting to making a mistake is a notion we don't want to cozy up to, do we, Eddie? It makes you look bad, but we all make mistakes. We all look bad at one time or another. We all do things we wish we hadn't. It's in our nature to fall from grace. That's what Fr. Elias would say confession is for; to get it off our chest and move on. But to do that, we need to take accountability for our actions. If we don't, the remorse grows deeper and deeper until we can't get away from it, and we eventually give up on fixing what's broken. When that happens, our lives become the mess that Howie's was. A regular kerfuffle!"

"That's all well and good, Thurm, but what's the use in confession when we go right back and do it again..." Eddie replied in his defense, "...I don't know a single person who doesn't tell the priest the same things every time they go back to confession, every single time."

Eddie's observation made people laugh, but Thurmond knew he had deflected the conversation. He wanted to stay on point and addressed Eddie's comments briefly before he moved on.

"Confession is not a turnstile Eddie. It's a car wash. An opportunity to clean yourself off by admitting to a mistake. The car's probably gonna get dirty again, but you keep going back to clean yourself off."

Thurmond wasn't sure Eddie understood his analogy, so he explained, "Fr. Elias once told me that we're supposed to approach confession with the intention of not repeating what we did wrong. That's the important thing. That's where you must start. Without that, there is no hope you will ever become who you want to be. Who you were meant to be."

The Diner had become noticeably quieter during Thurmond's discourse until it had gone almost entirely silent. A newspaper columnist eating breakfast at the counter became intrigued and listened intently. Thurmond continued, and the columnist began taking notes.

"Most people repeatedly make the same mistake, but the admission that we failed allows us to hit the reset button. If you try to change and make your life better by being nicer, more charitable, and kinder, you don't get bogged down, but you need to dedicate yourself to it, which I can tell you from my experience is not easy."

Thurmond paused for a moment to accentuate the importance of what he was about to say, then continued.

"Admitting we've done something wrong is difficult, but trying to keep from repeating our mistakes is the real battle. To keep from doing it again is nearly impossible. It becomes a habit, a cycle. A vicious vortex that grows stronger and stronger until it's impossible to escape. It would help if you dedicated yourself to changing your behavior from a selfish pursuit to a noble one. If you can manage that, it will push you past your mistakes and give you the strength you'll need to avoid making them again or at least enable you to recognize when you're making them. But we gotta push our pride aside and rise above the guilt and self-loathing to do it. But it's not easy. Howie never learned that lesson. His failures became who he was, and that cost him his life."

Thurmond's mouth had gone dry, and he paused to sip some ice water. He noticed how quiet the Diner had become and wanted to make sure that what he said next was precisely what he wanted to say; he wanted to get it right. He put his glass down and continued.

"People would say Howie had no dignity, but I say he did. He couldn't get his life on track by admitting he had made mistakes, and the result was a fate worse than anyone should have to endure."

Thurmond suddenly realized his entire argument was based on his own struggles to overcome his mistakes. His defense of Howie was a cathartic confession, making him suddenly uncomfortable with having exposed himself. He wanted to end his impromptu oration quickly and return to the safety of silence. He looked at his friend Emerson who nodded in agreement and smiled with the knowledge of his support. Thurmond concluded, "Look, Howie may have been the furthest thing from dignified, but his dignity as a human being was innate, not earned. It's inherent in us and not bestowed by people who didn't care for Howie or his actions. Howie may have made a hash of his life because of his pride, but he was still a human being, and no matter what you thought of him, he didn't deserve to be humiliated in death just because he made mistakes in life. No one does."

Thurmond's exposé of the human condition amazed people in its relevance to their own lives. The columnist furiously wrote down everything Thurmond said, determined to publish an article he intended to call 'The Pride and Dignity of Man.'

The newspaper's weekend edition published a thought-provoking article about Thurmond's shocking defense of Howard Mallory, which attracted tremendous attention. The columnist referenced an ancient oration on man's dignity to build upon what Thurmond had said fervently, if not less eloquently. The premise was whether human beings deserved respect simply for having intelligence and the free will to enable them to shape their own lives, for better or worse. The columnist focused on Thurmond's distinction between man's inherent abilities and the outcome of its application, which was what he had tried to communicate about Howard. The article suggested that Howard Mallory should be pitied, not ridiculed, for failing so miserably at being a human being.

Ehndale was made aware of the article and, after reading it, considered Thurmond's speech on the 'Pride and Dignity of Man' entertaining, believing it helped make the case that Howard had gotten what he deserved. The paper had pointed the blame for what had happened straight at the poor wretch's terrible decision-making and not at him. People didn't suspect Ehndale had anything to do with Howard's demise, and given that Howard was no longer a problem, the situation suited him perfectly.

Ehndale called his contacts at the paper to congratulate them for the piece and suggested they continue the lesson by publishing articles debating the differences between the Nature of Man and the Dignity of man, competing elements of the human condition.

~

Although Bradley barely knew Howard, he was shocked to hear of the poor man's demise. The details were gruesome, and when he read that the wretch had been found at 'Le Château de Bartholomé,' he knew that Ehndale had something to do with it. Bradley clearly remembered that name, and it was hard to forget. Following Becky's passing, Ehndale had suggested that he travel to the Château to get away for a while until things cooled down, but that had thankfully never come to pass.

Bradley remembered Howard's glib attitude towards Ehndale and recalled how he had stated his intention to make the man's life miserable and 'make him pay,' which had given Brad a chill of fear for Howard's sake at the time. He had warned Howard against confronting Ehndale with demands, but apparently, Howard hadn't heeded his warning, which may have been what cost him his life.

Ehndale was amazingly capable of orchestrating things and could have easily created the circumstances that led to Howard's demise.

That thought frightened Bradley because he knew he was just as susceptible. He knew that if he made a change somehow when the time came, Ehndale could do away with him as well, but now that he knew, Bradley would not allow that to happen if he could help it.

Bradley had also read the 'Pride and Dignity of Man' article and admired Thurmond's attempt to find something worthy about Howard's life. He was inspired to become noble in his intentions and not selfish, but to do so, he needed to take charge of his life if he had any hope of salvaging something admirable about it. To achieve this, Bradley knew his efforts started with Ehndale, whom he had avoided for fear of reprisals. Still, he was resolute in his convictions and decided to face his fears, which he believed was the only way he could salvage whatever was left of his dignity, for whatever it was worth. Bradley also hoped to confirm his suspicions about Ehndale's involvement in Howie's death which would help justify his feelings and encourage him to stick to his resolution to change.

~

Now that Howard was no longer a concern, Ehndale turned his focus to Monica. He had something in mind for her that required assistance, and when Ganneau returned from his trip to France, Ehndale began to discuss his plan of action with his handsome associate.

During one of their meetings, they were unexpectedly interrupted when Balaam told them that Bradley had reappeared unannounced and was unapologetic in his demand to speak to Ehndale. Ehndale excused himself and followed Balaam to the front door, where Bradley had been impatiently waiting for them.

Ehndale was impressed that Bradley had the nerve to show up alone but had become indifferent to his absence. He had considered punishing the wretch for disobedience, but there was no immediate use for him, and more pressing matters required his attention.

It was easy to discern from his manner that Bradley was uncomfortable, so to intensify his anxiety, Ehndale invited him in to join his other guest in the library. Bradley was afraid it could cause him to lose his nerve, so he immediately declined the offer. Ehndale mocked Bradley by laughing out loud.

"You reek of wavering confidence, my dear boy..." Ehndale began, "...What is it you have come to say? Speak up. Don't be shy. You had no problem rudely interrupting. Go on, then, speak up! Why are you here?"

Ganneau heard Ehndale belittling Bradley and exited the library to find out what was happening. When he stepped into the hall, he heard Ehndale continue.

"I should say that I am impressed, my dear boy, that you would think what you say matters to me; it does not. Your opinion means nothing. You are a minion, a plebe, a servant, my slave whose sole purpose is to serve me. Your very existence is at the mercy of my whim. If I desire it, you will cease to exist and disappear in humiliation like your friend Mr. Mallory."

Ehndale had unwittingly confirmed Bradley's suspicions that he was somehow responsible for what had happened to Howie, which made Bradley furious, and that fury gave him confidence. Bradley paused for a second to formulate his thoughts and replied.

"There is something you cannot control with all your power and money, and that's my dignity. That gift is divinely bestowed on everyone, and no matter how powerful you think you are; you can't take that away from me."

Ehndale laughed at Bradley's comment and knew that the impetus was Thurmond's silly premise, which Bradley had obviously read in the newspaper. Ehndale coolly cleared his throat.

"Oh, but I can control it, my dear boy, and I have. You see, you are standing here undignified, cringing at my doorstep, like some sniveling adolescent begging for forgiveness for your transgressions against me for fear of reprisals. Why else would you have hidden from me? Just look at your friend, 'Howie.' I took his dignity by humiliating him. I took his life and exposed his worthlessness for all to see. Dignity, you say? There is nothing dignified about your worthless life! And Mr. Mallory? Nothing could be more undignified than his death, which is all because of me. I choose who has dignity and who does not. It is as I will."

Ganneau listened intently and was surprised at the ferocity of his benefactor's argument. He didn't understand why Ehndale said he had meant for Howard to die and began wondering if he was somehow responsible. He had always trusted Ehndale, but a sudden chill of remorse ran down his spine at the prospect that any of his words could be true. He remained unnoticed while Ehndale continued to 'educate' Bradley.

"What you don't seem to understand, my good man is that the very nature of man is to be consumed by the 'self.' People are innately selfish. Whether or not you consider it divinely ordained, any 'dignity' is subject to this. Your friend was selfish, as are you. It's in your nature. However, the difference is that when you understand this to be true, you can temper your selfishness and extend beyond yourself to others. That's Dignified. Not this nonsense about it being divinely ordained. That argument is made by men who consider themselves intellectuals to justify their mistaken belief that there is dignity in every human life, which is categorically false. Not every life is dignified. It is not innate or divinely bestowed upon you at birth. That's absurd! It is earned rather, and not everyone has earned it. Suppose you somehow managed to earn it by some stroke of luck. In that case, it is not retained in perpetuity if you cannot dignify yourself by spreading the benefits of your selfish nature beyond yourself. Even if that is your ambition, you still must endeavor to retain it."

While Ehndale continued admonishing him, Bradley noticed Ganneau standing in the hall and could see by the look that he was not alone in his doubts about Ehndale and his motivations. Ehndale noticed Bradley's distraction and turned to see Ganneau, who he assured was just about finished and would rejoin him in a minute. Ganneau smiled but looked back at Bradley in such a way that showed Bradley he was not alone in his doubt. Ganneau then disappeared back into the library.

"Was there anything else, my good man?" Ehndale asked smugly.

"There was one more thing…." Bradley replied, "…I came to tell you I'm out. I am dignified, no matter what you say. My existence and worth are not at your discretion or your whim."

Bradley almost couldn't believe what he was saying but had to say it. It was the reason why he was there. He swallowed the lump in his throat and continued.

"I am no longer interested in working for you, Mr. Ehndale. I am not your slave, and I refuse to be your minion. I quit!"

Ehndale smiled before laughing and replied.

"We'll see, won't we, my good man? We shall see…."

14

Conversion

The weather on the drive home from Ehndale's estate reflected Bradley's melancholy. Torrential rain pelted his windshield, creating translucent waves of water that seemed to melt the glass, making it difficult to see the road and keep the car from veering into a ditch. The rhythm of the vehicle's wiper blades furiously pushing aside the water allowed Bradley's mind to wander.

Bradley had started that evening by confronting Ehndale, which he had struggled mightily to convince himself he needed to do. Although he had been afraid of the consequences, Howard's death scared him enough to make it evident that he needed to face his fears to begin making things right in his life, and the first thing he needed to do was to terminate his relationship with Ehndale. He had hoped that his anxiety about reprisal from Ehndale would dissipate once it was done, but it didn't.

Headlights from an oncoming vehicle created a tremendous glare across Bradley's windshield, forcing him to squint to keep from being blinded. His squinting revealed the shape of the oncoming headlights, which looked remarkably like those on Thurmond's truck. That brief thought of Thurmond reminded him of the only person he could truly call a friend, who, unlike himself, had selflessly acted on another's behalf without consideration of remuneration. Unmotivated by envy or greed, Thurmond was an honorable and worthy man. Selfless and generous, often at great personal expense.

Bradley considered how Thurmond and Ehndale could not have been more different. He recalled Thurmond's courageous courtroom speech about honor during the foundry trial, for which he was unjustly held in contempt of court and arrested. And the newspaper article about Thurmond's commentary on pride and dignity to defend Howie, a man Thurmond despised. These were selfless actions in support of others without regard to potentially harmful repercussions to himself. They were also directly opposed to Ehndale, a despicable man who manipulated everything around him for his own benefit and justified his vindictive and selfish actions with deceptive logic.

As he drove, Bradley thought about what Ehndale and Thurmond had said about the differences between a man's nature and his dignity. As he understood, human nature was what you were inclined to do naturally, without thought or consideration. In contrast, dignity was derived from the ability to do something or the actual act of doing it. Whether you did it or not was inconsequential. That quality, in and of itself, deserved respect.

Bradley began to consider his own life and believed he had failed to establish a dignity he could be proud of. He had chosen to be motivated by selfishness, pride, envy, jealousy, and greed, so these vices had come to rule his life. As a result, he was proud of nothing and ashamed of everything. He would probably have had more friends had he thought less about himself and listened to Kate, and had he heeded Thurmond's warnings about Ehndale, Bradley would have had nothing to fear from the man, and Becky could still be alive.

Bradley suddenly realized he envied Thurmond because he wanted to be more like him. He wanted people to think of him as they thought of Thurmond, but even that thought was selfish. Being honorable and generous were new concepts to Bradley, and he knew it would take some time before he got the hang of it. Still, this envy generated an earnest desire to change, and he committed himself to the exercise and wanted to start immediately.

~

Bradley was still thinking about Thurmond when he arrived home, and after parking his car, he walked deep in thought to his front door without caring about the driving rain. Soaked to the skin, he threw his keys on the counter, grabbed a beer from the refrigerator, and flopped on the couch. He put his feet on the coffee table, pushed his wet hair out of his face as he drank his beer, and watched the water drip from his pant legs onto the hardwood floors. He considered his predicament and his next course of action and knew it undoubtedly involved a conversation with Kate. He guzzled his beer and left immediately for the Diner to catch Kate before she went home for the evening.

~

As Bradley expected, the Diner was closed when he arrived, so he pressed against the glass to peer through the front window and saw Kate alone, mopping the floor. He tapped on the glass to get her attention, and when she saw him standing in the pouring rain outside, Kate put down her mop, rushed to the door, and invited him in out of the pouring rain for some coffee.

Except for her son Hunter, no one had seen or heard from Bradley for some time, and Kate was relieved to see him. She assumed Bradley was there because he was in trouble with his boss. With all the rumors about Ehndale's involvement in the horrific incident with Howie and her firsthand experience of the kind of man Ehndale could be, Kate was concerned for Brad's safety.

Dripping wet, Brad apologized for the hour, and they settled in at the front counter as Kate put on a pot of coffee, and Brad began to explain why he had come.

Clearing his conscience sounded like a wonderful idea, but owning up to his mistakes was a painful way to do it. His actions had caused so much pain and suffering. He was embarrassed and fearful of Kate's reaction to his confession, but thankfully she was not judgmental. Her response was calm, and her counsel straightforward and genuine. She intended to help him, not punish, or scold him.

Bradley sat at the counter, sipping the coffee Kate had prepared for him, considering where he should start.

"So many things, Kate. I know I need to take responsibility for my actions, even though I was put up to it. I still decided to do it. I could have said no, but I didn't."

Kate touched his shoulder and asked, "Do you remember our conversations, sweetie? Ever wonder why you wanted to talk to me? Why did you think it was a good idea?"

"Yeah..." Bradley replied, "...I guess I had always considered myself lacking in some way and needed to prove myself worthy; the problem is that I went about it the wrong way, and I knew it."

"Yes, honey, you did..." Kate replied, kindly chastising him.

"I guess I thought I needed to defend myself to you. Like you were the principal at school or something."

"Like, why you came here to talk to me tonight?"

"Yeah...I guess. But I wasn't looking for forgiveness then, and it was more like I was making excuses trying to justify myself."

Bradley had always assigned blame to justify his actions. He blamed women for his fear of inadequacy and objectified them to eliminate his fear of rejection. He treated them like their opinions of him didn't matter. He blamed his parents for his lack of opportunity and Becky for their failed marriage. He blamed Thurmond for his inferiority complex and Thomas for his lack of popularity. He knew it wasn't their fault, but he lacked confidence and was envious of those who had it. People like Thurmond, Becky, and Thomas were popular and respected, which made him jealous. He tried to be like them, to be liked by them, but he had never actually learned how to do it, and that failure made him angry. They had confidence, and his lack of it scared and humiliated him. It exposed his inadequacies, so he belittled them and acted like their opinions didn't matter.

When Ehndale came along, he seemed to be the answer to all his prayers. He was popular and respected, but more importantly, he was powerful. He could have what he wanted, and it seemed like there was no limit to what he could do or get. When he offered to share that with Bradley, he couldn't say no, and without realizing it, Bradley succumbed to temptation and sold his soul, which he regretted now more than anything.

Nothing Brad confessed surprised her. Kate had always known these things about him but could never help him. She was sorry he had come to the point where he felt overwhelmed by them, but Kate was happy that he had finally realized that he needed to address them. She sat patiently listening, waiting for her opportunity to give him counsel. When he paused to take a long sip of coffee, she replied, "I appreciate your sharing this with me, Bradley. I know it isn't easy, but you must come clean with everyone to make it right. You have to admit your mistakes and apologize."

That prospect scared Bradley, but he knew she was right.

"You won't regret doing it, honey, I guarantee it...." Kate told him, "... it'll make you feel so much better, but I'm not gonna sugarcoat it. You've got a lot to make up for; it's gonna be difficult, and it won't be pretty. Make no mistake about that, but nothing worthwhile ever comes easy, darling. "

"Isn't there something else I could do?" Bradley pleaded, "...I mean, isn't there another way?"

"None I can think of..." Kate replied before refilling his coffee cup and pushing a menu in front of him. "Have something to eat, dear. You look like you haven't slept or eaten in days. It's on the house, my treat."

Although he had confessed the underlying reasons for what he had done, Bradley had not been entirely honest with Kate. He had held back details of things he was especially ashamed of for fear that she would not be able to forgive him.

He accepted her gracious offer of something to eat and thanked her for being so kind. When Kate left to make him something to eat, Bradley sat quietly, deciding where he should start. There were so many things to confess, but two gnawed at him the most; the truth about Becky's accident and his role in hindering the plane crash investigation by hiding the black box.

Brad considered all his relationships and decided that Kate, Thomas, and Thurmond were the closest thing he had to friends and determined that he would return the following day to Kate's for breakfast and see who showed up so he could start trying to make things right. For that evening, however, he would enjoy sitting and chatting with Kate as he thought through how to make his confessions.

~

Vikki enjoyed Kate's company and made a point of sharing a cup of coffee with her to start her day and was amongst the first of the customers trickling in that next morning. She was surprised to see Bradley sitting by the front window staring out into the street, as she had never seen him at the Diner before, except for the free lunches he enjoyed at the expense of the women he had treated so poorly. When Kate saw Vikki, she joined her at her table and Vikki quietly asked her if she knew why Bradley was there.

"I think you should ask him yourself..." Kate whispered, "... he has something he wants to get off his chest, and he's waiting for Thomas and Thurmond."

With coffee in hand, Vikki approached Bradley, who had been staring out the window and hadn't noticed her. She was curious about what he would say and was not shy about asking."

"Good morning Mr. Ballard! Do you mind if I join you?"

"Well, I was actually expecting someone..." Bradley replied nervously.

"Yes, I know. Kate told me. Thomas and Thurmond. I'm waiting for them as well. Do you mind if we wait together?"

Bradley would typically send her away, but he thought it was probably a bad idea. He didn't know what to say, and before he could answer, Vikki had already sat across from him at his table. She smiled at him and began asking questions.

"So then, how have you been? I haven't seen you since you stayed at Mr. Ehndale's cottage. Are you still there, or have you moved out? Are you still in his employ?"

Her questions were quite forward, but Bradley couldn't figure out how to thwart her attempts to extract information from him. He was nervous enough about telling Thurmond and Thomas why he had come, but admitting his mistakes to her would entail an entirely different level of remorse. She knew too much and was too powerful. She was Ehndale's protégé, a shining example of his mentorship. Bradley wanted to sever that connection and thought confiding in her was not the way to accomplish that.

"I don't think I should be talking to you about this...." Bradley began, "...and I mean no disrespect, but I don't think it's really any of your business."

Vikki knew she had hit a nerve and wouldn't let up. She smiled at him and continued, "If this is regarding Thomas or Thurmond, you should know Thomas and I are dating, and Thurmond is an essential person at my company. If there was anything that should affect either of them, I believe it would be of concern to me. So, respectfully, I believe it is certainly my business."

Bradley knew she was right, but he didn't know how to answer her. Vikki continued, "You see, Mr. Ballard, I have every right to be interested in whatever you say to them. They are both very dear to me. Furthermore, I believe your relationship with Mr. Ehndale may have something to do with this, and I don't have to tell you about my relationship with him, now do I?"

"Ok, Ok..." Bradley stammered, "I get your meaning, but I don't feel comfortable telling you things about my personal affairs. They have absolutely nothing to do with you."

"Ah, but as I have already explained, they do..." Vikki replied, "...which is why I am going to sit here with you and remain while you have your little conversations with the men most important to me."

Bradley knew there was no way around it. He had always feared strong women and avoided them since he had no success belittling them. But he was trapped. He thought of leaving, but what was the point of that? What he needed to say, he wanted to say, and he wanted to say it as quickly as possible. He looked out the window, hoping that either Thurmond or Thomas would be coming in to help him escape this mess, but they were nowhere to be seen. He looked at Kate for help, but she was busy with other customers streaming into the Diner. Bradley was alone and had no way out. He considered what would happen if he opened up to Vikki and ultimately decided it didn't matter. It would all get back to her eventually, anyway.

"Alright then, if you really must know." Bradley began as he formulated his thoughts, "...I came here to apologize."

"Apologize?" Vikki asked quizzically, "...apologize for what?"

"Apologize to Thomas for lying about the night of the accident with Becky. Apologize to Thurmond for hindering the investigation into the plane crash. Apologize for everything. I guess I should apologize to Kate and to you too. I should probably apologize to everyone. I had no idea how my actions could be so far-reaching in their adverse effects on people. I would apologize to Becky if she were still here, but I had no idea that Becky would take her own life. I guess I just ignored how miserable she had become."

Vikki was not surprised at the number of things Bradley had confessed. He was a miserable person capable of despicable things. Still, his admission to hindering the investigation into the plane crash was potentially criminal and stuck in her mind as something she found particularly troubling.

"How did you hinder the investigation into the plane crash exactly, Mr. Ballard?" Vikki asked.

Bradley hung his head as he contritely replied.

"I hid the black box so no one could find it."

"That's despicable!" she shouted, "...Why in the world would you do that?"

Bradley's first reaction was to do what he always did; blame it on someone else. After all, Ehndale was the one who had told him to do it.

But the truth was the decision was his, and he knew it was wrong, yet he did it anyway. He also knew that implicating Ehndale could result in some form of retaliation. The man was probably planning ways to humiliate or even kill him anyway, so he didn't want to make it any worse by giving him another reason.

Bradley nervously sipped his coffee as he thought of a plausible excuse for the despicable act and said, "...No, ma'am. It was me. I didn't want people to find it because I wanted to sell it. I figured someone would be interested in it and willing to pay. I needed the money."

Vikki was furious and scolded him out loud, "Do you know the magnitude of the pain and anguish you caused? You could have ruined people's lives! Probably did! Those victims' families deserved answers, and the foundry almost went out of business because of it! Thurmond near killed himself because of you. You should be ashamed of yourself!"

Bradley was ashamed and hung his head as she scolded him. People looked on in disdain, and when Vikki had finished admonishing him, she told him that she would report him to the authorities and that he would likely end up in prison.

"Are you proud of yourself?" Vikki asked as she stood to leave.

"No, Ma'am..." was all Bradley could muster as a reply, "... I am not."

Kate had begun watching Bradley when Vikki became upset and believed he had started to admit his mistakes. Kate knew it would be painful but hoped he wouldn't be discouraged by this experience with Vikki and would continue making amends.

Bradley felt he had no reason to wait for Thurmond or Thomas. He would continue his confessions with them some other time. He had done enough of what he had come to do and left some money on the table before leaving the Diner.

~

Bradley saw the flashing lights reflecting on the wall inside his dark house and grabbed his coat as he answered the knock at the door. He knew full well that it was the police coming to arrest him and glanced around his home, possibly for the last time, as if he were taking pictures to bring with him to jail. He imagined he would have little to look forward to besides memories of his freedom.

What happened next was a blur. Bradley didn't want to make a fuss and admitted everything to the authorities, including some things about the night of his car accident with Becky and Hunter that he had not shared with Vikki. He pleaded guilty and waived his right to a trial, mainly to keep Ehndale from becoming aware of what was happening. The process took less than a week, and Bradley became prisoner No. P1-7131417 before anybody knew what had happened.

~

Bradley had always been an insufferable louse, but Vikki was surprised at how contrite he had been during the entire process. She questioned the ferocity of her reaction to his admission of guilt and the appropriateness of his ultimate incarceration. She was conflicted about her feelings and sought advice from Thomas and Kate, who assured her that she had done the right thing. Their assurances helped confirm that she hadn't overreacted, but she was not entirely confident that they had put the person in jail who was genuinely responsible.

Thurmond had since returned to Taipei and was unaware of everything. When Vikki told him of Bradley's incarceration, he was surprised and disappointed, but Thurmond didn't believe a single word when she told him the reasons Bradley had given her for doing it. They agreed it was unlikely that things were as simple as Bradley had made them appear. He had to be hiding something, like the real reasons he had done it or, as Vikki suspected, who was really behind the theft.

Thurmond knew he could talk to Bradley, so he asked Vikki to arrange for him to visit Bradley in prison. Vikki was determined to discover the truth, no matter the consequences, and arranged for Thurmond to visit Bradley in jail on his next scheduled rotation home from Taipei. She had intended to accompany him, but Thurmond requested that he see Bradley alone, and Vikki reluctantly agreed.

15

Confession

Modest in size but foreboding in its appearance, the old prison was perched on a hillside in full view of the interstate. The irony was that the inmates could watch people move freely from their confinement, which was commonly believed to have been done intentionally to remind them of what they had lost, hoping they would reform to regain it.

The buildings were encircled with miles of razor wire atop two perpendicular chain-linked fences, which rose and sank with the topography. There were no trees to block the view of the place's entirety, and other than an occasional person riding a mower, there wasn't another soul to be seen on the expansive property.

Bradley slowly became accustomed to the daily routines. An alarm would sound every morning to awaken the inmates, and after a few minutes, the cell doors would slam open to allow them to line up outside their cells for roll call before breakfast. The inmates were assigned their daily chores when they'd finished eating, and after completing their assignments, they were rotated into the yard for exercise. After exercise, the inmates were given free time in their cells before dinner and a short quiet time afterward before the lights went out. This process repeated itself day after day, with the only fluctuation being for those inmates who were allowed to have visitors.

One benefit of Bradley's incarceration was the protection it gave him from Ehndale, even though the man seemed capable of almost anything. Being in prison also gave Bradley plenty of time to reflect on the dismal failure that his life had become. Envy, lust, and desire for wealth had essentially destroyed any semblance of dignity he may have had, but Howie's death made Bradley re-evaluate his priorities. He considered Thurmond's defense of Howie, which made Bradley believe there was still hope for him, and his conversation with Kate gave him confidence that he could at least try to atone for his behavior.

~

The Warden had read stories about Thurmond in the newspaper and had come to admire him, so when he saw his name on the visitation request, he approved it immediately. These visits were typically scheduled for the afternoons in locations determined by the Warden, but because of his admiration for Thurmond, the Warden instructed the guards to grant Thurmond access whenever he arrived and take him to a private conference room customarily reserved for attorneys or other VIP visitors.

Thurmond had left early that morning to visit Bradley and found the prison's parking lot empty when he arrived. He parked beside a single-story brick building with a giant antenna and a large sign that read 'Visitors' and made his way toward the building's entrance.

Once inside, Thurmond was received by a guard stationed at a table who had orders from the Warden to grant Thurmond immediate access. The guard radioed for assistance, and an escort soon appeared and led Thurmond out of the small building and then through a series of narrow exterior walkways defined by chain link fence and razor wire. One after the other, the guard escorted him through a series of manned checkpoints until they entered the main prison building. As Thurmond progressed through the security perimeter, the weight of confinement grew around him.

Thurmond was then escorted through a restricted passage used only by the Warden, guards, and other dignitaries visiting the prison.

They followed signs directing them through this passage until they reached what appeared to be a lounge just outside the cell block where Bradley now lived. The guard opened a heavy wooden door to a modest room off to one side of the lounge and announced, "Prisoner 71425 is at breakfast, Mr. Joseph. He will be brought by presently. You can wait for him here."

The room had a small kitchenette, a conference table surrounded by sturdy chairs, and a large monitor mounted with a telephone beside it on one of the walls. The guard walked over to the kitchenette, opened an undercounter refrigerator, and removed a bottle of water that he placed on the table in front of Thurmond. He then told Thurmond to pick up the phone when he was done and closed the door behind him, leaving Thurmond alone in the room.

~

After breakfast, Bradley was notified that a visitor had come to see him, and when he asked who it was, he was informed it was Thurmond Joseph. Although he was happy, Bradley was concerned Thurmond would ask him questions he wasn't sure how to answer.

Bradley admired Thurmond's defense of Howard Mallory, which had inspired him to introduce some dignity to his miserable existence before it was too late. It would undoubtedly have been easier had he not been in prison, but Bradley didn't regret his imprisonment and believed it was a fair price for his crimes and a first step in his rehabilitation. Remembering what Kate had told him about atonement, he saw this as an opportunity to begin making things right with Thurmond.

Bradley was separated from the other inmates and escorted to the room where Thurmond anxiously awaited him. Thurmond stood when the guard escorted Bradley into the room, and Bradley immediately became nervous and defensive. The guard reminded Thurmond about using the telephone to tell them he was ready to leave and closed the door behind him, leaving the two men alone.

Staring at Thurmond, Bradley sat directly across the table from him and said, "If you came to ask me about my confessions Thurm, you're wasting your time. Look around. I believe I've said everything that needs to be said. It seems a decision has already been made on how to deal with me."

"Slow down, Bradley. Take it easy." Thurmond replied, "...I didn't come here to interrogate you."

"Didn't you?" Bradley asked sarcastically, "...I can't imagine why anyone would want to see a degenerate like me unless it was for information."

"I actually thought we could start with an apology." Thurmond waggishly responded.

"OK, Thurm, I'm sorry. I was wrong. I apologize, but I didn't think..."

Thurmond interrupted, "That's right, Brad, you didn't think. You rarely do! That's the problem; you act without considering the consequences, which gets you into trouble. That's why you're here!"

Bradley welcomed Thurmond's blunt honesty and recognized how difficult it must have been for him not to pass judgment, which he had every right to do. Bradley smiled, shook his head, and said, "You know, the funny thing is, you have no idea how much I admire you, do you, Thurm?"

"That's welcome news, to be sure, Brad. Thank you..." Thurmond replied, "...but what's that got to do with anything?"

Bradley valued that his compliment meant something to Thurmond, and even though he had done nothing to deserve it, he wanted to earn Thurmond's respect. He didn't know how to tell him the truth without jeopardizing his own life and began to fidget, which conveyed to Thurmond that he was nervous. Thurmond continued, "I know it's probably against your better judgment to tell me, but I need to know who was behind all this, and you can spare me the lie that you were acting alone. We both know that's not true."

Bradley sat quietly, staring at the floor, thinking about what to say. Thurmond assumed his apprehension had something to do with his fear of Ehndale, so to lessen Bradley's anxiety, he said.

"No one needs to know how I got the information, Brad."

Brad wrung his hands together and asked in a whisper, "Not even Vikki?"

Thurmond could appreciate Bradley's concern and replied, "I won't tell you that she's not going to find out anyway, but if you need me to promise that I won't be the one to tell her, then yes, I promise, I won't tell her."

Bradley knew Thurmond was a man of his word, so when he said he wouldn't betray his confidence, Bradley knew if Ehndale found out, it wouldn't be because of anything Thurmond had said or done.

"Thank you, Thurm, I trust you," Bradley confessed, "…but the thing is, I don't feel like I've been unjustly treated. I mean, prison is probably where I belong, and my life in the world is worthless anyway."

"That's ridiculous," Thurmond protested, "… Everyone's life is worth something!"

"I don't know, Thurm; what do I have to look forward to then? I've made a mess of my life. Becky's gone, and I don't have a job. I have no family and no friends. I deserve to be in here, and that's the truth!"

"I get that, Brad, and I agree, you screwed up. How many times did I tell you? For that matter, how many times did Kate tell you?"

"I know, I know," Bradley replied, "…Kate warned me; kept telling me I would come to regret the way I was acting, the things I was doing, the people I was associating with, and how I was treating Becky. And now, that day has come."

"We all have our problems, Brad," Thurmond said empathetically, "…but that's hardly a reason to give up. That's the easy way out. You need to fight for it if you want your life back, and why wouldn't you?"

Bradley paused to swallow the lump that had formed in his throat and said, "You don't understand, Thurm..."

Bradley clenched his hands together and placed them on the table in front of him, then looked Thurmond straight in the eye.

"I thought I could make some money by selling the flight recorder Thurm; that's why I hid it."

"Yes, I know, Brad. Vikki told me you'd say that."

Brad was surprised by Thurmond's mild reaction, so to shock him, he continued.

"That's not all of it; there's worse..."

"I see," Thurmond calmly replied, "...and what would that be?"

"Becky wasn't driving the car the night of the accident with Hunter; I was. She was dead drunk and passed out in the back seat. I put her behind the wheel, then left. I wanted to make it look like it was her fault. Then I lied about it, so you see, I killed her, or rather, she killed herself because of me."

Thurmond had no idea how to reply and stared blankly at Bradley, thinking that prison might be where he belonged, but there had to be a reason he had done these horrible things. There were rumors that Brad was involved somehow, but none were as heinous as what he had just confessed. Brad may have been a lecherous scoundrel, but he wasn't evil, which made Thurmond suspect that Ehndale had some part in it.

After a brief silence, Thurmond placed his arms straight out on the table in front of him and grabbed Bradley's hands.

"You're not a monster, Brad; you're a fool!"

"I guess I deserve that..." Bradley admitted as Thurmond continued.

"You and I both know this has to do with Ehndale!"

Bradley was unsurprised that Thurmond had figured it out but was still reluctant to admit it. His reaction to being exposed had always been to deny things, and without hesitation, he replied, "What makes you say that?"

Thurmond let go of Bradley's hands, leaned back in his seat, and asked, "I thought we were being honest here, Brad?"

Bradley thought this might be his chance to do something noble with his life. He knew Thurmond would honor his promise not to reveal his confession, and so he answered.

"Yes, Thurmond. Ehndale advised me, and I followed his advice like the fool you say that I am. That doesn't absolve me of my part, but he told me what I should do."

Before Thurmond could respond, a guard suddenly appeared and notified the men that the visit was over. Thurmond promised he would return, and as the guard escorted him away, Bradley was overcome with remorse and began to cry.

~

Vikki was anxious to confirm her suspicions and asked Thurmond to report back to her after he visited with Bradley. Thurmond did not want to betray his promise and told her that Bradley had revealed nothing they didn't already suspect.

"So, he admitted there was someone else?" Vikki asked, "...Did he say who it was?"

Thurmond suspected that Vikki also believed that Ehndale was involved, but he didn't know how to confirm her suspicions without betraying his friend. Thurmond sat thinking about how to answer, and Vikki could tell he was being evasive. She trusted Thurmond had a good reason for it, so she stressed the importance of getting all the information they needed to protect the foundry rather than pressing him for an answer.

Thurmond thought Brad might open up to Vikki, so he suggested she return with him on his next visit. Vikki was concerned that Bradley might feel intimidated by her and suggested Thurmond revisit him in prison alone before he returned to Taipei.

"I'd like to get as much information as possible from him," Vikki explained, "...but I don't want Bradley to feel like he's being cornered.

I think he will open up to you more than anyone else. My being there may make him nervous, which may hinder things, and the sooner we know the who and the why, the better our chances are that we can limit any damage to the foundry from it."

"Agreed," Thurmond replied, not knowing what else he needed to know besides what Bradley had already told him.

~

Early the following morning, Bradley received another visitor but did not welcome this one. The sound of a guard juggling through a ring of keys had awakened him, and when Bradley opened his eyes, he saw Ehndale smiling at him through the bars of his cell. He dismissed the possibility that Thurmond had broken his promise and sat on the edge of his bunk, anticipating what he assumed would be an uncomfortable affair.

After letting Ehndale in, the guard closed the cell door and left the two men alone. Bradley did not want to converse with the man and remained silent as Ehndale paced the tiny cell. Feigning concern Ehndale began:

"Bad business this, my dear boy, being arrested. I was concerned when I heard of it, but when I read about your confession, I was shocked!"

Bradley remained silent.

"I have to admit that although I consider it foolhardy, I was impressed with your bravery," Ehndale proclaimed, "…but I fail to see the logic in admitting to crimes you did not commit."

Ehndale stopped pacing and leaned against the wall across from Bradley, who sat silently staring at the floor. Ehndale continued.

"The newspaper did not elaborate on details other than to say you had admitted to interfering in a federal investigation."

"…and lying under oath. Yes, I did," Bradley added softly.

"Well, I find that curious because you were not implicated in the theft of the flight recorder, so for all intents and purposes, you had nothing to do with it."

"But I did," Bradley again added softly.

"Yes, well, I would suggest that one does not admit to something they are not being accused of. Wouldn't you agree?"

Bradley was scared but felt compelled to refute Ehndale's argument. He remembered Thurmond's words about being noble and wanted his friend to be proud of him.

"What about Becky then? They accused me of criminal mischief in that case. Should I admit to being responsible for that?"

"Ah, yes, that bit of business..." Ehndale replied as he began pacing again. "You were acquitted and exonerated of any wrongdoing, so there is nothing for which to admit. A confession, therefore, would be foolhardy and improper. Any counselor would tell you the same!"

Bradley knew Ehndale would continue to justify their dishonesty and being that he was no match for the man's wit, Brad wanted Ehndale to get to the point, and he asked him.

"Why are you here?"

Ehndale laughed at Bradley's forthrightness.

"You may feel noble in admitting responsibility for the crimes you have inexplicably confessed to having committed, but the implications of reopening an investigation into them can put others in an awkward position, which is undesirable."

Bradley was uninterested in discussing anything with the man and wanted the visit to end. He waited for the threats he knew were coming and listened as Ehndale continued.

"Do you believe that being in prison protects you from prosecution? From persecution? You understand that you are not in a position to divulge any information without repercussions?"

"I understand..." Bradley whispered as if speaking to himself.

Ehndale smiled, patted Bradley on the shoulder, and smugly said, "Splendid! Then, I guess there's little else to discuss other than to let you know that I will be back if I ever have some use for you. Until then, I would make the best of your time here!"

Ehndale looked around Bradley's cell with insincere admiration and wiped his fingers on the wall. He inspected the grit deposited on them, wiped them off on Bradley's jumpsuit, then walked to the front of Bradley's cell and called through the bars for the guard. As he watched the guard approach, Ehndale concluded.

"It could be worse. You could be alone in some damp and dingy crypt, tied to some pillar, naked and bleeding. Dirty business that!"

There it was, the admission and the threat, all in one.

Bradley had been worried about Ehndale's reprisals, but his belief in redemption helped him overcome his fear. He was committed to his new quest and felt reassured in his decision to make amends, no matter the cost. He knew Ehndale would come after him, but that didn't matter anymore. He would continue to shelter himself in prison and attempt to make amends from there.

As Ehndale left with the guard, Bradley decided he would not hold Thurmond to his promise and permit him to convey everything he had confessed. Bradley considered these confessions as the beginning of his reparations, which he hoped would positively affect someone's life who deserved it, unlike himself and Ehndale, who certainly did not.

~

On the day of Thurmond's second visit, he wanted a feel for what Bradley was experiencing and asked if he could visit Bradley in his cell. The guard looked puzzled but agreed and escorted Thurmond there. When they reached Bradley's cell, the guard announced, "I've been informed that Prisoner 71425 is in the exercise yard, Mr. Joseph. We've notified him you are here and are returning him to his cell. Should be here momentarily."

"Thank you," Thurmond replied as he stepped into Bradley's cramped cell.

"You have as much time as you need, Mr. Joseph, Warden's orders. You can also get some chow in the officer's mess if you get hungry. Give a holler or tap on the bars if you need anything."

"Thank you, and thank the Warden for me, will you?" Thurmond replied.

"Yessir!" the guard said as he shut the cell door behind Thurmond and left.

When the cell door clicked shut, Thurmond cringed at the thought of anyone spending their life there. He looked around and noticed that Bradley hadn't attempted to personalize his cell in any way. He had a bunk with a pillow, blanket, sink, toilet, and a small night table with a Bible. Thurmond sat on the edge of Bradley's bunk, picked up the Bible, and noticed a slip of paper holding a page. He opened the book to that page and began reading a noted passage.

'... *Here is a trustworthy saying that deserves full acceptance: Christ Jesus came into the world to save sinners—of whom I am the worst. But for that very reason, I was shown mercy so that in me, the worst of sinners, Christ Jesus might display his immense patience as an example for those who would believe in him and receive eternal life.*'

Thurmond heard someone approaching and looked up to see Bradley standing with a guard at the cell door. He closed the Bible, placed it back on the small night table, and stood to greet Bradley.

"Find anything interesting?" Bradley asked as the guard closed the cell door behind him and left.

Thurmond was embarrassed at having been caught snooping and had nothing to say, so Bradley continued.

"You were right about Ehndale. He's a dangerous man with bad intentions; he was furious with me for helping Kate and Monica find you at the airport. I was so scared of what he would do that I avoided him by hiding in Becky's old house and only went out to get groceries. Almost drank myself to death with all the liquor Becky had stored up in the basement."

Bradley was remarkably calm and surprisingly contrite; a quality Thurmond did not know Bradley possessed. Bradley continued.

"Ehndale apparently found out I was here and came by to threaten me yesterday. I had hoped to escape his attention, but I expected he'd eventually find out."

"Threatened you with what?" Thurmond asked.

"Told me to be quiet and said I'd end up like Howie if I didn't."

"So, why are you telling me all this? Aren't you afraid?"

"Yeah, I'm afraid, Thurm, but I'm also responsible for much of this mess. I should have listened to you and Kate and stayed away from him, but I didn't, and the result is my life is in shambles."

Bradley paused, walked over to his nightstand, picked up his Bible, and opened to another page he had dog-eared and read.

"Oh, what joy for those whose rebellion is forgiven, whose sin is put out of sight! Yes, what joy for those whose record the Lord has cleared of sin, whose lives are lived in complete honesty! " — Psalm 32:1-2.

Thurmond was flabbergasted and asked, "When did you start quoting scripture, Brad?"

Bradley closed the Bible and placed it back on the table, then sat beside Thurmond on the bunk, rubbed his face in his hands, pushed his hair back out of his face and leaned back on his elbows.

"It's the only place I find solace these days, Thurm. When you've sunk to the point where no one wants anything to do with you, it hits you that you've spent your entire life doing things you regret. I have nothing but time here to think. To me, the Bible was like an instruction manual. I started reading it and began to find answers. I don't know if it's too late to salvage my life, but I must try. Even if I never leave this place, I must make amends."

Bradley looked and acted the same, but he was entirely different somehow. Thurmond was amazed.

"What made you decide to make things right, Brad? What made you decide to change? Did somebody say something to you?"

"Well, I talked to Kate…." Bradley replied as he sat up, folded his hands, rested his elbows on his thighs, and continued, "…the funny thing is Thurm that I always talked to Kate, but this time was different. This time I listened and understood what she said."

"What made it different?" Thurmond asked.

"Howie's death." Bradley admitted, "… that was the moment for me, Thurm. That could've been me and probably should've been me."

Thurmond closed his eyes and shook his head.

"As you know, Brad, I didn't much care for Howie, but what happened to him was horrible. He didn't deserve that; nobody does."

"Can't imagine…." Bradley agreed. "…when I heard the news, I immediately thought of Ehndale. I knew he was somehow involved. He admitted it to me when he was here. Mentioned it to threaten me."

"Didn't know you even knew Howie, Brad?" Thurmond asked.

"Yeah, I saw him around," Bradley replied, "…I had no reason to talk to him, but I ran into him at Ted's bar before his accident…"

Bradley made air quotes with his fingers when he said the word 'accident' and continued, "…he was bad-mouthing Ehndale. It made me cringe to hear him talking about Ehndale like that. I told him to be careful, but he was drunk, so I guess he didn't listen. Why would he? I'm not someone who has a lot of credibility, but I know about Ehndale."

"Such a shame," Thurmond replied.

"Yeah, I figured if I heard any bad news about Howie after that, it had to involve Ehndale. That's the kind of guy he is."

Bradley paused for a second, then continued with a degree of satisfaction, "…I went to see Ehndale afterward to tell him I didn't want to work for him anymore."

"That took some nerve..." Thurmond admitted, "... How'd he take that?"

Bradley looked straight at Thurmond and coolly replied, "To tell you the truth Thurm, he left me with the distinct impression that I was next."

16

Wrinkles

Vikki was concerned about Bradley's confessions and Howard's recent actions, not because they exposed the Foundry's vulnerabilities, which was no small thing, but because she knew these two men were not savvy enough to figure out how to benefit from these actions. She was anxious to establish measures to protect the company, but her next steps depended principally on who had been responsible for the actions of these two men and why. She had uncovered Ehndale's interest in the company's finances and understood why stealing confidential information could prove profitable, but she had no idea how anyone could benefit from hiding the Flight recorder. It made absolutely no sense. If Ehndale were responsible, as she suspected, she needed confirmation before she confronted him, as he would undoubtedly retaliate for being exposed, and she wanted to be prepared.

Bradley had decided not to hold Thurmond to his promise to keep the substance of their conversations confidential. Still, out of concern for Bradley's safety, Thurmond was frustratingly evasive whenever Vikki pressed him for information. Instead, he would elaborate profusely on Bradley's remarkable conversion but divulged nothing further about their conversations, making Vikki wonder if Thurmond was genuine or equivocating to protect Bradley. Whatever the reason, she respected Thurmond's decision not to divulge any information and decided she needed to talk with Bradley alone.

Vikki tried to schedule a visit, but her request was inexplicably denied. Curiously, the Warden had become reluctant to grant Bradley visitation and said it was because he was uncomfortable with the amount of attention the new prisoner had been getting recently. When Vikki confronted the Warden, he accused her of challenging his authority and indefinitely revoked Bradley's visitation privileges. Undeterred, Vikki redirected her efforts to less cordial means and began putting pressure on the Warden through various methods, which she had learned to be effective from experience. She was confident that she would meet with Bradley one way or the other. It was just a matter of time.

~

The expansion initiative and its repercussions, coupled with the increasing production demand at home, had kept Vikki extremely busy at the Foundry. Additionally, the troubles she had been experiencing with Howard, Ehndale, Bradley, and now the Warden had monopolized what was left of her time, so she had asked Thomas to give her some space to focus, and although he missed her, he had reluctantly agreed to keep his distance.

Thomas knew convincing Thurmond to head up the Taipei operation must have been stressful enough for Vikki, but he couldn't imagine how exhausting it must have been to manage the overseas expansion while dealing with the foundry operation here at home. While they were apart, Thomas followed the events at the Foundry to be aware of what Vikki was going through. He heard about Bradley's shocking confessions and the security breach caused by Howie's thefts, but he was most concerned that Howie's tragic death had affected her somehow. Thomas had suspicions about everything, which he would happily share if Vikki allowed him.

With Thurmond home temporarily to look after things, Vikki organized a strategy to deal with everything to free up some time. Vikki believed she had neglected her personal life long enough and decided to take a desperately needed break from work. While she waited for the Warden to come around, Vikki invited Thomas to her office for some company, and he enthusiastically accepted without hesitation.

The evening Thomas came to her office, Vikki had take-out Chinese food delivered and laid it out on the coffee table alongside the couch like a buffet. They used chopsticks to eat from the paper cartons and talked about what they both had been up to since they had seen each other last. Thomas had an uncanny ability to relieve stress, so after Vikki managed to relax, she began to talk about what was most pressing on her mind.

"I believe Ehndale's got his fingers in all this somehow…" she began, "…I just need to figure out 'how' and 'why' so I can alleviate my risk if any exists."

Thomas was concerned and warned her to be careful, "Take a little time to think before you confront him, V..." he began as she calmly ate her noodles. He continued, "...I don't know exactly what he's capable of, but whatever he has in mind will be for his benefit and no one else's. I wouldn't even put it past him to try to hurt you somehow while he's at it. I believe he would hurt anyone who interferes with his plans. You know that better than anyone, so be careful!"

With a furrowed brow, Vikki curled her legs up under her and replied, "I'd stop worrying about me, Thom. If anyone was to worry, it should be whoever was responsible!"

In as threatening a manner as she could muster, Vikki pointed her chopsticks at Thomas and added, "Especially if they're doing something I don't like! You know what they say, 'Hell hath no fury like a woman scorned!'"

Vikki flirtatiously poked Thomas in the ribs with her foot and said, "...Who knows? Maybe it wasn't Ehndale. Maybe it was YOU behind everything after all!?".

Thomas knew she was making light of his involvement in the crash investigation when he had illegally helped Thurmond try to solve that mystery and was thankful that she found humor in it.

They both appreciated speaking openly and spending hours enjoying their food, some wine, and each other's company. After much discussion, Vikki took Thomas's advice and put off her confrontation with Ehndale. Instead, she would talk with other influential people who stood to gain from Bradley's actions and the information Howie had gathered about the company to narrow down the possibilities by eliminating them as suspects, which she believed would ultimately confirm her suspicions about Ehndale. That would be when she would confront him, but she needed to keep her intentions a secret to prevent Ehndale's suspicion.

When they discussed the methods she intended to employ, Thomas suggested meeting with these other associates individually to prevent suspicion about why they were there. This way, she could learn about what they knew and identify it as common knowledge or confidential information. Vikki liked the idea and said she could portray these meetings as inquiries into their interest in investing in the foundry expansion. That would assuredly lead to discussing the company's financial position and activities.

Thomas knew this meant they would see little of each other until Vikki had come to a conclusion. Still, he enjoyed every minute they had spent together and assured her that whenever she felt like taking a break from 'running the world,' he would be available for her.

~

Vikki relied upon Thurmond to help run things when he was home, leaving him little time to spend with his friends, but he was always happy to be there. He wasn't sure where his relationship stood with Monica and was too afraid of her answer to ask, but he nevertheless made a point to call her each time he was home. Her response was typically polite but often aloof, and she always seemed too busy to spend time with him. He knew she was unhappy about his decision to go to Taipei and hoped that, in time, things could return to how they had been before accepting his new role in the Foundry's expansion.

Thurmond consequently occupied his time at home primarily engaged in the foundry business. He met with workers to ensure protocols were followed and reviewed operational standards and contracts. He scoured through orders and met with customers to strengthen relationships. Vikki routinely took advantage of this and left the Foundry's operation entirely up to him when he was home, which he appreciated. As a result, Vikki was free to spend the better part of her time engaged in other affairs, which she used to conduct her investigation.

Many of the executives Vikki met with were curious about her interest in talking with them. Most believed she was maneuvering to solidify her company's position globally and conducting these meetings to explore mutually beneficial financial relationships that could assist her. Vikki concluded after each interview that although the executives were interested in becoming financially involved, none seemed to possess any knowledge of the information contained in the reports that had been stolen from Thurmond's office. She knew they would have most assuredly used that information to strengthen their negotiating positions, but none did. They also seemed entirely unaware of Bradley's role in hiding the flight recorder, which supported the case against the Foundry and weakened the company's position in the Van der Staar suit. One by one, Vikki eliminated each executive as a potential suspect until she was more convinced than ever that Ehndale had to have been responsible. Now she was ready to find out why.

In preparation for her confrontation with Ehndale, Vikki tried to ascertain the advantage Ehndale would realize from Bradley's actions. She studied the records that had been reported compromised to accumulate information that she planned on using to trick Ehndale into admitting he was responsible. He had admitted soliciting Howie to steal the documents, but Vikki needed to connect the two actions. Once she made the connection, she would be ready to confront him.

Vikki asked Sheila to gather copies of the compromised documents and put them on her desk. She then began clearing her desk to make room for them and noticed a handwritten letter from her sister Veronica in a pile of useless junk mail. Vikki hadn't heard from her sister in years, and although she was interested in seeing why her sister had written, it had to be personal. Consequently, it seemed of minor importance and, therefore, a low priority. She pulled the letter from the pile, slipped it under the corner of her leather desktop pad, and continued clearing her desk, intending to read it after finishing her work.

Vikki spent hours organizing the folders Sheila had placed on her desk into ordered piles, and when she was about done for the day, she noticed the letter from her sister that she had put aside. She picked it up, opened it, and began to cry after reading it.

~

While on night patrol, Thomas was surprised to see Vikki's car parked outside Kate's Diner since it had closed hours earlier. He stopped to ensure everything was OK, but the front door was locked. The streetlamp's glare in the glass made it difficult to see inside, so Thomas put his hands on either side of his face and pressed up against the window, peering inside. He saw a faint light glowing from behind the counter, which appeared to emanate from the doorway that he knew led to several rooms beyond it. He assumed Vikki was inside talking to Kate in her office and wondered if he should leave them alone but determined that something had to be wrong, given the late hour.

Thomas banged on the door loud enough to be heard from inside, and moments later, a female silhouette appeared in the doorway that Thomas made out to be Kate. Thomas stepped away from the door and waved as Kate walked toward him. When she was close enough for Thomas to see her face, he noticed she had been crying. She opened the door, looked up at Thomas, and said:

"Vikki's Mom passed away, Thom, and she didn't know. She's distraught. Her sister sent her a letter weeks ago with the news, but Vikki didn't open it until today and missed it all. She feels terrible, and she could probably use a hug from you about now. Come in if you have time, hun; she's back in my office."

Kate held the door open as Thomas entered slowly. He hugged Kate and kissed her on the cheek as he passed. On his way to her office, Thomas thought about what he would say, and memories of his own Mom suddenly flooded his mind. As he stepped into Kate's office, he thought about what someone could have told him that would have helped him deal with his Mom's passing.

When Vikki saw him, she jumped out of her chair and flung herself at him. She threw her arms around him tightly, and he held her without saying a word. When Vikki released him from her embrace, he saw her eyes swollen from crying. Her hair and clothing were slightly disheveled, and her mascara had begun to run. For the first time since he'd known her, Thomas thought Vikki looked frail and vulnerable, like a little girl. He wanted to help remove her pain but didn't know how to fix this.

~

Wondering what she would say to her sister about the terrible news of their mother's passing, Vikki spent hours staring at her phone before she mustered the courage to pick it up and call her. Her heart raced as the phone rang, and when someone picked up the phone, Vikki didn't know what to say and remained silent. After a few seconds, the person on the other end of the phone asked, "Is that you, Viv?"

Vikki stumbled for her words and said, "Yes, Ronnie, it's me. I don't…that is, I can't.…"

"It's OK, Viv…" Ronnie replied cordially, "…I know what you mean. It's OK."

Ronnie had always seemed emotionally detached, but Vikki realized when they were still relatively young that her sister was extremely level-headed. Ronnie had always been calm, even in the most stressful situations, which was an attribute that Vikki came to admire and emulate. Both sisters employed this ability to deal with their turbulent home life during childhood. Still, the difference was that Ronnie accepted her parents' disinclination to change, and Vikki resented their lack of fortitude to improve their circumstances.

"I'm guessing you finally got my letter about Mom, Viv." Veronica began, "…When I didn't hear from you, and you didn't show up for her funeral service, I wasn't sure you received it."

"I didn't see it until after the funeral, Ronnie…." Vikki replied defensively, "… I've been so busy with work that I haven't read my mail in months. I would have come. I loved Mom; even though I was mad at her, I always loved her."

"I know you did, Viv. Mom knew that. She loved you too. She understood why you left and prayed for you every day."

'Don't tell me that, Ronnie…." Vikki replied, "…that makes me feel even worse about missing her funeral."

Ronnie began laughing, which surprised and confused Vikki, who wondered if her sister had changed over the years and become callous. After a few moments of silence, Vikki continued, "I would have certainly been there for Mom had I known…." Vikki emphasized, "…I was only calling you out of courtesy to apologize for not being there for you and for Dad."

"Dad didn't come…." Ronnie coldly replied.

Vikki immediately became angry and shouted, "Why the hell not!"

"You've been gone a long time, sis. A lot has happened over the years that you have no idea about. I figured Dad may not come and wasn't surprised when he didn't show."

Ronnie paused briefly, then continued, "…I thought you'd be there, though. You and Mom had differences, but you two still loved each other. It's a shame you missed it."

Vikki was surprised at how upset she had become. Vikki had never considered her parents anything besides mere extensions of each other, so the news of her father not attending their mother's funeral was unconscionable. In her mind, their divorce didn't change that. They were still basically one in the same person, just in different packaging.

"Like I said, Ronnie, I didn't get the letter until it was too late. Had I known sooner, I certainly would have come."

"Not too late, Viv...." Ronnie returned, "...I mean, Mom passed away in the dead of winter, and the ground was still frozen. They couldn't bury her because they couldn't dig her grave. They held her in a receiving vault at the funeral home until the ground thawed. It should be a few months before they can dig her grave, and we can bury her."

Vikki was relieved she hadn't missed everything but appalled at the notion of her mother being stuck in a freezer, which she considered barbaric.

"You mean to tell me they can't bury her or won't because it's too much trouble."

"Well, all I know, Viv, is what they told me. I've been told it's actually quite common."

"Common?" Vikki replied, "I've never heard of it before."

Ronnie knew that her sister would be upset whatever she said, so she changed the conversation's focus and suggested something different.

"It's been so long since you and I spent time together, Viv; why don't you plan to come out early to visit, and we can make the preparations for Mom together? You're good at that. You may even have a chance to visit Dad and talk some sense into him. Maybe he'll change his mind."

Vikki hadn't considered her sister's suggestion, but it all sounded reasonable. She was about to tell her sister she'd make plans to come to join her but remembered she had several upcoming events that required her to attend, which were beyond her control to cancel or reschedule.

"When do you think they will be ready to dig Mom's grave, Ronnie?"

"Should be in the next month or so if I were to guess, Viv. Why? Are you considering coming out?"

"I'm sorry, Ronnie, but I'm in the middle of a few things right now. I don't think I'll be able to get out early to help you with all the arrangements, but I should be able to attend the burial. I hope that's not a problem?"

As she listened to herself apologize to her sister, Vikki became disappointed. It was always the same; she was too busy. She had recently taken time away from work to be with Thomas, which was a welcome relief, but she wanted to reconnect with her sister and didn't know how to arrange it.

"Tell you what, Viv…." Ronnie replied, "… I'm not doing anything I can't take a break from right now, so why don't I visit you? We can make all the arrangements for Mom from there. That way, you can finish what you need to get done, and we can still visit when you have time. What do you think? It'll be fun, and we can catch up. I've missed you. It would be great to spend a little time with you. C'mon, it'll be fun."

Her mother's loss meant Vikki would never be able to resolve her frustrations with her, but this was an opportunity to do so with her sister. She couldn't think why Ronnie's proposal wouldn't work and wanted to jump at the chance. She became excited and said, "I think it's a great idea! I'll buy the tickets. You can stay with me!"

"Perfect!" Ronnie replied, "…just let me know the details as soon as possible, Viv. I need to make arrangements here before I leave so my time away doesn't put anyone in a bind at my work."

"Done!" Vikki exclaimed at the unexpected development.

"I'm very excited!" Ronnie replied, "…I can't wait to hear about your business exploits and tremendous achievements. I've always been amazed at what you could do, and it's hard to imagine anyone can be so successful. I brag about you all the time."

Vikki was surprised to hear that her sister was interested in what she did, never mind feeling proud enough to brag about it.

When they ended their call, Vikki immediately began planning for her sister's visit. While doing so, she reminisced about their childhood, and warm memories flooded her mind. The angry episodes that had torn her family apart suddenly disappeared. Suffocating memories that infuriated her transformed into childish fantasies with insightful glimpses into her sister's motivations and decisions for what she had chosen to do with her life. Even her sister's devotion to faith seemed to make sense to Vikki and became almost admirable somehow, which made Vikki wonder if she had been unfair to her older sister all those years ago.

17

Serendipity

Vikki had a complicated relationship with her sister. They had always been friends but had never been close, and though the experiences in their childhood bound them together, their divergent philosophies had pushed them apart. Both were unwavering in their convictions, but they harbored no resentment towards each other whatsoever. They had pursued their lives without regret in their own unique way, and now that tragedy had brought them together again, Vikki wanted to know what had become of her sister and wondered if Ronnie felt the same way about her.

As a child, Vikki had typically confided in Ehndale regarding her feelings about her family, but over the years, she deferred more readily to her instincts. Given her suspicions about his recent actions, those instincts told her that if she confided in Ehndale, he would devise a way to exploit her anxiety for his personal gain. In this instance, that possibility seemed a certainty. Accordingly, Vikki needed to talk to someone without an agenda who wouldn't make her feel vulnerable. Thomas and Kate immediately came to mind.

No one was more thoughtful than Thomas, but Vikki was concerned that revealing her insecurities may affect their relationship, which she didn't want to risk. He had never discussed his family or mentioned any siblings, which made her question whether he could understand her emotionally complicated relationship with her sister.

On the other hand, Kate had become the closest thing she had to family and a proxy through which she could resolve complex emotions, especially regarding her mother. She was sweet and brutally honest but never judgmental. This made her better suited than anyone to help Vikki deal with her sister's visit and the loss of her mother, so Vikki began confiding in her, and their conversations went as Vikki expected.

"You do realize that she's not the same little girl you used to know, don't you?" Kate asked.

"Of course!" Vikki insisted, "…why would you ask me that?"

"I just want to ensure you managed your expectations, dear."

"And what expectations would those be, Kate?" Vikki asked reprovingly.

"I could be wrong," Kate began, "…but based on my experience, people change, and not always for the better. I don't want you getting your hopes up that you two will magically become best friends again when it's more likely that you have drifted further apart than you've imagined."

Vikki knew Kate was probably right. The sisters would likely bury their mother, then drift apart again until the next time fate brought them together, if ever. Vikki appreciated Kate's candor and replied,

"I'm sure you're right, Kate, but allow me the hope that something good can come of this opportunity to reconnect with her. She will arrive a week from tomorrow. I'm just finalizing the arrangements."

"I assume she'll be staying with you?" Kate asked, as more of a suggestion than a question.

Vikki laughed and said, "Of course!"

"Good!" Kate replied, "… you'll want to show her around then, I imagine? Take her out to eat?"

"Well, I wasn't really planning on cooking much…" Vikki offered, "…so I suppose we would go out to eat."

"Of course, you will…" Kate agreed and added, "…at the Diner, I assume?"

Vikki laughed and replied, "Of course!"

It was apparent Kate wanted to meet Ronnie, and Vikki enjoyed how politely Kate steered the arrangements to do so. Her passive-aggressive approach was precisely what Vikki's mother would have done, which made Vikki smile.

Vikki's anxiety subsided after conversing with Kate, and she decided she was ready to share the news of her sister's visit with Thomas. Thomas immediately offered to help when they spoke, knowing Vikki had a lot on her plate. He suggested picking her sister up at the airport, but Vikki politely declined. Thomas didn't understand her apprehension but took no offense and respected her decision. He said if she changed her mind, his offer stood to help in any way he could, for which Vikki was grateful but unsurprised.

~

Ronnie's flight was not due to touch down until late afternoon, but Vikki wanted to be sure to be there early. It had been some time since they had seen each other, so Vikki had no idea what to expect and wasn't sure if she would be able to recognize her sister. She wondered if life had been good to her, if it had worn her down, and, more importantly, if it would show.

Vikki arrived at the terminal well before her sister was scheduled to disembark and parked her unmistakable Lamborghini GT in the arrivals area queue. She spent her time watching the throngs of travelers' stream in and out of the terminal and began to fantasize about their lives. She wondered where they came from, where they were going, and why they were going there.

Airports had always fascinated her. Vikki considered them portals through which one could experience other cultures without leaving home. Strange clothing, different languages, and unusual customs excited her. It was an escape, making Vikki wonder how different things would be if she abandoned her life and got on a plane.

Vikki's thoughts turned to Thomas, and she wondered what it would be like to travel with him as her escort or husband. As she tried to imagine her life alone with him, a handsome couple that looked happy together caught her attention when they strolled out of the terminal, chatting and laughing. She studied them, supplanted herself and Thomas for the couple, and became lost in her thoughts, fantasizing about their lives together.

However, the fantasy abruptly ended when the couple suddenly stopped, turned to face each other, and separated with a perfunctory handshake. The man then walked away and disappeared inside the terminal without the woman giving him a second look. Instead, she stood on the curb, examining the cars in the queue waiting to pick up their travelers.

The woman appeared incredibly fit, and her hair was neatly styled in a loose French braid that fell just below her shoulders. She had a sizable leather shoulder bag and a small carry-on suitcase beside her. Wearing a clay-colored coat with a high waist belt and a large straw hat, she removed a pair of sunglasses she'd been wearing to glance through her shoulder bag. When she looked up, she began adjusting her hat, and Vikki immediately recognized her as her big sister, Veronica, although she was noticeably taller than Vikki had remembered.

Ronnie quickly spotted her sister's car, which she believed she would have guessed to be hers even without the description, which made her smile as she made her way toward it.

Vikki wanted to make a good impression but was incredibly self-conscious and nervous. She fumbled to release her seat belt and clumsily exited the car. After adjusting her clothing, Vikki calmly opened the trunk and stepped on the curb to greet her big sister.

Vikki had been through this moment a thousand times in her mind, and even though she had discussed it with Kate, she felt like an insecure little schoolgirl. Vikki had wanted to say so many things to her sister, but her mind went blank, and she couldn't think of one. She felt inadequate and vulnerable but stood silently, trying to portray confidence as she watched her sister approach.

Ronnie stopped a few feet away, removed her shoulder bag, placed it on top of the small suitcase beside her, and walked towards Vikki, wearing a genuine smile with arms wide open. When the two women embraced, Vikki inexplicably began to cry.

"What's the matter V? Did I step on your foot?"

"No, Ronnie, it's not you. It's me…" Vikki replied as the two women released their embrace and stepped apart to talk.

"…I had a sudden rush of emotion. It's fine, and I'm over it now."

Vikki wiped her nose and eyes with a kerchief she had pulled from her pocket, then said.

"It's so great to see you, Ronnie. How long has it been? Ten years, maybe twelve…?"

"Sixteen…" Ronnie replied without the slightest hesitation.

Ronnie retrieved her luggage and neatly packed it in Vikki's tiny trunk. When Vikki offered to help, Ronnie replied, "Thanks, V, but I got it. I only packed a few things to tide me over. Besides, I wanted to make sure I had enough room to pack a few of Mom's things that I put aside for you. I can always pick something up if I've forgotten anything."

'Very thoughtful, Ronnie. Thank you." Vikki replied and continued, "What about Dad? You saved some of Mom's things for him, right? "

"No…" Ronnie replied, "…I asked him, but he didn't want anything, so I got rid of everything else.

Vikki didn't understand why her Dad didn't want anything to remember their mother by and asked why. As she put the last of her things in Vikki's trunk, Ronnie explained, "Dad's still bitter about their divorce. I told him he should get over it, but he won't listen. He has a new life now with a new wife and grandkids."

Vikki was surprised and slightly upset to hear the news. Her father had always been the one to stress the importance of family, yet he had abandoned them for a new life with someone else. She considered him a hypocrite but wondered if she hadn't done the same thing when she left her family for Ehndale.

"Is he still working?" Vikki asked as she closed her trunk. Ronnie replied, "He's been retired for a while now but still drives a school bus to supplement his pension."

"What's his new wife like Ronnie, and what do you know about her?"

"Her name is 'Marlene,' and I don't think she works," Ronnie replied as they both slipped into the car and fastened their seatbelts, "...she seems nice enough, but I can't bring myself to call her ' Mom' like she wants me to. They moved away after their wedding to be closer to her grandkids, so I moved back home to be near Mom, so she'd have someone nearby to visit."

Vikki was angry with her father but became increasingly introspective and listened to her sister. A wave of guilt suddenly came over her when she realized she would have never been willing to move back home to look after their Mom herself, which made her feel incredibly selfish.

Ronnie continued, "...Even though they were divorced, Mom tried to stay friendly with Dad, but he didn't want any part of it. He couldn't get past the fact that she was the one who had filed for divorce, even though she was heartbroken when she filed the papers "

"I never understood why Mom ended their marriage," Vikki replied.

Ronnie remained silent for a moment while she thought of how to reply, then said, "Mom believed that Dad's happiness was more important than their marriage. She didn't believe in divorce as a solution, but she loved him and couldn't stand him being so unhappy."

Vikki remembered her Mom teaching her that selflessness was the key to all virtue and that a virtuous life would help her achieve her goals, even if she didn't recognize her ambitions.

Ehndale had told Vikki that her mother's logic was rubbish. That the life her mother advocated was like a prison sentence, where people suffered and sacrificed, expecting to be rewarded for their trouble when their life was over. He defined virtue as doing what's best for yourself, not others, but Vikki suddenly realized that there was more to it than that. There was a different kind of reward in sacrifice, and you didn't have to wait until your life was over to realize it. That kind of reward wasn't tangible because you couldn't have it or hold it like a possession or an asset. It was recognized in the consequences of your virtuous actions. In the instance of her parent's divorce, her mother had sacrificed her marriage to a man she loved to relieve his suffering.

Vikki began to remember the terrible fights she had had with her parents, and although she never regretted defying them, she wondered if her actions had contributed to the break-up of her family, which was something she had never considered before. She felt a more profound respect for her mother and sister than she had ever felt and was only sorry that she wouldn't have the opportunity to share that understanding with her mother now that she was gone. Vikki wouldn't allow that to happen again with Ronnie and wanted to seize this opportunity to reconnect with her.

~

Through his previous conversations with Vikki, Thomas had learned that although the sisters were close when they were younger, they had drifted apart over the years. Vikki hadn't shared what had come between them, but he believed that rekindling that relationship could be an emotional benefit to Vikki, especially when dealing with the loss of her mother, which, unbeknownst to Vikki, Thomas understood all too well. He wanted them to enjoy their visit together and gave them space to allow them a chance to reconnect, hoping that rekindling a bond between them may help Vikki reconcile issues she had with her past, whether she realized she had them or not.

Thomas's past had always haunted him, but he never discussed it other than answering a few questions that he didn't consider too personal. He had always hoped to have an opportunity to reconcile with his family, as Vikki did now, but believed that if it had ever existed for him, it had passed long ago and certainly didn't exist for him anymore.

~

Ronnie had never shown any interest in material things, but Vikki had hoped that even though it wasn't something her sister aspired to herself, she would appreciate the measure and breadth of her success. Vikki mentioned a few of her achievements to make a good impression, but Ronnie remained silent, and Vikki could tell that her sister was not interested in discussing any of them.

Vikki offered to take Ronnie on a tour of the Foundry to see where she worked, but Ronnie said she was tired from her trip and asked if they could look around after she got settled in. Ronnie closed her eyes and fell asleep as Vikki drove straight to her home, disappointed.

When they arrived, Ronnie awoke and thought her sister's home was remarkable, but that was as she expected. Although she was proud of her, she was curious about what Vikki had been willing to sacrifice to achieve such success. She did not want to be judgmental, so she complimented Vikki on her home but said nothing more about it as Vikki showed her to the room where she would be staying.

This lack of similar interests made Vikki concerned about reconnecting with her sister, so she changed focus. When Ronnie had settled into her room, Vikki brought her some food and suggested she get a good night's rest to help her refresh.

"We'll grab something delicious to eat in the morning when you're ready..." Vikki suggested, "...I know a great little place called 'Kate's' that I know you'll like."

"Sounds wonderful, V, thank you. I'll see you in the morning. Good night."

Vikki left her sister to rest, confident that Kate would make her feel welcome. Hopefully, their meeting would also be able to ease her anxiety.

~

Kate stopped what she was doing when she saw Vikki's car pull up in front of the Diner. She thought about calling Thomas, but he had asked her to see how things were going between them before she did. Honoring his wishes, Kate hastily approached the front door to welcome the two sisters. Vikki held the door open for her sister and was delighted to see Kate coming as she followed Ronnie inside.

"Good morning, and welcome! "Kate bellowed, "...I imagine this beautiful woman is your sister, Veronica?"

Vikki had told Ronnie about Kate on their drive to the Diner, so her friendliness was not unexpected. Ronnie appreciated Kate's kind manner and politely replied.

"Hello, Katherine. Nice to meet you. I don't know what my sister has told you but call me Ronnie. I can't recall the last time someone called me 'Veronica.'"

"Done!" Kate enthusiastically replied, "And you can call me Kate. The only people who ever called me 'Katherine' were my mother when I was in trouble, and my divorce attorney, whom I rather forget."

Kate wiped her hands on her apron, exchanged kisses with Vikki, and offered her hand to Ronnie.

"So very glad to meet you...." she said as she shook Ronnie's hand, "...Sit anywhere. I'll have one of the girls come over to take your order. Would you like some coffee to get started?"

"Yes, please. Thank you..."; the sisters simultaneously returned.

Kate motioned to a young waitress as Vikki led Ronnie to the table where she regularly sat with Thomas. Kate spoke briefly with the waitress, who grabbed two mugs, a carafe of coffee, and two menus before quickly making her way to the sister's table. She began filling the mugs and spoke.

"Miss Kate says if you want something not on the menu, don't hesitate to ask. Our Chef can make anything, and that's the truth."

"Thank you," Vikki replied as the two sisters chuckled about the idea of a 'Chef' in a Diner.

The waitress placed the carafe of coffee on their table, smiled, and told them she'd be back in a few minutes to take their orders. When she had gone, Ronnie whispered,

"That girl is so sweet it makes my teeth hurt."

"Get used to it, Ronnie," Vikki replied, "… there's a lot of that around here."

Kate knew Thomas was anxious to meet Vikki's sister, but he had expressed concern that his presence might interfere with their reunion. To determine when she should call him, Kate watched the sisters closely and was pleased with how things seemed to be going. After a short while, she thought Vikki might consider Thomas a welcome distraction, so she decided to call him when the sisters had almost finished their meal.

Thomas had been filing paperwork at the station house when he received Kate's call and was excited to hear that things were going well. He decided to take a few minutes out of his day to say a quick hello and hopped in his patrol car to head straight to the Diner. When he arrived, he parked around the corner to be less conspicuous and put his hat under his arm before entering the restaurant.

He spotted the sisters laughing and chatting but decided he would rather be invited over than abruptly introduce himself. He pretended not to notice them and walked directly to the front counter. He sat at a stool, ordered some coffee, and was almost immediately engaged by an angry man, who began furiously complaining about a parking ticket he had been issued.

"There ain't no-one ever parked in that handicap spot…" the man shouted loud enough to get a few customers' attention.

As a waitress placed his coffee cup in front of him, Thomas replied, "That may be true, Fred, but rules are rules, and the law says without a handicap sticker, you can't park in those spaces."

Thomas took a sip of his coffee as the angry patron replied more furiously than before.

"Them rules ain't always right; you know, 'officer,'" he said condescendingly, "…there ain't no-one in this town in a wheelchair, but Chauncey and it's his store! He doesn't even drive anymore, either! It's ridiculous, Thomas! You know it ain't right!"

The man had raised his voice so that everyone in the Diner couldn't help but hear it. When Vikki heard him yell 'Thomas,' she looked up, and although she was happy to see Thomas, she immediately began thinking of a way to extricate him from the situation. Ronnie noticed the sudden shift in her sister's attention and, wondering why she had become so interested, began watching the events at the front counter unfold.

Thomas sipped his coffee as he waited for the man to finish ranting, then coolly replied.

"Let's say a disabled person was visiting town and needed to pick something up at Chauncey's market, and they couldn't use the curb ramp because you took the space right in front of it. Don't you think they have as much right to go to the same places as you? Do you think it's right for you to prevent them from being able to use the ramp just because you want to save walking another 15 feet?"

"Gibberish Tom and you know it. Ain't never going to happen!"

Kate was also watching the altercation, and although she wanted to de-escalate it, she knew Thomas could handle it and left him to it. Vikki was waiting for the right moment to assist when her sister Ronnie suddenly stood, grabbed the bill from the table, and walked calmly but directly up to the counter where the two men had been arguing.

Standing directly behind them, Ronnie held up her hand to get a waitress's attention and then leaned across the counter between the two men to hand the waitress some money with their bill. Ronnie then stepped back as she smiled at each of the two men and waited there for the waitress to return with her change. When the waitress returned, Ronnie placed a tip on the counter and leaned in to quietly say something to the angry customer before returning to her table. The irate customer glared at her for a few seconds, reached into his pocket, begrudgingly pulled out some money he placed on the counter, then unceremoniously excused himself and stormed out of the Diner.

When Ronnie had made her way back to the table where she had left Vikki, she said.

"Where to next, sis?"

Vikki was dumbfounded and asked, "What did you say to that guy?"

"I asked him to consider whether he would feel the same way if his mother was inconvenienced by his callous insensitivity?"

"That's it?" Vikki asked.

"Yup. That's it…" Ronnie replied, then continued, "…so now that we've had a little excitement and a fantastic meal, which I must say was delicious, are we heading back to your place, or did you have something else in mind?"

Vikki usually took charge, but her sister just diffused an escalating situation instantly, without emotion or incident. Vikki and Thomas were both surprised and impressed as Thomas started going over to Vikki's table to join her and her sister, whom he was now more anxious than ever to meet.

18

Synergy

Monica understood why Thurmond accepted the position in Asia but was upset that they hadn't resolved their unexpected 'engagement' before his departure. She knew she needed to provide him with answers regarding her commitment to their relationship but struggled with how to relay that concern to him, and as a result, she avoided him whenever he came home. Kate suggested their separation may help bring clarity, but Thurmond's absence only left Monica with more questions.

Her feelings for him were never in question, but her worry was whether he could resist the same temptations he had succumbed to in the past and whether she was strong enough to forgive him if he couldn't. She understood that it was only a matter of time before she'd lose him if she couldn't figure out how to communicate these fears and knew her reticence would likely give him the wrong impression.

On her way to work one morning, Monica noticed Vikki's car parked outside Kate's Diner and decided to stop in and ask if she knew when Thurmond might be coming home again. She had missed him on his latest visit and wanted to be sure she could prepare herself for the next time he returned home. She jogged across the street, peered through the Diner's front window, and was immediately spotted by Kate, who rightly assumed she had seen Vikki's car and might be looking for some news about Thurmond.

When Monica stepped inside, Kate discreetly waved at her until she got her attention. Then, she pointed towards a table where

Vikki was sitting with Thomas and another woman Monica didn't recognize. Undeterred by Vikki's company, Monica waved back to thank Kate and quickly made her way toward Vikki's table. Thomas noticed her approaching and pushed back his chair to stand and welcome her, but Monica wanted to be quick about her business.

"There's no need to get up, Thomas. I'll only be a minute..." she politely said, then turned her attention towards Vikki and continued, "Did you happen to know when Thurmond might be coming home again? I didn't get a chance to see him last time he was here, and I needed to talk with him in person about something."

Vikki was not interested in becoming involved in the couple's problems but was sympathetic toward Monica's position. She knew when she assigned Thurmond to handle the Asia project that her decision could create tension between them, but Thurmond's involvement was critical to the success of her operation. Abandoning what was best for the company's expansion to preserve the couple's relationship was not an option, especially since Thurmond confessed that they had problems with their relationship before his departure.

Thurmond had also mentioned his frustration with her reluctance to see him, so Monica's sudden urgency to see him indicated to Vikki that Monica might have come to some conclusion and was looking for an opportunity to resolve their difficulties or possibly end their relationship—an unfortunate but unsurprising consequence of the situation.

Monica was uncharacteristically abrupt and visibly distressed, so to settle her down, Vikki politely replied.

"Nice to see you, Mona..."

Monica realized she was being blunt and took a short breath to relax and replied, "Nice to see you, Vikki. I'm sorry to barge in, but I saw your car out front and thought I'd come in for a minute to ask you about Thurmond."

Vikki calmly replied, "Thurmond hasn't shared his intentions with me, but I expect we'll speak again soon. I'll let him know you were asking about him."

Monica considered Vikki's response somewhat patronizing but had no interest in confronting her and politely returned, "I'd appreciate that. Thank you!"

Thomas remained silent as the two women spoke while Ronnie waited patiently to be introduced. When the brief conversation appeared to be over, Ronnie became concerned that she would miss her opportunity to meet her sister's anxious acquaintance and asked, "Is anyone going to introduce me?"

"Of course! How careless of me!" Vikki declared, "...Monica, I'd like you to meet my sister, Veronica."

Monica was genuinely surprised and stared briefly at Vikki's sister to see any resemblance. She turned her attention back to Vikki and indelicately said, "You've never mentioned you had a sister?"

While Vikki was sympathetic to Monica's emotionally fragile state, she wanted to end the unwelcome interruption and became impatient with Monica. She was more interested in continuing her morning with Thomas and her sister than engaging in a lengthy dialogue with Thurmond's distressed girlfriend and replied unctuously, "Why would I?"

As far as Ronnie could tell, Monica was genuinely surprised and meant no offense by her remark, but the tension seemed to be growing between the two women, so she quickly responded.

"You seem to be in a hurry, Monica, so I won't cause you further delay."

Ronnie stood, stretched out her hand, and continued.

"You can call me Ronnie. I'm only in town for a few days and just wanted to introduce myself. Hopefully, we'll meet again before I leave. Perhaps for some coffee or tea?"

Monica said nothing in return, shook Ronnie's hand listlessly, then immediately turned her attention back to Vikki.

"I'd appreciate knowing Thurmond's schedule as soon as you knew anything."

"I'll be sure to let you know," Vikki replied tersely.

Monica flashed a wry smile at Vikki, nodded at Ronnie, and patted Thomas on the shoulder as she politely excused herself from the table. She waved back at Kate as she approached the door, then disappeared out of view down the street. Ronnie stood as she watched Monica leave, then sat back down and asked, "Thurmond's girlfriend, I take it?"

"Fiancée…" Vikki clarified, then continued, "… Thurmond's working for me in Taipei at the moment, and the two rarely get to see each other. It appears she is having some difficulty with the arrangement."

Ronnie frowned at her sister and replied, "Can you blame her?"

Vikki wasn't interested in defending herself, so she changed the subject. Thomas had offered to help, so Vikki turned to him and asked.

"Do you mind showing Ronnie around town, Thom? I have some errands and don't want to bore her."

Then, before Thomas could answer, Vikki turned to Ronnie and continued, "Thom knows everything about this town. Would you mind spending time with him while I finish my chores?"

Vikki's manner reminded Ronnie of their mother, which amused her since they were very different and had always been at odds. Ronnie smiled, looked at Thomas, and replied, "Absolutely! I'd love it!"

"Splendid!" Vikki returned, "…then it's settled! Thom can show you around in his patrol car while I run errands. We can meet up later at the police station. I'll see you both there!"

Vikki grabbed her purse, slapped down some money, and left Thomas and her sister at the table.

~

As they drove through town, Thomas told Ronnie stories that he thought might entertain her, and when they reached the town green,

Ronnie commented on how difficult it seemed to navigate. Thomas was happy to explain.

"Your sister found that odd as well," he began, "...but it's been that way for as long as I can remember..."

"Pray to tell," Ronnie replied.

"As the story goes, a fella named Ernie, the town's Traffic Engineer, changed the traffic patterns to prevent cars from driving around the green."

Ronnie looked puzzled and asked, "Why on earth would he want to do that?"

"...Well..." Thomas continued, "...it seems that Ernie's wife, Angela, had a terrible sweet tooth and would spend hours slowly driving her car in circles around the green, stopping at every sweet shop to sample all the treats. She'd drive to a shop, park, get a treat, then sit back in her car, eating whatever she had bought before driving a few yards to the next place to get another treat. As a result, she became horribly overweight, and Ernie changed all the street directions and traffic signals, hoping she would become frustrated and either start walking between the shops or go home."

Ronnie laughed and asked, "Did it work?"

"Not really…" Thomas replied, "…Angela started using a little scooter to get around on the sidewalks, and Ernie got so mad that he refused to correct the traffic patterns to how they had been. It's just one of those quirky things about the town. People eventually became accustomed to it. They even named a sweet shop after her that sells every sweet you could imagine. It's called 'Angela's Appetite.' That really drove Ernie up the wall."

"How ridiculously quaint!" Ronnie chuckled before suggesting they honor the frustrated engineer by stopping for a quick treat at Angela's.

Thomas found a place to park, and they ordered some ice cream cones, which they enjoyed while strolling around the green. When they finished, they returned to Thomas's patrol car and continued their tour of the town until Thomas believed they had seen everything he could think of to show her. They then went to the police station, where Thomas decided to show Ronnie around to pass the time while they waited for her sister.

Thomas introduced Ronnie to his fellow officers, who teased him mercilessly about bringing his new 'girlfriend' to work. Ronnie found his acceptance of their playful chiding to be a bit naive but was impressed with the charming way he handled it. She was not offended, as it was all in good fun, but she was surprised that her sister would tolerate that aspect of her boyfriend's personality since it made him ripe for ridicule, which she knew her sister abhorred.

Vikki arrived shortly afterward and was not surprised that Ronnie had enjoyed her time with Thomas. She was grateful for his help and thanked him with a kiss, then suggested they finish their day with a tour of the Foundry. Ronnie agreed, and the sisters departed. On their way, Vikki went into detail about how she had acquired the company and explained her reasons for expanding the operation into Asia.

Ronnie knew that Vikki had always measured the value of her life in material terms, even though their parents had tried to instill in them the notion that being virtuous and maintaining one's principles was more important than any financial success. Ronnie listened quietly as her sister elaborated on her achievements and began wondering if Vikki had considered the consequences of her decisions beyond the material success they provided. Ronnie had always been concerned about her sister's willingness to sacrifice her principles to realize a financial gain, and based on what she heard, she could tell that nothing had changed, and their ambitions were still something they did not share.

~

After an extensive tour of the facility, they retired to Vikki's office, where Ronnie plopped into the chair behind Vikki's desk. Vikki sat on the couch and laughed as Ronnie clasped her hands behind her head, put her feet on the desk, and looked around the office.

"This is all very impressive, Viv, but I don't know how you see the potential. I mean, how do you know where to look, when to act, and what to do?"

Flattered that her sister was impressed, Vikki happily replied, "Thank you, Ronnie. I've learned through experience that although many strategies are involved, like calculating return on investment and the company's profitability potential, the most important thing you need is someone who lives and breathes the operation. A person with intimate knowledge who is familiar with the business to help navigate the company's acquisition, transition, and transformation. That's a critical component in the success of any venture. You identify that person, engage them, and rely on their expertise. The rest is pure tenacity."

Ronnie removed her hands from behind her head and pulled her feet off the desk. She clasped her hands on the desk and leaned forward on her elbows. Then, quoting a line from Shakespeare's Hamlet, she replied, "'Therein lies the rub!' I mean, even with your vast experience and resources, it still comes down to the simple 'Joe' engaged in the toils of everyday life to be successful."

Ronnie now understood the animosity between Monica and her sister; Thurmond was that 'Joe', and the two women were competing for his attention—Vikki for profit and Monica for love.

~

Ronnie began planning for their mother's burial and only intended to involve Vikki as much as she showed interest. She had hoped to use this opportunity to become reacquainted with her sister, but Vikki was busy running her business, so she handled all the arrangements herself. When that was complete, Ronnie began looking for other ways to occupy her time while she waited for her sister to become available.

After scheduling an additional Foundry tour to gain insight into her sister's life, Ronnie visited a few places Thomas had pointed out. She caught a movie at the local theater, visited a bowling alley, and went to a few bars to get a feel for some of the younger locals. She also had dinner at Cay Pham one evening for a change but returned to Kate's Diner when her experience there disappointed her. She had been impressed with the simple elegance of St Anselm's church when Thomas pointed it out and stopped in to look closer, where she met Fr. Elias, with whom she had a brief but interesting conversation.

One afternoon Ronnie stopped by the library and was pleasantly surprised to run into Monica. Being respectful of the library patrons, Ronnie approached Monica at the front desk and spoke with her quietly. While they began planning to do something together, a few patrons with unreasonable expectations admonished Ronnie for being too loud. When they started 'shushing' her to be quiet, Ronnie surprised Monica when she reacted with a smile. Then, she changed her voice to an exaggerated whisper that was decidedly louder than if she had been typically speaking, which Monica found particularly amusing.

Although Monica sensed the same confidence from Ronnie that she had seen in Vikki, she was astonished at the differences between the two women. Vikki was ambitious and arrogant, while Ronnie was modest and easygoing. Just as self-assured as her sister but much more agreeable. Monica admired this appealing combination of attributes and was instantly attracted to it, which made her anxious to learn more about Ronnie.

They felt remarkably at ease in each other's company and agreed to get together while Ronnie was in town. They quickly became friends, and as they spent more time together, they began offering each other more personal information about themselves.

Ronnie relayed things about Vikki and her family, which inspired Monica to be more forthcoming with her own confessions. Monica expressed her concerns about Thurmond and spoke about her relationship with her sisters, which she had always considered too personal to discuss with anyone, including Thurmond.

Apart from Kate, Monica couldn't remember meeting anyone like Ronnie, and without an earnest attempt to do so, Monica began gaining insight into managing her insecurities and was appreciative of the opportunity to do so. This blossoming relationship did not go unnoticed.

Thomas admired how much the two women seemed to enjoy each other's company, and Kate recognized Monica as happier than she had been for some time. Vikki recognized their connection and envied how easily Monica related to her sister, which made her wonder if she had taken her sister for granted all those years and had missed out on her opportunity to get to know her.

~

Thomas had always been interested in learning about Vikki's youth. Now that her trip home was rapidly approaching, he implored her to allow him to accompany her to her mother's burial in her hometown.

"Why would you want to attend such a depressing event?" she asked.

"It's only depressing because you look at it incorrectly..." Thomas replied, "... I consider it a matter of paying respects, honoring the memory of the deceased. I want to share that and help you if I can."

Vikki was honestly bewildered, and Thomas continued.

"...I didn't know your Mom, V, but I would consider it an honor and a privilege to accompany you and help you celebrate her memory."

Vikki had heard these sentiments before and considered them empty words. She believed that the deaths of others reminded people of their own mortality, which frightened them, but did nothing to honor the memory of the deceased. Besides the burial business, Vikki considered the entire affair altogether useless. She believed that after the ceremonies, people would return to the life they had known as if nothing had happened.

Vikki didn't deny that some people struggled with losing a loved one, but she believed it was likely for selfish reasons and considered all the rhetoric disingenuous. She also considered the ceremonies ridiculous pomp, organized by the bereaved to suggest they cared. However, Vikki's cynicism did nothing to dissuade Thomas, who remained adamant about going. She ultimately granted him the 'privilege' to appease and relieve him of his constant requests to accompany her.

Kate also expressed an interest in going, primarily to assure Vikki that people cared about her, but she hadn't felt well and decided against making the trip. However, Kate was comforted when she learned Thomas was going because she knew he would do well to represent them in Vikki's time of loss. She only regretted she couldn't be the one to comfort Vikki, as she had grown very fond of her and thought of her as her own daughter.

~

Ronnie had booked a round-trip flight and expected her sister to accompany her on the return trip home, but Vikki hired a private jet for the journey. Ronnie argued it was an unnecessary expense, but she knew it was useless to try and change Vikki's mind and agreed to accompany her on the private charter.

Thomas had never flown in a private jet before and was excited to be along for the ride. He spent most of the flight looking at the clouds out the window and trying to locate himself from landmarks on the ground below. While Vikki attended to some paperwork she had brought, Ronnie spent her time reading, and the three hardly spoke a word during the flight.

Their plane landed smoothly and taxied across the regional airport's modest runway before stopping outside the only building in the tiny airport besides airplane hangars. Vikki briefed her sister and Thomas on the protocols for exiting onto the tarmac and described how to navigate their way to the terminal, an exercise she had performed countless times.

After exiting the plane, Ronnie walked ahead quickly with Thomas as Vikki lagged behind them, talking with the pilots. When Vikki finished, she hurried to catch up with her companions, who had entered the terminal ahead of her. When Vikki stepped inside, she saw her sister digging through her purse while Thomas intently surveyed the tiny terminal. Vikki wondered what Thomas found so fascinating, looked around, and noticed that the airport was quite handsome.

The furnishings were ergonomically shaped wooden forms with cushions that looked as comfortable as they did interesting. Stone-tiled floors were set in a diagonal pattern, and white-washed, ship-lapped wood plank walls were adorned with enormous bulletin boards and meticulously framed photos of pilots and planes.

Brightly colored banners announcing several local celebrations hung between muted ductwork that navigated through massive wooden purlins and collar tie beams held together by gusset plates and tie-rods painted a high gloss black. In the center of the terminal was a large cupola stretching between the principal rafters, which flooded the building with light, creating a delightful sense of drama.

Vikki had typically ignored her airport surroundings, even when the terminals forced themselves on her like an assault. She had usually followed the signage to get to her next destination without noticing her surroundings, but this terminal surprised her. The ceiling was busy, but it was orderly and uncluttered. The practical design made for a pleasant experience, so she decided to resist the temptation to ignore her surroundings and look for thoughtfulness in design in the future.

~

The ride from the airport was short, and when the taxi pulled up to Ronnie's house, Thomas jumped out of the front seat and jogged behind the cab to retrieve their luggage from the trunk. Vikki got out to join him while Ronnie remained in the cab, rummaging through her purse for money to pay the driver.

Vikki surprised Thomas when she told him to leave their bags in the trunk. Thomas stopped and stood still, waiting to see what was happening. Vikki then walked around to the driver's window, told the driver not to take her sister's money, and asked him to wait.

When Ronnie asked what was going on, Vikki explained that she had made reservations at the Whitehorse Inn, then threw in the fact that Thomas snored as an excuse for doing so. Thomas pretended to be offended, which made Ronnie laugh.

"We appreciate the offer Ronnie, but we don't want to crowd you." Vikki added, "… it's not like we're kids and can crowd everyone into a little room. I think we all could use a little space. "

Ronnie knew the reason was they would be sharing a bed, which was something Vikki's parents would never approve of. Ronnie decided to make light of it and said, "Are you saying my house is too small to entertain guests? I'm offended!"

Vikki fumbled to explain her reasoning when Thomas came around from behind the cab and said, "Ronnie's only kidding, V. She's not being serious."

Slightly embarrassed, Vikki replied, "I knew that."

"No, you did not," Ronnie insisted playfully, "… you're always so serious."

"No, I'm not…." Vikki said in protest.

"She's right, I'm afraid…" Thomas confirmed, "…but that's one of the things I love about you."

Vikki felt like an insecure adolescent. She was defensive when there was no need. She was worried about her sister's opinion of her sharing a bed with a man who wasn't her husband, as her mother had warned her against all those years ago with Ehndale.

Ronnie sensed tension and light-heartedly remarked, "I'll see you two in the morning. I told the funeral home we'd be there around eight to sign the papers to release Mom from the receiving vault."

"Why so early?" Vikki asked.

"The funeral home has to release Mom's body before the cemetery digs her grave," Ronnie explained. "…and they need our signatures before any of that can happen. I thought we'd have a little ceremony for Mom before the burial, so I arranged a Mass for Mom, so her friends could pay their respects. Father Andrew is performing the ceremony at Philip Neri Church. So, you see, we need to start early, especially if you plan to leave tomorrow evening."

Vikki felt she could say nothing about the arrangements since Ronnie had made every effort to include her in the planning, but Vikki had neglected to help plan anything other than her room at the Inn and her flight.

"Sounds fine to me…" Vikki replied, then turned to Thomas, "…can you help my sister with her luggage?"

Thomas grabbed Ronnie's luggage as Vikki hugged her sister.

"See you in the morning, sis," Ronnie whispered as she kissed her sister on the cheek and released their embrace.

Vikki watched Ronnie run to catch up to Thomas, then got back into the taxi. Moments later, Thomas came trotting out of the house, and Ronnie stood at her front door waving as the cab pulled away from the curb.

Thomas watched the town go by out the side window of the cab on their way to the Inn, and when he saw an elementary school, he asked if it was the one she had attended, but Vikki stared straight ahead and said nothing.

"You OK 'V'?" he asked.

"I think so…" she replied, "…it didn't hit me until just now that we're burying my Mom tomorrow, Thom. I miss her, I do. I mean, I never knew I felt that way before now. It's all so final, and I'll never get the chance to talk with her again, make things right between us, and apologize for making her so miserable…."

Thomas shifted closer to Vikki and put his arm around her. She leaned against him and nestled in under his arm, and continued, "I know she never had anything but the best intentions for me, Thom, but now I've missed my opportunity to tell her that I appreciated it. I'll never have the chance to tell her I loved her, and I wonder if she ever knew I felt that way?"

Thomas hugged Vikki tightly and confidently replied.

"She knew."

19

Homecoming

Thomas awoke well before dawn, as was his regular routine, but his surroundings were unfamiliar. Sitting up in bed, he tried to recall where he was and remembered they were in Vikki's hometown at an Inn. Vikki was still sound asleep, so he decided to go for a walk to get a 'feel' for the place before returning to wake her. Ronnie had said they needed to be at the funeral home by 8 am, so they had plenty of time.

Dressing quietly but quickly, he grabbed his coat and hat as he left the room and went to the lobby, where he saw a young attendant busily preparing breakfast. He asked her if she was familiar with the places he was scheduled to visit that day and rattled off a few he remembered. When he mentioned the church where the services were to be held for Vikki's Mom, she told him it wasn't far from the Inn and gave him directions. Thomas looked at his watch to note the time and determined he could walk to the church and then say a few prayers for Vikki's Mom before he needed to return. He thanked her, then immediately left for the church.

Walking briskly through the chill of the early morning air, Thomas instinctively studied everything around him. Unattended bicycles, skateboards, and scooters were indiscriminately scattered on every yard and sidewalk. Parked cars and homes had wide-open windows, and many porch lights had been left on, which Thomas presumed was intended to aid in a teenager's late-night return home rather than to deter potential intruders. Being a policeman had trained him to take note of these things, which he saw as clues, giving him a clear picture of what life was like in the town, but he wondered if this was what it had been like for Vikki when she was young.

After a short while, Thomas saw a steeple capped with a cross behind some homes. When he reached the corner, he glanced at the street name overhead to confirm what the Inn attendant had told him. Looking down the street, Thomas saw the church and knew he had found St. Philip's. When he arrived, Thomas removed his hat and quietly entered the church's narthex through enormous front doors.

Thomas thought the church seemed smaller inside than it had appeared from the exterior. Still, he estimated it could seat a few hundred parishioners, which didn't seem particularly odd for that type of town. He walked out of the narthex and into the murky atmosphere of the church, illuminated by a series of dimly lit ornate lamps hung on long chains from the principal roof rafters and from vaulted ceilings along the side aisles.

Thomas slowly walked up the center aisle towards the altar, looking for a place to pray, and childhood memories flooded his mind. Votive candles arranged in rows on iron stands flanking either side of the altar rail reminded him of when he had lit hundreds of them when praying for his brother. Large candles in golden holders illuminated the sanctuary, and tiny, hidden lights accentuated the statuary in an elaborate marble reredos behind the altar.

As he drew closer to the altar, Thomas became lost in his memories of his brother until he noticed someone kneeling in front of a statue off to one side in a transept. He wasn't sure if the person had seen him, but he wanted to respect their privacy and picked a pew a few rows back from the front of the church. He gently slid into the pew, but when he sat, his weight caused the bench to creak loudly, so he quickly lowered the kneeler, dropped to his knees, and closed his eyes to begin praying for Vikki and her Mom.

Thomas continued to pray until he heard another rickety pew and opened his eyes. No one had entered the church that he could tell, so he looked to where he had seen the figure praying earlier and noticed that the person had moved to a pew just outside the transept, much closer to him. He looked at his watch to see how much time had passed and decided he needed to return to the Inn and wake Vikki if they would be on time at the funeral home.

He blessed himself and was preparing to leave when he saw the figure in the transept genuflecting in the aisle before exiting the church through a side door. Thomas stepped out of the pew, bowed, and headed towards the massive front doors. When he reached the exit, he noticed dawn was approaching and strolled out into the morning's brisk air.

Putting on his hat, Thomas began walking back towards the Inn, but in seconds a chilly wind blew his hat off, and he began running after it. When the hat flew into the middle of the street, Thomas looked up and down the road to ensure it was safe and saw a car's headlights approaching. He waited for the vehicle to pass before stepping out to retrieve his hat but was surprised when the car mysteriously stopped just in front of him.

Thomas stepped into the street, picked up his hat, then approached the vehicle, trying to see who it might be. When he'd gotten close enough to see inside the car, he recognized Vikki's sister Ronnie sitting behind the wheel, smiling profusely.

"Lose something?" she quipped as she rolled down her window.

"Good Morning Ronnie…" Thomas replied, dusting off his hat, "… I'm surprised to see you out and about so early?"

"Every morning Thom…." Ronnie responded, "…I like to get my rosaries in before dawn."

Thomas put on his hat, and Ronnie continued, "Why don't you hop in? I was going to grab a bite before heading over to pick you guys up at the Inn. You may as well join me."

Thomas could think of no reason not to agree and opened the passenger's side door, then slipped into the front seat. He removed his hat and wedged it tightly between the windshield and the dashboard, making Ronnie laugh. The two drove off to get something to eat before returning to the Inn to wake Ronnie's sister.

~

The tender rays of the dawning day peeked through Vikki's window and landed gently beside her on the bed. They grew in intensity as they slowly washed across her pillow, and when they landed on her face, the sudden shift in light and temperature awakened her.

Thomas was nowhere to be seen, so she rolled out of bed, went to the bathroom, slipped into the shower, and became lost in memories of her mother and her insufferable 'addiction' to religion and relentless focus on faith.

Vikki remembered how her mother's pronouncements of piety promoted suffering, which suffocated most of Vikki's aspirations. She also remembered how angry and frustrated she had become with her sister for adopting these notions, which had driven a wedge between them. Hence, she sought Ehndale's advice, which had become a voice of reason for her then.

Ehndale explained how devotion to her mother's philosophy would thwart any possibility of success and insisted it would promote misery and pain, which Vikki recognized in her parents' constant struggles. He emphasized how Ronnie would never amount to anything if she lived according to these principles. Still, Ronnie seemed very different now than Vikki had ever imagined she would be.

Vikki could tell that her sister was engaging, confident, and fun to be with. She was an intelligent, happy, and well-adjusted woman, not the miserable, brainwashed 'God-Squad' automaton Vikki had imagined she'd become, and this perplexed her.

When Vikki had finished showering, she turned off the faucets, reached through the open shower door, grabbed a towel, and dried herself while wondering what the new day was to bring.

~

After sharing breakfast at a local coffee shop, Ronnie and Thomas returned to the Inn. When they entered the lobby, they saw Vikki sitting in one of the comfortable armchairs arranged in the Inn's foyer, smartly dressed, and sipping a cup of coffee.

"Look who I found…." Ronnie said as she approached her sister.

"Where'd you find him?"

"Chasing his hat down the street…." Ronnie replied as she sat in a chair beside her sister.

Vikki laughed as Thomas stepped into the kitchen to grab some coffee for Ronnie and himself. When he returned, he handed Ronnie a mug and sat in a chair across from the two sisters.

"Do you know how far the Funeral home is from here?" Vikki asked.

"I'm not exactly sure." Ronnie replied, "…twenty minutes?"

Thomas looked at his watch and remarked.

"If that's true, we should consider getting over there soon."

They all agreed and took one last drink of their coffee. Thomas collected the mugs and placed them in the kitchen sink. When he returned, he took Vikki's hand to help her out of her chair and kissed her as they followed Ronnie into the parking lot. Thomas helped Vikki slip into the front seat when they reached Ronnie's car and sat in the back. Vikki saw Thomas' hat stuffed between the windshield and the dashboard, pulled it out, and tossed it to him, saying, "Keep an eye on that, Thom. Seems determined to separate itself from you."

Both women laughed as Thomas stuffed his hat into his pocket, and they headed out to the Funeral home.

~

As they drove through the town, Thomas began to ask the sisters questions about their life growing up there. They each took turns answering while reminiscing about their childhood.

"Remember Abner Francis?" Vikki asked.

"Abner Francis?" Ronnie replied, "…what in the world made you think of him?"

"That!" Vikki said as she pointed at a young boy in a school uniform standing beside a car idling in a driveway.

"Why would he remind you of Abner Francis?" Ronnie asked.

"Look at his feet…." Vikki replied.

Ronnie looked intently, then began to laugh hysterically. Thomas struggled to see what Ronnie found amusing about his feet and asked, "What's so funny?"

"His shoes…" Ronnie responded, "…look at his shoes!"

Ronnie slowed the car slightly to give Thomas a better view, and he noticed the top front of the young boy's shoes had been cut off, and his toes were sticking out in his socks.

"Why in the world would you do that?" Thomas asked incredulously.

"Never asked Abner, Thom…." Vikki replied, "…so it remains a mystery!"

"Must be Abner Junior'" Ronnie offered as they all enjoyed a good laugh.

A few moments later, Ronnie asked, "Remember coach Foley?"

"I do!" Vikki replied, "…I always liked him. He was a nice man."

"Well, he always asked me why you didn't run track…" Ronnie replied, "…he said you were faster than everybody…". Ronnie looked over at her sister, then added with a wry smile, "… everybody except me, that is…"

"You were not faster than me…" Vikki insisted, "…and that's the truth!"

"You wanna race?" Ronnie joked.

"You sound like a couple of teenage boys!" Thomas returned smiling.

The sisters laughed together for a moment, then Ronnie continued.

"I guess we'll never know. Maybe if you didn't spend all your time going to parties with what's-his-name? Wendell, Kendall? We would have found out. I mean, you were always off with him. How much older was he than you? 30 years?"

Thomas noticed a distinct change in Vikki's demeanor but didn't want to interrupt to ask about whom they were speaking. Vikki knew Ronnie was referring to Ehndale, but she felt no need to be defensive about him as her sister's comments were obviously meant in jest. Yet, they had struck a nerve, and Vikki suddenly didn't feel like talking anymore.

"Remember how much Mom hated him?" Ronnie asked.

"I remember," Vikki replied as she began to relive unpleasant memories of her mother's lectures.

"I mean, he wasn't even good-looking..." Ronnie remarked, "...I told Mom you were infatuated with him, and you'd get over him, but she was relentless. Said he was a bad influence. and you should stay away from him...."

"I remember..." Vikki said somberly.

Vikki remained conspicuously silent as they drove through town, but Ronnie continued to talk about Ehndale. She described his tremendous influence over her and reminded her sister of their parents forbidding her from seeing him. Thomas could tell that Ronnie had unintentionally made Vikki uncomfortable and wanted to change the subject. When they arrived at the funeral home, he thought for a second, then asked.

"Is your Mom here, or do we have to retrieve her from somewhere else?"

"She's here..." Ronnie replied, "...The mortician said their receiving vault was on-site, and although I haven't been down there, I assume that's in the basement."

Vikki was typically forthright when something bothered her, but she hadn't participated in the conversation for some time and remained aloof, which Thomas found peculiar. He knew Vikki had strong feelings about her mother, so her disengagement concerned him. Thomas decided it was probably the wrong time to discuss what was bothering her and decided to talk to her about it whenever the time seemed right. He was focused on helping Vikki deal with the emotional task of burying her mother.

When they entered the funeral home, they were greeted by the mortician, whom the girls both knew from their youth. After introductions and some reminiscing, the mortician took the three of them into the basement to visit the girl's mother and file the paperwork to secure her release.

~

The church ceremony and the burial were well-handled straightforward affairs, which Ronnie had arranged splendidly. Some neighbors and family friends had learned about the services and had come to pay their respects. They expected to see Ronnie and relayed their condolences to her but were surprised and delighted to see Vikki. They gathered around her and barraged her with questions, which Thomas could tell annoyed her.

Concerned about her emotional state, Thomas watched Vikki closely and politely interjected himself to protect her from being overwhelmed. Most people understood, and eventually, people ceased interrogating Vikki, and the burial proceeded without comment or incident.

After the priest prayed over the casket, it was lowered slowly into the grave. The mourners lined up to select a flower from a basket provided and tossed it on top of the coffin. The priest gave some encouragement in the form of scripture, then relayed his condolences to the two sisters before leaving. The small gathering quickly began filtering out behind him until only Thomas and the two sisters remained.

Ronnie mentioned dinner plans she had arranged for later that evening and hugged Vikki and Thomas before leaving them alone beside the open grave. Ronnie left her car for the couple to use and slipped into the limo provided by their friend at the funeral home. Thomas held his arm around Vikki as he watched the limo drive away and turned his attention back to her when the limo disappeared.

Vikki stood quietly, staring at the casket settled into the bottom of the open grave, and Thomas squeezed her gently and then asked, "You Ok, V?"

"I couldn't say Thom, really. I have all these feelings that I can't figure out. I don't know what they all mean. I never felt like this before."

"Allow yourself to mourn the loss of your mother. Forget the things that make you question why you're feeling what you're feeling and allow yourself to feel something that's not guarded or tempered. Don't shield yourself from the emotions; embrace them. You don't have to control them. Let them be what they are without asking why."

As they stood quietly beside the grave, the wind picked up and pushed the quick, low, darkening clouds across the sky until they had wiped any sign of blue from it. Vikki finally surrendered to her emotions and leaned into Thomas as she began to cry. Thomas was upset for her, but he was also happy. He was pleased that she had allowed herself to grieve for the loss of her mother, which was something that he had not allowed himself to feel for the loss of his brother.

20

Duty and Desire

Vikki's reaction to the news of her Mother's passing concerned Kate, primarily because of their estranged relationship. Kate understood the burden of burying a mother and desperately wanted to accompany Vikki home to provide the emotional support she knew Vikki needed. Unfortunately, the specter of leaving the Diner without someone to oversee its operation made that impossible, a genuine concern that Kate had never considered.

Between this recent incident and her ongoing health issues, Kate concluded that she needed to train someone she could trust to run things at the Diner when she was not there. She had offered co-ownership of the Diner to her son in the past, hoping that he would be interested in taking over the family business. However, Hunter had unequivocally always said no and told his Mother that he didn't want her help. He wanted to create something for himself to have as his own.

Kate did not want to worry anyone but knew her health had worsened. She tried to hide her infirmities, but the symptoms she had been experiencing had become debilitating. Abdominal pain, intense indigestion, fatigue, and a persistent cough made working extremely difficult and sleeping nearly impossible. It had been almost a month since Kate felt well enough to perform her regular routine without help, which left her with no choice but to confide in Hunter that she had become ill and would need his help running the business.

When she told Hunter, he felt bound by duty and obligated to help, so he reluctantly agreed to work with her on the condition that it was only temporary. He was emphatic about his lack of interest in running the Diner and was very clear that he was only willing to help until she felt better or found someone else to help. Kate understood her son's apprehension, appreciated his aspirations, and explained that helping her didn't have to be a career choice, just a temporary situation to help her when she needed it.

Kate was incredibly proud of the business she had built and had always wanted to pass that legacy on to her son. She hoped that his working with her might change his mind or make him less resistant to inheriting the business one day. Still, she was realistic about her expectations and never mentioned how excited she was that Hunter had finally agreed to work with her.

~

When Vikki returned from her Mother's burial, Kate was relieved that she and Thomas were back home safe. Thankful that Thomas had taken some time off from work to be with Vikki, Kate hoped that Vikki was able to reconcile some of her resentment towards her Mother. She also wondered if Vikki had rekindled her relationship with her sister Ronnie, whom Kate had come to hold in high regard.

Excited to hear about their trip, Kate asked Hunter to invite the couple to the Diner for a private dinner to celebrate their safe return later that week. Kate asked him to tell them that the chef would prepare something special just for them. When Hunter relayed the invitation, Thomas respectfully declined, noting that Vikki was working on an important project and had fallen behind while she was away and needed some time to catch up. Thomas asked Hunter to tell his Mother they'd take a 'Rain Check' and make plans to come by when Vikki managed to catch up on her work if that was even possible.

Thomas had noticed before his trip that Kate hadn't been feeling well and was concerned about her health. He didn't know how to bring it up but didn't want to let this opportunity slip away.

"By the way, Hunter, when did you start working at the Diner?"

"Only recently..." Hunter replied dejectedly, "...Mom hasn't been feeling that well lately and asked me to help her until she feels better."

"Sorry to hear that. I'm sure your Mom appreciates your help. How's she doing?"

Hunter didn't like being reminded of his work at the Diner, but the matter at hand was his Mother's health, not his professional aspirations, so he respectfully replied, "She's been having difficulty sleeping, but her cough seems to be improving. Thanks for asking."

"Glad to hear it...." Thomas replied, "I hope she feels better soon. Please tell her to take care of herself. We'll figure out a time to come by."

They shook hands, and Hunter said, "Will do!" then he left to relay Thomas's response to his Mother.

On his way back to the Diner, Hunter couldn't stop thinking about what Thomas had described as Vikki's "important project." He had always wanted to be involved with something meaningful and began to wonder what it would be like to oversee a company that big. To have that kind of responsibility and that much power.

Hunter had been attracted to Vikki since he had seen her drive her Lamborghini into the parking lot where he worked, but now that he knew her, he was even more envious of her success. Vikki had achieved everything he had ever wanted, and Hunter was determined to find out how to manage the same thing, even if he had to leverage his Mom's relationship with Vikki to do it.

~

When Hunter told her what Thomas had said, Kate understood but was disappointed. She asked him to follow up with them on their 'raincheck' offer until they committed to a date.

This was an opportunity that Hunter planned to use as an excuse to meet with Vikki, but whenever he spoke with her, she was surprisingly dismissive, which made him feel insignificant. Hunter was dejected and blamed his Mother for putting him in a position where he held no authority, which garnered little if any respect. Hunter knew that if he hoped to get anywhere with Vikki, he couldn't allow his frustrations to stop him. Hunter wouldn't let Vikki's apathy get in his way. He reasoned that if she considered him more important, she might come to respect him.

Accordingly, to prove his worthiness, Hunter believed he needed to become more vital to the operation of the Diner and began working harder. Without explaining his motivation, Hunter assumed more responsibilities, showing up early and staying late to do all the extra things he thought would earn him respect and Vikki's attention. Kate noticed immediately and told him how much she appreciated it. Even Thomas complimented Hunter on his efforts, but nothing worked with Vikki. She always seemed too busy to notice. Her apathy made Hunter consider whether he needed to abandon the notion of developing a relationship with her and find another mentor. Still, Vikki was the most successful person he had ever met. Who else could educate, expose, and introduce him the way she could? If he was ever going to gain any traction on his ambitions, he needed to rethink his approach and develop a different plan of action to get her attention.

After much thought, Hunter concluded that since the Foundry was the focus of Vikki's attention, he would have greater luck impressing her if he worked there and began scouring message boards and help-wanted ads, searching for positions, and feverishly submitting applications. The rewards for his efforts were polite letters of rejection, citing deficiencies in his skillsets and his lack of experience. Disappointed but determined, Hunter changed his approach and increased his efforts to spend as much time at the Foundry as possible.

Hunter involved himself with every connection between his Mom's Diner and the Foundry and used this exposure to become familiar with and friendly towards many people working there. He handled each delivery personally when foundry staff ordered lunch from Kate's. When the Diner was hired to cater events at the Foundry, Hunter volunteered to work them all in any capacity, no matter how small.

This abundance of time spent at the Foundry had another effect Hunter hadn't anticipated; it kept him away from the Diner, which made his Mother's work there much more difficult. Kate appreciated her son's efforts, but his absence continued to take its toll on her health, but she never mentioned it. She was just happy that her son was working there with her.

~

Eager to make headway in his efforts to exact his revenge on Monica, Ehndale planned to ingratiate himself by beguiling her with his generosity and kindness. Once she had accepted his deceitful benefactions, he would entrap her, giving her no option but to surrender to his will. He could then strip her of her piety and execute his revenge on her. However, Monica was justifiably suspicious of him, so it was exceedingly difficult to get anywhere near her.

While considering his options, Ehndale concluded that he could execute his plan if he managed to keep Monica separated from Thurmond, but to achieve that, Ehndale needed the knowledge of what was happening with the company's progress in Asia, so he could ensure Thurmond remained away as long as possible. This meant having someone inside the company with access to their files, but Bradley was unavailable, and Howie was gone, which left only Vikki to help him. However, her discovery of his surreptitious involvement in her Asian initiative meant she might be unwilling to help him without an explanation, which was something he was reluctant to give.

Unexpectedly, an equity partner associate, Randall Jacobs, relayed some exciting news to Ehndale.

"It's a breakthrough, Mr. Ehndale..." Randall exclaimed, "... one of the greatest magnitude!"

"Mr. Jacobs, I am certain you believe what news you have to relay may be of interest to me, but you'll need to be a bit more specific before that can be ascertained," Ehndale replied smugly.

"Well, sir, I've been following the news in Taipei and read only just this morning that the building commission in Taipei approved the application for a regulatory commission exception. Now they have no choice but to award the building permit. To do otherwise, in my opinion, would be considered an undue hardship."

Ehndale was encouraged but put little faith in Randall's 'opinion' and asked, "Who determines whether or not it's a 'hardship,' my dear boy?"

"Well, sir…" Randall began, "…an 'undue hardship' is an unreasonable determination or condition imposed that requires significant difficulty or expense."

"Is it an objective decision or someone's opinion?"

"Well, it's actually both.…" Randall explained, "…you see, the Authority having jurisdiction, the Regulatory Agency, in this case, has to review the development in terms of the codes and standards that govern all development in their municipality. Those codes and standards change periodically but are the governing criteria in every case. When an exception is granted, it's usually because it satisfies at least one of the prescribed conditions in the code. When it is not as prescribed, an official offers their subjective judgment, presumably with the knowledge and experience, to make an educated assessment. However, those judgments are defined in terms of limitations or conditions that need to exist to grant the approval."

Ehndale appreciated Randall's attempt to clarify but was never impressed with people's attempts to sound intelligent. Randall's explanation was verbose, which Ehndale considered a weakness in his character to compensate for his lack of confidence. He wanted a quick, definitive answer and politely interrupted to ask.

"Please, answer first, my good man. Answer first. Let me rephrase the question. Has the undue hardship been determined already, and is the exception granted? If so, is it binding?"

"Yes, sir. That's correct." Randall replied excitedly.

"Splendid!"

Ehndale saw an opportunity to manipulate the situation to his benefit. He knew Vikki wouldn't let something like this go without a celebration, for which Thurmond would undoubtedly be brought home, as he was likely entirely responsible for its success. Ehndale anticipated they would lavish Thurmond with praise for all his efforts, which could be used to insist that Thurmond be stationed in Asia indefinitely to oversee the operation. This would accomplish two things, First, Thurmond's indefinite assignment in Asia would keep him away from Monica, allowing Ehndale to work on heightening Monica's doubts about the viability of their relationship. Through empathy and compassion, Ehndale would use Monica's malcontent to turn her away from Thurmond.

Second, Thurmond's absence would also create the need for a replacement to step in for him at the Foundry while he was gone. That person could be someone Ehndale selected who would be instrumental in helping retrieve information, so Ehndale knew what was going on at the Foundry.

The celebration was the perfect opportunity to laud Thurmond's accomplishments and suggest his continued presence in Asia was critical to the venture's success. However, given Vikki's displeasure over his recent activities, Ehndale suspected he might not receive an invitation, and even if he did, Vikki would be suspicious of his motives. This created the need for a surrogate.

Accordingly, Ehndale invited a few select associates to his house to relay the good news about the company's progress in Asia, and, as expected, the equity partners were all excited. They agreed with Ehndale's assessment that Thurmond's presence in Asia was critical and supported his idea of providing incentives to make it attractive for crucial personnel like Thurmond to deploy overseas to help with the progress. This would create a host of vacancies Ehndale could choose from to plant someone on the inside just in case his strategy regarding Thurmond did not work out.

They all agreed this was the best course of action, drafted a letter to be delivered to Vikki, and appointed Randall Jacobs to represent the equity partnership. They told him to insist these demands be a condition of the equity partner's ongoing financial support. Vikki's receptiveness to this demand was critical to his strategy, so Ehndale planned to meet with Jacobs as soon as possible afterward to find out how things had gone.

As anticipated, the Foundry announced that CMC Enterprises, now branded CInc., had been approved to expand operations in Asia. A celebration was planned, and the company began offering employees bonuses and promotions to entice them to relocate overseas to help with the development. A flurry of new job openings appeared in the paper for their local replacements at the Foundry, which Hunter immediately noticed. He then began submitting applications for openings he thought looked interesting, and Ehndale continued to pressure Randall Jacobs to insist on the necessity of Thurmond's leadership overseas.

~

Vikki knew Kate had wanted to hear about how things had gone at her Mother's burial back home in Potters Hollow and had meant to get back to her but could not find the time. Thomas often reminded her about their dinner invitation, but it wasn't until he mentioned that Kate had not been feeling well that Vikki made plans to stop by the Diner herself for a quick visit.

When Vikki pulled up, Hunter noticed her car and immediately told his Mom, who was overjoyed to hear the news. Kate hurriedly finished what she was doing and asked the chef to prepare some treats while she set a table for her visit with Vikki.

"First, let me say I know you're busy with everything, so I don't expect you to stay very long...." Kate began, "... but I am thrilled to see you and happy that you found some time to come by."

"Of course, Kate...." Vikki returned, "...I feel terrible that I have let it go this long."

"Never you mind, dear. I've been up to my eyeballs with work lately and hardly noticed how much time has passed since you and Thomas returned."

Kate was truthful about being busy, but she had been counting the hours since Vikki's return.

"So, tell me, how'd it go? I want to hear all about it!" Kate said enthusiastically as she turned and raised her hand to get a waitress's attention, then continued, "What was it like to be back home? Did you get to enjoy any of your time with your sister? Did you see anyone you knew? Did Thomas behave himself? "

Though it was easy to see how eager Kate was to hear about her trip, Vikki was concerned about how tired she appeared. Vikki wanted to inquire about her friend's health but began their conversation with an amusing anecdote about Abner Francis, the little boy in the driveway, and his ridiculous shoes. As they enjoyed a laugh, two waitresses appeared with a coffee carafe, a couple of mugs, a plate with two croissants, and some grilled bacon rolled in pineapple leaves the chef had prepared for them.

Vikki continued by acknowledging that her intention had been to remain emotionally detached, but some strong emotions had surfaced that she hadn't expected, which made that impossible. She confessed how Ronnie had innocently brought things up about her past that made her feel angry and foolish at the same time and described the emptiness she felt when it dawned on her that she would never be able to make amends with her Mother now that she was gone. Kate was happy to hear Vikki say that Thomas had helped her manage these emotions and listened quietly, only interjecting when she felt Vikki needed encouragement to continue.

As Vikki spoke, she studied Kate's face. She noticed deepening wrinkles and dark circles surrounding her eyes. Her face had become gaunt, accentuating the pronounced bags under her eyes. Vikki paused and asked, "How are you feeling, Kate? Thomas told me you were a bit under the weather. How is it going with your son here to help?"

"Couldn't be better!"

Kate responded without being specific about which question she was answering, and Vikki was sure she had intentionally answered it that way. Vikki didn't want to be impolite by asking Kate to be more specific and replied, "I'm glad to hear it!"

Vikki finished relaying what she felt comfortable discussing and then told Kate she had to get going, and Kate thanked her for coming. As Vikki gathered her things to leave, she stopped suddenly and spoke.

"I almost forgot, Kate! We're having a celebration for Thurmond at the Foundry next week, and I want you to come as my guest. I'd also like to hire your Diner to be the caterer. It will be a big affair, requiring a lot of preparation. I can hire additional staff to help if you feel you need it. I don't want you to work or worry, so maybe you can have Hunter handle everything. I'm confident he would do a smashing job!"

Kate was overjoyed to hear the news and replied, "I'm honored, Vikki. Thank you! Hunter will be delighted and is more than up for the job…." Kate quipped, then added with a smile, "…with a little of my help, of course."

"I've seen Hunter at the Foundry a lot lately…" Vikki replied, "…which should make him familiar enough with everything to make it easier. It'll be perfect!"

"Yes… Kate replied, "…and I think he's even developed friendships with some of your employees, so he'll probably be excited to show them what he can do!"

Close enough to overhear most of his Mother's conversation with Vikki, Hunter was both honored and insulted by what he heard. Their faith in his abilities to handle the celebration for Thurmond was encouraging but being 'lead caterer' was nothing more than a glorified position amongst the service staff, an assignment Hunter believed well beneath his abilities, and he felt he deserved better.

Still, Hunter recognized that it was also an opportunity to impress Vikki and other company decision-makers with his professionalism and skills. He could leverage that impression to secure a more dignified position at the Foundry, which would finally allow him to begin to realize what he had always dreamed of, being a success!

When Kate told Hunter of the commission, he reacted excitedly but did not share the reasons for his enthusiasm. Hunter was sure his plan would work and didn't believe he'd be seen as a servant for much longer. Thrilled with the prospect, Hunter immediately began preparing for the celebration.

21

Avidity

On the day of the celebration, the Foundry grounds buzzed with activity well before dawn. The event wasn't scheduled to begin until twilight, but Vikki wanted to give those financially vested in the company's success a chance to celebrate privately beforehand so they could personally congratulate Thurmond for all his hard work. Accordingly, she arranged for an exclusive pre-party earlier in the afternoon and invited only important clients, company executives, and equity partners who had been instrumental in financing the impressive expansion project.

People were still busy with preparations when the VIPs began to arrive. Cars lined up quickly along the front of the main building and were greeted by valets and company volunteers, who escorted the guests to the entry hall, where they enjoyed cocktails and hors d'oeuvres while they waited. Ben, the enthusiastic young Foundry attendant, referenced a list on a clipboard he was carrying, tracking the arrival of the distinguished guests so he could notify Vikki when they had all arrived.

When the entire group had assembled, Ben notified Vikki. Minutes later, she appeared atop the grand lobby stairs, then descended to the mid-landing, where she delivered a brief but compelling welcome speech. When she had finished welcoming her guests, Vikki asked the group to join her in the company museum, where they were to continue their celebration with an awards presentation. The group happily obliged and followed Vikki up the grand stairs and to the museum.

The museum's exhibits had been slightly rearranged to clear a gathering area in front of the company's achievement gallery, which featured portraits of some of the most distinguished employees. Hunter and his attendants busily distributed champagne flutes to the guests as they gathered around an ice sculpture Vikki had commissioned in honor of the occasion. After everyone had been given a glass, Vikki gently tapped hers to get their attention. When the murmur subsided, Vikki stood on a small podium and began to speak.

"I want to thank all our distinguished guests, families, and friends for being with us today to help celebrate an enormous and amazing accomplishment, the implications of which I cannot even begin to fathom. This town, this company, and this humble executive…." Vikki said as she bowed and put her hand on her breast to acknowledge that she was speaking of herself, "…are grateful and indebted to the hard work and dedication required to realize this dream…."

To make a good impression Hunter and his wait staff circulated amongst the VIPs replacing empty champagne flutes to ensure everyone was prepared for the toast he knew Vikki was sure to make. While Vikki elaborated on the company's difficult transition from a local business to a global entity, a nagging resentment crept into Hunter's mind. He believed he was capable of the hard work and dedication Vikki spoke of and would prove it if given a chance. He watched the executives' reaction to the speech and was jealous that it wasn't him that they would soon be toasting.

Vikki continued.

"So, without further ado, I'd like to introduce the man primarily responsible for the company's successes thus far in Asia…". She paused, acknowledged the honoree standing behind her, and said, "I present Thurmond Joseph. A man whose accomplishments not only include our expansion initiative into Asia but whose hard work and dedication can be seen stretching across the remarkable history of this company on the wall of portraits behind me…."

Vikki stepped aside to reveal Thurmond emerging from a row of company executives behind her. As Thurmond stepped forward, people shook his hand and patted him on the back as a round of applause ensued that was loud enough to be heard in the parking lot. Vikki kissed him on the cheek, then retreated to leave him standing silently before the applauding crowd. After a few seconds, Thurmond held up his hands to silence the group, and when the applause subsided enough for him to be heard, he began to speak.

"I am humbled and grateful for the support and acknowledgment you have shown me today, but I do not consider myself worthy of the praise. I am happy that I could contribute, in some way, to something that may benefit the company, its partners, and, most importantly, the people of this town. Still, it's the hard work of all the company's employees and the insight of our new chief executive that has made this dream a reality."

Jealous of the attention Thurmond received, Hunter seethed with envy. Here was a man, he thought, who had made the most of his opportunities, but instead of embracing the accolades that were rightfully bestowed upon him, he lauded the accomplishments of others. Hunter saw it as a pathetic attempt at humility, which he considered dishonest, and decided to leave the hall.

Thurmond continued

"I am ever so grateful for having been given a second chance to prove that I was worthy of helping lead the company into the next phase of its evolution."

Hunter instructed his wait staff to keep the guest's glasses full and then left the room and listened to Thurmond's words echo as they faded away.

~

Hunter jogged down the main stair towards the entrance lobby to check on the preparations for the main event that evening and noticed Ben standing at the base of the stairs staring at him.

Ben had been running around, ensuring everything was progressing smoothly, and had just returned from the parking lot when he saw Hunter coming down the main staircase. He recognized Hunter as the lead caterer and was waiting patiently to offer his assistance. When Hunter reached the bottom of the stair where Ben was standing, the enthusiastic attendant began, "Good day, sir. My name is Ben. I'm the assistant events coordinator and here to help in any way I can...."

Hunter was in no mood to chit-chat and callously replied, "Hi, Ben. I'm Hunter...The caterer."

"Yes, I know...." Ben returned with a big smile, "...I wanted to let you know that they just finished erecting the main Pavilion in the parking lot. The freezer trucks are parked around the back, and the food deliveries have begun to arrive. The cafeteria kitchen is humming with activity, and I'm here to assist you in any way I can. Let me know how I can help."

Ben's enthusiasm entertained Hunter, which began to ease his anxiety. Hunter's focus shifted from his self-pity to the matters at hand, and he replied, "Thank you, Ben. I must ensure all the equipment is here and set up in the main Pavilion. I also need to inspect the freezer trucks and check on the deliveries to make sure we're still on schedule."

"Certainly, sir. How can I help?" Ben asked.

"Can you see if they have everything they need in the Pavilion? I'm going to check on the deliveries. I'll meet you by the stage afterward."

"Certainly, Mr. Hunter..." Ben answered, then added, "...you certainly do have a handle on things. It's nice to see that it's all so well organized. Your hard work and dedication will ensure today's celebration is a smashing success!"

"Thank you, Ben...." Hunter replied, "... It's nice to know someone noticed and that they appreciate it."

"Certainly, Mr. Hunter. No problem. I'll see you at the stage!"

Hunter was amused at how important Ben considered his menial job and wondered how someone could be so satisfied with that.

When Ben disappeared into the vast parking lot, Hunter looked around the lobby, noticed all the decorations on display, and wondered what it would be like if it was all there for him. Hunter admired Thurmond but was confident he could accomplish similar achievements if only given a chance. He longed for the day when he would have a celebration like this, where people would honor his achievements.

~

During her speech, Vikki mentioned that Thurmond would be instrumental in a company initiative to incentivize relocation. She also suggested that he would be personally engaged in a vigorous local hiring program to fill the vacated positions at home. This made Thurmond wonder what that meant in terms of where he'd eventually wind up and what effect that may have on his already tenuous relationship with Monica.

Thurmond had just arrived from Asia that morning, and because he was only in town for a few days, he was understandably anxious to spend as much time with Monica as possible. His past few visits had not gone well, which made him concerned that his being away was making it worse. When she declined the invitation to the company celebration, Thurmond called her to make other arrangements to get together and was encouraged when Monica sounded excited to see him.

When the ceremony honoring Thurmond had ended, everyone moved to the main lobby, where Thurmond circulated with Vikki, shaking hands, and accepting congratulations. Most VIPs did not intend to stick around for the main event and, after congratulating Thurmond, began filtering out into the parking lot to leave.

Vikki had not insisted that Thurmond stick around for the entire main event, but she did ask him to stay there for a bit to greet the employees when they arrived. He reluctantly obliged but was looking for his first opportunity to leave.

~

After Hunter finished checking on the deliveries, he began making his way to meet Ben at the stage, which had been set up for a performance scheduled for later that evening. On his way, Hunter noticed dozens of expensive vehicles parked in an area designated with traffic cones.

One car stood apart from the others and made him curious, so he took a few minutes to have a closer look. When he was near enough to make out the vehicle's markings, he was excited to find that it was one of his favorites; a convertible Bentley Continental Drophead Coupe. He had read a good deal about the car in his magazines and navigated past the other vehicles towards it to get a better look.

As he slowly walked around the convertible, he marveled at the beauty of the exquisite vehicle and wondered what kind of person could own such a beautiful car. He looked around to see if anyone was watching, then opened the car door and sat behind the wheel to get a feel. He grabbed the wheel with both hands, closed his eyes, sunk into the leather driver's seat, and began to imagine himself driving it.

Just then, a voice called out to him, and Hunter opened his eyes. When he saw Ben jogging towards him, Hunter was slightly embarrassed and did not immediately respond.

"I thought that was you…." Ben said as his jog slowed to a walk.

Hunter stepped out of the vehicle and closed the car door, waiting to see what Ben wanted.

"Is this your car?" Ben asked exuberantly, "I didn't know Caterers could afford that kind of thing."

"We can't…." Hunter replied dejectedly as he began walking away from the vehicle, "…I just never saw a car like this in person before and wanted to know what it felt like to sit behind the wheel."

"OK, well…" Ben continued, "…the pre-party ceremony just ended, and the VIPs will be coming out soon. Excuse me for saying so, but I don't know if they would appreciate your sitting in one of their expensive cars."

Hunter didn't consider being discovered sitting in the vehicle to be anything of Ben's concern and became slightly agitated by his comment. He changed the subject and asked, "Did you make sure they had everything they needed in the Pavilion?"

"Yessir! I believe so." Ben enthusiastically replied.

"Good. Then I could use your help checking on the cleanup of the Pre-party ceremony. Why don't you go back to the museum and the main lobby and see if you can help them clean it up?"

"Yessir!" Ben happily agreed, "…anything to help!"

Hunter had been entertained by the zealous assistant but had become annoyed that the bumptious imp felt it was appropriate to criticize anything he had done. Hunter sent Ben on his way, watched him disappear around the corner of the building, and left for the Pavilion.

~

Ehndale suspected that Vikki disapproved of his recent actions, which was confirmed when he did not receive an invitation to the Foundry celebration. In anticipation of such a development, Ehndale selected Randall Jacobs to represent the equity partners in his stead and directed him to express their congratulations. He also directed Mr. Jacobs to insist that it was imperative to their ongoing interest that Thurmond remained in Asia, which he knew was a request Vikki would have made herself, had she been in his position.

When Randall conveyed this to Vikki, it created a dilemma for which she was unprepared. Vikki knew that without the equity partners' financing, the operation would come to a standstill until she found alternative financing options, which could take time they did not have.

Vikki had promised she would bring Thurmond home at the first opportunity and knew he would be disappointed to hear that it would have to wait. Vikki reluctantly agreed to Randall's condition and relayed the news to Thurmond, and although he was flattered that everyone thought so highly of him, he was not keen to be kept apart from Monica. He did not mince words about his desire to remain home permanently.

"You said you would bring me home!" Thurmond demanded, "… you promised! The project manager in Taipei has it all under control. We can send Stan over to get things up and running. He knows the drill. Besides, they don't need me to build the blasted thing. They only need me to show them how to run it. I can fly back and forth, but I want to stay home. You said you would bring me home! "

"I know, Thurmond, and I agree…." Vikki replied, "…but Stan has not accepted the compensation package, and there's no indication that he ever will. He told me his wife had said flat-out that he couldn't go! Other than you, I'm not sure who else could run the show over there."

Thurmond struggled to come up with an alternative, and Vikki continued.

"I wouldn't think you'd want Eddie to go. Even here at home, he needs a watchful eye. You've told me as much. We can't afford to make mistakes while we're just getting started. The equity partners expect results. We need someone running the show who knows how to do it and, like it or not, that someone seems to be you!"

Vikki could see the disappointment on his face and continued, "I promise things will be different once the construction is complete. In the meantime, we will aggressively ramp up production here at home and promise to do the same once the Asia facility is operational, so the equity partners will realize their investment is safe. Believe me, I understand your concerns and will do everything I can to bring you home as soon as possible. You will only be there until we're operational. I will find someone to replace you. I promise!"

Thurmond had nothing to say and began thinking about relaying the news to Monica, but there was no easy way to put it. Thurmond hoped Monica would understand, but he knew remaining in Asia would not sit well with her. His being away had strained their relationship, and this development would undoubtedly exacerbate the situation, which was already tenuous. Still, there didn't appear to be another option, so although he was disappointed, he reluctantly agreed and told Vikki to aggressively search for a replacement.

Vikki didn't know who could replace him but began considering her options. She remembered how anxious Monica had been to see Thurmond on his next trip home and wondered if she had decided to end their relationship, which would be a shame, but it would solve all her problems. Still, she knew the sacrifice she was asking of Thurmond and understood it went against her promise to bring him home, which she was determined to do at the first opportunity.

~

Not long after the executives departed, the employees began arriving at the Foundry in throngs. The vast parking lot became chaotic, making it clear that the number of volunteers assigned to monitor and direct traffic was insufficient. Ben had been trying to assist but reported the chaos to Thurmond when he realized he needed help. Thurmond mentioned it to Vikki, and although he was supposed to meet Mona, he volunteered to help instead. Vikki knew Thurmond needed to spend time with Monica and said, "I don't want you to be late, Thurm. Monica has been patient, and I don't want her to think I kept you from her unnecessarily."

Thurmond was conflicted but knew there was work to be done. He wasn't meeting with Monica for a few hours and replied, "I hate standing around when I could be helping..." Thurmond said confidently, "...besides, it was Monica's choice not to be here."

"Are you sure?" Vikki replied.

"Positive! It shouldn't take long. I'll be done in no time!"

Vikki was concerned but thought his handling of the chaos would be the perfect way to honor him. Directing the employees personally would make them feel connected to him, like a general on the battlefield, amongst his troops. She agreed, and Thurmond quickly took charge.

Thurmond directed the valets to gather the volunteers greeting people at the main lobby and have them report to the main entry's guard booth. He then contacted Clarence, the security guard stationed there, and explained how to deploy the staff. Thurmond then asked Ben to gather the caterers cleaning up after the VIPs inside the main building and have them all report to the main Pavilion in the middle of the parking lot, where he would work out a plan with their manager to help untangle the mess.

Hunter was finalizing the food service assembly in the main Pavilion and became infuriated when some of the wait staff began mysteriously gathering there. Afraid that shirking their responsibilities would put him in an unfavorable light with Vikki, he intended to reprimand them for being irresponsible, even threatening to terminate them if they didn't immediately get back to work. As he approached them, he saw Thurmond in their midst and realized something else was happening. The catering staff noticed Hunter coming toward them and began pointing at him.

Thurmond looked to see whom they were pointing at, and when he saw Hunter, he shouted excitedly, "… Just the man I was looking for! I'm so glad to see you! We have a problem, and I will need your help to fix it! Can I talk to you for a minute?"

Being recognized by Thurmond as the person in charge genuinely pleased Hunter. He felt important for the first time that day and was eager to help.

The two men devised a strategy to utilize the wait staff and sent them out into the vast parking lot to perform various duties. Hunter reminded them to return to their regular duties as soon as they heard back from him or when the band began to play, whichever came first. Thurmond thanked Hunter, then left to check back with Clarence to see how the effort was coming along, and Hunter went out into the lot to ensure his staff was doing a good job.

The organized effort quickly turned the chaos into order. Thurmond told Clarence to let the volunteers know they had done an excellent job and could now enjoy the party. The wait staff returned to their stations, and Thurmond then went to the Pavilion to thank Hunter but did not find him there.

Now that things seemed to be running smoothly, Thurmond was anxious to leave. So, rather than continue his search for Hunter, he asked one of the catering crew to let Hunter know he appreciated his help, then returned to the Main building to tell Vikki he was leaving.

Hunter had been frantically darting around to ensure the food service ran smoothly while his staff directed traffic in the parking lot. When the band began to play, Hunter realized his team would soon be back, which meant he could finally relax. Upon returning to the Pavilion, one of his crew told him what Thurmond had said, which initially made Hunter proud, but when he thought about the recognition Thurmond would receive for his efforts, his pride dissipated.

'Thurmond came to me for help,' Hunter thought to himself, 'It was our plan and my staff, but I won't get any recognition because I wasn't in charge! Everyone will think it was all him!'

Hunter became resentful and angry. He envied Thurmond's position and believed there would be no acknowledgment of his effort and no compensation for his trouble. Hunter left the Pavilion to clear his head and stepped into the shadows behind the main building to listen to the band warm up while he had a smoke.

Leaning up against the brick building, Hunter stared into the crowd gathering in front of the stage while he enjoyed a cigarette, then returned to the Pavilion to check on his staff. When he entered the tent, he was told that a woman had been looking for him. Hunter assumed it was Vikki but was assured by his staff it was not. They pointed towards an attractive young woman standing near a bar set up in the center of the Pavilion, and curious to see who she was, Hunter immediately approached her.

The young woman was busily scanning the crowd and fixed her gaze on Hunter when she saw him approaching. She smiled at him but made no attempt to move toward him. Hunter was immediately enamored with her. She had a beautiful face with extraordinarily white teeth, pouty lips, thick dark shoulder-length hair, bright eyes, and tawny skin. She was impeccably dressed and wore a wide-brimmed floppy straw sun hat.

"I understand you wanted to see me?" Hunter began, not knowing exactly how to initiate their conversation.

"Good afternoon, sir. My name is Naomi, and I was sent by my father to get your contact information. You are the food service director here today, are you not?"

"Yes, Ma'am, I'm the caterer…." Hunter replied.

The woman then smiled at him and said, "Well, my father and I are terribly impressed with how you have organized today's event. The food, and the service, were wonderful. We would like to discuss the possibility of your catering a private gathering at our home next month."

Hunter stared at the attractive young woman and noticed little things about her. She had perfectly straight, dazzling white teeth and eyes that seemed to smile as she spoke. Her silky dark hair willowed in the breeze, and she lifted an eyebrow slightly for emphasis while speaking. Hunter listened to the sound of her voice rather than to what she was saying, which the woman took notice of and asked, "Is there something the matter?"

Hunter had become so enthralled by her appearance that he didn't realize she was waiting for his response. After a few awkward moments, she repeated the question, and at a loss for how to respond, he stuttered in reply, "Sorry. I've just been so busy I'm a little out of sorts. You caught me by surprise, is all. I apologize."

"No worries…" the young woman replied, reaching into her soft saddle leather tote bag, and pulling out a card she handed Hunter.

"Here's my card. Let me know if you are interested in providing catering services for our party."

Hunter thanked her as she excused herself before leaving promptly.

Hunter didn't want her to leave, but he didn't know why she would stay. As she walked away, Hunter glanced quickly at the card she had given him, then slowly followed her out of the Pavilion at a distance just to see where she went. When she arrived at the area that had been cordoned off with traffic cones, he realized she was a VIP of some sort.

An older gentleman stood beside the convertible Hunter had been admiring earlier and opened the passenger door for her. After she got in, the older man got behind the wheel, and they slowly exited the parking lot. As Hunter watched, he wondered who she was and who was the man with her. He looked at the card again and determined it would be his mission to find out.

22

Muddlement

Monica's feelings for Thurmond were never in question, but she had serious concerns about his ability to resist temptation and her ability to forgive him again if he couldn't. In her mind, the future of their relationship was uncertain, and his remaining in Asia only created opportunities to test his resolve, her capacity to forgive, and their commitment to each other.

Her shocking announcement of their engagement had not necessarily conveyed her genuine desire. Instead, it was a jealous reaction borne from anger and resentment. Had the situation not forced her into it, Monica questioned whether it was something she would have wanted otherwise, even if it had been Thurmond who had proposed.

Monica was reluctant to convey these concerns to Thurmond for fear of being misunderstood, but her reticence was undoubtedly sending him mixed messages. When she received an invitation to attend the celebration at the Foundry honoring Thurmond, she wondered whether this was her chance. Monica was always proud of Thurmond's achievements and wanted to celebrate with him. Still, she feared they would spoil the event by arguing, so she regrettably declined the invitation.

Understandably disappointed, Thurmond accepted her decision but asked if he could see her afterward. Monica knew she owed him an explanation, so she agreed to see him, believing the time had come to put this all behind them and move on as a couple or as just friends.

~

Monica carefully considered what she would say to Thurmond when she saw him, but her mind went completely blank when his truck pulled into her driveway. She decided to allow things to unfold as they may and grabbed her purse, then hurried out to keep him from waiting. When Thurmond saw her coming, he leaned across the front seat and pushed the passenger's side door open from the inside. She tossed in her purse, sat beside it, and then politely kissed him before fastening her seatbelt.

Neither said a word as they drove away from her house, which created a slight tension they each wondered how to alleviate. Thurmond was excited to see her but wanted to avoid getting her upset. Monica knew he was being careful and decided to break the ice.

"How'd the celebration go? "Monica began.

"You know Vikki…." Thurmond replied. "…she made a big deal of it. Did an excellent job selling the idea that things were going smoothly over there?"

"Are they Thurm? Running smoothly over there, that is?"

"Not sure if I would call anything over there smooth…" Thurmond returned, "…I will say it's different. Everything is different. The language, the people, the climate, the houses, the food, the customs…everything!"

Monica wanted to be careful, but the conversation lent itself to discussing the elephant in the room, so she went with it.

"Do you have to go back right away?"

"No, but I should…" Thurmond responded, "… that's what I wanted to talk to you about, Mona. I mean, I don't want to go back, but the investors insist I need to be there, at least until we get everything rolling, and we're close to that now."

"Do you have a choice?"

"I do, but I don't necessarily disagree with their thinking. If I'm there, I can speed everything up. I could have all the permits in hand in the next couple of months and be pushing dirt soon afterward. The construction isn't difficult and shouldn't take more than a year before the new plant is up and running."

"Do you have to be there the entire time?"

"That's what the investors are insisting on," Thurmond answered.

"Why is it that you have to be the one, Thurm? Can't someone else handle it? I mean, no offense, but you're not even in construction. How would you know the first thing about it?"

Thurmond smiled and said, "… it's not really a matter of being able to direct the construction, Mona. It's more a matter of knowing what's important. I can choose equipment, materials, and methods on the spot. I know what to look for and what to approve. I can talk to the suppliers, direct the construction managers, and deal with the authorities there. It's just handy for someone familiar with the whole operation to be on the ground. That's what the investors are insisting on, and honestly, we can't send anybody in my place other than Stan, but Flo won't let him go."

"Want me to talk to her?" Monica asked half-jokingly.

"That's not necessary, Mona…."

"I mean it, Thurm…" Monica replied, "… I'm sure I can persuade her to let him go."

"What would you say that would convince her?" Thurmond asked.

Monica thought for a second, then replied, "There are incentives, right?"

"Yes."

"Well, then I would play them up. Better pay?"

"Of course…" Thurmond replied.

"A promotion?"

"Certainly…"

Monica's enthusiasm entertained Thurmond, and he told her to go on, so Monica continued.

"I would remind Flo that it didn't have to be permanent, and they could keep two houses with the extra money he'd be making. I'd tell her about all the wonderful things she could experience in Asia if she wanted to visit him there and elaborate on all the vacation spots she could visit. I would show her brochures of Japan, Indonesia, the Philippines, Tahiti...."

Thurmond enjoyed listening to Monica's plan, but he couldn't help but laugh when she mentioned Tahiti.

Suddenly frustrated, Monica asked, "What's so funny?"

"Don't take this the wrong way, Mona, but your excitement may be getting the better of you."

Monica wasn't sure what Thurmond was referring to and became annoyed by his amusement at her expense.

"I'm quite sure I don't understand what you're talking about."

"Mona. Tahiti is in the middle of the Pacific Ocean. You know that, right? It's 7,000 miles from Taipei. I think we're closer to Tahiti from right here than we would be from Taipei."

Monica was embarrassed and became uncharacteristically furious rather than laughing about her mistake.

"You know what I meant, Thurm. Just because you get to travel around the world for your job doesn't mean you know more than I do about geography. For heaven's sake Thurmond, a year ago, you couldn't locate China on a map!"

"I'm sorry, Mona. It just sounded funny to me, that's all. I meant no offense. I know you're smarter than me. I just happened to know where Tahiti was, and it sounded funny. Like you meant it to be funny. I apologize."

Mona couldn't understand why she had become so upset, but rather than accept Thurmond's apology, she allowed her anger to escalate and was suddenly entirely disinterested in spending another minute with him. She remained silent for a moment, then said.

"You should take me home, Thurm. I'm suddenly not feeling so well. I guess I didn't realize how tired I was."

Thurmond was astonished.

"You're not serious, Mona, are you? I mean, I said I was sorry. I didn't mean anything by it. Don't let my mistake ruin our evening."

Mona was consumed by the sudden urge to be by herself and said, "We can spend some time together tomorrow if you want. I just need to go home and lie down. I'm suddenly feeling fatigued. There's a bug going around at the library that I may have caught and may only just be beginning to feel the effects of it."

Thurmond pulled over to the side of the road and parked the vehicle. He turned towards Mona and spoke.

"I miss you, Mona. I've been away for so long. I've been counting the days until I returned. I was looking forward to spending some time with you, and now that I am back for a couple of days, you want to cancel our date because I made some dumb remark?"

"Please, Thurm? I don't want to argue. I just don't feel well suddenly, is all. I need to lie down. I just want to go home and crawl into bed. Please take me home. We can spend the entire day together tomorrow, I promise."

Thurmond knew he would not change her mind, but he suspected it was something else and began pressing for an explanation.

"What else is on your mind, Mona? You couldn't possibly be this upset about one dumb comment I made."

Monica was annoyed by Thurmond's persistence, which became evident in the tone of her voice, which changed from apologetic to antagonistic. She continued.

"I'm not sure what you want me to say, Thurm. It's not for you to decide what is or isn't possible regarding what angers me. I told you I don't feel well and would like you to take me home. Period. That's it! Why is that so difficult to understand?"

Monica knew she was being unreasonable but didn't care; she was angry. Angry that Thurmond was away all the time and angry that he had left her home alone. Did Thurmond expect her to put her life on hold while waiting for him to return? His career had become more important to him than she was, and he didn't seem to need her anymore. He was visiting places and experiencing things that she had only dreamt of. He had changed and seemed more worldly and independent. He had grown beyond the limitations of their hometown, and she was just the same old Monica, which made her mad.

"For crying out loud, Thurmond, just take me home or let me out! I'll walk home if I must!"

Thurmond believed that while it may have been true that Monica was not feeling well, something else was bothering her. He wasn't interested in arguing with her and didn't want to make her any angrier than she had already become, so he stopped pressing for answers and reluctantly agreed to take her home.

Monica became lost in her anger and Thurmond in his confusion, and they both remained silent for the entire trip. When they reached her house, they both said good night without a kiss or an embrace, and Thurmond left before Monica had even reached her front door.

~

Vikki was excited that things were finally moving forward in Asia and convened the company board along with the equity partners for a briefing early the day following the celebration. Images of renderings, flow charts, maps, plans, schedules, and spreadsheets splashed across a large projection screen behind Vikki as she spoke.

"Now that we have received the necessary approvals, we expect to begin construction immediately. Support staff who have accepted positions to assist Mr. Joseph in Taipei have been notified and are making their final preparations for departure."

Vikki paused to drink from a glass she had placed on a shelf inside the podium from which she spoke, then continued, "We expect to have operations online in less than a year and anticipate production to begin shortly afterward if all goes according to schedule."

Vikki noticed a few grimaces from some board members when she mentioned the word 'schedule' and quickly diverted her presentation to address what she considered their concern.

"As you all know, we have experienced some delays due to environmental concerns. This caused the schedule to slip, but Mr. Joseph has adjusted the construction plans and rescheduled some activities to perform them simultaneously rather than in sequence to compensate for the delays. We do not anticipate any significant changes in the design during construction, which will also help keep our schedule on track, not to mention our financials."

Several executives applauded her remark, but the equity partners remained skeptical and silent. Thurmond also remained quiet but for an entirely different reason. He was considering instead what he should do about Mona. He knew she needed time to figure out whatever was bothering her, and his waiting around for her answer would be insufferable for them both, which meant his return to Asia was likely the best way to give her the time she needed to figure it out on her own.

Vikki wrapped up her meeting and shook hands with all the executives as they left the boardroom, but Thurmond was quietly lost in thought, sitting at the boardroom table, and never moved. Vikki closed the doors and approached a small bar concealed behind a panel in the corner of the room. She removed a small ice bucket from an under-counter refrigerator and two crystal sifters from a shelf beside it. She dropped several ice cubes into each of the glasses, then filled them to the brim with some Kentucky bourbon.

As she approached Thurmond with the two drinks, she evaluated his mood. She placed one of the glasses in front of him, then walked to her chair at the head of the table and sat facing him. She kicked off her shoes and put her feet on the table while taking a long sip of her drink.

"What's wrong, Thurmond? You've been awfully quiet?"

"Nothing Vikki. I just have a lot on my mind, is all." Thurmond replied as he took a drink and leaned forward in his chair.

Vikki assumed it had something to do with Monica and wanted to ask Thurmond directly, but she knew it was a delicate matter and didn't want to be presumptuous. She had anticipated some resistance from Monica about Thurmond's return to Taipei, and her absence from the celebration was evidence of that. Vikki needed to know what Thurmond was thinking, so to persuade him to talk about it, she decided to discuss upcoming events, knowing that the topic of Monica would undoubtedly come up without asking him anything directly about her. Vikki began.

"I'd like to assemble the volunteers before you leave Thurmond so we can go through their travel itinerary. You can talk to them briefly about the culture and living conditions they should expect there. They will need to know. I'm sure you can attest to that?"

"Of course." Thurmond curtly replied.

"Excellent!" Vikki exclaimed, then continued, "…I will make arrangements, but I need to know what works for you. Did you have plans before you left?"

"I thought I did, but I don't, at least not now. I was going to see Emerson for a few beers tonight and visit with Brad tomorrow if that's okay. Can I let you know tomorrow?

"Of course!" Vikki replied, confident that whatever had happened between him and Monica the previous evening did not go well since he did not mention her in his plans.

~

"Tell me all about it!" Kate said enthusiastically.

"It was crazy but manageable…." Hunter returned as he sat at the Diner counter eating breakfast while his mother set up tables for the day's work.

"Details, baby! I need details! Why do you say it was crazy? How many people were there? Did the service go well? Did you have any complaints? Any compliments? Did you have enough food? Enough help? Did…"

"Okay, Mom, okay… I get the picture. You want details well, let me see. Where do I start…."

"Did you get a chance to talk with Vikki? Did she think it went well?"

"I'll get to all of it, Mom, if you stop interrupting me."

"I'm sorry, baby. It's just such a big thing for us. It could mean bigger and better things."

Hunter knew his mother was right, but he resented that she assumed he was okay with the Diner being a 'family legacy' sort of thing, which was something he had spent his entire life trying to avoid.

"Actually, I didn't get a chance to speak to Vikki, but I did get a compliment and a potential lead on a new catering job from some big shot."

"That's fantastic, baby! I'm so proud of you! I knew you would do a great job. I'll talk to Vikki when she comes in tomorrow. I think she's having breakfast with Thomas in the morning."

"Sounds like a plan, Mom…." Hunter replied, then commented on something she had said, "…and do me a favor, Mom…."

"Anything, baby."

"Stop calling me 'baby'? Nobody will take me seriously if they hear you calling me that!"

"Sorry…" A bit embarrassed, Kate replied, "…it won't happen again. I know you're a man, son. A bright, capable, and independent young man."

"Don't patronize me, Mom."

"Who's patronizing? I'm just stating the truth."

"Yeah, right…" Hunter returned as he took the last mouthful of breakfast and placed his plate in the dishwasher before joining his mother to help prepare for the morning rush.

23

Deployment

On the evening of the Foundry celebration, Ehndale invited the same associates back to his house that had selected Randall Jacobs to present the group's demands to Vikki. They discussed their options regarding their investment in the Taipei project, but much of what they planned depended on how receptive Vikki had been to their condition that Thurmond remain in Asia. They all concurred that it was essential for their continued financial support for the project, so they waited until almost dawn the following day to receive word from Jacobs. When no one heard back from him, they concluded their meeting and agreed to reconvene after they had learned of what Vikki's response had been to their desires.

Just after dawn that following day, the house staff began thoroughly cleaning the property as Balaam shuffled around busily directing them. Balaam lumbered throughout the manor, and when he stepped out onto the veranda, he heard someone calling out to him from behind. Balaam turned to see where the call had come from and noticed Ganneau, one of Ehndale's semi-permanent houseguests, on a balcony above, summoning him inside.

After trudging up to the second level, Balaam was told by Ganneau that Ehndale wanted to go for a drive and needed a car to be made ready. Balaam immediately dispatched a house staff member to retrieve a vehicle from the carriage house. When Ehndale appeared at the massive front door, Balaam was attending a car waiting under the Porte-cochere. As he was leaving, Ehndale paused momentarily to speak to his manservant.

"I'm going to the club to discuss some business," Ehndale explained, "...call Mr. Jacobs and tell him I expect him there presently."

"Very good, sir," Balaam replied as Ehndale slipped into the car and quickly disappeared down the drive.

Balaam returned inside to relay Ehndale's request, but Randall Jacobs' daughter Naomi answered the phone when he called.

"I'm sorry..." she began, "My father is exhausted and still sound asleep. I'd hate to wake him unless it's urgent."

"I believe you misunderstand, my dear...." Balaam calmly explained, "...I don't believe the master's request was optional."

Naomi knew Balaam through her father's association with Ehndale and had come to pity him and his menial life. She despised his blind obedience to Ehndale's wishes and considered his lack of self-respect loathsome. Naomi knew he was an extension of his employer, whom her father had asked her to respect. She loved her father and always tried to honor his wishes, even if she disagreed.

"My apologies," she replied, "I'll check on him again and see if I can rouse him. Do you mind holding on for a minute? I will be right back."

The lack of response suggested Balaam's displeasure, so after an awkward moment of silence, Naomi continued:

"Never mind, I'll just wake him and tell him he must head to the club immediately. Sorry for the misunderstanding."

"Thank you," Balaam replied, then hung up the phone to return to his other duties.

~

The stress associated with losing her mother, Howard's demise, Bradley's imprisonment, Ehndale's covert activities, and the dilemma she faced with Thurmond's deployment had Vikki riding an emotional rollercoaster. The pile of work she had neglected while she was away had Vikki working feverishly to catch up, but there had been so many things happening at the Foundry lately that it became difficult for Vikki to keep track.

Hirings, firings, and relocations at the Foundry seemed to bundle up into an enormous pile of 'things to do,' where items were checked off only to be replaced with new ones, which appeared to be endless. Orders were coming in faster than they could handle, and the pressure from the investors to expedite the Asian expansion made Vikki wonder if it was all worth it.

However, the exciting news about the developments in Taipei demanded a celebration. Since Thurmond had been instrumental in the company's success in Asia, Vikki wanted to ensure it was memorable for him and put everything else aside to prepare for it. As a result, Vikki was mentally and physically exhausted and decided after the celebration it was time to unwind.

The first thing she planned to do was to take Kate up on her offer for a lavish meal with Thomas, so she scheduled to meet him at the Diner the morning after the celebration, which was expected to end early, but things did not go as planned. People enjoyed the music, which delighted the Band, who rewarded the audience by performing well past midnight. Hunter was keen on making a good impression and had prepared more than enough food to continue feeding the remaining guests. Vikki could have sent everyone home, but she did not want to disrupt the festivities and allowed the celebration to continue. After the Band finally finished playing, Vikki returned home so exhausted that she fell asleep in her clothes, face down on her bed.

~

Thomas sat alone for over an hour at a table at the Diner, sipping coffee and checking his watch, wondering why Vikki had not yet arrived. He called her home several times and became concerned when there was no answer. He went to the front counter to speak briefly with Kate, who insisted that Vikki was probably fine but suggested that if he was that concerned, he might go to the Foundry or her house to check on her.

While busily attending to other customers, Hunter overheard his mother's conversation with Thomas and wanted to help. He genuinely liked Thomas, but he also saw this as an opportunity to make an impression on Vikki. He stopped what he was doing and approached his mother while she was still talking with Thomas and said, "I'm on my way to make some deliveries, but I can stop somewhere if you need me to help you look for Vikki."

"That's very kind, Hunter...." Thomas replied, "...where are you headed?"

"I'm making a delivery to the maintenance crew at the club."

Thomas knew Vikki went to the club occasionally and asked.

"I'll probably find her asleep at her desk, but can you see if anyone's seen her while you're there? I appreciate the help."

"My pleasure," Hunter replied as he picked up several large bags stuffed with food and left the Diner to make his delivery.

~

Kate was still under the weather, which did not escape Thomas' notice, and although he was concerned, Thomas did not want to mention it until Hunter had gone. Thomas gathered his nerve when Hunter was gone and brought it up as delicately as possible.

"If you don't mind me saying, Kate, you must take care of yourself. You've not looked well since before I left town with Vikki to bury her Mom."

With a smirk, Kate jokingly replied, "Are you suggesting something, Tom?"

Embarrassed that he had unintentionally linked Kate's infirmity with the death of Vikki's Mom, Thomas was still determined to make his concern known. Blushing, he continued, "Certainly not Kate!

But have you seen a doctor? You could be more than a little run down. You know pneumonia can creep up on you, especially when overtired. It's happened to me."

"I've been meaning to, but I haven't had the time."

Thomas wasn't satisfied with Kate's answer and continued, "You should make time, Kate. I mean, your health is the most important thing."

"I know, and I will, Tom…." Kate replied with a smile, "…my concern is that the doctor will tell me to take time off from work, which I'm not sure I can do just yet. Hunter is a tremendous help, and I can let him run things if I must, but I don't think he's ready to run the show yet. He hasn't been here for very long, so I think he needs a little time to get accustomed to it, so he doesn't get overwhelmed."

"As long as you have a plan, Kate. Hunter is a smart and capable kid. He's a quick study…." Thomas answered and continued, "…he handled the celebration by himself, and I haven't heard any complaints."

"True enough, Tom. True enough. I'm very proud of him. It won't be long. I promise. I'll keep an eye on him and make an appointment when I feel he is ready to take charge."

"Sounds like a plan, Kate…." Thomas replied, "…now I'm headed to the Foundry. I'll let you know if I find Vikki there, but can you have her call me if she shows up here?"

"Certainly, Tom."

"Thanks, Kate. We'll have breakfast another day. I'm off…." Thomas said as he took a bill from his wallet, placed it on the counter, and left Kate at the Diner.

Kate knew she needed to take better care of herself, and Thomas' inadvertent reference to the death of Vikki's Mom scared her. She went back to her office and immediately scheduled a doctor's appointment.

~

Hunter was instructed by the facility supervisor to use the club's rear access road to the maintenance shack, where he was to make his delivery. The workers eagerly awaited his arrival, and when they saw him approaching, they ran out to meet him and lined up before he reached them.

"Took you long enough!" grunted one of the older workers,"... did you get lost or something?"

"Don't mind him, son..." another worker remarked, "... he's just sore he didn't order meatloaf!"

The crew lined up to get their food, and as Hunter handed it out, he asked if they had seen a Lamborghini that morning.

"Not today..." one worker returned, "...but it was here yesterday..." said another as if finishing his coworker's sentence.

"Are you sure?" Hunter asked.

"Yup..." both men answered in unison.

"I seen some other fancy cars this morning..." another crew member offered, "... a couple of Rolls Royce's or something if I ain't mistaken. Didn't see them leave, but I been out back most of the morning, so I couldn't say for sure. They could still be parked out front."

Hunter wasn't convinced the crew members could tell a Lamborghini from a Fiat and thought they could have missed Vikki's vehicle, so he decided to see for himself while he was there to be sure. He thanked them and finished his delivery, then drove away from the dreary gray metal maintenance shed down the back access road to the road's intersection with the main entry drive to the club.

The beautifully landscaped roadway had tree-lined roadside paths, which separated parking lots on either side and led directly to the clubhouse entrance. Fully matured sugar maple tree's branched over herringbone brick footpaths and arched across the main roadway, creating a canopy that provided shade for vehicles and pedestrians along its entire length.

Hunter parked in a remote location and pridefully strode down the brick footpath towards the main clubhouse, pretending to be a club member while scanning the parking lots on either side for Vikki's car.

He finally spotted the 'fancy' cars the workers had mentioned parked beside a colossal Porte Cochere that extended from the second level of the main building to a beautifully planted island in the middle of a traffic circle directly in front of the Clubhouse entrance. As he approached the expensive automobiles, he fantasized about what it would be like to call them his own.

The exquisite cars were parked awkwardly across striped parking stalls, occupying two spaces each, which appeared to have been done intentionally to protect them from other vehicles. Hunter recognized one of the cars as the same convertible he had seen at the foundry celebration and remembered the pretty young woman he had met there.

Hunter walked around the vehicles and stopped to peer into the convertible, whose roof and windows were closed tight. He pressed his face against a side window and shielded his eyes from the sun's glare as he studied the interior features to confirm it was the same car he had seen before. Suddenly, a deep, bellowing voice startled him.

"Did you know it is one of the most exclusive Bentleys ever made?"

Hunter was embarrassed and quickly backed away from the vehicle as he began apologizing profusely. He turned to see a tall, slender, well-dressed older gentleman wearing a bowler top hat standing perfectly still and smiling at him. The man had one arm folded across his midsection with his other elbow resting on it. He pinched his chin with the thumb and forefinger of his hand, appearing deep in thought.

Hunter didn't know what to say as the man suddenly clasped his hands behind his back and began strolling around the car. The well-dressed older gentleman continued speaking.

"Less than 500 of these cars were ever produced. A 'Masons Blac' exterior finish and black leather interior trim with grey piping…."

"I'm really sorry, sir…." Hunter replied, "… I didn't touch anything. I was just looking…."

"… lamb's wool car mats, Brazilian Dalbergia woodwork, bespoke door-mounted twin mini-bars with leather-bound Tudor crystal glass and decanters sets."

A woman's voice suddenly rang out from behind Hunter.

"You're terrible, Ehndale!"

Hunter turned to see who had come to his rescue and recognized the same young woman who had given him her card at the foundry celebration. Ehndale smiled and politely replied.

"My dear, I was simply pointing out the finer points of the vehicle. The young man seems to have an affinity for it, and I just wanted to let him know what he was looking at."

Naomi smiled back at Ehndale and said: "Respectfully, sir, you were trying to intimidate him."

Ehndale laughed, "Of course, you're right, my dear…." He then turned to address Hunter.

"I apologize, young man. I didn't mean to intimidate you. I just thought you should know what it is you are admiring. "

Hunter regained his nerve and, to impress Naomi, he confidently replied, "My name is Hunter, sir, and no, I wasn't intimidated. Thank you for telling me about the car. It helps me to appreciate it even more now than I had before. Thank you."

"Splendid!" Ehndale exclaimed before addressing Naomi, "… you see, my dear, the young man understood my intentions after all."

Naomi was impressed by Hunter's fortitude and smiled at him in recognition. Her smile gave Hunter the confidence to approach the car once more.

Ehndale admired Hunter's cockiness but felt compelled to restrain it and asked, "Are you a member of the club, my dear fellow? Haven't seen you here before".

Hunter was unsure how to answer and intended to lie to protect his pride, but Naomi understood Ehndale's intention and responded with half-truths to defend him.

"Hunter came to the club at my request to meet Father…" she began. "…he catered the foundry celebration yesterday and did such a splendid job that Father and I asked him to cater our gathering next month."

Naomi's explanation was perfect. It made Hunter feel important without portraying him as anything other than who he was, and his attraction towards Naomi became more pronounced than it had already been.

A puzzled look came over Ehndale's face.

"I'm a bit confused, my dear…" he began, "…I was under the impression that Vikki had hired her friend Kate to cater the affair. Is that not true?"

Hunter responded without taking his eyes off Naomi.

"Kate is my mother, and she asked me to handle the affair."

The news delighted Ehndale, and all sorts of things ran through his mind. He could use Hunter to get back at Kate for her role in foiling his plans for Thurmond and believed he could use the young man's affinity for beautiful things to solicit his assistance. Ehndale could also try to secure a position for him at the Foundry to help retrieve the information Ehndale needed to influence decisions there. It all seemed to work. He just needed to get the wheels in motion.

Ehndale reached into his pocket, pulled out the keys to the Bentley, and flipped them to Hunter.

"Here, you go! Why don't you two take a ride? I have some business to discuss with Naomi's father, so I'll ride back with him."

"But I have to get back to the Diner," Hunter insisted, knowing his mother would be waiting for him to return.

"No worries..." Ehndale replied flippantly, "... your mother will be just fine and very proud of you, I should think! She'll be impressed when you drive up in this exquisite automobile!"

Hunter tried to convince himself that there had to be a reason why this was too good to be true and asked about his own car. Ehndale calmly replied, "It'll be fine. I'll have your car taken to the Foundry. It will be waiting for you there."

Hunter had no problem showing up in that beautiful car at the Foundry with Naomi. It would certainly make an impression, but he didn't understand why Ehndale had wanted his car to be taken there and asked.

"I appreciate that, but you can drop my car at the Diner. I wasn't planning on going by the Foundry unless they needed a delivery or something."

"Well, actually, my dear boy...." Ehndale said smiling, "...I need someone to deliver a letter to the chairman there, and I would appreciate your dropping it off for me. There's no rush, so take your time and enjoy your ride with Naomi. You'd be doing me a tremendous favor!"

Ehndale reached into his pocket, pulled out an envelope with Vikki's name on it, and scribbled something on a piece of paper he had pulled from inside it. He folded the paper, placed it back inside the envelope, sealed it, and handed it to Hunter.

Hunter was excited about being given an important task and more excited about being able to impress Vikki. He assured Ehndale he would make sure she got the letter.

"I trust you," Ehndale said with an almost sinister grin, "Naomi will drive the Bentley back to Beechwood after dropping you off at the Foundry. So, go ahead, enjoy yourselves! Have some fun!"

Hunter was excited, but Naomi suspected Ehndale was up to something. She took the keys from Hunter and tried to hand them back to Ehndale, but he gently pushed her hand away and said, "The young man seems more than capable, my dear. Besides, given his appreciation of the automobile, he deserves to know what it feels like to take it for a spin. Don't you? Go ahead, have some fun! I'll see you at the Beechwood Manor house, Naomi. Your father won't mind. Go ahead. Enjoy!"

Ehndale patted Hunter on the back, kissed Naomi on the cheek, and left. Hunter was excited. He put the envelope in his pocket and exclaimed, "Let's go!"

24

Tangibility

Vikki was not in the habit of being late and never missed an appointment. In the rare instance that she couldn't make an appointment, she would call to reschedule. This was the main reason her absence that morning at the Diner concerned Thomas, who feared something was wrong. Because he was not on duty until later that evening, he had no plans other than to spend the day with Vikki, so he took Kate's advice and began looking for her.

Thomas drove out to her house, imagining terrible things but reminded himself to consider plausible scenarios where nothing was seriously wrong. When he found Vikki was not home, he searched for clues but found nothing and immediately headed to the Foundry. When he arrived, he was relieved to see Vikki's car in front of the main entrance, and he quickly parked his vehicle and then went directly to her office.

Anxious to see some trouble hadn't befallen her, his fears were alleviated when the receptionist told him that Vikki was indeed at the Foundry. Still, he became disappointed when he learned Vikki was in a board meeting and could not be interrupted. When Thomas asked how long she would be, the receptionist told him the board had ordered lunch, so they were not expected to be done for some time.

Thomas considered what he should do, looked at his watch momentarily, and then asked who was providing lunch. When he was told it was Kate's, he decided to wait so he could help make the delivery. That would give him a moment with Vikki to kid her about ruining their plans.

He sat in a comfortable lounge chair, quietly reading the paper for over half an hour before the receptionist's phone rang, breaking the silence.

"Nothing yet..." the receptionist said, "... I've been watching and waiting, but no one has come by yet...No, ma'am. I've been here the whole time. Never left. You can ask the gentleman sitting here waiting with me."

Thomas deduced that the call was likely from the board room inquiring about their food delivery.

When the receptionist held her hand over the receiver and motioned for Thomas to come over, he assumed it was to corroborate her story. He put down the paper and approached the receptionist. When he drew near, she asked.

"I'm sorry, sir. What did you say your name was?"

Thomas believed it was Vikki on the other end of the phone and decided to have some fun.

"Tell her it's the police, and we're here to see her."

The receptionist stared at Thomas for a moment, then lifted her hand from the receiver and said, "He says he's a policeman and here to see you, Ma'am."

There was a pause, which made Thomas laugh as he assumed Vikki had suddenly remembered their plans and was probably embarrassed. He stood smiling as the receptionist replied, "Yes, Ma'am, I'm sure...Yes, Ma'am, I will."

Thomas was very curious about Vikki's reaction, and when the receptionist hung up the phone, he asked, "What did she say?"

Without the slightest hesitation, the receptionist replied, "She asked if you were here with their lunch."

Thomas laughed as he knew Vikki was having some fun at his expense, which was a good sign of her humor. Thomas told the receptionist that he would check the status of the delivery and headed immediately back to the Diner.

~

Thomas saw Kate packing a rather large delivery in the rear seat of her car when he arrived back at the Diner, which he assumed was for the foundry board meeting. He parked his car, jumped out to help Kate, and noticed she appeared to have been crying. Thomas did not want to be nosy, but he was genuinely concerned and asked:

"Is everything OK, Kate?"

Kate stopped loading her car and, with her head down, tersely replied, "No, Thom, it's not," "Why? What happened?"

Kate wiped her hands on her apron and angrily replied.

"Hunter was supposed to be here an hour ago to make this delivery, but he only showed up a few minutes ago."

"Where is he now?" Thomas asked, looking around.

"Gone, in some fancy car with some girl I've never seen before."

"In a fancy car with some girl? Do you know who she was?"

"Like I said, I never saw her before...." Kate answered as she resumed struggling with the large order, "... Hunter introduced her as 'Naomi.'"

When Thomas began helping Kate load the food containers in her rear seat, she stopped what she was doing and wiped her face with her apron to remove the tears.

"Hunter said he had met her at the Foundry party and just ran into her at the club." Kate continued,"...he said they got to talking, and he lost track of time."

"Why did he leave without helping?" Thomas asked.

"Hunter said he had to drop the girl off and return the car. That's when we got into an argument. He told me he might be back later...." Kate replied, emphasizing the word 'might' when she said it.

Thomas was surprised and suspected there was more to it than Hunter had told his mother. He may be young and impetuous, but Thomas didn't consider Hunter irresponsible, especially when it came to helping his mother.

"Let me take this delivery to the Foundry for you, Kate...." Thomas offered, "...I just came from there. Vikki sent me back to pick this up."

"You're such a dear, Thomas, but I couldn't ask you to do that."

"No. Really. It's no trouble, Kate..." Thomas replied, "... I'm playing a little game with Vikki, and this will give me a chance to turn it back on her."

Thomas could see the confusion on Kate's face as he spoke and explained, "It's a long story, Kate, but I wanted to give Vikki a little grief about missing our date this morning and making me worry. But rather than apologize, she sent me on this errand. It would help me if you let me make the delivery. I'm happy to help."

"OK, Thomas, thank you."

Kate leaned back against her car and continued, "... I'm feeling a little worn down today anyway, and things get a little difficult when Hunter's not around to help. I didn't realize how much I had come to rely on him."

Thomas began transferring the delivery boxes and bags into his car as Kate watched him make the switch. When he was done, Thomas turned to her and asked.

"Can you tell me anything about the car Hunter was driving, Kate? Did he say to whom it belonged and where he had to return it?"

"He did say something about the man it belonged to. Can't remember all the details. I was pretty upset. I do remember he said he met him at the club. Where he ran into that girl, Naomi."

When Kate mentioned the name 'Naomi,' her dislike for the girl was evident in her voice. Kate continued:

"The car looked really expensive. I didn't like him driving around like that, with some floozy I'd never met before. Seems like a recipe for trouble. I didn't like it one bit."

As Thomas listened to Kate, he became suspicious of Hunter's behavior, the car, the girl, and the man at the club. It all seemed strangely familiar somehow, but he was more concerned about how tired Kate appeared.

"Thank you, Kate…." Thomas replied, "… I'll take it from here. I'm sure there's an explanation for what Hunter was doing. You probably know better than me, but he's young and impetuous. Driving around in a fancy car with a pretty girl isn't uncommon for kids his age. I'm sure it will all be fine. I'll talk to you later."

"I'm sure you're right, Thom…." Kate said softly, "… I don't like surprises, and our customers don't like waiting. I'll talk to him when he returns. Thanks for your help. I'm much obliged."

Kate slowly walked back into the Diner, waving goodbye as Thomas pulled away from the curb.

~

Thomas wanted to follow up on his suspicions, but first, he needed to figure out how to deal with Vikki, who had gotten the better of him back at the Foundry.

When he arrived, he saw Thurmond talking with other executives milling around the plaza and assumed the board may have taken a break in anticipation of the food delivery. Thomas hadn't devised a plan to get back at Vikki for sending him on his little errand, but he decided against doing anything that affected the food delivery. It was well past lunchtime, and people were obviously hungry.

Vikki had told Thurmond that Thomas had gone to get the food, so when he saw Thomas pull up, he solicited a few other men to help unload the delivery. He knew Thomas was doing Kate a favor by making the delivery, so when he was close enough for Thomas to hear him, he said jokingly, "You're late!"

Both men laughed as they began unpacking Thomas's car.

"Where's Hunter?" Thurmond asked, "…I think he'd be making the delivery. If he keeps this up, he may have to look for another job!"

Thomas didn't think Kate would appreciate everyone knowing her business and decided against telling Thurmond what he had learned about Hunter's activities.

"He's been helping his Mom…" Thomas replied, "… she's been trying to help him learn the business so he can take over when she calls it quits. He still has a lot to learn."

"Well, keeping people waiting for their food is not the way to go about it…" Thurmond added, "… don't matter how good it is. If Hunter wants to be successful, he must make sure his customers are happy 'cause happy customers are repeat customers. Keeping them waiting for food ain't gonna do that."

"I don't disagree…" Thomas replied, "…Hunter still has a lot to learn if he's going to be successful. But he is trying. Besides, Kate is a dynamo. He will learn much from his Mom, whether he likes it or not."

One of the men helping them unload the car overheard their conversation about Hunter and said,

"He was here about half an hour ago."

"Who was here?" Thomas asked.

"Kate's son, Hunter. That's who you're talking about, isn't it?"

"Yeah, it is…." Thurmond confirmed.

Thomas was disappointed to hear that he had missed Hunter. He wanted to ask him questions, like who was the girl he was with and who lent him the car. Thomas also wondered why Hunter didn't make the delivery if he was coming there anyway? The man continued.

"Yeah, The kid was all about the show, if you know what I mean. Drove up in some fancy car with a pretty girl asking to speak with Vikki. Kind of like he was someone important. Wouldn't leave until

Vikki agreed to see him. That's why we broke the meeting. We knew lunch was coming, and she wanted to deal with him."

"How do you know that?" Thurmond asked.

"A call came in during the meeting, saying the kid was here to see Vikki. She sent me down to talk to him. When I got back, I told her what he had said. She broke the meeting, told everyone they should wait downstairs for lunch, and asked me to bring him up."

"What did he say to you?" Thomas asked.

"That he was there on an urgent matter."

Thurmond was tired and hungry and hadn't paid much attention to the events in the boardroom, but the man's explanation seemed accurate enough, based on what little Thurmond remembered of them.

"Where's Vikki now?" Thomas asked.

"Still in her office, I imagine…." the man replied, "…she saw your car pull into the lot and sent me out to help with the food."

Thomas excused himself, went into the lobby, asked the attendant what Vikki had ordered for lunch, and separated it from the rest of the delivery to bring to her office.

Thomas knocked but entered Vikki's office without waiting for a reply. She was standing in the corner looking out the window and, without turning to face him when he entered, said half-heartedly, "Hello there…"

"Hello yourself…." Thomas replied as he placed the food on the coffee table before the couch, "…got your lunch here!"

Vikki turned and saw that Thomas had opened her lunch box to see what she had ordered. When he began picking at her lunch, Vikki asked, "Any good?"

"Always is from Kate's!" Thomas assured her, "…want some?"

"You can have it…." Vikki responded, "…I lost my appetite."

Thomas tried to be light-hearted to help cheer her up, but he could tell something was wrong. When he asked her what the matter was, she sat behind her desk across from him and replied, "Ehndale."

"Ehndale?!" Thomas exclaimed.

"Yes, Ehndale…" Vikki replied, "…Hunter came by with a letter from him that is troubling because it puts me in an awkward position."

"What was the message, and how is it affecting you?"

Vikki stood and began to pace around the room.

"As you already know, I've been interviewing people to replace the team I have to send to Asia with Thurmond…."

Thomas nodded that he understood and folded his arms across his chest as he listened intently.

"Well, in the letter, Ehndale recommended I hire Hunter for a key position."

"Hunter? Why Hunter?" Thomas asked, suspicious of Ehndale's motives.

"Didn't say…" Vikki returned, "…but the Equity partners have made it abundantly clear that they would pull funding if I don't do as they ask. They have insisted that Thurmond is on the ground in Asia. At least for the foreseeable future."

Thomas was a little confused and asked, "What does that have to do with Hunter being hired to work at the Foundry? I don't understand?"

"Apparently, Ehndale has taken a liking to Hunter," Vikki replied.

Thomas didn't understand the connection but thought this development might explain Hunter's unusual behavior with his mother. He became angry with the possibility that Ehndale was trying to corrupt the kid somehow for his own purposes and asked,

"Can't you say no?"

"I could…" Vikki replied, "…but Ehndale has a controlling interest in the Equity partnership, and I would risk losing funding if he's already convinced them I should hire Hunter."

Thomas knew Ehndale wouldn't do anything that wouldn't benefit him directly, but he couldn't see how Kate's son could help him in any way. Vikki continued, "The worst part is that Ehndale is forcing me to hire an unqualified person like Hunter to perform an essential role. It will only cause problems I must fix unless I bring Thurmond home, which they say is not an option."

Vikki walked back over to the window she had been looking out of when Thomas had arrived, stared out into the parking lot, and then turned to face Thomas.

"Don't get me wrong, Thom, I like Hunter. I've come to know him much better lately, and I think he's a great kid. He's competent, but I know Kate wants him to take over at the Diner, and I have a soft spot for her, as you know."

"I know..." Thomas returned.

"Well, I don't know if you knew, but Hunter has been trying to get a job here for a while now...."

"No, I didn't know," Thomas answered, and Vikki continued, "He has applied numerous times for various positions, but I have turned him down every time because of his lack of experience...." Vikki paused briefly, then added, "...and because I know Kate can use his help at the Diner."

Vikki walked over to where Thomas had begun eating her lunch, picked up a few morsels, and put a few of them in her mouth. When she finished chewing them, she continued.'

"I know Hunter would not consider that fair, but I must consider everything in my decisions. Kate is important to me, and I don't think she can manage without his help. Have you noticed how frail she looks? I'm becoming concerned about her."

"I have noticed..." Thomas replied, "... and I feel the same way.".

Vikki returned to her desk, sat down, and began to nibble on the bits of her lunch that she had taken in her hand. Thomas brought the rest of her order over to the desk and joined her.

"I'm curious what position Ehndale recommended for Hunter?"

"That's the thing, Thom. Ehndale insists I hire Hunter to stand in for Thurmond while he's away."

"That's ridiculous!" Thomas replied.

"I agree…" Vikki replied, "…but Ehndale is using his association with my equity partner on the Asian expansion deal to force his hand. The letter he sent with Hunter was basically a veiled threat."

Thomas could feel his anger surge, so he took deep breaths to suppress his immediate reaction. If he showed how upset he was about Ehndale's involvement, Vikki would stop relaying information, and he wanted to know everything. He took a long sip of the drink from Vikki's lunch as she continued.

"Besides recommending I hire Hunter, the letter suggests that the equity partners may consider pulling their funding if I don't do what they ask."

Now it was Thomas' turn to pace around the room. He stood slowly, turned away from Vikki so she couldn't see his face, and began walking towards the bookcases, where he indiscriminately began pulling and pushing books in and out of their places on the shelves. Vikki continued.

"That doesn't mean I can't do the deal without their funding, but their terms are ideal. I'd never get that kind of deal anywhere else, and it's mostly because of our mutual relationship with Ehndale that I'm getting it. Souring that deal could increase my financial exposure, which could delay the whole process and extend any return on investment. That equates to losing money, so you see, I am in an awful position."

"I see the dilemma," Thomas replied, trying not to focus on his anger at Ehndale's meddling, "…. but what are you going to do?"

"Not sure yet, Thom, but I have to decide soon. Thurmond's off to Asia with the entire team in less than a month."

25

Quandry

Since the moment he had met him, Thomas had been wary of Ehndale. The mere mention of the man's name evoked a defensive response, which heightened Thomas' sense of awareness and angered him. Ehndale's meddling was a threat that had not been resolved, even after he lost his influence over Thurmond. Now that his interest in Vikki and Hunter was abundantly clear, Thomas wanted to protect his friends but was unsure of exactly what to do.

Ehndale's tendency seemed to be to ingratiate himself into people's lives and then exploit any leverage he managed to accumulate for his own benefit. To protect his friends, Thomas decided to keep a watchful eye on Ehndale while pretending that everything was normal. He didn't want anyone to know his concerns but was determined to thwart any attempt by Ehndale to manipulate his friends.

When it came to Vikki, Thomas understood that she likely needed a little space to deal with her planning for the Taipei project, so he agreed to give her whatever time she needed and intended to use that time to observe Ehndale's meddling from afar. He also wanted to use that time to address some of his other concerns, including Kate's health and Hunter's worsening attitude.

~

As part of his daily routine, Thomas stopped by the Diner twice daily to check on Kate and try to talk some sense into her son. Thomas quickly learned that Kate had been missing time at work, and Hunter was becoming increasingly impudent when he was there.

It was evident to Thomas that Hunter was shirking his responsibilities, and his indignation was exasperating, particularly to his mother. Thomas considered it inappropriate and infuriating and believed Hunter's behavior was contributing to his mother's deteriorating health, which Thomas found inexcusable. He decided it was time for an intervention, whether Kate wanted it or not, and decided to confront Hunter about it at his next opportunity.

One morning Thomas stopped by in his patrol car after his shift and found that Kate had taken the day off, which had become a regular occurrence. He ordered a cup of coffee at the counter and asked Midge, the querulous cashier, if Hunter was around. She told him that Hunter was in Kate's office rifling through some papers looking for an invoice and would be off to deposit it in the bank once he found it. Thomas waited 10 minutes, then walked behind the counter and into Kate's office.

Hunter was sitting behind Kate's desk, looking through a pile of paper, and was not surprised when he looked up and saw Thomas enter. Thomas asked him if he had a few minutes, and Hunter invited Thomas to sit down. Hunter continued methodically looking through papers for a few minutes, then pushed them aside when he couldn't find what he was looking for.

"Exasperating!' Hunter remarked, "… can't make heads or tails of my mother's filing system!"

"I'm here about your Mom, Hunter…." Thomas began, "… I've noticed she's missed a lot of work lately, and when I have seen her, she didn't appear to be feeling very well."

"Yeah. She's been going to the doctor…." Hunter explained, "… he's been telling her to take some time off from work, which only means more work for me."

Thomas had been involved in interventions before, and one thing he learned was not to beat around the bush. He needed to say what he felt needed to be said.

"Hunter, your Mom is a treasure around here, and you treat her like she's a bother."

"What do you mean?"

"What I'm saying is your Mom knows she's fortunate to have you to help her, but I'm not sure you understand how much she needs you right now. Your taking time off while she's home convalescing is bad for business, which is not good for her or you."

Hunter looked at Thomas quizzically and replied, "I'm not sure I follow?"

Thomas continued, "You see, Hunter, people know who your Mom is and genuinely like her. They'd do just about anything for her. But you, well, people don't know who you are other than you're your Mom's son. If you neglect your work, it will show and may affect people's opinion of you."

Hunter took offense to Thomas' remarks and replied.

"Neglect work? I'm here now, aren't I, while my Mom's taking another day off!"

Thomas tried to explain.

"Hunter, if you have a bad attitude, it will give people a reason not to like you, and if their opinion of you is not good, your business will suffer."

"I don't care, Thomas!" Hunter said forcefully, "...people can keep their opinions of me. Why should I care? It has no effect on me whatsoever! It's not my business. I'm just here helping my Mom until she feels better. Once she comes back, I'm gone! I have opportunities just waiting on me to wrap it up here! This is only a temporary setback."

"That's where you're wrong, son...." Thomas replied, "...you see, you aspire to be successful, but there are no guarantees. People with low opinions of you could be in positions to either help you achieve your desired success or prevent you from achieving it. Take your desire to work at the foundry, for instance. I know you have applied to work there. Perhaps aspire to replace Mr. Joseph someday...."

Hunter interrupted Thomas mid-sentence and shouted back, "Who told you that?"

"I know more than you think, son. It shouldn't come as a surprise. Now, if you permit me to finish, as I was saying…."

"Respectfully, Thomas, I won't permit you to finish. I've heard all this before from my mother. It didn't make sense to me coming from her, so why should it matter if it's coming from you?"

Thomas tried to think of the best way to relay his concerns about the perils of lofty aspirations and questionable associations. As he considered what he should say, Hunter continued, "Don't think I don't know the deal, Thomas. I may be the son of a waitress working at a Diner, but I have lofty goals. I also have the support of a powerful and wealthy advocate. An extremely successful person who is willing to help me achieve everything I ever wanted. You can't offer me that, can you? Didn't think so. Neither can my Mom, so I don't know why I should be listening to you when I can take the advice of someone who has made something of their life. Not someone who settled for being a policeman or some other menial job like waiting on tables. I want to be the one who is being served. That's my measure of success!"

Thomas was literally speechless. Here was a young man he had watched grow from a respectful little boy into a selfish twit. Thomas became irascible, but not at Hunter for his disrespect, but at Ehndale for his wrongful influence over this impressionable young man.

Thomas was determined to do something about it, but he needed to set the record straight with Hunter first before he engaged with Ehndale.

"You are not being counseled by your so-called 'Advocate' in a way that will ultimately benefit you in the long run, Hunter. You're being manipulated!"

"Yeah, right…" Hunter responded as he resumed shuffling through the papers on his Mom's desk. Thomas continued, "I know you think I'm just some dumb cop, but I had a life you know nothing about. So did your Mom, as do most people. Our choices for our occupations result from those lives, for better or worse. Some people are 'stuck' in a job because of bad choices they have made, but not everyone, even if you perceive it that way, because you don't think very highly of what people have chosen to do.'

Thomas could tell he had Hunter's attention even though Hunter pretended otherwise. To take advantage of it, he continued to relay information about his past that no one knew, not Kate nor Vikki. Thomas continued:

"I grew up in an abusive household with an alcoholic father who beat my mother and me. I had an older brother named Iggy, who died when I was young. It was a tragic accident; my dad blamed everyone, especially my Mom and me. My Mom never got over my brother's death and eventually had to leave the house to protect herself from my father's drunken rage. She wound up in a sanatorium, and I joined the military to get away from my dad. I served in two wars and was awarded a Purple Heart, a Bronze Star, and a Distinguished Service Cross. So, you see, I didn't settle for being a cop. I chose to be a police officer because I wanted to protect people from their enemies and keep them safe. I wanted to protect them from people like my dad."

Hunter listened but seemed to become increasingly disinterested. He began shuffling through papers while Thomas was talking, and when Thomas had finished, Hunter replied, "At least you had a dad. Mine couldn't be bothered with me. He wanted my mother to abort me. How's that for feeling like you don't matter?"

"That's not true…." Thomas returned.

"Sure is. Ask my Mom. She'll tell you."

Thomas was at a loss for words, and as he thought of what to say, Hunter pulled an envelope from the pile of paper, stuffed it in his pocket, and continued:

"Don't lecture me on life's decisions and suffering hardships, Thomas. I've had my share, even before I could recognize how hard my life would be. My Mom settled for what we have, but I don't want to settle. I want to succeed and become more than an unwanted child. More than a delivery boy. I want to be more than a stooge at my Mom's Diner, pretending it's all admirable. It's not."

"That's where you're wrong, Hunter…." Thomas interrupted, "…admiration is not something you can quantify by assigning value to your achievements. It's something people give you like a gift. It's something you earn, Hunter, regardless of how you feel about your actions. That's what motivates people to give it to you. It's a gift. Like a cold drink offered without asking after working hard on a hot day."

"Nonsense!" Hunter replied, "…you make it sound like I should appreciate being given an iced tea as much as I would a Ferrari. They're not the same. One certainly means more than the other. It is totally quantifiable. The measure of gratitude is directly related to the value of the reward."

Thomas immediately recognized the logic. Ehndale had certainly done his job and was corrupting Hunter's thinking. Before Thomas could reply, Hunter continued.

"My Mom wants me to help her; fine. I owe her that much for caring for me until now, but that's not enough. I want more. I need more and won't stop until I get the admiration, reward, and gift I deserve. I want to be successful. I'm capable, and I'm ambitious. Once the opportunity presents itself, I'm gone. Mom or no Mom. She would probably agree this is not for me. I don't belong here. My legacy is not working in or owning a Diner when my Mom's gone. Nope. No sir."

Thomas knew he was not going to get anywhere with Hunter, so he ended their conversation with a thought.

"Sounds like you've got it all figured out, son. Good for you. I hope it works out how you want it to, but I'm here to tell you that things are not always what they seem. Be careful not to be blinded by your ambition. You may find yourself on a road that dead ends at a cliff with no way back. All the possessions in the world can't help you then. That's when you'd trade everything for a way home. If she still wants you at that point, you'd trade your Ferrari for a warm bed in your mother's house."

Hunter began clearing the papers off his mother's desk and pretended that what Thomas had just said didn't matter, but it did. He struggled with the contradiction between what Ehndale had told him and the advice that Thomas had just given him. He respected the officer but didn't believe Thomas understood his motivations.

Thomas knew their conversation was over and reached out to shake Hunter's hand.

"Give your Mom my best, Hunter, and remember what I said. You'll never be a hero at home, but you are always welcomed back, even after you've worn it out."

Thomas left the Diner, and Hunter stood wondering what the officer meant by his last statement.

~

After much consideration, Vikki had the foundry human resources office schedule Hunter for an interview. She had counseled Thurmond on the possibility that this may happen, and although Thurmond liked the boy, he was less than thrilled at the prospect of having to train his replacement, especially someone who knew so little of the operation. Vikki argued that it made sense for many reasons, not the least of which was the ease with which they could shift Hunter out of the position when Thurmond returned from Asia.

"Anyone with enough experience to warrant the promotion would be hard-pressed to give it up when you returned, Thurmond…." Vikki argued. "I can appreciate that your being away is putting pressure on your relationship with Monica, and because of that, I want to be able to pull you back quickly with as little disruption to the operation as possible."

Thurmond let Vikki know he appreciated her consideration, and she concluded:

"When the time is right, Thurmond, I want your return to life here to be easy, quick, and seamless. Both for your sake and for mine."

Thurmond reluctantly agreed and continued planning for the relocation of his staff.

~

Excited and nervous, Hunter wanted some advice on approaching the interview and called Ehndale, who promptly invited him to his manor house for dinner.

"Splendid news, my boy. Splendid indeed!" Ehndale crowed.

"I had a feeling they were going to call me…." Hunter admitted, trying to sound humble.

"Nonsense…" Ehndale replied, "…of course, they called! They should consider themselves fortunate you are even considering the position."

"I don't know about that…." Hunter replied, suddenly feeling like Ehndale was being overly bombastic.

"Of course, they should, my boy!" Ehndale emphatically replied, "…do you think a hard-headed factory worker with no ambition deserves to be more successful than you?"

Hunter assumed he was speaking of Mr. Joseph, and although he respected Thurmond, Hunter tended to agree with Ehndale's assessment regarding his ambition. Ehndale continued.

"Why shouldn't you have the same opportunities? You're certainly capable, and I can tell you're ambitious. Those are the qualities required to succeed. That and resourcefulness. Look at my protégé, the CEO, Miss Vikki. I found her when she lived in a dirt shack with her family. That's right, my boy, literally dirt-poor, but she was resourceful, intelligent, and ambitious. She worked hard, and now look at her. That could be you! Can you see it?"

"Yes, sir…" Hunter returned as he thought about the possibilities.

"Splendid!" Ehndale said, "… let's have a drink to celebrate the commencement of a rewarding adventure!"

As instructed, Balaam had set out two snifters and a bottle of Napoléon Cognac for their celebration. Ehndale popped the cork and filled the glasses before handing one to Hunter. As they prepared to toast, Ehndale considered the advantages he would enjoy, with Hunter being the one to help him manipulate things. It was perfect. Hunter's absence at the Diner would punish Kate by eliminating the family business legacy she undoubtedly desired. It could also make life difficult for Thurmond by putting severe demands on his time, keeping him away from Monica, and allowing Ehndale to corrupt her. Those demands would also distract Thurmond during a critical time in the foundry's resurgence, making Vikki miserable, thus allowing Ehndale to punish his protégé for ignoring his bidding. It was all a win for him, and he was elated with the prospect.

"To a heroic success!" Ehndale offered as he raised his snifter.

"Cheers…" Hunter replied, and they both drank.

"Funny you should say 'heroic,' Mr. Ehndale…." Hunter said as he wiped his mouth with a napkin Balaam had left on the table.

"How's that, my dear boy?" Ehndale asked.

"Well…" Hunter began, "…just the other day, Officer Thomas told me, '… you're never a Hero at home….' I didn't know what he meant by that, but I guess it means you must be away from home to be a hero. Funny, isn't it?"

"Yes. Funny." Ehndale responded and asked, "…did he say anything else?"

"Well, he's upset because my Mom isn't feeling well, and I've been, let's just say, less than enthusiastic about helping her around the Diner. He even got mad at me for skipping a delivery to his girlfriend's office the day I was with you and Naomi. I mean, it's really none of his business. He's always full of advice on how I should live my life. I don't know why he needs to advise me on how to approach it."

Hunter paused to take another sip from his snifter, then continued.

"He told me about how difficult my Mom's life had been and how much she had sacrificed for me, but when I told him about my dad leaving me, he began to talk about how difficult his life had been. Like it had some bearing on mine."

"What did he say about his life?" Ehndale asked.

Hunter relayed what he could remember of what Thomas had told him in confidence. Details about his life, including his relationship with his parents and the death of his brother.

"Interesting…" Ehndale replied, "…makes you wonder why he feels qualified to advise anyone on anything, doesn't it?"

"Sure does!" Hunter replied.

Ehndale finished his cognac and placed the snifter on the table.

"Will you excuse me for a minute, my dear boy? I must check on something. I shouldn't be more than a minute."

"Of course," Hunter replied as Ehndale left the room.

Ehndale had had enough of Thomas and decided it was time to do something about it. It was bad enough his protégé did not leave him when he had first asked her to, but the annoying officer was now counseling Ehndale's new 'project' against his wishes, which could ruin everything. Ehndale would not let that happen again and quickly devised a plan.

26

Bernard

Thurmond struggled to select the staff to accompany him back to Taipei, and unlike Hunter's interview, which resulted in his immediate hire, the process proved arduous and frustrating. Through the generosity of the equity partnership, tremendous incentives were offered, which created a flood of applicants and a large pool of volunteers. Vikki encouraged Thurmond to conduct training sessions to familiarize the volunteers with the local building process, customs, and living conditions, hoping it would whittle down the numbers once people realized how different things were there. Thurmond also stressed how they would miss their family, friends, and loved ones while away.

When these strategies didn't work, Vikki began hiring locals in Taipei to reduce the number of employees required to relocate. With any luck, she may even be able to identify a suitable replacement for Thurmond, which could expedite his return home. This would be ideal since Vikki was convinced that Hunter would make a mess of things if his tenure as Thurmond's replacement wasn't limited. Besides, she had promised to bring Thurmond home as soon as possible, and she wanted to make good on her promises.

Meanwhile, Ehndale was pleased with how things were going. Leveraging the Equity partnership's influence had assured Thurmond would be away and provided Ehndale with an agent in Hunter, who had unlimited access to the Foundry's information. Hunter's acceptance of this new position also meant abandoning his mother's dream, undoubtedly leaving Kate heartbroken. The only obstacle remaining was the incessant meddling of Vikki's boyfriend, Thomas, which Ehndale intended to remedy by any means necessary.

Quite by accident, Ehndale had learned of Thomas's troubled childhood, including a tumultuous relationship with his father. Ehndale surmised that the reintroduction of his family would likely keep Thomas preoccupied and, therefore, too busy to interfere with his plans.

Ehndale began searching for Thomas's family and found his mother first. She had been a long-term patient at a sanitarium but was recently transferred to a psychiatric asylum after her diagnosis was re-evaluated. Thomas had not visited her in some time, so he was probably unaware of her transfer. This meant the new facility may have never met Thomas, so Ehndale had an associate pretend to be him and retrieve the files he needed to track down Thomas' father, Bernard.

After a circuitous expedition, Ehndale eventually found Bernard living in squalor and offered to buy him a meal. At first, Bernard was skeptical, but he hadn't eaten a full meal in some time and accepted Ehndale's offer. As Bernard devoured his food, Ehndale continued his solicitations, offering him some money and a place to stay. Though cautious, Bernard accepted on the condition that it was only until he had earned enough money to find a place of his own.

Bernard was set up in the cottage where Brad had stayed and cleaned himself up before having a good long rest in a proper bed. When Balaam reported seeing Bernard walking around the cottage, Ehndale visited him and invited him to dinner at Cay Pham. Ehndale intention was for Bernard to cause a ruckus, ensuring the police would be called, which would make Thomas aware of his father's presence in town. This was all Ehndale needed to initiate his plan.

While they enjoyed their dinner, Ehndale offered Bernard a menial job, which he immediately accepted. Aware of Bernard's propensity for alcohol and violence, Ehndale ordered drinks to celebrate. Bernard mentioned that he was a recovering alcoholic who had repeatedly failed to manage his addiction. Despite this modest protest, Ehndale convinced Bernard that a single glass was harmless and warranted, given the circumstances. One drink led to another until Bernard became drunk and belligerent, and things spiraled entirely out of control, as Ehndale had intended.

Bernard became too much for the waiter, so he implored Albrecht, the maître d', to do something about the situation. The intoxicated man was clearly upsetting the other patrons, so Albrecht left his station to address the problem.

"I'm going to have to ask you to leave…." Albrecht announced, "…or I'll be forced to call the police…."

Bernard shoved his chair away from the table and stood face to face with the maître d' before pushing him. Satisfied that he had created enough trouble to suit his intention, Ehndale stood, excused himself from the table, and left the restaurant before the police arrived. He knew Bernard would never notice his absence.

Bernard began shouting violent threats and throwing punches at anybody within arm's length. He tried to free himself as he was wrestled face down to the ground. Albrecht called the police, and within a few minutes, a pair of officers arrived to find the situation had deteriorated beyond reasoning with the inebriated man. They immediately arrested Bernard and took him away in handcuffs.

One officer placed Bernard in the rear seat of the squad car while the other called the station house. They had taken Bernard's wallet to get his identity and recognized his last name. Because it was an uncommon name, the officer mentioned it to the dispatcher, who called Thomas to see if there was any relation.

"It can't be!' Thomas replied.

"Yessir. Says right here, Ignatius Bernard Arnaud."

"Is he drunk?" Thomas asked sheepishly.

"You could say that" the dispatcher confirmed.

Thomas was mortified, not because his father was arrested for public intoxication and criminal behavior, which was nothing new, but because this terrible part of his life that he had put behind him had now come home. Thomas had not seen his father in quite some time and was not too happy about the possibility of reintroduction. Still, against all his natural inclinations to let his father sit in jail, Thomas decided to bail him out after he had a night to sleep it off, if for nothing else than to be rid of the man.

~

Bernard was passed out in the holding cell when Thomas arrived early the following day.

"Looks peaceful now, but you should have seen him when they brought him in last night. Never seen anything like it..." said the officer who let Thomas in to see his father.

"He's an alcoholic...." Thomas stoically returned, "... I'm sure he won't remember any of it."

"If you say so..." the guard replied, "... I'll get the paperwork to release him into your custody if that's what you want."

"Not a matter of what I want. It's a matter of what I need to do as a son." Thomas replied dejectedly.

The guard left Thomas, who stood watching his father sleep. He began thinking about all the horrible things this man had done to him and his mother. He had made his mother suffer for the loss of their son and unfairly blamed Thomas for the death of his brother Iggy. Thomas missed Iggy as much as anybody, if not more, and had always longed for the kind of connection that Iggy had with their Dad, but that connection was never to be for him, which made him wonder how he would feel at that moment if things had been different.

The guard returned with the necessary paperwork, and Thomas signed it as the guard opened the holding cell to release Bernard. Thomas stepped in and jostled his sleeping father. When Bernard awoke, Thomas was not surprised by his cheerful disposition. He was hungover but genuinely happy to see Thomas and threw his arm around him as the two men left the jailhouse together.

~

As they drove through town, Thomas tried to figure out what he would do with his father. He was not going to take him to his house. Thomas would never be rid of him if his Dad knew where he lived. There weren't many options, so Thomas wanted time to think and asked, "You hungry?"

"Thought you'd never ask, Tommy. I'm famished!" Bernard replied, then added, "…and thirsty. Can we get a good cup of coffee around here? I have a hell of a hangover and could use me a little pick-me-up."

"I know a place…." Thomas said, then pausing a second to consider what to say, and added, "…good coffee, good food, and good folks. I'm just going to have to ask you to behave yourself."

Bernard snapped back, "What the hell is that supposed to mean?"

"You know what I mean, Dad. This is where I live and work. My life is here. You were arrested yesterday for assault and being a public nuisance."

"That's because I was drinking…." Bernard offered as an excuse, "…you know how I get when I get to drinking. Don't worry, Tommy, I'll behave."

None of this was new. Thomas had heard it all before.

As his childhood memories flooded his mind, Thomas couldn't decide if he should confront his father about his drinking. He wasn't sure it would do any good and could cause an argument he didn't want to have.

The two men sat silent as Bernard stared out the car window as they headed for the Diner. After a few minutes, Bernard tried to initiate a conversation and asked,

"You like living here, son? I guess it could be a good a place as any to hang my hat. I may have to look around to see if I can't find somethin' tolerable."

Thomas remained silent as his father continued, "Been doing pretty good myself. Straightening my life out. Trying to work regularly, but there ain't much work around these days. You know anybody hiring, son? I'm good with my hands. Haven't had a drop to drink 'til last night."

Bernard slapped Thomas on the back and joked, "...and I don't have any more warrants out for my arrest, I don't think. At least none that I know of."

Bernard laughed, but Thomas did not find the humor in his father's comment. Bernard sensed his son's indifference and changed the topic, "Was staying with a lady-friend till she kicked me out about a month ago. Met her at the AA group I was going to. She was quite a looker...."

"Enough!" Thomas shouted, "...I don't want to hear about your love life. As far as I'm concerned, you're cheating on Mom. When was the last time you visited her?"

"That's not fair, Tommy. Your mother and I have been over for a while now. She's gone, son. You're gonna have to come to grips with that."

"Gone? What do you mean gone?" "Thomas barked back,"... she's in a sanitarium because you tortured her, mentally and physically. You did that to both of us. You're the one who must come to grips with reality, Dad. You're the one who must admit you're a screw-up. You're a terrible father and a lousy husband."

"That may all be true, son...." Bernard said perniciously, "... but I'm not the one who killed Iggy. That tore the family apart, and that's all you!"

Bernard was trying to defend himself by deflecting blame, but his cruel words hurt Thomas more than he could ever know. Iggy was Thomas' best friend. They did everything together. The memory of his death brought on a flood of emotions like a tsunami that Thomas couldn't deal with.

"Get out!" Thomas screamed as he pulled over beside the bus station, "… I'm tired of your hyperbole!"

"Fancy word, son. Wonder if you even know what it means. Did you read it somewhere and were waiting to use it?"

"Here's some money…." Thomas said as he stuffed some bills into his father's shirt pocket.

"Thank you, son. Appreciate the cash…." Bernard began, "… but as far as leaving, well, you see, I may have just got a job here, and I ain't got no plans on going nowhere."

His father smiled, tapped the money in his pocket, and stepped slowly out of the car as he continued:

"I'm actually thinking of staying. I kinda like being back in town. Suits me. I guess that means you'll be seeing me around then. Bye, son!"

Bernard smiled as he tapped the top of Thomas' car, then turned to walk away.

Thomas was livid and didn't know how to respond. His father had always been able to push his buttons, but Thomas knew arguing with him would only escalate the encounter. He wanted to speak with Vikki, but he had promised not to bother her. Kate was the only other person he could think of that he could trust to keep their conversation confidential. She was considerate and nonjudgmental and would be helpful even if she only provided a shoulder to cry on, so Thomas decided to continue to the Diner.

The Diner was just finishing with the breakfast rush when Thomas arrived, but he didn't see Kate. He walked up to the counter and sat beside the register, where Midge smirked a preposterous smile at him.

"Morning, Midge. Kate here?"

"I'm sorry, honey, she's not. She wasn't feeling well again this morning and took the day off."

Thomas thought that Kate hadn't looked well, and now that he knew she was missing work, he became more concerned. He wanted to visit her at home but needed to check with Hunter first to find out when would be a good time to go by and see her. Thomas was also curious about his recent conversation with Hunter and interested to find out if it had made an impression on him. He scanned the Diner to see if Hunter was there, and when he didn't see him, he turned to Midge and asked her if Hunter was around.

"Nope…" Midge replied as she began ringing up another customer who had stepped up to the register to pay, "… he's been out so much lately that I'm beginning to forget what he looks like."

Hunter's absence clearly indicated to Thomas that his advice had fallen on deaf ears. Curious to hear who had stepped in to help, he asked Midge who took care of things whenever Kate was out sick.

Snapping her gum as she spoke, Midge replied, "Ronnie."

"Ronnie?" Thomas repeated.

"Yeah, Honey, Ronnie…." she confirmed, "Kate decided to call her to see if she could help out, and she came straight back to town and jumped right in!"

Midge paused to blow a bubble and let it pop. As she snapped her gum, she dipped her head and looked at him over the glasses perched on the end of her nose and said, "She's no Kate, mind you, but I will say that it doesn't suck having her as a boss if you'll pardon my French."

Midge's response made Thomas laugh, which felt good, especially after his morning. After enjoying a good chuckle, Thomas thanked Midge for the information and the levity and asked her to say hello to Ronnie for him.

"You can tell her yourself…." Midge replied, "… she's probably in the back doing the books, ordering supplies, or cooking. She's always back there helping. You don't see her out front much."

"Think she'll mind if I stop back to say hi?"

"Don't see why she would?" Midge replied.

Thomas thanked Midge, stepped around behind the counter, and walked back to the office.

Ronnie was sitting at a desk in a room illuminated by a single desk lamp. All the other lights had been turned off. Her head rested against one hand supported by her elbow as she wrote in what Thomas recognized as a ledger because of its shape. Humming along with the radio that played quietly beside her, Ronnie twirled her fingers through her hair as she wrote.

Thomas gently knocked on the open office door jamb and softly said, "Hello there, stranger…."

Ronnie turned to see who had come in and replied: "Why hello there yourself, Thomas!"

"I hope I'm not disturbing you?"

"Nonsense…" she replied, "…come on in!"

Ronnie placed her pencil in the ledger to keep her page before closing it and stood to greet her visitor. After exchanging a quick hug and a kiss, Ronnie invited Thomas to sit on a couch Kate had put in her office.

"Would you like a cup of coffee? A piece of pie? Maybe a sandwich or something?"

"Coffee would be wonderful, thank you!" Thomas replied as he sank into the cushy couch.

"Wonderful! I'll be right back!" Ronnie cheerily replied.

Thomas settled on the couch, wondering what he was doing there. He had come to seek counsel from Kate about his resentment towards his father and didn't know Ronnie well enough to discuss something so personal. Something he hadn't even shared with Vikki.

A moment later, Ronnie returned with Thomas' coffee.

"Here you go…" she said as she handed Thomas a cup she had filled to the brim, "…two lumps of sugar and a splash of cream if I remember correctly?"

"Perfect!" Thomas replied as he sipped his coffee to keep it from spilling.

Ronnie plopped back into her office chair, picked up a glass of water she had on the desk, took a drink, and asked:

"So, how goes it, Thomas? How are you?"

Thomas deflected her question to avoid discussing why he had really stopped by.

"As good as can be expected, I guess. How about you?"

"There's never a day goes by that something doesn't kick me in the pants…" she said.

"I know what you mean…." Thomas replied, thinking about his father. Ronnie continued:

"Kate told me you come by in the mornings to have coffee or breakfast with my sister, but I know Vikki's busy with the whole company expansion. Don't imagine she has much time for you these days, does she?"

"Nope…" Thomas agreed as he sipped his coffee. Ronnie continued:

"Well, Kate called me this past weekend and told me her doctor suggested she stay home and rest. She asked me to come by and help her out, which I'm happy to do. I'm a teacher by trade, which gives me a lot of free time when school is out. I'm always looking for ways to supplement my income."

Ronnie spun in her chair and flailed her hands out as she added:

"I wouldn't mind doing this all the time, actually. I like running a business. It's fun, and the people here are great!"

"What about Kate's son?" Thomas asked. "…Why isn't he helping out? I thought he was helping his Mom?"

"Hunter has been M.I.A. recently…." Ronnie replied, "…I guess he's got something else going on. Had a terrible fight with his Mom the other day on the phone. Hasn't been back since. Thought I heard him say he quit but don't quote me on that."

Thomas felt that Ehndale had something to do with Hunter's recent behavior, and the thought made him visibly upset. Ronnie noticed and asked:

"Everything OK, Thomas? "

Thomas didn't want to gossip about his feelings on Hunter and Ehndale, but he knew Ronnie's question was warranted and deserved an answer.

"Well, to be honest, I came here to talk with Kate about something personal that was bothering me. Your news about Hunter reminded me of it. I'm sorry. I don't mean to be upset. I would talk to your sister, but she's too busy, and I promised not to bother her for a bit."

"I'm sure it won't bother her if it's important. I don't think she would mind."

"Well, you're probably right, but I promised to give her space while she handles her business in Asia, and I'd like to stick by that. We can talk about it later. It may just work itself out in the meantime. I would talk with Kate about it, but I know she's not been feeling well, and I don't want to bother her. She has issues of her own to deal with. I can probably get through it on my own anyway."

Ronnie sensed Thomas was a person in need of someone to talk to. Something was bothering him, and the least she could do was offer to listen. It couldn't hurt, and she had the time.

"OK. I'm not as worldly as Vikki or as experienced as Kate, but I am a good listener. I'm more than willing to listen if you want to talk about it."

Thomas reluctantly agreed and, for well over an hour, unloaded the sordid history of his family. He described his feelings about his brother and mother and his painful relationship with his father. Ronnie was sympathetic and sat patiently listening. As Thomas spoke, she began to think about her own family history.

27

Presage

Even though Hunter shared information he had learned about Thomas with Ehndale, he did not share his feelings. While he pretended to be disinterested and apathetic, he was honestly touched by the officer's story. Hunter empathized with Thomas's difficult life and admired his fortitude and achievements. He also understood Thomas's resentment of his father because he had those same feelings towards his own father, Roy, who had left the family when Hunter was still young.

Hunter considered staying at the Diner to help his mother, as Thomas had suggested, but Ehndale was as unrelenting in his efforts to keep Hunter away from his mother as he was in keeping Thomas preoccupied with his father.

Hunter attended numerous training sessions with Thurmond to prepare for his new position at the Foundry. He also attended social gatherings at the behest of Ehndale, where he was introduced to a litany of social elites. Ehndale stressed the importance of establishing relationships and told Hunter it would benefit him in his new position because he could leverage them when the time came that he needed them.

To Ehndale's delight and his mother's chagrin, Hunter never missed a gathering, but his motives for doing so were not for the reasons his mother nor Ehndale suspected. Hunter looked forward to attending these gatherings because he knew Naomi would be there.

The only relationship Hunter cared about establishing was with Naomi, who had secretly expressed the same sentiment to him.

The two would secretly break away at these gatherings to talk about life and their plans. They established a rapport that grew stronger each time they were together. Naomi admitted that she only attended these functions to satisfy her father's wishes. The truth was she didn't much care for Mr. Ehndale or the company of most of his guests, including her father's associates. She joked that she would rather spend her time in a tee shirt and jeans, skipping stones or swinging from a tire hanging from a rope tied to a tree than rubbing elbows with the phonies she met at Ehndale's soirees.

Hunter was totally infatuated with her. His mind frequently wandered with thoughts of her, which contributed mightily to his making several significant missteps in his training at the Foundry. He readily admitted that he had been daydreaming when his mistakes were pointed out. Luckily, Thurmond understood.

"I've done my share of daydreaming, son…." Thurmond began, "…mostly about women, but take it from me, you have to be careful! What you do here can have an impact beyond your wildest imagination, whether you realize it or not."

Hunter shrugged, and Thurmond continued: "…I had bumped into the rill plate press one day when I was daydreaming about a girl, and I knocked it out of alignment. I forgot to go back to fix it, so they had to halt the entire operation, and I got docked pay because of it."

Thurmond watched Hunter's reaction and wasn't convinced his anecdote sufficiently relayed his point, so he continued, "Well, remember that terrible plane crash? Well, I thought I was responsible for it because of mistakes like that, and until the real cause was revealed, I thought it was entirely my fault, which it could very well have been. So, you see, you can't imagine what could happen if you're not careful. "

Hunter understood Thurmond's point and considered whether he should reveal anything about his feelings for Naomi, and said, "Yessir. I understand. But…it's just…."

"It's just what, son?" Thurmond inquired.

"Promise you won't say anything to anyone?" Hunter asked sheepishly.

"Depends…" Thurmond replied.

"Depends on what?" Hunter asked.

"Depends on what it is…." Thurmond added.

Hunter had always admired Thurmond, but now that he had spent time with him, he genuinely liked him. Hunter stood silent while he considered what to say next, and after a few awkward seconds, a smile crept across Thurmond's face.

"I promise not to say anything, son. Scouts honor!"

Thurmond gave a stern look to show Hunter he was being serious. He held up three fingers in one hand and placed the other over his heart.

"Well, sir…" Hunter began, "… it's about a girl…."

"Of course, it's about a girl!" Thurmond trumpeted.

Both men laughed, which made Hunter feel more at ease, and confessions of his feelings for Naomi began to pour out, reminding Thurmond of Monica and their happy times together. Thurmond became discouraged when he thought about how things stood between them now, and as he listened to the joy in Hunter's voice, he decided it was time to make things right with Monica, especially since he would be going away soon, and they could be apart for quite a while.

~

Things at the Foundry had finally gotten on track. Thurmond's dutiful mentorship had Hunter's training ahead of schedule, and Vikki had finalized her staffing schedule by narrowing down the list of employees to accompany Thurmond to Taipei. Local replacements were hired, and a staffing service was engaged in Taipei to find qualified staff to fill any vacancies Thurmond may identify, including his own. Vikki also considered moving up the scheduled departure date but left it as planned when Thurmond expressed severe reservations about it, primarily for personal reasons, which Vikki understood.

Having isolated herself for months, Vikki was finally comfortable enough with how things were progressing to let go of the foundry reigns and take some time off to decompress. She hadn't seen Thomas in weeks and was anxious to let her hair down and spend some time with him. Thomas was overjoyed to hear that she was taking a break and instantly agreed to her invitation to meet at Kate's the following morning for breakfast.

Vikki arrived early and sat by the front window at a table she usually shared with Thomas. As she looked out the window for Thomas's car, she was surprised when her sister Ronnie came out to greet her.

"Meeting Officer Thomas this morning, are we?"

"What in the world are you doing here?"

"Well, Kate told me I could help her now and again if I felt like I needed a change, so here I am!"

Vikki had missed much of Ronnie's adult life, but she knew her sister and Ronnie wasn't there because she needed a change. There was another reason, and though Vikki hoped she was wrong, she was afraid she knew what it was. Rather than asking her sister about it, she replied, "I think Kate was just being nice because you helped her a few months ago. I didn't think you took it seriously."

"Well, I discovered I liked it!" Ronnie returned, "... I'm on a break from work anyway and figured, why not? I can always use some extra cash. Besides, I get to spend more time with you...when you're not working."

Vikki wanted to know what was going on and asked, "Where's Kate? I know she wasn't feeling well, but isn't she back at work yet?"

"Setbacks..." Ronnie replied, "...You know how cautious doctors can be. Their prognosis changes like the weather. One minute she's fine, and the next, she's not."

Vikki had her suspicions about Kate's lingering infirmities, and her sister's ambiguous answer made her believe there was more to it than she was letting on. Vikki knew her sister could keep a secret, so there was no use in pressing her directly about Kate's condition, so she changed her tact and tried to ascertain the information another way and asked, "How long have you been here helping out?"

"On and off for a couple of weeks. More on than off recently..." Ronnie replied.

"I had no idea. Why didn't you tell me?"

With a wry smile, Ronnie replied, "I didn't think I needed any advice."

Vikki knew her sister was right and decided not to address her remark.

"How long are you planning on staying?" Vikki asked.

"Don't know. I kind of like it here. I'll stay as long as Kate puts up with me."

"What about your position at school?"

"I have plenty of vacation time saved up."

"What happens when that runs out?"

Ronnie anticipated this type of reaction from her sister, which was why she didn't notify her that she was back in town. She also knew more about Kate's health issues than she was letting on, but Kate had made her promise not to tell anyone. Ronnie focused her responses on money since that would be the one thing her sister would understand and accept.

"Truth is, I left my position at school and came out here to help when it became clear how much money I could make working for Kate."

Vikki was shocked.

"I can't believe you would leave your teaching job to work at a Diner?"

"At first, it was easy…." Ronnie began, "…a day off here, a day off there, but when I realized how much money I'd be making, it was an easy decision."

"What kind of hours is Kate giving you? It seems a bit presumptuous that you'd think you get enough to make it worthwhile."

"That's a curious way of looking at it…." Ronnie remarked, "…Whatever do you mean by that V?"

"It's presumptuous of you to assume that there's any future for you at Kate's place beyond helping her out while she's sick. That's not enough to leave a solid teaching job for. What will you do when she's better and comes back?"

Ronnie believed that if the discussion continued in the direction it was headed, she would probably reveal too much.

"I'll deal with that when the time comes, V…." Ronnie replied, "…I really do like working here. I'm even considering opening my own place. I have a little money saved up. Besides, I may hit up my little sister for a business loan. She's got plenty of money!"

When Vikki began to laugh, Ronnie knew she had managed to change the tone of the conversation and took the opportunity to extricate herself to get her sister some coffee and two menus.

Vikki came by that morning hoping to see Kate and ask her how she was feeling, but the surprise that her sister might be around for a while was a welcome one, which pleased Vikki.

~

Thomas had mentioned his concern about Kate's health, and because of the evasive conversation she had had with her sister, Vikki now shared that concern more than ever. It appeared the only way Vikki would get the answers was by looking for ways to check in on Kate at home herself. She intended to suggest to Thomas that they swing by Kate's house after breakfast to see how she was doing. Thomas agreed.

When they arrived at Kate's house, Thomas thought it unusual that Kate would leave her porch light on during the day. When he went around the back of the house, he found that the rear flood lights were also left on. Thomas joined Vikki on the front porch, placed his hands on either side of his face, and pressed against a front porch window beside the front door. When he didn't see anything unusual, they knocked gently and waited. After a few minutes, they knocked again, only louder this time. When no one answered, Thomas walked around to the side of the house to look through the side windows while Vikki waited for Kate to answer at the door.

"Maybe she's still sleeping?" Vikki suggested as Thomas rejoined her at the front door.

"At half-past ten in the morning?" Thomas laughed nervously, "…I don't think so. I've known her my whole life and never known her to sleep past six. She's been waking up early her whole life."

"She's not feeling well, so maybe she's sleeping in?"

Thomas hadn't seen anything noteworthy through the side windows either and was trying to remain calm. Vikki, however, was becoming visibly worried.

"Maybe she's with Hunter?" Vikki asked, "…should we call him?"

Thomas inexplicably chuckled, which Vikki found odd.

"Kate is definitely not with Hunter…." Thomas replied, emphasizing the word definitely, "… he's at the Foundry training with Thurmond. Besides, I don't think Kate and Hunter have been getting along recently. I know rather than helping his Mom at work, he's been going out with some girl and hanging around with your friend, Ehndale."

It was no secret that Thomas disliked Ehndale, but his comment reminded Vikki of the power Ehndale seemed to have over everyone. Being forced to hire Hunter as Thurmond's replacement was not easy for Vikki to swallow. However, she still didn't like Thomas's insinuation that Ehndale had anything to do with Kate's deteriorating health.

"That's unfair and unappreciated, Thom," "Wait? What?" Thomas replied, unclear about what Vikki was referring to. "All I meant was…."

Vikki interrupted, "Never mind, Thom. It's not important. I'm just worried about Kate."

Vikki approached a window along the front porch and pressed her face against the glass to look inside, and asked, "Do you think it would be OK if we went inside? To see if she's OK, I mean? Maybe she fell, and she can't answer us?"

"We don't know if she's even home…." Thomas replied, "… besides, there's no indication that anything's wrong other than us knowing she's sick and not answering the door."

"Please, Thom?" Vikki implored as she clutched his arm to emphasize her eagerness to enter the house, "… we're here. We may as well check in on her. Who will it hurt? She wouldn't mind. No one would if they knew we were only trying to be conscientious."

"I guess if I called it into the station and let them know that we are just concerned about a friend and only entering to check on her…."

"They may send a squad car, Thom…." Vikki pleaded, "… I'm not sure Kate would appreciate the fuss. Let's just go in, you know, like concerned friends. I'm certain that Kate wouldn't mind that at all."

"OK. But it's still breaking and entering, V. You're my witness. I wanted to call it in first."

"Yes, Thom. I'm your witness." Vikki returned, patronizing his reluctance to deviate from formal police procedure.

They turned the handle and found that the front door was unlocked. Thomas slowly opened it, and Vikki rushed past him and ran throughout the house, calling Kate's name. As Vikki ran up the staircase, Thomas looked around for signs of anything unusual and noticed a milk carton on the counter in the kitchen and picked it up. He sniffed it and found it had soured, which meant it had been there for some time. Thomas then went to the base of the stairs to see where Vikki had gone. That's when he heard her scream.

"She's up here, Thom! Call an ambulance!"

28

Calamity

Vikki demanded to be in the ambulance with Kate, but because the medical technicians needed room to attend to her, they would not allow Vikki to ride along. Accordingly, she rode with Thomas, who followed closely behind.

The ambulance lights flashed as the sirens blared, and the vehicle ignored all traffic signals. As a result, Thomas found it difficult to keep up, so rather than trying to chase it down, he did his best to stay close but quickly lost sight of it.

Vikki began reaching out to people she thought should be notified about Kate's condition and called Thurmond's office at the Foundry, hoping that Hunter was with him. When no one answered, she had Thomas call the police dispatcher to see if they could track either of them down. While speaking with the dispatcher, Thomas also asked them to contact Fr. Elias in case things were as bad as they seemed.

The dispatcher contacted the foundry switchboard, who immediately summoned Thurmond to the operations office. When Thurmond picked up the call, he was told that Kate had been taken to the emergency room in an ambulance. Thurmond feared the worst and saw that same fear in Hunter's eyes when he relayed the news. They stopped everything they were doing and immediately left together for the hospital.

Thomas and Vikki wanted to be there when Kate was admitted, but the ambulance had gone by the time they arrived. They checked on Kate's status with the front desk and were told that Kate had been admitted and taken straight to the intensive care unit, so the despondent couple stood sullenly at the entrance to the emergency room, waiting for others to arrive.

Fr. Elias was the first to arrive and, after speaking briefly with Thomas, checked in at the front desk momentarily and promptly disappeared through a set of double doors. A short while later, Thurmond's truck pulled up in front, and Hunter jumped out before it stopped. He dashed toward Vikki and Thomas, shouting, "Where's my Mom? I need to know where she is!"

"She's in Intensive Care, Hunter…" Vikki replied.

"Take me there!" Hunter demanded. "Take me there now!"

Thomas put his hand on Hunter's shoulder and said:

"The doctors are taking good care of her son. Fr. Elias is with her right now. Let's give them a minute before we rush in."

"Fr. Elias?" Hunter screamed incredulously, "…what the hell is a priest doing in there? What aren't you telling me? Is she going to be OK? I want to see her now. Take me to her NOW!"

Hunter pulled away from Thomas and said, "…never mind. I'll find her myself…."

Thomas tried to grab Hunter's arm, but Vikki gently restrained him and softly said, "Let him go, Thom. He needs to be with his Mom."

Hunter ran wildly through the hospital, following signs directing him to the intensive care unit, and when he arrived, he found a small group of people seated in a sizable waiting room. A nurse's station was situated at the far end of the room, which stood guard in front of a set of double doors displaying a sign warning 'Authorized Personnel Only".

Hunter headed towards it immediately, and a large male nurse stepped in front of him and asked.

"Can I help you?"

"Yeah, you can get the hell out of my way, you idiot! My mother's in there, and I have to see her!"

The nurse was an imposing figure, more than capable of restraining Hunter, but was sympathetic to his urgency and replied kindly, "I completely understand, sir, but I can't let you run in. Other people have loved ones in there too."

"I don't care about them; I must see her!" Hunter yelled as he attempted to push past the nurse.

The nurse grabbed Hunter forcefully by the arm, and Hunter realized he couldn't get by. Hunter went limp from frustration and whimpered, "I have to see her..."

"I understand, sir. Let me help you find her. What's your mother's name?"

"Kate..." Hunter replied, "...Kate Harrington. My Mom's name is Katherine Harrington."

"Thank you..." the nurse said as he let go of Hunter's arm, "... if you have a seat, I'll check the log and let you know what room she's in and whether the doctor will allow you to see her."

Hunter preferred to stand and paced back and forth while the nurse scanned down a lengthy list of names on a clipboard. Hunter was impatient.

"She has a priest with her..." he said nervously, "...Please, you must let me see her. I'm very worried."

Thurmond had parked at the entrance and stepped out of his truck to talk to Thomas and Vikki. A guard stationed there told him he couldn't park there and asked him to move his vehicle away from the building. Before Thurmond left, Thomas told him they were going to the ICU and that he should meet them there after finding a place to park.

Thomas and Vikki then went to the ICU and saw Hunter at the far end of a waiting area, talking to someone at the nurses' station.

They decided to let him be and found some seats while they waited for Thurmond. A few minutes later, Thurmond came panting and asked what had happened.

"We went by Kate's house to check on her and found her in her bedroom…." Thomas explained, "…she was unconscious on the floor beside her bed. She had a terrible fever, and I think she'd been that way for a while."

"How could you tell that?" Thurmond asked.

"I found a carton of soured milk on the kitchen counter," Thomas replied.

Vikki squeezed Thomas's hand and left the two men to check on Hunter, who had stopped pacing. When she reached the nurse's station, Vikki put her arm around him, but Hunter was preoccupied and did not react. She hugged him and whispered in his ear that they were there for him, then rejoined Thomas and Thurmond in the waiting area.

The nurse found Kate's information, checked Hunter's identification, then escorted him into the ICU.

~

When the call had come into the parish office from the police dispatcher Fr. Elias excused himself from a young couple he was counseling and rushed to the hospital, where he was given a dire diagnosis of Kate's condition. She was suffering from stage IV ovarian cancer, which Fr. Elias knew meant she was terminally ill.

Kate's records showed that she had been in treatment for some time and was in remission until recently, when she experienced an aggressive recurrence. Her cancer had apparently metastasized, and the prognosis was that she didn't have much time left. The ICU doctor counseled the Priest and told him Kate's family should be notified immediately, as every effort should be made to get her affairs in order, post-haste.

Unfortunately, this was familiar territory for the Priest, and although it was heartbreaking, he knew what to do. He reached out to Kate's doctor to see who had been aware of her condition, and the doctor explained that, despite his objections, Kate had expressed a desire to keep her condition secret. Fr. Elias asked if anyone knew about her condition, and the doctor told him that Kate had made him swear not to tell anyone about it, not even her son, Hunter.

When Fr. Elias had arrived at the hospital, Thomas had told him that Hunter was on his way there with Thurmond, so it seemed the people who would need to be notified were already on their way, so it was pointless to reach out to anyone else: Things would just have to unfold as they may, Fr. Elias removed a purple silk stole from his bag, draped it across his shoulders, then pulled out some anointing oils and a pair of rosary beads, which he wrapped around his hand. Kate regained consciousness as he made the sign of the cross over her, and tears began streaming down her face.

"I need to see my son Hunter before I go," Kate whispered.

"No need to worry, dear..." the Priest reassured her, "I'm sure he's already on his way if he isn't here already."

"But he doesn't know, father..."

"You needn't worry yourself, my dear."

"Thank you, Father..." Kate replied, "... it's just that we haven't been getting along lately, and I want to tell him how much I love him and how much I'm going to miss him."

"He'll be along presently, I'm sure..." the Priest told her, "...now, do you want to make a confession?"

~

The nurses in the ICU had seen situations like Kate's many times before and were well-versed in preparing relatives for a loved one's passing. They knew it would be a roller-coaster of emotion for Hunter and did their best to calm him down so he would be prepared for what they knew was coming.

To make himself presentable, Hunter visited the lavatory before entering his mother's room, and a nurse took that opportunity to inform Fr. Elias that Kate's son would be in momentarily. The Priest thanked the nurse, then quietly mentioned Hunter's presence to Kate, which lifted her spirits.

Fr. Elias wiped the hair away from Kate's face and tidied her gown, then sat in a chair in the room's far corner. Opening his Bible to a tasseled page, Fr. Elias read as he waited for Hunter.

~

For almost an hour, Vikki, Thomas, and Thurmond sat quietly, listening half-heartedly to the hospital staff banter about work and their personal lives. Thomas knew it was their way of dealing with the stress of working in an intensive care unit. When a nurse peeked out from behind the ICU doors, she made eye contact with Thomas and motioned him over.

"You can see Mrs. Harrington now..." the nurse told him, "... but it can only be one at a time. She's very frail, and a few people are already in the room with her."

The nurse disappeared behind the doors, and Thomas looked back at his friends, who were both staring at him.

"We can see Kate now..." Thomas explained, "...but we can only go in one at a time."

They were all fearful of what they would find in Kate's room and glumly looked at each other, considering who should be first. After a few moments, Vikki suggested that it be Thurmond.

"You've spent the most time with Hunter lately, Thurmond. You should be the one in there with him now. He could use your support."

Thurmond disagreed.

"Who knows what frame of mind he's gonna be in? Besides, Kate will probably want to thank you two for helping her. You're the ones who found her and brought her here. I think it's only fitting that one of you should go first.

"I'll go..." Thomas volunteered.

Vikki couldn't allow him to bear the burden of what she expected to find. Thomas was always the one with that obligation, so she put her hand on his shoulder and said, "No, Thom. I'll go…."

There was nothing else to be said, and the two men watched as Vikki slowly entered the ICU. They silently wondered what she would find when she disappeared into the authorized area.

Vikki was directed to Kate's room and saw Fr. Elias talking to what turned out to be Kate's doctor in the hallway outside Kate's door. When they saw Vikki approaching, they stopped talking and waited for her to arrive.

The Priest's presence scared Vikki, so she wanted to focus on speaking to the doctor, but when she was close enough to talk to them, Fr. Elias was the one who greeted her.

"Nice to see you, Vikki. Thank you for coming. Kate will be happy to see you."

Vikki was more interested in answers from the doctor than exchanging pleasantries with the parish priest, so without taking her eyes off the doctor, she replied,

"Yes, hello, father, thank you…." then asked the doctor, "Before I go in, doctor, what can you tell me?"

It was evident to the Priest how determined Vikki was to be informed of Kate's medical condition, so he smiled and stood silently aside.

The doctor informed Vikki that he was Kate's physician and explained that while he had been treating Kate for her condition, she forbade him from telling anyone of her illness. He then told Vikki everything about Kate's treatments and said this wasn't a surprise. He explained that Kate knew it was only a matter of time before she was gone but had chosen to keep it a secret.

Vikki was shocked. She assumed that Kate's condition wasn't good, but she didn't expect to hear that it was terminal. She stood silent, staring blankly at the doctor in disbelief, and Fr. Elias remarked.

"In times like these, we find comfort in knowing that Kate's pain will soon end. She will be at peace in a better place, which should give us all solace."

The Priest's words provided Vikki with no comfort and served only to anger her. Resisting the temptation to lash out, Vikki pushed past the Priest and into Kate's room, where she saw Kate sleeping peacefully while Hunter stood staring out the window.

"I'm so sorry, Hunter…." she began.

Without looking at her, Hunter whispered barely loud enough for Vikki to hear him and asked, "Did you know?".

"No, Hunter. No one knew. Except for her doctor, who told me in the hall that your Mom made him promise not to tell anybody."

"Idiot!" Hunter replied, a bit louder, "How could you agree to not tell anyone that their patient, a mother, someone's friend, is dying?"

Hunter turned and walked to his Mom's bedside, where Kate lay motionless. He sat in a chair he had pulled over and took her hand while staring at her and said, "How could she be so sick, and yet no one knew? Why would she want to keep it a secret? How could I not see? How could I not know?"

Vikki empathized with Hunter. His emotions reminded Vikki of the regrets she felt when her Mom passed. But unlike Hunter, Vikki knew the answers to those questions. By choice, she had abandoned her mother and never felt the need to reconcile with her until it was too late, which was something she feared would haunt her for the rest of her life.

"You're here now, Hunter, and she knows that…." Vikki began, "…this time you have with her now is a precious gift, so make the most of it and tell her how much you love her. Tell her how much you appreciate her and everything she did for you. Tell her how much you are going to miss her."

Vikki realized she was chastising herself and began to cry.

Hunter suddenly stood and leaned over his mother. He put his ear to her lips and frantically called out for a nurse when he heard no breath. Hunter implored his mother to answer him, and Vikki ran out of the room to get a nurse's attention. When someone noticed her waving wildly, a nurse immediately rushed past her and into Kate's room.

Vikki stood out of the way and watched things progress as if in slow motion. Several more nurses rushed into the room before one burst out and ran down the hall calling for Kate's doctor. When the doctor ran back past, Vikki pushed herself up against the wall and wondered what she was supposed to do. Should she be consoling Hunter? Should she go out and tell Thurmond and Thomas what was happening?

Just then, a nurse came out of the room and ran directly up to Vikki to tell her that Kate had gone into cardiac arrest, and they were doing everything possible to resuscitate her, but they needed to get Hunter out of the room. He was frantic and, in the way, which was preventing them from trying to save Kate's life.

"We have to get him out of that room, and we have to do it now!" a nurse demanded.

Vikki nodded in acknowledgment and ran into the waiting room to get Thurmond and Thomas to help. When the two men saw Vikki crash through the doors and wave for them to follow her back into the ICU, they knew it was a bad sign and immediately jumped up and ran to meet her.

On their way to Kate's room, Vikki explained that they needed to get Hunter out of the room as quickly as possible so the doctor could help her. When they arrived, Vikki pushed the door open, and the two men rushed past her. Hunter was forcibly shoving nurses away from Kate as he shook her and yelled, "Wake up, Mom! Don't do this to me! Wake up, damn it! Wake up!"

The nurses unsuccessfully tried to restrain Hunter and immediately released him when Thurmond and Thomas entered the room. Thurmond grabbed Hunter in a bear hug as Thomas removed Hunter's grip from his mother's gown. Hunter kicked and screamed as the two men lifted him off his feet and whisked him out of the room.

When they reached the waiting room, they were met by a nurse who injected Hunter with a sedative. As they waited for the sedative to kick in, Thomas and Thurmond held Hunter until he eventually settled down.

Vikki returned to join them shortly afterward, and a doctor appeared less than ten minutes later. The friends knew the news would not be good after seeing his expression and body language. The dire prognosis of her condition was unbearably accurate, and Kate was gone by morning the following day.

29

Virulence

After his mother's death, Hunter was furious and lashed out at everyone who attempted to console him. He threatened to sue the doctor for withholding the severity of his mother's condition and the hospital for incompetence in her care. He also resented Fr. Elias for trying to convince him that this tragedy was all part of some divine plan and that his Mom's death was appropriate in some bizarre way. The priest's contention that a benevolent God had ordained it made Hunter question whether this divine being, if it even existed, wasn't just some mischievous Omnipotent that delighted in people's misery.

From Fr. Elias's experience, Hunter's unfortunate sentiment was not unusual, as doubt was a common reaction when disappointed by an unwelcome outcome. However, the priest remained steadfast in his counsel and tried to reason with Hunter while recognizing the need for consolation.

"There is no way of knowing why we should consider something like this just, my son..." the priest began, "...but there is a reason for everything under heaven. God's plan is beyond human understanding, so we must accept everything on faith."

"Bullshit!" Hunter replied, "...all I know is that my mother spent her whole life serving others, believing her hard work would pay off, and now she's dead. I don't see any reward! No payoff! Just dirt and death and nothing else."

The priest continued, undeterred.

"The pain of losing a loved one cuts deep, but we cannot presume to understand why the Lord has chosen to call your mother home. We can only have faith that there is a reason for it that we do not understand. Something may yet result from this that may never have come to pass if this had not happened. Your mother trusted in her faith and embraced the frailty of her humanity, and you can be sure she will be rewarded for it, my son."

Fr. Elias thought quoting scripture may help explain the mysteries of faith and began, "Romans 8:38-39 says, *'For I am sure that neither death, nor life, nor angels, nor principalities, nor things present, nor things to come, nor powers, nor height, nor depth, nor anything else in all creation, will be able to separate us from the love of God in Christ Jesus our Lord.'*"

"Love?" Hunter asked sarcastically, "…what kind of love justifies my Mom's death, father?"

"You misunderstand me, my son…" the priest persisted, "… God allows suffering because He knows how powerful it is to our spiritual lives. It helps us to embrace His infinite love and mercy."

The priest thought for a second and continued, "1 Peter 5:10 *'And the God of all grace, who called you to his eternal glory in Christ, after you have suffered a little while, will himself restore you and make you strong, firm and steadfast.'*"

Despite all Fr. Elias' efforts, Hunter took nothing away from his conversations with him except resentment. Hunter was not interested in continuing any dialogue with the priest, but Fr. Elias repeatedly attempted to console him. Hunter saw nothing benevolent about his mother's demise and dismissed the notion that faith had any value whatsoever. Nothing could justify his mother being taken from him or the suffering he experienced because of it. God, if there was one, had simply abandoned him and condemned him to pick up the pieces his mother had left behind. Hunter felt he was doomed to run his Mom's Diner and would be forced to abandon his lofty aspirations.

While discouraging everyone who tried to console him, Hunter showed little interest in making special arrangements for his mother's wake and funeral until Thomas and Vikki asked permission to organize something in her honor. Hunter disagreed with celebrating his mother's death, but rather than arguing with them, he reluctantly agreed and offered to assist them only if they needed his help. Nothing more.

Hunter became hardened and mechanical, handling one affair after another with dispassionate efficiency. He met with attorneys to settle his mother's affairs and remodeled her house for his use. He continued training with Thurmond at the Foundry, focused intensely on learning the business, and quickly picked things up. He had asked Ronnie to stay on at the Diner indefinitely, and because she had offhandedly expressed interest, he considered the possibility of her assuming ownership. Hunter would also disappear occasionally, which everyone thought was to spend time with his girlfriend Naomi, but that only turned out to be partially true.

~

Thurmond had been avoiding Monica at her request but felt the circumstances warranted his calling her. When he notified her of Kate's passing, Monica was devastated by the news and became understandably distraught. After reflecting for a few days on what that might mean, Monica's thoughts quickly turned to Hunter, and she decided to go to the Diner to see him and express her condolences for his loss.

Hunter had notified Ronnie of his Mom's death shortly after Kate's passing and said he would not be coming in. He asked Ronnie to take care of things at the Diner until after the burial and told her they would discuss what would happen with the business then. Ronnie hardly knew Kate, but she could tell from her customers' reactions that her loss profoundly affected the entire community.

When Monica arrived, she found that Hunter was not there and was told he had not been since his Mom's passing. She also learned that Ronnie had been running things in his absence, which was a welcome surprise. Monica remembered Ronnie mentioning that she intended to return to town, and though she was surprised to find her working at Kate's Diner, she was excited to see her new friend.

Ronnie was in her office when she was told by a waitress that Monica had stopped in to see Hunter. She immediately left the office and saw Monica at the register talking with Midge. Ronnie decided to take a few minutes to share coffee with her friend, and when she made eye contact with Monica, the two friends calmly approached each other and warmly embraced.

"How long have you been in town?' Monica inquired.

"A couple of weeks…." Ronnie explained, "Kate called to ask me to come to help her out. But I assumed she just needed a little help. I never considered it was because of her health. I could see she didn't feel well, but I had no idea how sick she was."

"What did she say?" Monica asked.

"Kate said Hunter accepted a position at the Foundry and was too busy training there to help her. She said the Diner had become swamped with business, and she couldn't manage without someone's help," Ronnie paused for a second, then continued, "I knew she was making frequent trips to the doctor, but I assumed it was for something less severe. She told me to say nothing about it, but had I known how bad it was. I would have said something. I feel foolish."

"How could you have known?" Monica replied, "From what I understand, no one knew. There's nothing you could have done."

"I didn't know her well, but I thought she looked ill…." Ronnie admitted, "…she never once mentioned how serious her condition was. I should have known, though. All the signs were there, but I never asked. "

"Nonsense, Ronnie. It's a shame, is all." Monica replied, "It's not your fault. It was all just so sudden. There was nothing you could have done."

"I guess..." Ronnie contritely agreed.

Monica wanted to shift the conversation away from Ronnie's guilt and asked how Hunter was handling the loss of his mother. Ronnie took a long drink of coffee and replied, "He's not been himself since even before his Mom passed."

"How so?" Monica inquired.

"When I first arrived, Hunter seemed a little annoyed by having to work at the Diner, but it got progressively worse. He argued with Kate about working more hours because of her absence and stopped coming in when he knew she was homesick. Eventually, Hunter stopped coming in altogether, and when I asked Kate about it, she said he had accepted a job at the Foundry. So, whether he's working there or not, I haven't seen him since Kate passed."

Ronnie stopped to take a sip of her coffee and continued, "... and from what I've heard, he also has a girlfriend, so I guess he's probably spending some time with her too."

As Ronnie spoke, she considered whether she should mention her brief conversations with Hunter about the possibility of her taking over the business but decided it was a bit premature and said instead, "Hunter's a determined kid. He is always thinking about what he's going to do next. Speaks with no one but me about the Diner and won't speak to anyone about his Mom's passing. He's still pretty angry about it. Fr. Elias came by the other day to talk with him, but Hunter threw the priest out of the Diner."

Monica had had her own issues with the priest, but she was astonished by Hunter's actions. She replied, "I'm sure Fr. Elias was only trying to help."

"Can't help those who don't help themselves..." Ronnie returned, "... I'd avoid Hunter until he's finished grieving. He's not himself and more than a bit unpleasant at the moment."

Monica took her friend's counsel to heart but was still interested in conveying her condolences to Hunter, even if she couldn't tell him directly. She concluded that since Fr. Elias had been speaking with Hunter, even though it was contentious, the priest was persistent and still likely her best approach. Monica thanked Ronnie for the coffee and company and left the Diner to make her way to the rectory.

~

"Everyone grieves in their own way, Mona...." the priest began, "... the young man is understandably distraught. His apathy seems to be his way of hiding his pain."

"When you spoke with him, Father, did he express grief?"

"He did..." Fr. Elias remarked, then explained, "...and frustration in accepting God's plan. Oddly enough, he was more upset about having been left with the responsibility of handling his mother's affairs than her loss, a callous and selfish reaction, to be sure. He'll get past that in time, though, and when he does, he can truly grieve for his mother and appreciate the Legacy she has left for him. Rest assured; God has a plan for that young man. Hunter just needs to surrender to God's divine providence. When he does, he'll be fine."

Fr. Elias gave Monica cause to think about her life and the recent odd turns it had taken. She thanked the priest for his kind and thoughtful words and asked him to relay her condolences to Hunter when he saw him. Monica left, reassured that Hunter would eventually be OK, wondering if the same could be said for her.

~

Kate's wake was held at Vikki's home for three days, where no expense was spared to make it a memorable experience for those that came to pay their respects. Though most of the town came, Hunter was not seen until the funeral. Gossip abounded, but Vikki and Thomas made every effort to focus on paying respects to Kate and not her son's unusual behavior.

The church filled beyond capacity for Kate's funeral, and people who could not get in stood on boxes outside in the pouring rain, peering through the windows to watch the ceremony. Though the weather wasn't cooperating, the stained-glass windows still glowed with brilliant colors that washed the entire inside of the church, including the mountains of flowers that adorned the altar.

Fr. Elias celebrated a magnificent mass featuring a fabulous choir that Vikki had brought in. Hunter sat stoically in the front pew staring blankly at his mother's casket with Ronnie and Vikki on either side. The sisters supported him by touching his hand and holding his arm without the slightest reaction from Hunter.

Thurmond gave a touching eulogy with help from his friend Emerson, who added a bit of humor that almost everyone appreciated. When the ceremony was complete, a stout bagpiper could be heard from outside the church wailing a Celtic dirge as he stood fast in the steady rain. The bag piper finished the lamentation and began playing Amazing Grace, instantly making people cry. A half dozen pallbearers, including Thomas, Thurmond, and Emerson, carried Kate's casket out of the church as everyone filtered out behind them. Monica approached Hunter to express her sympathy, but he didn't acknowledge her in any way and continued blankly staring at his mother's casket as he followed it out of the church and across the front lawn.

Mourners gathered around the Hearse as they loaded Kate's coffin into it. The funeral director had his staff load flowers from the church into the Hearse as the driver prepared to lead the procession to the cemetery. People randomly dispersed to their vehicles and lined up orderly behind the lead limousine, where Hunter should have been with Vikki and Thomas. Hunter, however, had unexpectedly slipped into the front seat of the Hearse, where he silently sat motionless, waiting for the burial procession to begin. Thomas rode with Vikki in the lead limo, followed by Thurmond in his truck with Emerson, then Monica and Ronnie behind them. Vehicles lined up until enough had assembled that the funeral director motioned for the hearse driver to begin Kate's journey to her final resting place.

~

A blanket of gray clouds ran low and swift across the cemetery treetops as the steady rain transformed into a light, swirling mist. The long train of cars navigated slowly through the cemetery behind Kate's Hearse along a modest gravel path. Thomas studied headstones for familiar names out the window of his limousine while Vikki reflected on her mother's recent burial. They became lost in their thoughts until their limo stopped beside a mausoleum.

When Thomas saw that the Hearse had gone ahead, he asked why they hadn't followed. Their driver explained that there wasn't enough space between the headstones for more than one car to park beside it, so they would have to walk from where they were. The driver then excused himself and began walking down the line of cars parked behind them to explain to everyone what was happening.

Thomas could tell from where the Hearse was parked that the gravesite was not far ahead, so he grabbed his umbrella, opened Vikki's door, and took her hand to help her out. Everyone behind them followed suit as Vikki stepped out under the umbrella. They waited for Thurmond, Emerson, Monica, and Ronnie, then led the procession on foot to where the Hearse had stopped ahead of them.

Hunter stood beside his mother's headstone, staring blankly into her empty grave as her coffin was carefully placed in a harness above it for the interment ceremony. As the group approached the gravesite, Thomas asked Hunter how he was doing, and without ever looking up, Hunter replied:

"That's a stupid question. What do you think?"

"We're just concerned about you, Hunter is all," Vikki replied, defending Thomas' honest concern.

"I don't need your sympathy or concern…." Hunter barked in reply as he moved his blank stare from the empty grave to Vikki, "…I need answers, and I don't have any."

"Answers to what, Hunter?"

"Why did this have to happen? How I'm going to manage without her? What I'm going to do now?"

Ronnie and Monica both interpreted Hunter's questions as a testament to how much his mother meant to him, but they soon changed their opinion when Hunter continued.

"Why did she do this to me? She knew she was dying. She did this on purpose. Why else would she ask me to help her? Damn her, she knew I didn't want to be stuck running her stupid Diner. My Legacy, my ass!'"… he said mockingly, then continued, "… You all remember what you want about my Mom, and mourn her how you please, but to me, she will always be the one who ruined my life!"

Hunter's shocking attitude towards his mother had all her close friends mortified, and none had anything to say. Still, his unjust comments made each of them consider their personal relationship with Kate, which they all felt to have been a privilege, regardless of her son's opinions of her. Her sage counsel, kindness, and tremendous generosity had provided them with material and spiritual comfort. Consequently, the group left Hunter to wrestle with his emotions and focus on paying their respects to their dear friend, which was why they were there.

~

Fr. Elias finished his final prayers for Kate, and the piper Vikki had requested to play at the gravesite flooded the cemetery with the song 'Going Home' in Kate's honor. Mourners lined up to pick flowers from the floral arrangements brought from the church and then tossed them into Kate's grave after her coffin had been lowered into it. People consoled each other by sharing tears, hugs, and kisses as the sound of bagpipes swept through the misty cemetery.

When the ceremony had ended, Thomas invited everyone back to the Diner for a repast prepared by Ronnie in Kate's honor. Ronnie left first with Monica and Emerson to greet everyone when they arrived at the Diner. As people returned to their cars, Thurmond remained behind with Hunter beside his mother's grave, waiting for him to acknowledge his presence before he said anything. Thurmond had spent a lot of time with Hunter recently and felt it was his place to talk to him about dealing with the loss of his mother. When the last of the crowd had all gone, Thurmond broke the silence between the two men.

"You know, son, your Mom only wanted what's best for you…."

"She had a funny way of showing it," Hunter replied, finally looking up from his mother's grave to address Thurmond.

"How do you mean?" Thurmond asked.

"Would she have asked me to work with her if she wasn't sick?"

Thurmond sympathetically replied, "As I understand it, son, you told your Mom you saw no future for yourself there, so your Mom respected your wishes when she didn't ask you for help until she absolutely needed it."

"Right, I think she planned to bring me back all along. She used her illness to lure me back there, like a spider. She knew if she was sick, I couldn't say no. I had to go back."

"But you already left the Diner when you accepted the position at the foundry…." Thurmond replied, "…you were already gone."

Hunter began kicking dirt into his mother's grave over the flowers that sprinkled color across the top of her coffin.

"It's actually pretty simple, Mr. Joseph…." Hunter began, "…my Mom made me think it was only temporary when her plan all along was to keep me there."

Thurmond was confused and asked, "How do you figure, son?"

"In a million years…." Hunter began, "…I would never have agreed to return if I knew how sick she was. She knew that but kept it from me anyway. It was selfish of her to keep that from me."

Thurmond began to get the distinct impression that Hunter was being counseled by someone. His logic sounded familiar. Hunter continued.

"…When I approached Ronnie about helping at the Diner so I could leave to work at the Foundry, my Mom got desperate and let her health deteriorate. She knew that would leave me no choice but to come back, where she could trap me and force me to live out her Legacy at the Diner."

Thurmond understood Hunter's logic but vehemently disagreed.

"You mean to tell me that your Mom planned to get sick and die just to stick you with the Diner? That's just plain wrong, son."

"Is it?" Hunter asked as he began kicking more and more dirt into his mother's grave. "Don't you get it? She knew what I wanted, but she didn't care. She did it for herself! She planned this! This is the life she wanted for me. Not the life I wanted!"

Thurmond was surprised at how selfish Hunter was acting and decided to give him some advice of his own.

"You can always sell the place, son. You're not stuck with it. Your Mom probably hoped you'd feel connected to it, seeing as she built it up from nothing, but you can do whatever you want. It's yours. Keep it or sell it. That's not a trap; it's an inheritance."

Hunter stopped kicking dirt, stood perfectly still, stared directly at Thurmond, and said:

"So, it's like Mr. Ehndale said then, just some sick joke God is playing on me. Taking my mother from me, I'm stuck making pennies running her stupid Diner when I should be making dollars out working on my own!"

Thurmond thought the logic sounded familiar, and mentioning Ehndale's name confirmed it. With an unmistakable tone of severity in his voice Thurmond replied.

"Listen here, son, and you listen good. That man is evil and will do anything to get his way. He doesn't care about you. He's the spider. He's the one who is luring you into his trap."

Hunter replied, almost laughing, "It's funny you say that because Mr. Ehndale told me you'd say something like that."

"If that man is giving you advice, then following it has a good chance of being beneficial for him and bad for you. That I know for certain from my own personal experience."

Hunter smirked and rolled his eyes, which Thurmond knew meant he wasn't getting anywhere with his argument about Ehndale. He decided to leave Hunter with some final thoughts and said:

"Listen, son, I know you're mad, but you can't be careless. You need time to think clearly. You should consider talking to someone who really cares about you. Someone like Fr. Elias, not Mr. Ehndale, blaming God for your troubles is irresponsible and wrong. That only serves to turn you away from the truth. I've learned that evil may be obscure, but it's out there, and Mr. Ehndale is one of its purveyors. He's skilled at muddying the truth and hiding behind lies and promises of easy success. His advice may seem well-intentioned, but following it can be dangerous, and it's never easily undone. Stay away from him, Hunter! That man is trouble! I'd even say he's evil!"

30

Lament

Kate's absence at the Diner was palpable. Everyone in town was saddened by her sudden passing, and initially, it was difficult to imagine the place without her. Hunter made no attempt to alleviate this sense of loss, and other than asking Ronnie to take over its operation while he figured out what he would do with the place, he did nothing.

Conversely, Ronnie embraced the opportunity and took over the operation seamlessly. She worked diligently to increase her familiarity with the Diner's patrons, and they slowly became accustomed to her running the place. Things eventually returned to normal, and in relatively short order, the customers stopped talking about Kate's absence and resumed their regular routines as if nothing had changed.

~

Thurmond drove Emerson to the Diner on his way to work every morning whenever he was in town. Emerson enjoyed his friend's company and listened to Thurmond confide in him about the things troubling him. One morning, Thurmond dropped him off after a lengthy conversation about Monica, and Emerson saw her sitting alone at a table near some of his friends, reading. Emerson hadn't seen Monica since Kate's repast and wanted to say hello. He thought she still looked glum, so he endeavored to approach her with care out of respect for her privacy and mollified his usual comedic entrance.

Monica never noticed him, but as he approached her, Emerson heard his friends at a nearby table discussing the benefits of pasteurization. He couldn't resist. When he was close enough to be heard by them, he interrupted their conversation and said, "Processed milk ain't milk, fellas. It's missing bits. It's like a creek without water. Don't know 'bout you, but I'd call that a ditch!"

A few of his friends smirked at his joke, and as he glanced at Monica, Emerson noticed her smile. Emerson pulled an empty chair away from his friend's table and sat on it to face Monica, and said, "Howdy, Mona. How's by you?"

Monica was happy to see her quirky friend but was not interested in any company. She could tell Emerson was only trying to cheer her up, so she politely replied.

"Morning, Emerson. I'm well, thank you, how are you?"

"Not as good as I'd like, but better than I deserve..." Emerson replied as he swept both arms down the front of his overalls and added, "...been getting more work than you can shake a stick at lately. Must look like I been through a goat roping."

Monica laughed at her friend and decided to invite him to join her, but after his conversation with Thurmond on the way in that morning, Emerson understood that Monica was probably just being friendly and likely preferred being alone. He shook his head and said:

"Thank ya kindly, Mona, but just thought I'd say howdy. I'm off in a minute. Elroy's pickin' me up. Needs help at school. Kids stuffed the toilets with all manner of things, and they been flowin' over ever since. Elroy's busier than a one-armed paper hanger and asked me to lend him a hand cleaning up the mess."

Emerson nodded at Monica, stood, returned his chair to his friend's table, and rejoined their conversation, which had morphed into a discussion about the benefits of animal fat in your diet. As she sipped her coffee, the thought of her ridiculous friend made Monica smile, and she slipped back into the book she'd been reading. Suddenly a familiar voice interrupted her concentration.

"Nice to see you again, Mona."

Monica put down her book and turned to see Ronnie standing behind her, wearing an apron and holding a mop.

"I didn't see you," Monica said apologetically.

"No worries, Mona," Ronnie replied, "I was going through some paperwork when one of the girls told me you were here. I just wanted to come over and say hello."

Suddenly, Emerson jumped to his feet, pushed his chair away from the table with the back of his legs, and excused himself from his friends. He hurried through the Diner, bumping into several tables and spilling various drinks. He rushed out the door and jumped into the front seat of a red pickup truck waiting out front, which Monica took to be the aforementioned 'Elroy.'

The two women watched in amusement, and Ronnie couldn't resist the temptation to add a bit of her own humor. She held out the mop in front of her and said:

"…they also told me Emerson was here, so I brought a mop, just in case."

Both women began laughing, and Ronnie asked if she could join her. Monica happily agreed, and Ronnie turned a chair around and straddled it precisely as Kate used to do. Ronnie looked towards the counter and motioned to a waitress, who brought a carafe of coffee and two mugs to their table. She filled both cups and pushed one in front of Monica, and said, "I enjoyed our conversation the other day and was wondering if you wanted to talk some more."

Monica had avoided Thurmond at Kate's repast, fearing they may quarrel over one thing or another, and gravitated to her new friend Ronnie, whose company she enjoyed. One topic they discussed was poetry, which Monica enjoyed immensely.

"Now that you mention it," Monica replied, "…I didn't want to say anything at the risk of appearing ignorant, but I was rather confused by some of the poetry you suggested I read."

"Which poet?" Ronnie asked.

"Donne…" Monica replied, "…I was intrigued by our discussion about the metaphysical poets and became interested in learning more about that genre. Being a romantic myself, I was curious about the difference between the two. I had difficulty interpreting some of his meanings."

Ronnie smiled. Being a teacher of younger students did not allow her to engage in discussions like this, and she relished the opportunity to do so. Ronnie turned her chair around and settled in for a deep dive into the metaphysical. She continued.

"I suppose you could say all romantic poetry is metaphysical, but Romanticism grew from an interest in promoting liberty and individualism. Metaphysical poetry is much broader than that, and it tends to be a bit ambiguous."

"So, the intention is to confuse you?" Monica asked.

"Not exactly…" Ronnie replied, laughing, "…I believe the intention is to stimulate debate. To persuade…or to argue. It's a matter of opinion when dealing beyond the physical, which leaves room for interpretation."

"I see…" Monica replied, then, from memory, began to recite one of the poems Ronnie had suggested she read:

As virtuous men pass mildly away,

And whisper to their souls to go,

Whilst some of their sad friends do say

The breath goes now, and some say, No:

So let us melt and make no noise,

No tear-floods, nor sigh-tempests move;

'Twere profanation of our joys

To tell the laity our love

When she had finished reciting the poem, Monica asked, "What do you think Donne meant by 'profanation of our joys? That's a bit confusing to me, I must admit."

"I'm impressed!" Ronnie said as she smiled at Monica's recitation, then repeated a small phrase, "Twere profanation of our joys, To tell the laity our love."

"Interesting, isn't it?" Ronnie remarked, "…metaphysical poems are very personal and subject to interpretation. To me, he's talking about faith, but my interpretation of Donne's meaning may differ greatly from yours."

"I can see that." Monica agreed, and Ronnie continued, "In the context of Donne's comparisons between the physical beauty of nature and the spiritual significance of our existence, his phrase 'the profanation of our joys' refers to the degradation of something worthy of respect, as I interpret it. In context to the entirety of the poem, I believe he's referring to a sort of cheapening, saying that regardless of what others think of your feelings for something, or someone, those feelings are sacred, and though they may differ from others, they do not require a defense."

"I see…" Monica replied, "…but is it solely about recognizing the importance of something or someone that is permanently lost, like to death?" Monica asked.

"You could certainly say that…." Ronnie continued, "…a lost connection, as Donne implies, could certainly be one caused by death, but I think it can be broader than that. As I said, I think he's talking about faith. Faith in something or in someone."

Ronnie's response made Monica wonder about Thurmond, and she asked:

"In the instance of a 'someone'…." Monica continued, "…can a loss be profound if the 'someone' that's lost is still living? Is that spiritual, physical, or both?"

"How do you mean?" Ronnie asked, and Monica replied, "I mean, I think it implies a lost connection or a distance that develops between people. Like when lovers are separated; by death, or for some other reason."

Ronnie was suspicious of Monica's line of questions and sensed it had something to do with Thurmond. She had seen the couple quarreling and felt a growing tension between them. She wanted to be careful not to impose her opinions by offering advice, so she just listened and waited for an opportunity to provide emotional support to her friend without giving her any suggestions about what she should do. Monica continued, "In the case of lovers being separated by death, I understand how physical separation can create distance between them. That kind of loss is unrecoverable, both spiritually and physically, but can a loss of love in a relationship be as profound?"

"I imagine so,' Ronnie responded, "…but I don't think that's profound enough for Donne. It seems too shallow, mostly because the loss could be recovered and is not necessarily permanent. It can be regained."

Ronnie picked her coffee mug up with two hands to take a sip, leaned back in her chair, and crossed her legs before continuing.

"For me, I believe Donne is saying some permanence is required for it to truly be profound. There has to be a permanent separation to make the loss of a spiritual connection profound. At least, that's how Donne presents it in the poem. "

Monica did not reply.

Ronnie's interpretation did not lend Monica insight into how she should approach the weakening connection she had been experiencing with Thurmond. On the contrary, it only made her question whether the expectations she had for her relationship with him were realistic, expecting him to somehow convince her that he wasn't capable of disappointing her again while she hung on to the doubt that he could ever be able to give her enough assurances.

Monica loved Thurmond, but she wanted to protect herself, and it seemed her forgiveness of Thurmond's transgressions had alleviated his anxiety, but it had only strengthened hers. She wondered if their deteriorating relationship wasn't entirely her fault. Whether she was just jealous of his new adventure because it didn't involve her, she thought perhaps she couldn't trust him because she could never truly forgive him for his indiscretions.

Whatever it was, Monica was unsure of herself and couldn't tell Thurmond what he needed to do to improve it, no matter how much he begged her to. She knew Thurmond would do anything to save their relationship, but there was nothing he could do. It was all her, and she knew it. Monica either needed to come to grips with her emotions and accept him and the situation for what it was or abandon him and move on.

Ronnie noticed Monica fall deep into thought and smiled. She took a long sip of coffee, then said, "Heavy, isn't it?"

Monica suddenly realized she had momentarily gotten lost in her thoughts and apologized for becoming distracted. Ronnie laughed and replied, "I'm always amazed at the poignancy of poetry."

"Very true," Monica replied.

Half-jokingly, Ronnie returned, "It also helps if you can find someone else who reads it. I've always had difficulty finding anyone I can converse with that would have any idea of what I'm talking about."

Both women laughed out loud.

"Thank you for that, Ronnie," Monica replied, "…I believe you have unmasked the riddle I've been wrestling with, at least regarding Mr. Donne's work."

"You are very welcome!" Ronnie replied, "My pleasure."

Both women sat quietly, thinking momentarily while enjoying their coffee.

Ronnie had noticed Monica's cautious and careful interactions with Thurmond during Kate's repast and sensed that something significant had either happened or was about to happen. She wanted to say something to comfort Monica but wasn't sure how to bring it up without being presumptuous.

The phone rang, and Midge waved at the two women to let Ronnie know the call was for her. Ronnie held up one finger, collected her cup and the carafe, stood, and said, "I believe someone once said that advice was like Castor oil, easy to give but terrible to take…."

Monica smiled, and Ronnie continued.

"I don't want to impose, Mona, and I know it's none of my business, but I can see you're hurting, and I don't believe it's only because of Kate. Don't get me wrong, I know that's enough to upset anyone, but I see how you and Thurmond have been acting towards each other lately, and I can sense that something's amiss."

Monica was not surprised by her friend's remarkably astute observation. She clasped her hands together before placing them in her lap and listened as her emotions began welling inside her. Ronnie continued:

"It's presumptuous of me to say, I know, but I care for you, and I just wanted you to know that there's always light at the end of even the deepest, darkest tunnel."

"Thank you for that, Ronnie…." Monica replied, as she began crying, "…you are an incredibly perceptive and kind person."

Ronnie had wanted to console rather than illuminate, so when Monica began to cry, Ronnie knew their conversation needed to end. Ronnie gently put her hand on Monica's shoulder, thought for a moment, and, before leaving to take her phone call, quoted Shakespeare and said:

"The course of true love never did run smooth."

~

Monica left the Diner to help clear her head and decided to go for a walk. She knew Thurmond was leaving for Taipei soon and didn't know what to do. There was a lot to consider and not much time to do so.

As she strolled down the street, she became lost in her thoughts again and unintentionally wandered toward her home. When she arrived there, she found a letter in the mailbox beside the front door and opened it with the nervous anticipation that it was from Thurmond.

It wasn't.

"You have been identified as the person to be notified in the event of an emergency or accident. Regrettably, we must inform you of your sister's untimely passing. Please contact our office for further details and to make arrangements for her remains."

Monica dropped the note and stood frozen in disbelief. After a few moments, she picked it back up to see if the message had changed somehow.

It hadn't.

31

Sisters

News of the untimely death of Monica's younger sister Isabella was heart-wrenching. 'Bella,' as she was affectionately called, was the third of four sisters and the closest to Monica in age. Intelligent and industrious, Bella was unrelenting in her pursuits and had always felt that others' needs were more important than her own. Although she was petite, she possessed a gargantuan personality and was well-respected by her peers. She was married to her work, so she never had time for a family, but everyone who met her loved her.

Bella had dedicated her life to helping others and worked through medical school without taking a penny from her parents. When she became a Doctor, she turned down several high-paying jobs at prestigious Institutions to join an international medical group committed to helping less fortunate people worldwide. That decision eventually cost her her life when a medical outpost she had been assigned to was viciously attacked in a regional conflict.

Monica knew that, given Bella's occupation, it was always possible that her life could be in danger. However, it was particularly disheartening to Monica that her prayers for her sister's safety had been in vain. She assumed she had been the only one notified of Bella's passing and immediately contacted her two remaining siblings to relay the news.

~

After her parents' death, Monica tried to remain close to her sisters, but their lives drifted apart as they grew older. Lynda, who preferred to be called Lynn, was the youngest sister, and Sydney the eldest. Their mother often referred to these two as the 'Bookends,' but the name inferred more than just their position amongst the siblings in age. They were considerably different in many ways and had always been at odds. Monica hoped they could put their differences aside when burying their sister Bella and invited them both home.

The sisters received the news of Bella's death quite differently. Lynda was shocked and saddened and immediately agreed to come home. However, Sydney reacted as if it were a nuisance that Bella had died and complained about the inconvenience and expense of traveling. She insisted accommodation be made for her, which did not include staying with Lynda. In fact, Sydney made such a fuss that Monica decided to pay for her sister's flight and booked a room at a fancy hotel to satisfy her demands.

As the eldest, Sydney believed she had the right to approve or deny every arrangement for Bella, even though she did not intend to make any of them herself. Disappointed but unsurprised, Monica told Sydney she had no say if she didn't help. In response, Sydney threatened not to accompany her sisters to receive Bella's remains at the airport if she wasn't in charge. Monica considered it unfortunate, but rather than acquiesce to her sister's typical bullying, she told Sydney she would let her know if she had any questions.

Lynn was particularly strong-willed and was fun to be around if she liked you. She often teased Sydney about being adopted and would remark that they shared nothing in common but being on the same planet. She believed that Monica should take the lead in making arrangements for Bella and offered to help however she could. When she learned of Sydney's demands, she warned Monica to 'avoid the gravitational negativity that emanated from her.'

~

Lynn graciously accepted the offer to stay at Monica's home after being assured of enough room for her and her husband. Lynn also mentioned that she was taking advantage of the opportunity and would drive there to see a bit of the country, so Monica had no idea when they would arrive.

Sydney was the first to appear in town and arrived on an early morning flight. Monica picked her up at the airport and drove her to the hotel where she would stay. Sydney demanded that she remain with her while inspecting the accommodations, then had Monica run errands for her while she settled in.

While juggling arrangements for Bella, Monica spent several days attending to Sydney's needs. On an errand requiring her to return home, she was surprised to see Lynn sitting on the porch, chatting with a man she assumed to be her husband. Monica had never met him and was anxious to know the kind of man her free-spirited sister would marry.

Monica slowly pulled into the driveway, and when Lynn saw her, she hopped off the porch and stood waiting beside her husband. When Monica exited her vehicle, the sisters immediately ran toward each other and embraced, sharing overwhelming grief for their tremendous loss.

"I can't believe she's gone." Lynn whispered as she released her embrace, "We never got to see her. Hell, I didn't even know where she was half the time. It used to be that just knowing she was alive was enough, but now she's gone, and we don't even have that."

"She gave her life for what she believed in Lynn...." Monica replied, wiping away the tears from her cheeks, ".... She would want us to celebrate her life, not mourn its loss. Bella knew the risks, and although there's little solace in that, who knows how many people she's helped? She's a saint! I have no doubt in my mind that she is in heaven."

"Yes, she is!" Lynn replied emphatically, "Makes me cringe to think of how much less a person I am compared to her."

"Nonsense, Lynn! Each of us contributes in our own way. Bella would tell me that every time I spoke with her."

"Even Sydney?" Lynn asked sarcastically.

"That's not fair, Lynn, and you know it. Sydney has had a hard life."

"A hard life caused by her own bad decisions and callousness!" Lynn replied, "…she has no one to blame for her troubles but herself. She's a victim of her own hostility!"

Monica knew Lynn was right about Sydney but wasn't interested in discussing it. To change the discussion, she looked to Lynn's husband, Jack, who had been standing at a respectful distance to let the sisters mourn privately, and with an enthusiastic smile, she exclaimed.

"It's nice to meet you, Jack! How was the drive?"

"I'm very sorry for your loss Mona…." Jack returned somberly, "…I can't imagine how difficult it must be for you guys. I'm glad we could be here, so you and Lynn have each other to go through this together."

"Thank you, Jack, and I'm glad you could make it here with Lynn. That means the world to me. I'm sure you had to make sacrifices to be here."

"It's really nothing, Mona…" Jack replied, "…this is more important than anything I was doing. I wanted to come. I actually asked Lynn if I could."

"And I'm delighted you did," Monica replied as she walked over and kissed him before embracing him tightly.

~

Lynn had married early in life but was widowed at a young age. Her first husband was tragically killed in combat overseas, and she was left alone to raise an infant son Stephen, named after his father. To support herself and her baby, Lynn took a job as a bookkeeper for a construction company, where she met Jack, a kind and respectful man with a rapier wit. After only a short while, Jack fell madly in love with her and eventually convinced her that marrying him was in her 'best interest.'

Monica had learned from Lynn that when Jack was a youth, his parents recognized that traditional schooling was not his strength and enrolled him in a trade school to learn how to be a carpenter, as his grandfather had been. After a brief apprenticeship, Jack became a journeyman and eventually opened his own home-building business, where he worked tirelessly to make it successful. He eventually sold his share of the company to his partners for a tidy sum and retired briefly before marrying Lynn.

Soon after their marriage, Jack started another construction company at Lynn's insistence, to 'keep him out of trouble,' as Lynn liked to say. They had a son together named Jonathan, who, at only 13, had already begun working for his father, along with his three older brothers, Simon, and Andrew, from Jack's previous marriage, and Lynn's son, Stephen.

Monica admired Lynn as much as she had her sister Bella, but for entirely different reasons. Bella was modest and mild, while Lynn was an extrovert with an infectious personality. Persistent, resilient, and fearless. Nothing was unattainable or unmanageable for Lynn; she was a force of nature.

The couple's gusto for life was insatiable and infectious. They were always up for an adventure and would take vacations to unusual places to experience new and challenging things. They were the perfect remedy for Monica's melancholy, and she was relieved they had come to help her through this difficult period.

~

Sydney believed that being the eldest fated her to fend for herself, which made her bitter and resentful of her sisters. She regarded Monica as weak and loathed her self-deprecating manner, even when Monica was trying to accommodate her wishes. She believed

Monica craved sympathy and thought her kindness was self-serving. Consequently, Sydney never expressed gratitude or appreciation for anything Monica did for her.

Jealous of Bella's appearance, friends, and occupation, Sydney viewed Bella's life as unfairly easy. She also resented her family's tremendous affinity for her and considered her spoiled and undeserving. And then there was Lynn, who served as a constant reminder of her shortcomings, if not with her words, then by her deeds and ability to enjoy her life, no matter what it threw at her.

Lynn believed Monica's consideration for their virulent sister, Sydney, was useless and said as much every time Monica made any concessions or accommodations for her whatsoever. This only exacerbated the situation and always precipitated a confrontation between Sydney and Lynn, which sometimes became physical.

Monica would try to play the peacemaker, despite Lynn's insistence that it was a waste of her time. It had always been this way between the sisters. None of them, including Monica, had any reason to believe it would ever be any different, although Monica would continue to try.

~

While her sisters made arrangements for Bella, Sydney decided to see if there was anything to do in her dumpy, yokel hometown. She put on a floral print dress, some costume jewelry, and an excessive amount of makeup she had brought with her.

Sydney exited the hotel and stood at the curb, trying to hail a cab, but was quickly discouraged when she didn't see any. She went back into the lobby and demanded they provide one for her, and the concierge had a cab out front of the hotel within minutes.

"Where to, ma'am?" the driver asked Sydney as she slipped into the cab's rear seat.

"I'm not sure…." Sydney said, looking into her compact to check her appearance, "…I don't know what to expect from a place like this. I guess just drive me around town until we see something worth looking into."

"Yes, Ma'am…" the driver said, and without making any suggestions or asking any further questions, he headed towards the center of town.

On the way, Sydney noticed the enormous Foundry smokestacks in the distance that she remembered from her childhood and asked the driver if he knew anything about how the company was doing. The driver explained how recent events at the Foundry had profoundly affected the local economy and mentioned how they had expanded operations to Asia. Sydney was shocked that there could be anything of interest in her hometown and asked him to drive by the Foundry.

The cab stopped where the road intersected another that ran along the endless chain-linked fence delineating the perimeter of the vast parking lot. Sydney stared at the enormous chimneys she had seen from miles away, which she saw sprouting from a cluster of expansive brick buildings.

"I never knew what they did there…" she admitted, "…what is it that they make?"

"Engine parts Ma'am… "the driver replied, "…airplane turbine engine parts."

Sydney sat peering out the cab window and suddenly realized she was hungry.

"I don't recall if we ever had any here, but can you take me to a nice restaurant? Nothing too fancy or expensive. Just someplace with a little ambiance where I can get something to eat that doesn't make me ill."

The driver made a U-turn and drove away from the Foundry towards the town center. When they arrived at Main Street Green, Sydney saw a church steeple behind some houses that she imagined marked the church where Monica had arranged for Bella's services. Sydney had abandoned her Christian faith long ago and had become what she called a 'committed non-practicing agnostic,' the meaning of which only she understood.

Sydney snickered under her breath about the foolishness of faith as they continued driving through town. They eventually turned down a side street, and the driver pointed at a restaurant's canopy and said, "Cay Pham, Ma'am…"

The restaurant's maître d', Kenny (aka Albrecht), was a classmate of Monica's who had always hopelessly pined over her. He remembered Mona's sister Isabella from high school and had heard about her passing. Kenny intended to convey his condolences for her loss but had not seen Monica for some time. When Sydney entered the restaurant, he immediately recognized the resemblance and wondered if this woman was a relative who had returned to town for Bella's funeral.

Kenny didn't know how to breach the subject of Bella's passing without being awkward about it and decided to ask if this woman had a reservation, hoping he could learn her name and confirm her identity. When he asked her about the reservation, Sydney quickly looked around the restaurant and sarcastically asked why a reservation would be required when no one was there.

While Kenny tried to figure out how else to ask her who she was, Sydney spotted an open stool near one end of the bar. Annoyed by the delay, Sydney curtly conveyed her preference to eat there and snatched a menu from Kenny's hand. Embarrassed, Kenny smiled nervously at the woman as she sauntered to the bar.

When Sydney settled in on the stool, she quickly ordered a drink and began fussily looking over the menu. A deep, bellowing voice addressed her as she critically studied the entrees.

"I pray you don't mind the imposition, my dear, but I will say that you bear a striking resemblance to someone I know."

Sydney turned to see who had addressed her and saw a tall, well-dressed, handsome man in a bowler cap standing behind her whom she hadn't noticed there before. He continued, "I don't suppose you are related to the town librarian, perchance?"

Sydney smiled at him and thought her evening might not be a total failure after all.

~

Ronnie had learned of Bella's passing from Monica and relayed the news to her sister, Vikki. Vikki assumed Thurmond had been made aware of the tragedy but was surprised when he became visibly upset after she mentioned it to him offhandedly.

Thurmond had never met Isabella, but he could only imagine the magnitude of Mona's loss because of how she had spoken of her little sister. He understood how difficult it must have been for Monica but was terribly hurt that she had not shared the news of her loss with him herself.

There didn't seem to be any way of expressing his sympathy without upsetting Monica, so as difficult as it had been for him, Thurmond decided to give her the space she had requested and allow her to grieve without him. He knew he could offer her emotional support and was frustrated that his help was being refused.

~

Lynn dreaded receiving her little sister's remains but knew Monica would not impose such an unwelcome task on her. Sydney's position was clear on the matter, so Lynn insisted on meeting the plane with Monica rather than letting her go alone. With Jack as their chauffeur, they followed an empty hearse to the airport to gather the remains of their beloved sister, Isabella.

After receiving her remains, Jack followed the hearse back to the funeral home, where Mona and Lynn planned for Bella with the director. When they'd finished, Jack drove them to meet Fr. Elias at St. Anselm's rectory to discuss the details of Bella's funeral services. They were graciously received and settled into the front parlor, where Mrs. McGillicuddy served them tea and blueberry scones.

Jack was not religious, and although he was not uncomfortable with being in the rectory, he spent his time there looking for an opportunity to excuse himself. Fr. Elias joined them a few minutes later and immediately began consoling them.

"Take heart, my dear friends…" he began, "… your sister may seem lost to us because she is no longer in our lives in the way in which we have grown accustomed to her being, but I believe she is still with us, in our memories and in her many good deeds, the effects of which will live well beyond our lives. You see, your sister has been transfigured into her natural state and shed the body God gave her to fight the battle that is life, and even though God may be the final judge, you should rest easy knowing that with those many good deeds, she has by all accounts won the battle for her soul. I dare say she is lost only to heaven, where the battle is over and where she can enjoy that which she has earned; her place in paradise."

Jack excused himself almost immediately when he heard Lynn giggle and went outside to have a cigarette while he waited for the sisters to finish their business. After a few minutes, Thomas drove his police patrol car into the parking lot and pulled beside Jack. He parked the car and stepped out into the glow of streetlights so he could be seen and said,

"I imagine that since you're waiting outside the church at this hour, you're waiting for Monica, which means you must be Jack."

Jack dropped his cigarette on the ground and extinguished it by stepping on it and replied, "That I am! And I imagine that since you're a cop aware of who I am, you must be Monica's friend, Thomas."

Thomas smiled and replied, "You can call me Thom."

The two men then heartedly shook hands, and Jack leaned against Thomas' patrol car, lighting another cigarette.

"Lynn always told me she was afraid it would end like this…." Jack said apologetically, "…not to be disrespectful about it, but Bella always put herself in harm's way. Her loss is a tragedy, to be sure, but not a terrible surprise, given the circumstances…."

Jack paused for a second to study Thomas' face to see if he was taking offense, and when he saw none, he continued, "I still think my wife will have difficulty dealing with this, though. Monica too."

"I believe you're right…." Thomas returned, "… Mona recently lost her friend Kate suddenly. And now her little sister? She may never truly recover."

The mention of Kate's name reminded Jack of what he had overheard at the funeral home.

"I can't even imagine…." Jack replied, "…I heard people talking about Kate. Such a shame. I understand she was a legend in town; God rest her soul."

"She was…" Thomas agreed, "…and she'll be sorely missed. She was a dear friend of mine as well. Her passing was a terrible loss for the community."

"Sounds like quite a woman," Jack added.

As Thomas nodded approvingly, he felt a surge of emotion welling up inside himself and decided to change the topic of conversation to avoid an embarrassing scene.

"So, I gather you took the ladies to the funeral home? Deerings, is it?"

"Yes. Deerings." Jack confirmed, "…seems like a nice place. The funeral director seemed to be a friend of Mona's. I think he likes her if that's not inappropriate to say."

"Not at all…." Thomas replied, "… Mona's a handsome woman. Lots of fellas have had their eyes on her over the years."

As the two men chatted, Jack noticed Monica and Lynn suddenly appear on the front porch of the rectory. He dropped his cigarette to extinguish it and said, "Here comes the lady's…."

Thomas looked at the rectory and saw that the women had finished their business. Jack extended his hand and said, "I guess it's good night then, officer."

"I guess so." Thomas returned, "… it's been a pleasure."

The two men shook hands as the women slowly approached, and when Monica noticed it was Thomas talking to Jack, she remarked, "Nice to see the two of you getting along…."

"Didn't know you knew each other?" Lynn added.

"Honey, this is Officer Thomas," Jack announced, "…Monica told us about him."

"Nice to meet you.," Lynn said as she offered Thomas her hand.

Thomas took her hand and gently kissed Lynn on the cheek as he offered his condolences. He then turned to Monica and said:

"Vikki's been terribly busy, but she wanted me to convey her deepest sympathies for your loss, Mona."

"Thank you, Thomas…." Monica mildly replied, "…that means the world to me. I'd like to introduce her to my sister Lynn and her husband, Jack, while they're here."

"Another time perhaps…." Thomas returned.

"Certainly!" Jack replied, "…perhaps after Bella's ceremonies, we can get together for a drink before we head home."

"Jack!" Lynn shouted as she swiped at her husband, feeling he was disrespectful.

"It's OK, Lynn…" Monica replied, "… there's no reason we shouldn't get on with our lives because of Bella. She'd want us to. I'm certain of that."

"Good!" Jack replied, "…then it's settled! We're on for drinks!"

32

Appraisal

Monica endeavored to make Bella's funeral mass something her little sister would be proud of, but when it had ended, Sydney openly expressed her disapproval. Lynn knew Monica was hurt by the spiteful assessment and assured her that Bella would've been pleased.

"Syd's opinion doesn't matter," Lynn declared, "She's just jealous that she had nothing to do with it. Besides, Bella loved St. Anselm's and would have treasured the reading you selected about the meek inheriting the earth! I thought it was perfect!"

"The Beatitudes..." Monica replied, "...I picked that one because it reminded me of her."

"Like I said, Mona, I thought it was perfect!"

Lynn put her arm around her sister and joined the line of people following behind Bella's casket out of the church.

"I wasn't sure about having a burial," Monica remarked, "...I didn't think it was necessary..."

"What's the point?" Lynn reassured her, "...Bella asked to be cremated, and her ashes scattered to the wind, so there really is no need. It's what Bella wanted."

Monica held her sister's arm as they watched Bella's casket delicately loaded into the Hearse that was to carry her to the crematorium. The thought of Bella's cremation was ghastly to Monica, but Lynn's geniality comforted her. Flowers sent in condolence were removed from the church and placed around Bella's casket until it was barely visible.

"Where do you think we should scatter her ashes?" Lynn asked in a whisper.

"I was thinking of Gallagher's Hill," Monica replied, "…Bella loved being up there. She'd spend hours sitting on that rock under that big oak tree."

"Bella would love that!" Lynn agreed, "That's perfect!"

The Hearse slowly pulled away, and the sisters stood silently watching it disappear. When it was out of sight, Lynn continued, "We can go to the crematorium later to finish caring for Bella. There's nothing we can do now, so let's go get something to eat. I don't know about you, but I'm famished!"

As had been the case for as long as the sisters could remember, a large tent had been pitched on the church's front lawn where people had begun to gather. Under the tent were tables loaded with food the parishioners had prepared for the occasion. A small crowd stood just outside the tent awaiting the sisters and respectfully conveyed their condolences as Monica and Lynn made their way to the food tables. When they stopped to try some pie, Lynn asked, "Remember when Bella and I would go to the bathroom during service?"

"I do!" Monica chuckled as they both picked up a small plate of pie.

"Well, we were actually sneaking out for treats before everyone else had finished them."

Monica smiled at the thought of her sister's hijinks, and Lynn continued, "We'd steal some pie when she wasn't looking, then hide under her table and eat it. I can't believe the old lady never figured out why she was always the first out of pie!"

"She knew!" Monica giggled, "…she just pretended not to notice."

"What makes you say that, Mona?" Lynn asked, "…the woman was half-blind!"

"I know because Mom and Dad told me."

"Really? If they knew, why didn't they stop us?"

Monica smiled and replied, "Mrs. Tillman told them it made her happy. She knew what you two were doing but let you do it anyway. Mom and Dad offered to pay her, but she wouldn't take a penny from them for it."

"So, we all got what we wanted?" Lynn asked as she began to laugh.

"Not exactly…" Monica replied, "When Syd found out, she got mad. She wanted to go with you, but Mom wouldn't let her. Mom told us that we were too old to be doing that, and Sydney would have gotten us caught anyway. Stealth was not a weapon in her arsenal."

"Well, I'm glad Mom didn't let Sydney ruin it for us," Lynn added, "…and I can't speak for Bella, but it was probably the only reason I never squawked about going to church!"

The two sisters began laughing, which got the attention of Lynn's husband, Jack, who was standing at a table nearby with Thomas, Vikki, and Thurmond. Jack politely excused himself to join his wife, and Thomas suggested they all pay their respects. Thurmond had been keeping his distance from Monica but believed this was a valid pretext to speak with her. When Monica spotted the group approaching, she said, "Never thought I'd be happy to see her!"

Lynn knew Monica was experiencing difficulties with Thurmond and was surprised that her sister's remark was about Vikki. When they all came together, Vikki and Thomas relayed their condolences as Thurmond cautiously approached Monica. Not sure what to say to him, Monica's mind wandered. Her uncertainty about their future together weighed heavily on her, and she wasn't sure if Thurmond was strong enough to handle the truth.

As Thomas, Jack, Vikki, and Lynn engaged in lighthearted conversation, Monica decided she had put it off long enough and suggested she and Thurmond go for a walk. Thurmond happily accepted, and they excused themselves, crossed the church lawn, and sat on either end of a stone bench beside a small cemetery.

To break the ice, Monica asked Thurmond what he thought about Bella's ceremony, and as he responded, she wondered how to express her concerns about their relationship. She became more confident in her convictions as he spoke, and when he paused, Monica changed the topic entirely and abruptly questioned his motivations for going to Asia.

Thurmond was relieved that they were finally discussing something which had plagued them both, but, to his surprise, Monica became increasingly contentious. She asked him about his intentions, reminded him of indiscretions, and confronted him with her concerns about his commitment to her.

"I'm glad we're finally talking about this, Mona…." Thurmond admitted, "…but I've been trying to talk to you whenever I come home, and you avoid me. All I ever wanted was what was best for you."

Monica suddenly became uncharacteristically volatile.

"What's best for me?" she shouted, "… that's interesting? How is your leaving me here alone best for me? Sitting here wondering if you're ever coming back!"

"I value your opinion, Mona, which is why I asked you if I should take this job…" Thurmond meekly replied, "…you told me I should. I would never have gone if you told me not to!"

Monica paused while she thought of what to say. She wondered if his asking her permission was his way of removing the guilt he felt for doing something he knew was wrong.

"I wanted you to make up your own mind!" Monica shouted back, "…you never do! You always ask me what to do, then use my advice as permission. I don't want to be responsible for making your decisions. You're a grown man, for heaven's sake! You need to figure out what you want and then decide what you will do, not ask me, and blame me when it doesn't turn out how you wanted! You make it seem like I'm responsible, but I'm not! You went to Asia because you wanted to. You only asked me so you could remove the responsibility for making that decision yourself."

Suddenly, memories of what Ehndale had said to her flooded her mind. She remembered Ehndale saying that Thurmond was probably the only thing of value in her life. How she was afraid of losing him to a more fulfilling life than the one she could offer him, but Monica was willing to prove her love for him every day of her life if he would just come home with her, yet he still decided to go.

Monica grew angry and became quite loud. She surprised herself with how visceral her argument had become. She was relieved to finally expressed her feelings, and now that she had, she wanted to see what Thurmond would do to earn her trust. To deserve her love.

Thurmond bowed his head in shame and continued.

"I just wanted to express my condolences for Bella. I know how much she meant to you. There's no need to crucify me for the effort."

"Crucify!?" Monica screamed incredulously, "…you don't even know what that means! Besides, we're not talking about my sister. We're talking about us!"

Ronnie was talking to Fr. Elias nearby and could easily hear Monica screaming. When she looked to see what was happening, she saw Monica arguing with Thurmond and could tell her friend was quite upset. Ronnie wanted to help but was unsure if, when, or how to intercede. She excused herself from the priest and carefully approached the unhappy couple.

The commotion had also attracted considerable attention from others. When Lynn heard Monica's angry voice ring out, she became alarmed and immediately ran toward her sister. Thomas, Vikki, and Jack followed behind, and by the time they arrived, they found Ronnie standing near the bench, looking like she was wondering if she should step in.

Monica had stopped screaming and hunched over on the bench with her head in her hands, sobbing inconsolably. Lynn immediately recognized Monica's delicate condition, hurriedly sat beside her sister, and put her arm around her.

Thurmond was in shock. He didn't know what to say that wouldn't make matters worse, so he stepped away from Mona. Thomas walked over to him and put his hand on his shoulder, then walked him away from the bench. As Thurmond began walking away, Monica looked up and screamed.

"I never want to see you again!"

Thomas was unsure what to do and looked over at Vikki. She had remained at a distance, believing her presence may be unwelcome, but she could tell Thurmond was heartbroken. He looked like a man wholly undone, and Vikki knew Thomas was asking for her help. Vikki quickly approached, and when she was near enough to hear him, Thurmond whispered to her that it was probably time for him to return to Asia.

~

Vikki and Thomas were astounded by Monica's behavior and believed she had been terribly unfair. Thomas wanted to bring Thurmond home but didn't think he should be left alone. It seemed Emerson might be the only person who could help at that point, so Thomas asked Vikki to stay with Thurmond while he looked for him.

Thomas found Emerson discussing the deleterious effects of electromagnetic radiation while eating cookies with Herb. The two were oblivious to everything that had just happened, and after Thomas explained, Emerson said, "Soon as I get Herb here to agree that high-frequency radio waves can cause biological damage, I'm headed over to Teddy's place to plow the froth off a couple!"

Thomas couldn't help but chuckle at Emerson's comment. The man was an enigma and a welcome levity to the distressing situation.

"I was going to take Thurmond home..." Thomas explained, "...but Teddy's sounds like a better idea. Can I give you a ride over with him?"

"Kind of you, Officer," Emerson said as he pointed at a car approaching them, "…but Stan's my ride and is pulling up as we speak".

Emerson shoved a cookie into his mouth and wiped his face on his sleeve, then slapped Herb on the back and said, "Gotta go! See ya'll at Teddy's! Tell Thurm I'll see him there!"

When Thomas returned, he saw Vikki standing alone, with no sign of Thurmond anywhere. He asked her where Thurmond had gone, and Vikki replied, "He left. Said he needed a drink and mentioned going to Teddy's Pub. I couldn't talk him out of it. Said that he planned on meeting Emerson there after Bella's ceremony anyway. You should probably go there to make sure he's OK. I'd go, but it sounds like a 'guy thing.'"

Vikki kissed Thomas goodbye, wished him luck, and departed.

Thomas looked over to see what was happening with Monica and saw Jack sitting alone on the bench with Lynn. He thought it was strange that neither Monica nor Ronnie was with them. He jogged over to see what had happened.

"I'm so sorry this turned out to be such a mess, Lynn," Thomas began, "…it was such a beautiful ceremony!"

Jack and Lynn both stood up. Lynn kissed Thomas on the cheek and said, "Thanks for saying so, Thom. Mona did such a beautiful job. It's a shame it had to end the way it did."

Jack shook Thomas's hand and added with a wink, "Not sure what happened with Mona & Thurm, but I wouldn't be surprised if Sydney didn't have something to do with it. She has a way of causing trouble."

Annoyed by his flippant comment, Lynn glared at Jack for a second, then elbowed him in the ribs and said, "You don't know anything, Jack! Mona's emotions just got the better of her. That's it! It's got nothing to do with Sydney. It's between Mona and Thurm. They're the ones having issues."

Thomas hadn't considered it, but now that Sydney's name had been mentioned, he thought it unusual that she was nowhere to be seen.

"I hope you don't mind my asking, Lynn…." Thomas inquired, "… but I wanted to convey my condolences to your sister Sydney before she left, but I haven't seen her since we left the church."

Jack snickered and said, "I overheard her talking to some guy. They were making plans to meet somewhere. It was weird. She was acting all sweet, which is not like her."

Lynn didn't like talking about her dysfunctional sister's love life, and since Sydney had nothing to do with their present situation, Lynn decided to change the subject.

"I need to check on Bella at the crematorium. Then I'm joining the girls at Ronnie's place to check in on Mona. She's an emotional train wreck right now. I'm sure you guys don't want to be around all that drama…"

"Hell no!" Jack vehemently concurred.

"Then why don't you two enjoy yourselves and have a drink somewhere," Lynn suggested.

"Suits me fine," Jack replied enthusiastically, "…what do you say, officer? Down for a couple of frostys?"

"Sounds great…" Thomas replied, "I know where to go. I'll drive."

~

Thurmond was just finishing his first beer when Stan and Emerson arrived. Emerson spotted Thurmond at the bar, hurried over, and hopped up on a barstool beside him. Digging his hand down deep into his pockets, Emerson pulled out a crumpled fifty-dollar bill, slapped it on the bar, and shouted, "This round's on me, Teddy! Filler up!"

"Thanks, Em…." Thurmond replied softly.

Emerson placed his hand on his friend's back and said, "T'aint no never-mind, Thurm…."

It was apparent that Thurmond was distraught, but rather than ask him why Emerson let Thurmond decide if he wanted to talk about it. Thurmond remained silent until their beers arrived.

"You know Em, Mona has every right not to trust me, and I hate myself for that."

"Cain't say as I agree, Thurm ...." Emerson replied as he clinked Thurmond's glass.

"Thanks, Em, but I don't blame Mona for being unable to trust me. It's my own fault. I'm the one who screwed up."

Emerson emptied half his beer in a single swig, wiped his mouth on his sleeve, and replied, "Sure did, Thurm, but that fancy fella you fell in with just couldn't quit being ugly. That's what got you into trouble. I mean, you lost your way, friend. No doubt about that, but Mona knows it. That's why she forgave you. Like we all knew, she knew that fella ain't no good."

"I know that now, Em...." Thurmond said dejectedly, "...but I'm sorry about everything, and I don't know how I can make it right."

"Ain't no never mind, Thurm. You can't change what's past. We all make mistakes, but we lick our wounds and move on. Life's like a creek. The way ain't never straight."

"No, it ain't," Thurmond replied, and Emerson continued.

"To be sure, Mona's hurtin' something fierce, Thurm, and she misses you, but she's afraid you're gonna hurt her again. That's why she's angry. She knows you're a good fella and that it ain't your inclination to treat people poorly, but she doesn't know how to resolve her fear of losing you without feeling like she's the only one who cares. Tain't anythin' you can say that'd make her think other-ways. So, you gotta let it be what it is. I mean, it's not you. It's her who's got to work it out. You do what you do. Be your best 'you,' and let her be her. Up to her to be the best 'she' she can be. Just keep your head clear, and don't let things get sideways again."

Thurmond was always surprised at how astute and profound his seemingly hapless friend could be. His words seemed to lift a weight off Thurmond, and he suddenly felt more at ease.

"Now, whaddya say 'bout wettin' our whiskers with some of that-there sippin' whiskey?" Emerson suggested as he began making circles in the air over his head to get Teddy's attention.

After his dose of Emerson's hillbilly wisdom, Thurmond felt much better and put his hand on Emerson's shoulder to let his friend know he appreciated him.

~

Thurmond noticed Thomas and Jack enter the bar and waved them over to sit with him. Thomas spotted Thurmond waving and led Jack to where he and Emerson were seated. Thomas was still concerned about Thurmond, but he seemed in much better spirits. Emerson twirled his hand in the air to get Teddy's attention and held up four fingers to order another round.

Teddy set out a round of beers and four bourbon shots as the men shook hands.

"What brings you two here?" Thurmond asked.

Jack knew how tense everything had been and tried to make light of what had just occurred.

"The girls are having a pow-wow at the Diner, and we weren't interested in all the drama..."

Thurmond was happy to hear that the women were all helping Mona and decided to take Emerson's advice and move on. Jack lifted his glass and offered a toast:

"Here's to the two secrets to a long-lasting relationship! A good sense of humor and a very short memory."

The men all downed their shots, and Jack continued, "You know, women only tolerate us men because we don't understand them, right? I mean, they see us as an amusement they enjoy torturing. They understand each other, so they're not always the best companions. They know what buttons to push, so they can easily offend each other. That's why they prefer the company of men. They find our ignorance gives them an advantage."

"That doesn't make any sense..." Thurmond insisted.

"That's cuz you're not a woman..." Emerson replied.

"That's correct..." Jack confirmed as the group of men began to chuckle.

Thomas was a little confused by Jack's logic and asked, "So, correct me if I'm wrong, but you're saying if we understood them better, they would find us less attractive?"

Stan and Teddy had been chatting nearby and overheard the men talking. Teddy felt he had something to add to the conversation and chimed in, "Actually, if we knew what they were thinking, we'd probably want to run away anyway!"

Everyone but Thurmond started laughing, but the lighthearted atmosphere had lightened his spirit, and he managed to smile. Jack noticed, slapped the bar top, and replied, "Speaking from experience, you should never try to figure out what a woman wants because they only know what they don't want, and even that is subject to change. It'll make you crazy."

Stan decided to join the conversation and said, "I never try to figure out what my wife wants. Rather, I just do the opposite of what I would do, and I'm right more often than I'm wrong."

"You guys met Lynn's sister Sydney, right?" Jack asked rhetorically, "...a miserable person, to be sure. Never has a kind word. Never smiles and has absolutely no sense of humor whatsoever. I called her out on it once, and she told me if she had a sense of humor, she wouldn't be able to stop laughing at me. It was actually kinda funny. I didn't expect that from her."

The group continued to drink and share stories about the unpredictability of women. At one point, Emerson related the topic somehow to the paradox between science and spirituality. He argued that telepathy and psychokinesis were not just perceived scientific phenomena or fraud perpetrated by charlatans but were biologically encoded traits in people's DNA, endowed by their creator.

When he'd finished, the other men looked at each other and began laughing hysterically. Emerson was unoffended and joined in on the laughter as the men continued to drink and talk until very late into the evening.

When Ted announced he was closing the place for the night, he set out a final round of drinks on the house. Jack paid the tab as the men slugged down their last drink of the evening. They then slid out of their barstools and stumbled towards the door, and when they made their way out onto the sidewalk, they spotted Lynn waiting outside in her car.

Jack threw his arm around Thomas and stumbled towards the car. Lynn rolled down the passenger's window broadcasting a smile that bordered on a smirk, and said, "We took Mona home hours ago, and when I didn't hear from you, I figured you'd probably need a ride home."

Jack took his arm from around Thomas and leaned up against the car. He began gesturing exaggerated kisses and making smooching sounds and replied, "You're an angel and a saint, dearest! Got room for us heathens in there?"

"Sure. Hop in, you drunken stumblebums."

33

Pernicious Courtships

Hunter was aware of the ceremonies for Monica's sister Bella but believed he had endured more than his fair share of grief. Although he felt sincere compassion for Monica and sympathized with her loss, that wasn't enough to compel him to attend. The weather was particularly notable to him, as the cold, damp, blustering day of his mother's burial starkly contrasted with the bright and sunny day of Bella's funeral. He believed this reflected the disparity of life's fortunes and represented some sort of cosmic proclamation about the quality and value of the decedent's life, a form of judgment from the Almighty, quantifying the value of the individual in the cosmos.

He regularly visited his mother's grave but not to mourn her loss. Instead, he did it to remind himself of what he was determined not to become. Hunter loathed his mother's lack of ambition and her satisfaction with mediocrity. He was determined not to make the same mistakes and imagined what his life could become if he was only given a chance. He bemoaned the situation his mother had created for him because he believed it shackled his ambitions. He knew if he did nothing, he would likely be buried in a nondescript grave on a cold, damp, blustery day, just like his mother.

Standing over his mother's grave, he read the epitaph engraved on her headstone and wondered what meaning it could give to the misery that was her life.

'All mourn the loss to death, but to the faithful, the loss is but to Heaven.'

'In Memory of our beloved friend & mother, Kate, may she rest in peace.'

After her burial, Fr. Elias counseled Hunter not to ignore how he felt about losing his mother but to embrace the emotions he was experiencing. The parish priest had said, "The loss of one as dear as one's mother is a significant event in anyone's life, to be sure. It can change your perception of the world and perhaps even force you to question your faith. No one is above that, not even a priest like me. It can lead you to question why God would take her from you. Why would he allow suffering at all? But we must have faith that God is merciful and benevolent. We may not understand why things like this happen, but there is a higher purpose beyond our ability to understand. God's love for us is everlasting, and His mercy is inexhaustible. Try to accept His wisdom and find solace in His mercy. Know that your Mom is in a better place than she has ever been. Have confidence that her kindness has been rewarded. Our beloved father has a place for her, with him, in heaven."

'Lost to Heaven?' Hunter thought to himself, 'What was that supposed to mean?' Love, Mercy, Faith, Solace, Benevolence? These were just words thrown around to ease the distressing and inevitable fact that death was an end, not a beginning of something. Final and guaranteed. A permanent and abrupt separation from life. That was the brutal reality of it all. Living your life as if it were a prelude to something better was nonsense to him, and Hunter wouldn't let that limit what he would do to get what he wanted.

Hunter believed the priest was right about one thing, though; his mother's death changed everything, most notably Hunter's faith in anyone but himself. He wouldn't let what became of her happen to him. He wanted more, and he was determined to get it.

~

After the women had managed to calm Monica down, they wanted to bring her home. She was exhausted from her emotional day and needed to rest peacefully until morning. They all agreed she should not be left alone, so Ronnie offered to look after her.

Lynn hadn't heard from her husband, Jack, and wasn't sure what condition he would be in when he came home. She believed it was unlikely that he could drive and decided she needed to go get him. She also thought his drunken compatriots would need a ride home, but Vikki had left, so they had only Lynn's car to taxi them.

Considering the alternatives, Lynn decided the best thing to do would be to bring them all to one place rather than drive them around town, so she took Monica to Ronnie's nearby apartment, where she fell soundly asleep on the couch and went to the bar to pick up Jack and his drunken friends.

It was late when Lynn finally packed the drunken hoard into her car, and when she explained that she was taking them all to Monica's house, Thurmond insisted that she drop him at his home. She explained that it would take too long to take them all to their separate houses, but Lynn could see how staying at Monica's house may be traumatic for him and agreed. She dropped Thurmond off at his house, then headed straight to Monica's house, where she asked everyone to find a place to lay their heads for the evening.

Jack's snoring was prodigious when he drank, making it improbable that Lynn would get any sleep if he stayed in the bedroom with her, so she laid Jack on the couch in the living room and threw a blanket over him to remedy this dilemma. Thomas immediately fell asleep in a chair, and Emerson visited the restroom. Lynn figured Emerson could take care of himself, so she retired alone to the bedroom for the evening.

Because of these late-night activities, Lynn hadn't gotten to bed until quite late. She knew the men would be sleeping off their hangovers in the morning and saw no need to rush into her day, so she decided to sleep in the following morning.

~

The weather had changed overnight and remained dark until late in the morning. When Lynn finally awoke, she lay in bed for a few minutes listening to rain slapping against the roof, then threw on a nightgown and headed downstairs to see how the boys were doing.

Lynn found Jack exactly where she had left him, but Thomas and Emerson were nowhere to be seen. She decided to put on some coffee, hoping the smell would generate some interest, and saw a note on the counter from Thomas letting her know he had left for work and thanking her for driving them home.

After preparing the coffee, Lynn went upstairs to get dressed, hoping the boys would awake while she was away, but when she returned, there was no sign of Emerson, and Jack was still sound asleep on the couch. She looked around for a second and decided it was time to get the day started, and announced with alacrity, "Rise and shine, boys! There are places to go and people to see!!"

Jack stirred on the couch and replied without opening his eyes, "Why so loud, love?"

Lynn smiled and replied, "Time to get moving, Babe!"

Jack tried to sit up, then laid back down and pressed his fingers into his temples, rotating them in a circular motion, trying to rub the throbbing hangover out of his head. Suddenly, a voice came from the hallway and said, "Mornin' Ma'am!"

Lynn looked to see where the voice had come from and saw a pair of legs covered in overalls unfolding out of a closet. Laughing, she replied, "There you are, Em! Been looking for you! How are you feeling this fine morning?"

"Not as good as I'd like, Ma'am…." Emerson mumbled, "… but probably better than I deserve. Common sense ain't a flower that grows in everyone's garden."

Lynn found Emerson's way of putting things charming, and even though she didn't know half the stuff he was saying, she somehow understood.

"What does that even mean?" Jack asked as Emerson tumbled out of the closet.

"Gettin' drunker than Cooter Brown has its price …" Emerson explained, "… if you don't want to pay, then you shouldn't go doin' it. Golly, I feel like I'd been rode hard and put away wet."

Lynn and Jack both began to laugh, but the pounding in Jack's head made him stop. He sat up on the couch, looked around, then placed his head in his hands and asked, "Where's Thomas and Thurm?"

Lynn brought two cups of coffee to the table beside the couch and replied, "I dropped Thurmond off at his house on our way home last night, not that I'd expect you to remember that. You guys were drunker than skunks!"

"What about Thom?"

Lynn handed Jack his coffee and explained, "He got up early and left a note saying he had to go to work."

"How'd he get to work?" Jack asked as he sipped his coffee, "… his car still at the bar?"

"Don't know…." Lynn replied, "…but he seems capable enough. If he woke up feeling anything like you two, he probably called someone to pick him up."

Emerson ran his fingers through his hair, then stood and wiped his hands down the front of his overalls to straighten them out. He walked over to Jack, sat next to him on the couch, and picked up the coffee Lynn had prepared for him. After a long sip, he said, "I ain't got the sense God gave a goose!"

Emerson put down his coffee, rubbed his feet, and continued, "I'm plumb worn out, but I should probably head over to the Whitehorse. Seems they always got plumbin' needs fixin'. They hired some kid to help, but he's blind in one eye and can't see out of the other, bless his heart."

The name Whitehorse sounded familiar to Jack, and he tried to remember where he'd heard it before. He thought for a second, then looked straight at Lynn and asked, "Isn't that the place where Sydney is staying?"

"It was…" Lynn replied, "…but she called last night and said she had made other arrangements. Said she wouldn't need the room anymore, so we could have it if we needed it."

Jack lifted his head and snickered, "Other arrangements? What the hell does that mean?"

"That's what she said," Lynn replied.

Lynn knew, for whatever reason, Sydney had done something unexpectedly thoughtful and offered to let her sisters use her room. Lynn wasn't sure how much she wanted to tell Jack, but, as painful as it may be, she believed it was worth mentioning that her sister wasn't all bad, and added, "I wasn't going to say anything about it, but Syd did offer to let us use it. We considered letting Mona stay there last night, but as it turned out, we didn't need it. Mona fell asleep at Ronnie's apartment, and Ronnie was happy to look after her. If that hadn't happened, though, we would have had somewhere to bring Mona. We certainly couldn't bring her here."

"Why not?" Jack asked sincerely.

"You're kidding, right?" Lynn replied incredulously, "…I couldn't drive a bunch of drunks around creation last night, so I had to bring you guys here. With the shape you guys were in, you would have certainly disturbed Mona, which was the last thing she needed! She needed peace and quiet. Let's just say that Syd was trying to be friendly and leave it at that, shall we? Now, why don't you two sots splash some water in your faces while I clean this place up?"

Jack stretched his arms over his head and asked, "Will you make us one of your famous omelets, love? I don't know about Em, but I'm starving!"

"I made plans last night to meet Ronnie and Mona for lunch today…." Lynn replied, "…You guys can use the car and do what you want, but you'll need to drop me off at the Diner first."

"I'm probably riper than a watermelon in summertime...." Emerson said as he clasped his hands behind his back and stretched, "...I reckon I could use a shower. Can you drop me at home on your way to the Diner?"

"Shower here, Em..." Jack suggested, "... I'll drop off the wife and swing back by to pick you up. We can go by Thom's precinct to see if he's free for lunch."

"Thank ya kindly...." Emerson replied, "... the Whitehorse ain't got problems bigger than a minnow in a fishing pond, so I reckon they can wait. Besides, I'm hungrier than a tic on a teddy bear."

Jack joined Lynn in laughter as Emerson made his way toward the bathroom.

~

Sydney did not intend to hide her burgeoning relationship with the handsome gentleman she'd met at Cay Pham. In fact, she had introduced Lynn to try and make her jealous. However, Sydney also did not plan to resist the romantic interlude she considered imminent and believed Monica would attempt to dissuade her from it had she known. It had been such a long time since any man had made her feel that way that Sydney wanted nothing to ruin it for her, so she mentioned nothing to Monica and, other than the initial introduction, kept her activities with him secret from Lynn.

~

When Lynn arrived at Kate's, Ronnie assured her that Monica felt much better. Monica apologized for her behavior the day before and told them she appreciated their efforts on her behalf.

Lynn thought it was worth mentioning that even Sydney had offered to help, which made Monica happy. Still, when Monica heard that Sydney had offered her room, she wondered if her sister had decided to leave town without saying goodbye. Lynn assured her that Sydney was still in town but said she had made other arrangements.

"My guess is she's staying with this guy she met in town…." Lynn explained, "His face is long and angular. You could say he's handsome enough, but he wears a frock coat and a stupid bowler cap. I mean, who does that? Apparently, he has money, but everything about this guy smells funny. Even his name sounds made up; Ehndale… what kind of name is that?"

Monica was surprised to hear that Sydney's new interest was Ehndale and debated whether she should mention what she knew about him but decided there was no point. The memory of Ehndale's actions against Thurmond had lost its sting, not only because of the time that had elapsed since those events had occurred but also because of Monica's recent sentiments towards her 'former' boyfriend.

Besides, Lynn would use anything Monica said about him to rebuke Sydney, and Monica wasn't interested in stirring that hornet's nest. More than likely, Sydney wouldn't believe her anyway, and even if she did, Sydney would probably accuse her of being jealous or intentionally trying to ruin her chances with him.

~

Lynn and Jack had no specific plans on when they would return home. Their sons were entirely capable of running Jack's business, so they intended to stick around for as long as they were welcome. On the other hand, Sydney intended to leave town as soon as possible and had Monica schedule her return flight accordingly, but when Ehndale invited her to stay with him, she changed her plans.

Fueled by romantic interludes with Ehndale, Sydney fantasized about their relationship. Always a perfect gentleman, he gave her his complete attention and lavished her with gifts, making her believe it was more than a passing fancy. Still, it had not yet become what she imagined, but she thought it would in time, and although it wasn't exactly what she had hoped for, the current situation still suited her quite nicely.

Ehndale invited her to extravagant parties as his guest, where she met some interesting people, some of whom were familiar to her from her youth. One was Thomas' father, Bernard, whom she had heard unflattering rumors about when she was a child. She recognized him when they were introduced and found him to be obnoxious. Unceasingly inebriated, his brash interaction with men and wanton interest in women was unwelcome, and his unusual fondness for physical contact made people uncomfortable around him.

Another person she recognized was Kate's son, Hunter, who had grown into a handsome and confident man, but she remembered him as a pesky little boy running around his mother's Diner. Hunter kept the company of a young girl named Naomi, who was obviously infatuated with him. Still, the couple seemed to go to great lengths to conceal their affinity for each other, which Sydney considered decidedly juvenile.

Sydney found Ehndale charming, but he exhibited some curious tendencies. He was wealthy, powerful, and worldly, but his generosity towards undeserving people surprised her, as did his unusual interest in her sister Mona, which she couldn't understand. Mona was shy, poor, and introverted, with no interest in change. Just a plain, dull girl with no interest in anything but books, religion, and Thurmond, who, as of late, did not appear to be of any interest to her whatsoever.

This interest in Mona, however, did not appear to be romantic. Still, he had talked about her since Sydney had first met him and even initiated their first meeting with a remark about the sister's resemblance, which Sydney found incredibly annoying. Still, Ehndale's kind and attentive manner towards Sydney made it easy for her to overlook these curiosities, so she ignored them.

~

As was his usual routine, Ehndale invited Sydney to have breakfast with him on the veranda. But on this particular morning, they were joined by a young man named Ganneau, who was charming and incredibly handsome, so much so that Sydney found it difficult to refrain from staring at him, which did not escape Ehndale's notice, though he never mentioned it.

The three were engaged in pleasant conversation when Ganneau accidentally spilled coffee on his white linen shirt. When he excused himself, Sydney reminded Ehndale that she was scheduled to leave town the following day.

"Nonsense, my dear!" Ehndale remarked, "...surely you are mistaken. Had I been aware, I would have insisted a party be held to honor your departure!"

The fact that the news of her departure should evoke such an emphatic response from her host gave Sydney a tremendous sense of satisfaction, and she replied with false humility, "That really isn't necessary, Ehndale."

"Nonsense!" Ehndale shouted.

Ganneau returned, wiping his shirt with a rag, and heard Ehndale's remark. When he asked what they were talking about, Ehndale exclaimed, "Our flower is leaving! We must commemorate this occasion and celebrate our becoming acquainted."

"Absolutely!" Ganneau agreed.

Ehndale addressed Ganneau as he reached out to take Sydney's hand, "Find Balaam, my good man, and tell him we are having a ball tomorrow evening in our guest's honor."

"Please let it be a masked ball!" Ganneau added suggestively, "Those are so much fun! "

Ehndale looked at Sydney, kissed her hand, and asked.

"What do you think, my dear? There may not be enough time for people to prepare properly, but I suppose it can be an option if they have a spare costume. What do you think? It's your party. It should be your choice."

"It does seem a bit much..." Sydney began before Ganneau interrupted.

"Oh, please? Let it be a costume ball. People only need to bring a mask. We can provide whatever they need, can't we, Ehndale?"

"I believe we can, my friend. What say you, my dear? What do you think?"

Being the center of attention delighted Sydney, and she haughtily replied, "Sure, why not!"

"Splendid!" Ehndale shouted, then turned to address Ganneau, "Tell Balaam to invite about 30 people. Tell him it will be a costume ball, but a full costume is optional as masks will be provided."

Ganneau nodded to express understanding and excused himself from the table, but Ehndale suddenly held out his arm to stop him.

"One moment, my friend, I completely forgot...."

Ehndale turned to Sydney, who was delighting in the attention she was receiving, and said, "I apologize, my dear. How clumsy of me. I've forgotten to ask whom you'd like to invite. Some close friends, perhaps? Maybe your sisters?"

There it was again, her sisters. Sydney couldn't get away from it. The mere mention of them put a damper on the entire affair, and her excitement deflated into a stressful decision about whether to agree to invite them.

The thought would have never crossed her mind if Ehndale hadn't mentioned it, and she struggled to understand what interest he could possibly have in Mona. She wanted to ask but didn't want to have to explain why.

"Sure..." Sydney said dejectedly, "...you can invite my sisters, but...."

"Splendid!" Ehndale exclaimed before she had finished, then Sydney continued, "Monica's not very sociable, and although Lynn's a trollop and loves a party, I think she's leaving tomorrow. I'm sure they won't come. Besides, Lynn won't come without her husband Jack, and I don't think he would be interested."

"Nonsense!" Ehndale remarked, "...of course, they'll come. How could they not? We'll make it so they can't say no."

"I guess...." Sydney replied, hoping Ehndale wouldn't be able to get her sisters to agree to come.

"Anyone else?" Ehndale asked, "...another acquaintance you've befriended in town? Monica's boyfriend, perhaps? Maybe a girlfriend?"

Ehndale's suggestion suddenly gave Sydney an idea. It was perfect. She didn't know why she hadn't thought of it herself. Thurmond hadn't left for Asia yet, and his presence should annoy Monica enough to make her decline the invitation. Even if she did come, Thurmond would probably ruin her evening and may even cause a fight between them.

"Certainly. Yes, I think that's an excellent idea...." Sydney replied, "...please extend Thurmond an invitation as well. Thank you for thinking of them, Ehndale. I appreciate your consideration, as I'm sure they would as well. Thank you."

"My pleasure, my dear," Ehndale replied, smiling.

He waved his hand over his head, and Ganneau was off again in a flash to notify Balaam about planning for the costume party the following evening.

34

Backwash

After Jack had dropped Lynn off at the Diner, he returned home to get Emerson at Monica's house, and the two men swung by the precinct to see if Thomas could join them for lunch. Jack parked across the street from the precinct, and Emerson followed him into the station. They asked the desk sergeant if Thomas was around, and after calling him on the radio, the sergeant told them to sit on a bench.

When Thomas came out into the reception area, the men could tell he was having a rough morning, which was no surprise, given their carousing together the previous evening. Thomas removed his hat, wiped the sweat from his forehead, and sat beside them on the bench.

"I don't ever want to show up here like that again," Thomas said unhappily.

"I heard that!" Jack replied, "…I thought my head was going to explode."

"Amen!" Emerson added.

"Truth be told…." Thomas began, "…I didn't think I'd be able to work this morning, and I considered calling in sick, but I agreed to work Jimmy's shift, so I couldn't back out."

"So, I guess you're not free for lunch then?" Jack asked.

"Nope," Thomas replied, "…but I'm meeting Vikki after my shift, then I'm going home to get some sleep!"

"No worries," Jack replied, "… we're heading to Thurmond's now to see if he wants to join us. We'll catch up with you later."

"Don't bother…." Thomas replied, "…I saw Thurmond taking out his trash this morning when I was out on patrol, and let's just say I don't think he's in the mood, if you know what I mean."

Emerson had been quiet and hadn't said two words together since Jack had gone back to pick him up, but he felt inspired to add to the conversation and said, "I read somewhere once that if getting drunk were how people tried to forget they was mortal, then hangovers was how they remembered!"

~

Thurmond had had a great time with his friends but was glad he had decided to come home. He couldn't imagine waking up at Monica's house and dealing with her anger at his being there, especially after she had told him she never wanted to see him again.

There was no trouble with falling asleep, but Thurmond was extremely restless. When he finally awoke, it was with a splitting headache, so he decided to skip work to recover. He was hungry, so he dragged himself out of bed to grab something from the kitchen and found the trash can full, so he decided to take it out to the curb for pick-up before going back to bed.

When Thurmond took out his garbage, he saw Thomas driving by on patrol and waved. Thomas spotted him and stopped for a few minutes to talk. They were both feeling miserable, which kept their conversation short, but they made sure to tell each other how much they had enjoyed the previous evening together, hangovers notwithstanding.

Thurmond had left his truck at Teddy's pub and asked Thomas for a ride later to pick it up. Thomas mentioned he was meeting Vikki after his shift and could give him a ride then. Thurmond accepted his offer, then returned inside. Thomas drove off, and Thurmond crawled back into bed and quickly fell asleep.

~

When the girls had finished their lunch, Ronnie took advantage of Monica's trip to the restroom and explained to Lynn that although she had enjoyed having her in her apartment, the accommodation was meager and the space incredibly cramped. She thought Mona should probably return home, but Lynn thought her sister might enjoy something different and suggested they take Sydney up on her offer and have Mona spend a few days at the Whitehorse Inn.

"It will give her some space and make her feel like she's on vacation… "Lynn reasoned, "… Mona's the one who paid for it anyway, so I don't see why she would disagree. Besides, I think she'll enjoy it."

Ronnie agreed, and when Monica returned to their table, the ladies presented her with their idea. Lynn explained all the amenities they had at the Inn, and although Monica was initially uninterested, Lynn convinced her it would be a nice break from her every day.

Monica wanted to go home to pick up a few things, but Lynn explained that she didn't have a car. Ronnie suggested they didn't need a ride since the Inn was nearby, and they could walk if they didn't mind a little rain. Lynn thought that was a good idea and said that after they had checked in, she would swing by the house with Jack to pick up her things.

Appreciative of everything Ronnie had done for her, Monica suggested she come with them, but Ronnie was expecting her sister Vikki at the Diner shortly and declined. Monica understood but encouraged her to join her at the Inn later that evening. Ronnie said she would see what she could do and, after relaying her goodbyes, disappeared into the kitchen as the sisters left for the Whitehorse.

On their way, Lynn considered everything bothering her sister and knew she had difficulty dealing with it emotionally. The loss of their sister and the passing of Monica's dear friend Kate were both terrible losses, but Monica also had problems with Thurmond, which seemed to be the tipping point.

Monica would likely be reluctant to talk about any of it, so Lynn focused their conversation on pleasant things and told her of the adventures she had been on with Jack. Lynn knew it would take time for Monica to recover and decided she couldn't leave town without the reassurance that her fragile sister would be OK.

~

Jack and Emerson had decided against going to the Diner, knowing the girls would probably appreciate the space, which Lynn had made very clear to Jack earlier. Now that Thomas and Thurmond were out of the picture, Emerson suggested they pick up some lunch from a food truck parked in front of the stationhouse and eat it on the town green.

Even though Jack only understood half of what Emerson said, he found him incredibly entertaining. An example of that was while they ate their lunch Emerson expounded on the nutritional value of his food choice. He equated the components of his lunch to characters, as in a book, and talked about how they all related to each other as if they had personalities. Jack had never met anyone like Emerson before and enjoyed every minute he spent with him.

When they had finished, Emerson asked for a ride to the Whitehorse Inn so he could help the inexperienced kid deal with their plumbing issues. Jack had no problem with that, but he wasn't sure if Lynn had a ride home from the Diner. Emerson explained that the Whitehorse was not far from the Diner, so it wouldn't take long to head over there after Jack dropped him off.

On their way to the Inn, Emerson explained that he wouldn't be long and asked if he could bum a ride home after he'd straightened out the plumbing issues at the Inn. Jack had no idea what Lynn had in mind, but he had nothing planned for the rest of the day, so he agreed to give Emerson a ride and then asked if he wanted to do something together afterward. Emerson suggested they visit Thurmond, and Jack happily agreed.

~

Lynn had just finished checking in when she saw Jack and Emerson pull up in front of the Inn. She stepped out onto the porch at the sight of them to let them know she was there. Jack parked in front of the Inn, and Lynn came out to explain that Monica would be staying there for a few days. She also mentioned that Monica would need a few things from home and asked Jack to give her a ride there to retrieve them.

Jack explained he had made plans with Emerson after he had finished his work at the Inn, which made Lynn thankful that her husband was keeping himself busy while she dealt with her sister. Lynn promised Emerson they would return as soon as they retrieved Monica's things, and Emerson jumped out of the car, thanking her, and disappeared into the Inn, looking for the hapless lad he had come to help. Lynn hopped into the car with Jack, and they left for Monica's house.

Monica was in her room resting peacefully, but Lynn didn't want to leave her alone for long, so she told Jack they needed to hurry. When they arrived at Monica's house, Jack burst through the front door and didn't notice an envelope wedged into the screen door. Lynn was following behind and saw it fall onto the porch beside it. It was a fancy envelope with Monica's name handwritten on it, so Lynn picked it up and put it into her pocket.

The couple rummaged through the house quickly, looking for what Monica said she needed, then jumped back into the car and headed back to the Inn. On the way, Lynn pulled the envelope from her pocket and noticed it was not sealed. She opened it and realized it was an invitation to a party in honor of her sister Sydney. She didn't want Jack to become aware or curious, so she carefully slid the invitation back into the envelope and shoved it back into her pocket before he knew what she was doing.

~

The rain began falling more steadily, and the sound through the open window in her room awakened Monica from her nap. When she didn't see her sister, Monica became curious about where she had gone and remembered Lynn had said she was going back to her house to pick up a few things.

Monica went downstairs to look around and stepped into the kitchen, where she saw an assortment of treats on the kitchen island. She grabbed a few with a cup of freshly brewed coffee and went to the front parlor, where she watched out the window for her sister.

Emerson had finished his business and was sitting on the porch so Jack could see him and was unaware that Monica was behind him looking out the parlor window. When Jack pulled up out front, they saw Emerson sitting on the porch but not Monica in the window behind. Lynn gathered her purse and umbrella and leaned over to give her husband a few last-minute instructions.

"You boys go enjoy yourselves, Jack. I'll be staying here with Mona for a while, and will likely be having dinner with her here, so there's no rush. You can check back with me after supper but go enjoy yourself!"

Emerson watched Lynn navigate the puddles that had formed on the sidewalk and waited for her to step onto the porch out of the steady rain before he clumsily splashed his way to the car. Monica left the parlor and quickly returned to the kitchen to retrieve a little something for her sister.

As Emerson buckled himself in before Jack began to drive away, Monica stepped out onto the front porch carrying two mugs of coffee and some Danish. She placed them on a tiny glass table beside some wicker furniture and greeted her sister with a kiss, then waved at the car as it pulled away. The sisters appreciated the laugh when Emerson rolled down his window to reciprocate and became drenched by the rain in the process.

"They seem awfully excited?" Monica remarked.

"Had a boys' night out last night…." Lynn replied, "… they're still half-drunk if you asked me."

Monica laughed, "It's nice to see that Jack has made friends with Emerson. I thought the two of them would get along."

Lynn thought it was promising that Monica was laughing, shook out her umbrella, then collapsed it and put it into an umbrella stand beside the front door. Monica picked up a mug and a Danish off the table and handed them to her sister, then invited Lynn to sit with her and enjoy the treats she had brought.

"Thanks, Mona…" Lynn replied, "How did you know I was craving something sweet?"

"Not hard to guess you could use something on a day like this, Lynn. Something hot to wash down, something sweet? It's sort of like Chicken soup. It's versatile."

"Decidedly that…" Lynn agreed, "…anyway, it was very thoughtful, thank you."

"Don't mention it…." Monica replied, "… I'm only trying to make your stay here as pleasant as possible."

"I should have liked to have been able to take a run around town with you to have one last look at everything before we go, Mona. Maybe we can stroll around the green for some sweets and a picnic tomorrow if it's not raining. It's a shame today had to be such a dreary day."

"I know…" Monica replied, "…but it's always great to see you, Lynn. I can't tell you how much your both being here has helped me cope with everything."

"Glad we weren't a nuisance." Lynn jokingly replied as the two women sat and began to enjoy their coffee and the Danish.

Monica appeared to have gotten over the emotional collapse she had experienced the day before over Thurmond, but Lynn was still worried. She could not have resolved the emotional effects of losing her beloved sister and her dear friend so quickly. It was going to take some time.

Lynn didn't want to get into a serious conversation just yet and began talking about the boys. She relayed the men's antics from the previous evening and the scene in her house that morning. Lynn mentioned how she thought Emerson was adorable, and Monica wholeheartedly agreed. They began discussing the lighthearted nature of the man, and Thurmond's name eventually came up. Lynn noticed Monica gulped a mouthful of coffee when it did and decided to dive into the matters that concerned her.

"I don't mean to pry, Mona, but you two having time away from each other may not necessarily be a bad thing. Could even strengthen your relationship with him…."

"Or kill it…." Monica replied.

"Yes. Or kill it. That's true. But you'd never know which until you go through it. You need to focus on yourself, Mona. With all this crazy sadness and drama you've been surrounded by, it's a wonder you get out of bed. It's a testament to you that you do, but you need to soldier on. You must try to step out of your box and experience life from a different perspective. One that allows you to enjoy yourself without worrying about how it affects others. I mean, when was the last time you took a vacation? Last time you took a day off from the library, that wasn't for someone else's benefit or because of some tragic event."

"I can't remember…." Monica replied.

"That's because it hasn't happened, Mona. I'd venture a guess and say that you haven't been out of state, at least not recently. I'll bet you've never been to Europe or Asia. You've never been anywhere but here. How can you appreciate what you have until you see what else is available? It can make you appreciate the things you have more or abandon them for something better. Either way, you come out better off than you started. At least then, you know. At least then you have a better idea of your options."

Monica did not change her expression or her demeanor, which surprised Lynn. She just ate her Danish, sipped her coffee, and listened to her sister expound on the joys in life she had been denying herself.

"Let's do something extraordinary…." Lynn said in an increasingly excited tone, "…something unique. Something crazy."

"I'm not you, Lynn…." Monica replied, "…I don't do crazy. It's not me. I'm safe, boring Monica. That's what I do. That's who I am."

"But it doesn't have to be that way, Mona…." Lynn said encouragingly, "…I mean, you only have to allow it to happen. Just go with the flow, and don't be so darned conservative. So afraid of change or anything new. Sure, it's a risk, but it is worth taking if you ask me. 'Joie de vivre' Mona, 'Joie de vivre'!"

Monica thought to herself for a moment, then stood, picked up her mug and the napkins, and asked her sister if she wanted more coffee or another Danish. She knew this complacency would provoke her sister, which was not her intent, but she did not believe what Lynn said was possible for her, even though it made sense. Even Ronnie had mentioned something of the same. Still, Monica was a homebody, engrossed in reading about the places Lynn talked about rather than going to visit them.

Because of her reaction, Lynn backed off lobbying for an adventure and handed Monica her empty coffee mug. Monica went inside to get two fresh cups of coffee, and Lynn pulled the invitation she had picked up at the house from her pocket and placed it on the table without a word.

When Monica returned, she gave Lynn her mug, and the two sisters remained silent for a moment as they enjoyed their coffee and listened to the rain fall on the porch roof. Lynn wondered if her sister would notice the envelope and about her reaction when she did. Monica suddenly picked up the envelope and began reading the invitation she had pulled from inside:

'A Costumed Ball is being held in honor of Sydney Berber-Johnston tomorrow evening at the Beechwood Downs Estate. Your presence is requested. Costumes will be provided in the form of masks, but all are welcome to bring their own. Drinks at 6, dinner at 8. Music and Dancing throughout.'

Without emotion, Monica returned the invitation to the envelope and placed it back on the table between them. She took a sip of coffee, turned to Lynn, and asked.

"Is that what you mean? That I should go to something like that?"

Lynn did not know what to say. She picked up the envelope and reread the invitation.

"Have you been to Beechwood Downs, Mona? Do you know who is throwing this 'Ball'?"

"The answer on both counts is yes …." Monica replied, "… His name is Ehndale, and I've been to his home before."

"I've met him. Syd introduced us, but I don't understand the problem?" Lynn remarked.

"He's not a very nice person…." Monica replied, "… he's partially the reason why Thurmond and I are not getting along. I've been to his house, and it wasn't a memorable experience, at least not in a good way. Kate hated him. Thomas and Thurmond also hate him, as I believe you would too."

Lynn was not in a hurry to encourage Monica to do anything that could jeopardize her emotional condition, but this was an opportunity to do something out of the ordinary. To venture out and enjoy herself.

"I know this may seem impossible, Mona, but you should consider going. Believe me, the last thing I want to do is go to a party celebrating Syd. She's been a pain since she's been here and deserves nothing of the kind, but if you could look past who this man is and what he represents, you may enjoy yourself. Use this as your first step in doing what you want without regard for anyone but yourself. Do it for you!"

"The only possible way I could go is if you went with me," Monica replied, "…but you're leaving tomorrow, aren't you?"

"Well, we haven't really decided when we're leaving yet, Mona. We were kind of feeling that out. I know guests are like fish and begin to stink after a few days, but if you're OK with us staying another day or two at your house, we'll let the boys know. They can handle the business."

Lynn paused for a second, then continued, "...besides, I think it would be fun! Jack would absolutely love to go. Are you kidding me? He lives for this kind of stuff!"

"I don't know, Lynn. I mean, Thurmond may be there. What about that? I don't want to argue with him. I don't think I can handle that."

"You can deal with your ex-boyfriend being there. Just be straight with him if he approaches you, Mona. Tell him upfront that you're there to enjoy yourself, not to be his date or be harassed by him. I can tell him if you want."

Lynn saw this as an opportunity for Mona to begin to think of her life differently and excitedly continued, "...besides, he and Jack have become friends, and I know Jack would love to spend time with him. If I ask Jack to make sure he doesn't bother you, it won't be an issue."

"I thought Jack abhorred Sydney...." Monica replied, "...and you don't even have an invite, Lynn, and given it's Syd we're talking about, you probably aren't going to get one."

"To hell with her!" Lynn replied, "...and to hell with the invitation! Jack and I have crashed better parties than this before, believe me, and he'll be excited to go! Jack loves parties."

Monica was encouraged by her sister's excitement but was still unsure. Lynn saw that Monica seemed to be considering the idea and continued to make her case.

"You can get past the fact that you don't like this guy Ehndale, and if it's Syd you're worried about, don't! I can handle her if she decides to make trouble. She'll probably just want to flaunt her new boyfriend anyway, to try to make me jealous. She'll love that I'm there! C'mon Mona. Let's do it! Let's go! It'll be fun!"

35

Anticipation

The impending exodus of Foundry employees scheduled to depart with Thurmond for Taipei created an urgency in training their replacements. Hunter saw this as his opportunity and wanted to take advantage of it while it lasted. As a result, he abandoned all interest in the Diner and needed someone to take over its operation while he decided what to do with it. Ronnie had learned a great deal about the place filling in during Kate's illness and had become integral to its operation since her passing. This made her the prime candidate to manage it, so Hunter offered her the job permanently, and she accepted without hesitation.

Ronnie had never thought of running her own business but became excited when Hunter surprised her by discussing her assumption of ownership. The two began discussing the transition details, and Vikki became concerned when Ronnie told her the news. Vikki thought the decision seemed too impulsive and asked her sister to consider what resigning from her teaching position would mean. Ronnie seemed perfectly fine with the idea.

"Don't get me wrong, 'V,' I love the kids,"...Ronnie began, "… but the idea of becoming my own boss is very appealing. Of all people, I'm sure you can understand that. Besides, I've made many good friends, and I like being back in town. It's comfortable and familiar. I also like the fact that we will be able to see each other more regularly. It's like an opportunity to become reacquainted. It just feels right."

Vikki understood the appeal of being in charge and could empathize with her sister's need for 'belonging.' She herself had developed an emotional connection with the town when she assumed control of the Foundry. The board seemed destined to destroy the company and the town along with it, but she saved both by wrestling control away from them, and although there was opposition at first, people eventually came to love her for it.

When she was a child, Vikki had a desperate desire to expand her horizons beyond where she grew up and had constantly been on the move chasing deals throughout her career, which Vikki hadn't regretted until she met Thomas. Quite unintentionally, she had found that focusing her pursuits on the single enterprise of the Foundry allowed her to nurture her relationship with Thomas and find comfort in the idea of being in a place where she finally felt she was at home, which was something she had never felt there before.

~

Ronnie had arranged to meet Vikki that afternoon to review some financials associated with assuming ownership of the Diner. They were having a late lunch when they saw Thomas and Thurmond drive up, and Vikki was happy to see them both. She was looking forward to hearing about what Ronnie was calling their 'boys' night out' and teasing Thomas about it.

Though the day was far from over, the two men's body language suggested it had already been a long day for them both. Neither seemed to care that they were dripping wet from the rain, and they labored as they sloshed across the Diner until they reached the table where Vikki and Ronnie were sitting. As they made their way, Ronnie tried to get a waitress's attention to bring them some coffee.

"Morning Ronnie…" Thomas said as he pulled a chair aside and kissed Vikki before he sat.

"Good afternoon, boys…." Ronnie replied as she shifted her chair to make room, "… How're things?"

"Swell…" Thurmond returned, "…but if you wouldn't mind, can you stop yelling, please? I have a headache that could split an atom!"

"She's not yelling Thurm…." Thomas replied.

Vikki put her hand on Thomas' shoulder, winked at her sister, and said, "Of course she is, Thom. Seems our friend Thurmond is experiencing the effects of dehydration. Probably the result of excessive alcohol consumption, from what I understand. I'm guessing that is true for you both, but you know what they say, to every action, there is an equal and opposite reaction. So, basically, It's the price you pay for overindulging."

"Yeah, like what she said…." Thurmond replied, holding his head, and pointing a finger at Vikki.

"Two black coffees, comin' right up!" Ronnie announced as she left to get coffee and a bottle of aspirin for the men. Vikki continued in a whisper, "I wanted to mention, Thom, that I only just received an invitation to a party being held tomorrow night for Sydney."

"Who's having a party for Sydney?" Thurmond mumbled wearily, "…I didn't know she even knew anyone?"

Before Vikki could reply, Thomas added, "I think it's in poor taste to celebrate anything with Bella's passing. Who's throwing the party anyway, and where is it?"

"It's a costume ball, but you don't have to wear a costume. You just have to show up. Masks are being provided."

Thurmond was not processing the information and didn't realize Vikki hadn't answered his question, but Thomas had the distinct impression she was leaving information out and repeated the question, "Who's throwing the party for her 'V'?"

Vikki continued, "Some important people are going to be there, so I have to go…."

Thomas suspected Vikki was intentionally keeping something from him, most likely because she knew he wouldn't like her answer, so he repeated the question with a bit more resolve.

"Who's throwing the party for her 'V,' and where is it?"

From the moment she received the invitation, Vikki wondered how she would tell Thomas about it because she knew he would become upset once he learned it was from Ehndale. She was also concerned that Thurmond would become angry and considered fabricating some story to make it easier to convey. Ultimately Vikki determined that the easiest way was to tell them the truth. She would just have to deal with the repercussions afterward.

Vikki took a deep breath and began to explain when a porcelain plate exploded against the terrazzo floor. The sound amplified the throbbing pain in Thurmond's head and attracted the attention of almost everyone in the Diner.

Everyone but Thurmond looked to see what had happened, and a momentary hush fell over the restaurant, followed almost immediately by awkward applause. Jack and Emerson were seen scrambling around on the floor, helping a waitress pick up the scattered dinner plate pieces. Everyone knew Emerson was somehow responsible.

"Afternoon, fellas!" Jack bellowed as he handed the last piece of the plate to the waitress, helping them attend to the mess.

"Hey, Jack…" Thomas replied, "… great you could make it. How are you guys feeling? Thurm here is less than ideal."

"That's putting it mildly," Thurmond added without lifting his head from his hands.

Jack smiled at him and replied, "Em, and I just came from the Whitehorse. Lynn's over there with Mona. She wouldn't make us breakfast this morning, so we stopped by to ask if you were free for lunch earlier, Thom. When you couldn't join us, we got something from the food truck and ate it on the green. But that wasn't near enough to satisfy our appetite! Ain't that right, Em?"

"Truer words ain't never been spoken. Wuz gettin' so my belly thought my throat's been cut."

Jack and Emerson pulled over several chairs and crowded around the table. Ronnie hadn't returned with the aspirin yet, so Vikki was the lone woman at the table. She was glad the interruption allowed her to avoid answering the question about Ehndale's party but knew Thomas would not let her off the hook that easily.

She decided it was probably best to tell Thomas in private and told the men she had a meeting at the office and wanted to say goodbye to her sister before she left. She excused herself and asked Thomas to come with her for a minute so they could finish talking away from the rest of the group. Thomas joined her, and Vikki began, "You probably already know what I'm going to say…."

"It's Ehndale, isn't it?" Thomas asked.

"Yes, Thomas, it is," Vikki replied.

Vikki could see the frustration on Thomas's face. She knew how he felt about Ehndale and was concerned about his reaction.

"What is it with that guy?" Thomas replied and continued, "Correct me if I'm wrong, but don't you think it is in poor taste that he should have a party for someone when the whole reason for their being here is to bury their sister? I mean, c'mon!"

"It could be that he is trying to cheer her up and let her know she's appreciated. I know Monica and her sister Lynn don't get along with Sydney. Lynn abhors her. Maybe Ehndale truly likes her. I mean, he's been spending a lot of time with her lately, and maybe he sees that she needs a little ego boost. Ever consider that he may actually be trying to help her?"

Thomas couldn't understand why Vikki seemed to be defending Ehndale, but he was not interested in arguing the point and changed the subject.

"So, are you really thinking of going?"

"Yes, and I'd like you to come with me," Vikki replied.

"Why?' Thomas asked.

"Regardless of how you feel about him, Thom, Ehndale has many powerful associates. Some of them are invested in my operation in Asia, and they'll likely be there. You see, I have serious concerns about their intentions and have suspicions about Ehndale's motivations. I already know he's involved, and I'd like to do some reconnaissance. Maybe one of them will slip and say something useful."

Thomas found Vikki's explanation reassuring. He had always questioned Ehndale's motivations, and it was nice to hear Vikki beginning to come around to his way of thinking, but he wanted to know more.

"Suspicions about what intentions, 'V'?"

"I believe Ehndale may be manipulating the equity partners."

"Manipulating them how and toward what end?" Thomas asked.

"I don't know for certain, Thom, but Ehndale approached me about Hunter...."

"Hunter?" Thomas interrupted, befuddled as to how the boy figured into her suspicions.

Vikki was concerned about revealing too much, but if she asked Thomas to come to help her, he had a right to know why. She put her purse on the counter, took a deep breath, and began to explain.

"The investors insisted Thurmond remain in Taipei indefinitely, to the point where they were willing to withdraw their equity if he didn't. But they also insisted that I hire Hunter to step in for Thurmond while he was away, and I can't figure out why. "

"You're right, that's odd...." Thomas replied, "...I get why they want Thurmond to remain in Taipei. He's the best man for the job. But why would they insist his replacement be Hunter?"

"Well, I know Hunter's been spending a lot of time with Ehndale since his Mom died, and he's been training with Thurmond since I hired him. I was hoping that Thurmond would have learned or even suspected something, but he hasn't mentioned a thing other than Hunter's particular interest in the daughter of one of Ehndale's associates."

"So why does that concern you, 'V'?"

"That's why I want to go to the party, Thom. To talk to Hunter in a setting where he may be more at ease and open to telling us about what's going on. I don't think he knows what Ehndale is up to necessarily, but he can tell us if he was asked to do anything unusual."

"Hunter's a good kid, V, and he's smart. I don't think he'll do something he's uncomfortable with."

"I'd like you to come with me, Thom, because Hunter may talk to you. I know he respects you, and he may tell you something he's not telling Thurmond or me."

"Like what 'V'?"

"Like if I should be concerned about Ehndale soliciting information from him as he did with Howie. I mean, Hunter will have access to sensitive information, and that information, in the wrong hands, can cause me a lot of trouble."

Thomas closed his eyes, nodded, and said, "I understand, 'V.'"

"Thank you, Thom…." Vikki replied, "You and Hunter have something of a friendship. I can tell he looks up to you. I just wish he would confide in Thurmond. That would make things so much easier."

Thomas began to think of how he would extract information from Hunter and asked.

"Do you know if Thurmond was invited to the party?"

"I'm fairly certain of it…." Vikki affirmed.

"How can you be so sure?" Thomas asked.

"Ehndale always has more than one thing in mind when he arranges these sorts of things. There's too much to be gained to waste such an elaborate affair for a single purpose. The celebration for Sydney is the excuse, but the workings of the Foundry are probably on his agenda, as is some sort of retribution against Thurmond, I'm guessing."

"Retribution for what?"

"Ehndale never came to terms with his failure to collect Thurmond into his employ. He considers that a major defeat, losing an asset like Thurmond. You can also be sure that taking advantage of Thurmond's availability infuriated him. I believe it changed my relationship with Ehndale, and now I'm concerned about what he's up to."

Thomas knew Vikki was right and nodded in agreement as she continued.

"I know Ehndale is connected to the equity partners invested in our Asian expansion. He's admitted as much, but I believe he is up to something, and I don't know what it is. He can't know if I'm suspicious of him, or he will change his tactics. If that happens, I may never find out what it is until it's too late."

"Fair enough…" Thomas remarked, then asked, "… Do you know who else is invited? I'm guessing Monica and Lynn, which means Jack may be going too?"

"Sydney and Lynn don't get along, so I don't imagine Lynn will get invited if Sydney has anything to say about it, but I wouldn't be surprised if Lynn crashed the party anyway. She seems the type."

Thomas was glad to hear Lynn may be there, mostly because he knew she would bring Jack.

"Do you think Thurmond would come with Monica if they're both invited, or are they still having a rough go of it?"

"I'm sure they're both invited, but I'd imagine for entirely different reasons, and based on recent events, I seriously doubt they'll be going together."

Vikki looked back at the table and saw Thurmond hunching forward while Jack was joking with Emerson. Thurmond had his elbows on the table and his head in his hands with a hood pulled up over it.

"From the looks of it…." Vikki replied, "…Thurmond probably doesn't even know what day it is. Not sure he's in any shape for a party."

Thomas was hoping that Thurmond would come and said,

"He needs to go home and sleep it off. He'll be better after he's had some rest."

"I don't know, Thom. Sometimes the effects can linger." Vikki suggested, "…maybe he'll feel better when he wakes up, but he doesn't really need the aggravation. He's leaving for Asia soon, and he needs to be fresh. This business with Monica is killing him. I think the two of them could use a break from each other. It'll do them both a world of good to be apart."

"You may be right, 'V'…." Thomas replied dejectedly, "…but Thurm's his own man and will do what he wants, regardless of reason or friendship."

Ronnie suddenly emerged from the office with an aspirin bottle in hand and saw Thomas and Vikki at the counter. As she approached, Vikki picked up her purse and tucked it under her arm, then placed her hand gently on Thomas' shoulder and said:

"You still haven't really answered my question, Thom. Will you come with me or not? Will you talk to Hunter?"

"I will 'V'…." Thomas replied, "… I'll go and talk to him. But I don't want anything to do with your friend, Ehndale, in any way…."

"Understood, Thom."

"Good…" Thomas answered with a smile that was more of a smirk and concluded, "… it'll only turn out badly… for him, I fear."

"Fair enough, Thom…." Vikki responded with a slight laugh, "…and you never know. You may even have some fun!"

~

Vikki told Ronnie she had to get going and agreed to schedule some time with her in her office to finish their conversation about assuming ownership of the Diner. When the sisters had said goodbye, Ronnie handed Thomas the bottle of aspirin and asked him over to Thurmond at the table, then disappeared back into her office.

After walking Vikki to the door, Thomas rejoined the men and found that some food had been delivered to their table. Jack and Emerson ate voraciously, but Thurmond hadn't touched his food. When Thomas asked if he was feeling OK, Thurmond said he was nauseous. Thomas offered him some aspirin and a ride home, and Thurmond immediately accepted.

~

On the drive back to his house, Thurmond nodded in and out of sleep while Thomas wondered how to approach Hunter without raising suspicion. Thomas knew Thurmond would be invaluable in that regard, but he wasn't certain Thurmond had received an invite. Thomas was worried that the mention of Ehndale may provoke Thurmond to anger, so he decided to let Thurmond sleep.

Thurmond awoke when they arrived at his home, and he groggily thanked Thomas for the ride. He trudged up the front steps and across the porch to the front door, then lifted the loose shingle beside the living room window where he hid the house key. Thomas waited until Thurmond had opened the door and began to pull out of the driveway when Thurmond waved to let him know he was OK.

Happy to be home, Thurmond returned the key to its hiding place, then stepped back inside. The screen door slammed shut behind him, amplifying his headache. He pulled off his wet hooded sweatshirt, tossed it on the back of a living room chair, and then leaned against the walls to steady himself as he made his way toward the kitchen.

When Thurmond entered the kitchen, he pulled a milk carton from the refrigerator and drank it furiously before tossing the empty container into the sink. He then headed back towards the stairs to go up to his bedroom to rest, but when he reached the base of the stairs, Thurmond saw an envelope with his name on it lying on the floor inside the front door that he hadn't noticed before.

He picked it up, entered the living room, and turned on the light to see what it was. He plopped into a chair and strained through his splitting headache to read it.

The letter was an invitation from Ehndale to a party being held in honor of Mona's sister Sydney. Thurmond laughed at the idea and immediately threw it in the trash, then went upstairs to lie down.

36

Invitation

Vikki was seriously concerned about the potentially significant financial consequences of Ehndale's meddling in Foundry affairs. Ehndale had used Howie to gather confidential information in the past, and Vikki suspected Hunter might have been selected to perform the same purpose.

She was relieved that Thomas had agreed to come with her to Sydney's party but wanted him to avoid raising suspicion. She asked him to delicately extract whatever intelligence he could from Hunter and stressed that it was imperative that he avoid confronting Ehndale directly, no matter the circumstances.

Thomas thought it would be evident to Hunter that his interest in Foundry affairs would be on Vikki's behalf and wasn't quite sure how to approach him. Although Vikki had assured him to the contrary, Thurmond was not guaranteed to be invited, so Thomas believed he was likely on his own. Thurmond had been working closely with Hunter, so his assistance would have been tremendously helpful.

The possibility that Lynn and Jack would attend was a welcome thought, even if they had to crash the party, as Vikki had suggested. It was not that they could help Thomas get the information he needed from Hunter, but Thomas appreciated their company. The couple had a knack for enjoying themselves and would undoubtedly be a welcome distraction.

~

As he tossed and turned, trying to sleep off his hangover, Thurmond couldn't stop wondering how things could have turned out so badly with Mona. He was confident that she would be at Sydney's party, and although he had no illusions about being able to make everything right with her, he believed this might be his only opportunity to talk with her before leaving for Taipei.

After a few hours of restlessness, Thurmond thought it was important that he at least said goodbye and returned to the parlor to retrieve the envelope he had thrown in the garbage. He seriously considered going and took the invitation upstairs with him and placed it on the night table beside his bed, wondering if he should bother.

Frustrated that he could not quiet his mind, Thurmond sat up in bed and grabbed the invitation. As he stared at it, he wondered what to do, and after a few minutes, he jumped out of bed, threw on a coat and stuffed the envelope in his pocket, then ran out of the house, headed for Emerson's trailer.

When he arrived, Thurmond saw Emerson reading at a table inside. He pulled his truck up beside the trailer, rolled down his window, and shouted out to his friend through the rain.

"Howdy, Em! You busy?"

Emerson looked out his window to see who had called him and spotted Thurmond sitting in his truck. He put down his book and made his way to the open window and shouted back.

"I'm finer than a frog hair split four ways, Thurm. C'mon in."

Thurmond laughed, parked his truck beside the trailer, then jogged through the light rain to the trailer door, which Emerson held open for his friend as he reached out his hand in welcome.

"Don't know 'bout you, Thurm, but 'til I got some vittles and a little shuteye, I felt like I'd been chewed up and spit out! To what do I owe the honor?" Emerson asked.

"Same here, Em, but I had something on my mind that's making it difficult to sleep…." Thurmond replied, shaking his friend's hand, then continued, "I was wondering if I could pick your brain for a few minutes, Em. Mind if we sit for a bit?"

"Not-at-all, Thurm…" Emerson replied as Thurmond stepped into the camper and sat at the table where Emerson had been reading.

Even though it was late, Emerson thought a little hair of the dog that bit him would do Thurmond some good, so he grabbed a couple of beers from a cooler on the ground beside the camper door, popped the caps with the wrench he had pulled from his side pocket and sat back down at the table. He replaced the book he had left on the table with the two beers.

"What can I do for ya?" Emerson asked as he placed the book he'd been reading on a nearby counter.

"What's that you're reading, Em?"

"Aristotle…" Emerson answered quickly before reading the title slowly in broken segments to be sure he pronounced it correctly, "NI-CO-MACH-EN Ethics…."

Thurmond laughed at his preposterous friend and remarked, "Sounds complicated Em…."

"Not so much…" Emerson replied as he stretched to the nearby counter and picked up another book with dozens of dog-eared pages.

"Now this here Plato fella though, he's twisted six ways to Sunday."

Emerson tossed the book back on the counter and clinked bottles with his friend as they both began to laugh. After a long swig of beer, Thurmond explained why he'd come.

"It's about Mona, Em. As if you couldn't guess."

"Figured out as much, Thurm. What's it that you got on your mind?"

"Well, I'm not sure where to start?"

Emerson smiled at his friend and replied, "Start at the beginning, Thurm. See where it takes ya. That's what I'd do. Seems like a good place to start."

Thurmond took another drink of beer and continued, "I got an invitation to a party for Mona's sister, Sydney. But it's at that fella Ehndale's house."

Emerson smiled and replied, "I kin see how that would be less than appealing, Thurm…."

"It's not just that, Em. I mean, I don't know what I should do or even what I want to do. On the one hand, I have no interest in Ehndale or his stupid party, but Mona's definitely gonna be there, and I don't know if this isn't the last opportunity I'll get to say goodbye to her before I leave for Asia."

"I thought you said she was needin' some space, Thurm?"

"Yeah, that's right, Em. Mona told me she needed a break to consider how our relationship fit into her future. The last time we saw each other, we got into a fight. Said she never wanted to see me again, but I don't want her to remember us that way. I wanted to leave on a good note."

Emerson leaned back in his chair, silently sipping his beer, listening as Thurmond continued.

"I don't want her to think I'm going to Sydney's party just to get to her. She accused me of that at Bella's services. Made me feel awful."

"Imagine it would, Thurm…." Emerson interjected.

"I hate to ask Em because I know you don't like this sort of thing, but if you're going, could I just stick with you? Mona wouldn't see that as me taking advantage, I'd just be going with my friend, and if I do talk to her, it won't be like I went there for that alone…."

"I weren't invited…." Emerson replied without the slightest hint of resentment for being excluded, "…besides, you know those stuffed-shirt parties ain't for me, Thurm. Full of feather dusters pretending to be roosters."

Thurmond understood his friend's meaning and took a swig of beer to wash down the lump in his throat. He wiped his mouth with the sleeve of his shirt and continued.

"So how do I make her understand what she means to me, Em? Make her understand how sorry I am for what happened. Make her believe I would never do anything like that to hurt her again. How do I make her believe I love her, Em?"

"I'd say nothin', Thurm...." Emerson earnestly replied, "... Mona knows you love her."

"How can I be sure, Em...." Thurmond replied, "...I mean, she's still angry about what I'd done when I hung around with Brad. You know, the things I'd done that hurt her. Things that she said she had forgiven. I guess she's had a chance to think about them, and now she's unsure. Probably thinks I could do it again, but I wouldn't, Em! I couldn't! Not ever. I love her, and I need her to know that. I can't have her hating me for the rest of my life!"

"What's past is past, Thurm. You can either be a prisoner to it or learn from it. Just give it some time, and Mona'll come around. You'll see. Memory is generous, and time heals all wounds."

"So, you don't think I should go?"

Emerson finished his beer and placed it off to one side between them on the table.

"As I recollect, you don't much care for that N'Dale fella anyways, is that fair to say?"

"Yes, Em, I don't care for him. I think he's been putting ideas in Mona's head. Trying to convince her I will cheat on her while I'm away. Trying to drive us apart."

"Forget him..." Emerson coolly replied, "...that fella don't matter a hill of beans less you let him Thurm, so don't let him. Now, cause of what you'd done before, Mona's gonna have doubts about you, but she's the one who needs to get over it, not you. You know where your heart is."

Thurmond knew his friend was right. He finished his beer in one long swig, took his empty bottle along with the one Emerson had placed on the table between them, and tossed them into the trash. He stepped out of the camper into the light rain, grabbed two more beers from the cooler, and placed them on the table between them. Emerson opened the beers with his pipe wrench and continued.

"People like this N'dale fella think the sun comes up just to hear them crow. They spend more time minding other people's business than their own, and that dog don't hunt in my book Thurm."

"Yeah, he's cocky and arrogant!" Thurmond confirmed.

"Bad combination if you ask me…." Emerson replied, "… you'd do well to remember he's all fluff and bluster, Thurm. Just got a big head 'cause he's livin' high in cotton, is all."

Thurmond thought for a second and managed a laugh before he replied, "…come to think of it, Em, he does have a pretty big head."

"As you know, I ain't one to throw stones, Thurm…" Emerson replied, "…but now that you mention it, I ain't seen a head that big since that snake oil fella come through town couple years back. Remember him? Had a head could throw shade!"

Both men began to laugh, and Thurmond felt his tension beginning to wane. He was glad he had decided to visit his friend. Emerson's company always had a way of making him feel better about everything.

After a few moments of laughter, Emerson returned to the topic and said," If you don't mind me sayin' Thurm, I think you're right. That N'dale fella is up to no good."

"What makes you say that?" Thurmond asked.

"Don't think for one second that there N'dale fella don't know that Mona's broken-hearted about losing Katie then Bella. I could tell from talking to Mona he's got her confused. Tellin' her things that ain't his place to say, even if they was true, which they ain't."

"What did he say, Em?"

"Mona didn't tell me much, Thurm, but I think she let some things slip she'd rather she hadn't."

"Like what?" Thurmond asked abruptly.

"Can't recollect exactly Thurm, but he was trying to cozy up to her with sympathy. Like he understood… and you didn't."

Thurmond became visibly upset, and Emerson immediately regretted telling him anything. Before Thurmond could speak, Emerson continued.

"If he's gettin' her riled up like that, Thurm, then you have two choices as I see it. You can make him stop, which ain't likely, or you can prove him wrong."

"Prove him wrong, Em? I'd rather string him up!"

"Ain't gonna convince Mona this fella's lying by stringin' him up, Thurm."

"I know, Em. Just makes me mad, is all."

"I heard that, Thurm, but you gotta be smart about this. You gotta show Mona he's lying, but you can't do that just by sayin' so, Thurm. He'll just convince her you're lyin'. His word against yours. No, you got to show her by giving her what she wants, as hard as that may be, and let things work themselves out. Then she'll see the truth. Then she'll believe you. That's when she'll come back. I won't lie, it's just gonna take a little time, and seein' as you're busier than a one-armed paper hanger with the whole Asia thing, that time should go by right quick."

"What I don't understand is why? How does he benefit from messing things up between Mona and me? Maybe he's still mad at me for bailing on his Middle East deal and wants to punish me?"

Emerson had a sudden urge to use the trailer lav. He picked up the book he had been reading and slapped it into his palm as he stood.

"This here Aristotle fella says that we ain't born good naturally Thurm. He reckons we must develop habits that a good person has to be a good person. The way I figure it is this fella N'dale ain't done that. Been bad from the get-go. Had more practice being bad than anything else and probably has fun messing with people. Tickled his fancy like it was entertainment for him."

Emerson tossed the book on the table before Thurmond and excused himself for a minute.

Thurmond picked up the book and began fanning through the pages, which stopped where it had been dog-eared. He noticed something highlighted on that page and paused to read it quickly:

'…Those who are quick to treat each other in friendly ways wish to be friends, but are not friends, unless they are also lovable, and know this. For though the wish for friendship comes quickly, friendship does not.'

Thurmond tossed the book back on the table and sat quietly, wondering what he should do or if he should do anything. A few minutes later, Emerson returned and picked up where he'd left off.

"Seems like this N'Dale fella probably did whatever he needed to do to get what he wanted, good or bad. It doesn't seem to matter much to him if he hurts people. Now that's just plain ugly, Thurm, and you know God don't like ugly."

"Do you think he's using Mona Em? Do you think she's in danger?"

Emerson sat down, sipped the foam from the top of his beer, then wiped his mouth and the bottle top with his sleeve and replied:

"I don't think she'd give up everything she's ever believed in for a 'good-time Charlie,' Thurm. She's smarter than that."

Thurmond recalled Ehndale's temptations and how he would manipulate people and situations for his benefit or the benefit of his choosing. Offering treasures in the present life in return for unwavering servitude in the next. Thurmond remembered how difficult it was to resist, especially when things weren't going so well, but Thurmond was confident that if it was his intention to try and corrupt Mona, it wouldn't work. Mona would never agree, given the strength of her faith.

Emerson saw his friend deep in thought and added, "…this here N'dale fella is just a selfish highfalutin Thurm. Don't let him get under your skin. He ain't worth it."

"But what about Mona Em? How do I protect her from him if she won't talk to me?"

"Mona's got her own demons to deal with, Thurm. Maybe this here N'dale fella's one of them, but she's a good person and strong. She'll come through it. You'll be happy you gave her space, and she'll love you for letting her have it."

"I know you're right, Em. It's just that I don't want her to make the same mistakes I did. I want to spare her the grief."

"Even if she does something stupid...." Emerson replied, "...there's always forgiveness. You know you love her, and that's all that matters. I'm not worried, and you shouldn't be either."

Thurmond was amazed at how clearly he could think after listening to his friend. He decided at that moment that he was going to Sydney's party for no other reason than to let Mona know that he loved her unconditionally. If she came back, Thurmond would know she felt the same, but if she didn't, it wasn't meant to be. Thurmond was not going to let Ehndale ruin this opportunity. He would express his feelings to her and then just walk away and get on with his life.

He thanked his friend and went home to prepare for Ehndale's party.

~

The invitations had been delivered to everyone on the guest list, but due to the short notice, the favor of a response had not been requested, so there was no way of knowing who would actually attend. Sydney wondered what her sister's reaction might be and, contrary to her initial reaction, hoped they would be there.

Early the following morning, streamers and banners announcing the celebration were hurriedly draped around town, fueling speculation that the event had something to do with the Foundry. Local merchants providing goods and services for the party packed their trucks and paraded through town on their way to the estate.

Beechwood Downs buzzed with activity as tents, lights, tables, and chairs were delivered and erected by several crews of laborers, who also constructed a stage on the rear lawn where musicians would perform. Vans filled with food were delivered to the service kitchen, which were either set up at prep stations under the tents or stored in a refrigerated truck, serving as a freezer. A wide variety of masks were also delivered, along with a dozen full costumes, that the costume shop threw in as a gesture of gratitude for the business.

Sydney was grateful that Ehndale was throwing her a party, and regardless of how many people attended, she looked forward to being the center of attention for a change.

37

Preparation

Hunter coveted his new position at the Foundry and saw it as the opportunity of his lifetime. It provided him with the liberation he desperately desired from what he considered to be the internment of his mother's business. Hunter understood, however, that this opportunity came at a price. A ransom he owed to the one responsible for facilitating this opportunity, and that ransom was not something that sat well with his new partner.

Early in the morning on the day of Ehndale's scheduled costume party for Sydney, the couple strolled through the light rain, enjoying each other's company. When the topic came up, Naomi squeezed Hunter's hand and asked, "So, what are you going to tell him tonight, sweetheart? You know he's going to want an answer."

"I know, Naomi, but I have half a mind not to go, honestly. I mean, I don't even like half the people that are going to be there. Besides, I'd rather just tell him without the hoopla and spend that time with you."

"...and I love you for that..." Naomi replied, "...but you must go. It's important."

"I guess..." Hunter replied, "...but I don't even know Mona's sister, Sydney. What kind of name is that, anyway? Syd? That's a guy's name."

"Hunter, stop. You're just coming up with excuses. Who cares whom he's pretending to honor? You know he's just using her as an excuse to have a party, don't you? It's a ruse. She means nothing to him."

"I know…" Hunter reluctantly agreed, "…but I don't want to pretend I like those people anymore. I have nothing to say to them."

Hunter thought for a moment, then continued, "No disrespect to your father, Naomi, but Mr. Ehndale's friends are all phonies. You even said so yourself. They don't care about anyone but themselves. They just want to make a good impression on Mr. Ehndale, so he'll throw them a bone and possibly make them some money."

"What about Mr. Joseph or Officer Thomas, Hunter? I thought you enjoyed talking to them."

"I do, but Thurmond will be all about work. Probably remind me of something I did wrong. And I like Thomas, but he can be boring. I just want to stay home and skip the whole damn thing."

Naomi stepped around in front of Hunter to stop their stroll. Facing him, she took both his hands in hers, stared straight into his eyes, and spoke.

"You're not going there to mingle, Hunter. You have something more important to do. You need to give him an answer!"

"And what would I say? That I don't want him to help me? That I don't want to be successful?"

"No. Of course not, and you know that's not what I meant. But you can't just give Ehndale everything he wants. It's unreasonable and highly inappropriate."

Naomi wanted to relay the importance of what she believed to be in Hunter's best interest, and the two began walking again. They remained quiet for a few moments, then she continued, "I'm just saying that you don't want to jeopardize what you've just started by doing something that can get you in trouble, do you? Look what happened to that man, Mr. Ballard. He wound up in prison for doing Mr. Ehndale's bidding. And then there's Mr. Mallory, God rest his soul. His life fell apart when he got caught doing the same thing

Mr. Ehndale asked you to do. Why do you want to take that chance? You need to say something to him, and tonight is the perfect time to do it."

Hunter smiled and playfully replied.

"The difference is I'm smarter than Bradley and Howie. I won't get caught."

"Seriously, Hunter. All kidding aside, why take that chance?"

"He's responsible for putting me in this position, and I owe him. You know that. Without his help, I wouldn't be where I am. Besides, you know what they say, nothing ventured, nothing gained. If I say no, nothing will change. I'll probably lose the position and always wonder what I could have become."

"You don't owe him anything but your gratitude, Hunter. He may have been instrumental in securing the position, but you can't let him manipulate you because of it. If you say yes and get caught, you'll be in a worse situation than before you started. You'll be in a hole that you'll have to dig out of, and the opportunities that could have been available to you will no longer be possible."

"The ends justify the means, darlin'. You can't expect the reward if you don't take the risk. I understood that when I accepted the position. I knew they didn't think I could perform the responsibilities of the job; they kept turning me down until Ehndale provided me with the opportunity to prove them wrong, and I will."

"I know you will, sweetheart, but you have to mitigate your risks, and this is a big one."

"Look, I don't agree with everything Ehndale says, Naomi, but he does make some valid points."

"Give me an example Hunter. Just one."

"I'll give you two…." Hunter replied defiantly, "… Ehndale said that the most common pitfall to becoming successful was a fear of failure. He also said that…."

Naomi interrupted, "You'll have to explain that to me, Hunter. I'm not sure how fear of failure relates to asking you to spy for him…."

"Let me finish, Naomi, and you'll see…." Hunter replied, "…take my Mom, for instance. She'd be retired and enjoying her retirement if she had expanded operations and added another location or two, as I told her. But she lacked confidence in her customer base and slaved her whole life to generate enough money to survive as a result. I think that's what eventually killed her."

Naomi understood what it was like to lose a mother, and although her loss was different, she knew how much it hurt him. She let him talk and quietly listened as they continued their stroll.

"My Mom's customers would have followed her anywhere, Naomi, but she never leveraged that relationship for her benefit or mine. So, you see, her failure was in being too careful. She worried she couldn't handle more than one location and justified it by saying that a smaller operation was more 'manageable.' All she had to do was trust, but she didn't. She was too careful, which is selfish when you think about it."

"How so, Hunter?" Naomi earnestly replied.

"She wanted to control everything, but she couldn't. As a result, her limited abilities cost her money and her health. It probably even cost her her life. It also left me stuck to her business, like fly paper, which could have been much easier to sell if it was seen as a successful operation with a history of expansion. Instead, it's just a dumpy little Mom-and-Pop operation with minimal earnings. I'd be lucky to give it away at this point."

Hunter was being evasive, but there was escalating anger in his voice. Naomi wanted to get back to the matter at hand but knew she had to console him first. She sat him down on a nearby bench to continue discussing Ehndale's offer but thought it was worth mentioning that she disagreed with his assertion that his mother had been selfish.

"I know what it's like to lose your Mom, sweetheart, but I'm sure you're not being fair..." she said cautiously "...I get that you don't think she had the same foresight as you and suffered as a result. But I'm sure she did not intend it to be a burden for you. She thought she was giving you a legacy. One that she built on her own."

"But I didn't want it!" Hunter exclaimed, "...but she didn't listen."

"That may be true, Hunter, but I don't see how any of that is relevant to the premise that the end justifies the means. What's your second example?"

Hunter unexpectantly changed his demeanor dramatically and startled Naomi when he excitedly stood to face her. He lifted his foot on the bench beside her, folded his arms, one across the other, and rested them on his knee, then said, "What if I told you that I could become the CEO of CInc? Ehndale believes I have the potential. Even Vikki and Thurmond recognize that!"

Naomi hadn't expected such a grand proclamation and was genuinely surprised. She was amused by his enthusiasm but confused by his pronouncement and asked, "How do you figure?"

"I was hired for a job that surrendered control of the facility's entire operation to me! I'm not sure how Ehndale managed to get me in the door, but they didn't have to hire me. They must have believed I was capable. Why else would they agree to do it? How's that for confidence in my potential?"

"I don't want to rain on your parade Hunter, but from what I understand, it's only a temporary position. They need you to stand in for Thurmond while he's away and will probably have people helping you run things. Besides, once he completes his assignment in Asia, Thurmond will be back. What then?"

"You're right, of course, but how long do you think that will be? A year, maybe two? A lot can happen in that time. Ehndale said if I worked hard enough, I could eventually occupy Thurmond's position permanently or become even more! I just need to remove the obstacles that may prevent that from happening."

Naomi was glad to see Hunter so happy and believed that he would work tirelessly, but she worried his ambitions were blinding him. He couldn't see that Ehndale may be manipulating him, not for anyone's benefit but his own. She had seen it happen with her father, who was now a shell of his former self, with many promises left unfulfilled.

"Ehndale said that if I help him secure the information he asked me to provide, he could use that to remove the obstacles holding me back! He said that if I played my cards right when Thurmond returned, he would work for me. I can become vital to the operation while he's away, so it can't run without me. That way, Thurmond would have to decide whether to stay in Asia or come home and agree to work for me!"

Hunter took his arms off his knee, lifted his foot from the bench, and paced back and forth as he spoke.

"Does that seem relevant to the premise that the end justifies the means?"

Naomi replied with a hint of disappointment in her voice, "…yes…".

"Well then…" Hunter replied, "…does that change your mind about my giving Mr. Ehndale what he wants?"

"Depends."

"Depends on what, Naomi?" Hunter responded defiantly.

"I'd say it depends on what happens to Thurmond," Naomi replied.

"Thurmond?" Hunter retorted, "He's one of the obstacles. Probably the biggest!"

"But I thought you liked him?"

"I do. I respect Thurmond, but the man is in my way, which he knows. He's old, Naomi. He's had his time. Now it's time for someone younger with fresh ideas. Better ideas. Someone ambitious, like me!"

"He's not that old, Hunter, and besides, he knows a hell of a lot more than you do about running things. That's what comes with age, experience, and knowledge. He may lack the energy you have, but you can't hold a candle to him regarding practical experience. You'll get there., eventually, I'm sure, if that's what you want to do, but he deserves your respect. He's earned it."

Hunter continued without hesitation.

"He feels threatened by me, Naomi, and he'll try to keep me down, not as punishment for my having done something wrong but as a matter of self-preservation. For that reason alone, I need to sidestep him. Don't get me wrong. I don't wish him any harm, but, as Ehndale put it, the most important thing for a young man is to establish his reputation, which I can't do while I'm Thurmond's flunky. He'll hold me down accidentally or on purpose, and I need to get around him. He's had his time. He needs to step aside."

"How about Ms. Vikki?" Naomi asked anxiously.

"Another obstacle...." Hunter replied, "...but at least she's only doing this to make a profit. She pretends to be emotionally invested in the Foundry, but you and I know that's a lie. Ehndale told me that once she gets what she wants, Vikki will sell the place for a tidy sum and be gone quicker than she came. That's what Ehndale taught her to do!"

Naomi realized Hunter was probably right about Vikki and nodded in agreement. Hunter continued.

"I need to be out there on my own and in charge, sweetheart. There is no disrespect to Thurmond or Vikki, but they're standing in my light, and I need them to move. I want the light to shine on me! If they can't or won't move out of my way, I must go around them. It's as simple as that!"

Hunter stopped pacing and put his foot back on the bench beside Naomi, assuming the same posture he had taken previously. He continued, "If I need to help Ehndale to make that happen...." Hunter concluded, "...then so be it. It's not like I owe him anything because of it, anyway. Once I get what I want, I'm done with him too. He's a means to an end as well. He's no different than Thurmond or Vikki."

Naomi understood and was excited about the opportunities in front of Hunter, but she could see Ehndale's influence on full display, as she had seen with her father. She knew nothing she could say wouldn't be interpreted as unsupportive, so Naomi decided not to argue, but she did want to warn him.

"I guess what you're saying is that you're accepting his offer, which is fine if that's what you want, but I'd be careful not to let Ehndale know you feel he's also an obstacle."

"I know. I know…" Hunter replied, "…but one day Naomi. It'll be just you and me! The two of us running our own lives. Realizing our own dreams! With nothing but possibility in front of us!"

~

Vikki decided it may not be in her best interest to attend Sydney's costume party with Thomas as her escort, as their activities would undoubtedly be monitored. She didn't trust that Ehndale wouldn't accuse her of conspiring with Thomas in his reconnaissance mission to ascertain what kind of mischief Ehndale had put Hunter up to and made plans to spend the evening with her sister. Lynn was determined to crash the party and followed along separately with Monica, while Thomas led the way with Jack.

Thomas remembered the way to the estate and didn't need the directions that came with the invitation until they got quite close. When they were in the vicinity, Thomas slowed to inspect the plaques mounted conspicuously at each entryway to identify the properties. After a short while, he spotted the "Beechwood Downs" plaque that confirmed the location of Ehndale's estate and pulled off the main road onto the entrance apron. He slowly drove between the open, enormous ornamental wrought iron gates as Jack marveled at the fish-scaled cobblestone apron and enjoyed how the up-lighting highlighted beautiful features in the landscape.

Slowly they navigated the circuitous drive, with Lynn and Monica following closely behind in a separate car. When they emerged into the central courtyard, Jack commented on the grandeur of the estate, but Thomas was more concerned about how he would extract information from Hunter without raising his suspicions or Ehndale's attention. Lynn also admired the estate, but Monica had come in honor of her sister, Sydney, for whom she felt a tremendous sorrow and a bit of envy for having had so much attention lavished on her for little more than her keeping the company of a wealthy man.

Twilight was painted on everything but slowly gave way to the light emanating from the courtyard's lampposts as the two cars pulled up to the monumental steps. Thomas and Monica noticed Valets scurrying about in compliance with directions being shouted out by a short, huddled man who seemed to be in charge.

After exiting their cars, they handed the keys to the valets, and a mumbled voice came from the shadows, directing them to the rear terrace, where costumes and masks were being distributed. Thomas offered Monica his arm, and they made their way around the fountain that occupied the center of the motor court, with Jack and Lynn following behind.

"Nice digs!" Jack whispered to Lynn.

"Yeah. Wonder what this guy does for a living?" she asked.

Having overheard Lynn's question, Thomas looked over his shoulder and quietly responded, "Manipulates people for profit, amongst other things…."

"That's not entirely fair…." Monica retorted in Ehndale's defense, "…just because you don't like him doesn't mean you have the right to judge him, Thom. It's not your place."

Thomas was more than a little surprised by Monica's reaction and replied.

"My apologies Mona. I didn't mean to judge him or offend you. I'm sorry…."

"Oh, but you did, Thom…" she shot back, "… you certainly meant to judge him. Just because you and Vikki are jealous of him doesn't give you the right to disparage his character."

"We're not jealous of him, Mona…." Thomas responded as he laughed at the insinuation, "…how can you say that?"

Monica let go of his arm and walked over to her sister, Lynn, and said, "… C'mon Lynn, let's go to Syd's party. I'm not interested in assassinating people's character."

Lynn reluctantly let go of Jack's hand to take her sister's arm, not so much as to show she agreed with Monica but to appease her sensibilities and extinguish the disagreement.

"See you inside…." Lynn said to her husband as she walked on ahead with Monica.

Thomas stood speechless. He had no idea what had just happened or why it had happened. Jack slapped him on the back before putting his arm around him and hugging him.

"C'mon Thom. Let's go plow the froth off a couple. What do you say?"

"I'm sorry, Jack. I'm not really sure what that was all about."

"No apology necessary, mate…." Jack merrily responded, "…I think she's still grieving for Bella and not thinking straight. She probably won't even remember what she said in an hour. Don't think about it. Let's go get drunk! Let the girls drive us home later! I wonder what kind of costumes they have. Let's go check it out!"

Jack put his hand on his friend's back as Thomas sluggishly nodded in approval, and the two walked past the fountain and followed the signs posted around the side of the house to direct them to the party in the rear yard.

~

Sydney was nervous but also very excited. She had never been the guest of honor before and was looking forward to the attention she would receive. Costumed as Marie Antoinette, she smiled, stepped up to the railing atop the main staircase, looked into the central stair hall, and saw Ehndale watching her from below.

"You look lovely, my dear!" he bellowed, "…splendid choice of character and costume, I must say!"

"Thank you, Ehndale…" she replied.

Sydney gripped the handrail tightly and steadied herself before descending the main staircase with a healthy degree of trepidation. When she reached the base of the stairs, she balanced the enormous, powdered wig on her head and spun in a circle to give Ehndale a view of her costume.

"Splendid indeed!" he repeated, "…other guests are arriving, my dear. Why don't we go welcome them? They'll love your costume. They may not even know it's you in it! You look smashing!"

Sydney wondered if he was complimenting her or insinuating that she only looked good because she was in costume.

Ehndale took her arm and escorted her onto the veranda, where Sydney scanned the guests meandering about the yard, trying to identify them. The costumes made that almost impossible, but she did recognize her sister Monica at the costume table with her wretched sister Lynn.

Sydney was glad to see that Monica had come but had explicitly requested that Lynn not be invited. She wanted to ask Ehndale to tell her to leave but hesitated when she considered the fuss that would cause. Sydney was delighted that it was her evening, and nothing Lynn could say or do would change that. Everyone was there for her, so she decided not to let Lynn's presence ruin her evening and said nothing.

~

"This is exciting!" Lynn remarked as she rifled through the options at the costume station beside the veranda. "Do you want a mask, Mona, or a full-on costume?"

"I think a mask will do just fine, thank you…." Monica unenthusiastically responded.

Lynn ignored her sister's melancholy and picked up a modest sequined Fairy Mask plumed with green and gold feathers. She held it before her face and asked, "How about this, Mona?"

"That'll be fine," Monica said listlessly as she took the mask from her sister and held it to her own face.

"Very nice!" Lynn replied, "…and it looks good with your floral dress Mona."

"Now, how about me?" Lynn asked as she immediately went back to rifling through the options on the table.

In rapid succession, she held a variety of costumes up against her body, glancing into the full-length mirror positioned at the end of the costume station to see how she looked.

"I was thinking of going full-on costume Mona, but now I'm thinking of something simple to go with my black dinner dress. It's the only formal thing I brought; besides, black goes with everything."

"You look fine, Lynn…." Monica lethargically replied as she fastened the leather ties of her mask behind her head.

"How about this?" Lynn asked as she picked up a full-faced mask designed to appear as wood with leaves and twigs intermingled around her eyes, forehead, and cheeks with spiral horns extending from the sides of her head.

Monica looked at her sister and smiled beneath her mask. Seeing her sister in that mask was the first thing that made her happy.

"What do you think, Mona? Do you like it? Do I look good? Is it me?"

"I think it's supposed to be 'Puck'…." Monica commented.

"Who or what is Puck?" Lynn asked as she put on the mask and picked up a hand mirror that had also been provided at the costume table.

"Puck is a mischievous pixie from a Shakespearean play, Lynn. It's called A Midsummer's Night Dream…." Monica replied.

"Well, is it me, Mona? Do you think it suits me?"

"Puck delights in pranks and practical jokes, Lynn. Kind of like you."

"I'll take that as a compliment, Mona. Thank you!"

Mona noticed Jack and Thomas arrive at the costume station as the sisters spoke, but she was not interested in their company. She was still upset with Thomas' comment about Ehndale, not because it was offensive, but because she believed it was accurate. The man was a manipulative ogre, but Mona had been taught it was wrong to judge people, even if they deserved it.

The recent emotional roller-coaster Mona had been on with Thurmond exacerbated the situation. She had no idea why she couldn't accept the possibility that he could be faithful to her while he was away, as he had promised. This uncertainty filled her with doubt, which made her wonder why she hadn't been genuine with Thurmond at the airport about her misgivings.

Lynn noticed Mona's moment of reflection when she spotted Jack and Thomas at the other end of the costume station. She wanted her sister to enjoy herself, so she gently took her sister's arm, then spoke.

"So now that we're both fairies, let's create a little mischief and start with a drink! The boys can try to catch up!"

38

Spectacle

Looking out over the crowd milling about on his rear lawn, Ehndale wondered if the guests were satisfied with the selection of costumes. He summoned Balaam to inquire and was assured that there were no complaints, and everything seemed to be going splendidly.

Sydney was noticeably uncomfortable around his servant, so Ehndale immediately sent Balaam to check on the food. As the strange little man scurried away on his errand, Ehndale slipped his arm around her waist to make Sydney feel more at ease and delicately kissed her.

"This is so nice..." Sydney gratefully remarked, "...I don't know how to thank you."

"My pleasure, my dear!" Ehndale replied, "... I'm delighted you are enjoying yourself."

"Makes me want to stay...." Sydney sincerely replied.

"Ah, if it were only that simple, my dear."

"Why can't it be that simple?" Sydney asked sincerely, "...why is it that we shackle ourselves to lives we despise? There's no happiness for me back where I'm going. At least here I have you. I don't know if I need more than that."

Sydney watched Ehndale to see his reaction, and with a wry smile, he replied, "While it is true, my dear, that you may consider yourself 'shackled' to a pitiful life, it is also true that it is easier to imagine a life than to live one. Once you alter the course of your life, if you find it not to your liking, supplications to undo that redirection may be fruitless."

To address his curious comment Sydney turned to face Ehndale, which forced him to remove his arm from her waist. She steadied the considerable wig on her head and asked.

"I'm not really sure what you're suggesting, Ehndale. Are you saying if I stay here that I will regret it? How would that change our relationship?"

Ehndale gently put his hand on her cheek.

"I would be wary of rearranging your life based on your expectations of others. You may be disappointed."

Sydney was confused. Was Ehndale suggesting that he had no interest in being with her? Did he see their relationship as whimsy? A fling to be discarded without concern or regret? Was their time together meaningless? Ehndale continued, "I would recommend relying on yourself to be happy and refraining from projecting your desires onto others. Even if you managed to entangle another into your fantasies about how wonderful your life could be with them, they might despise you for it when they realize their life is not their own but a role they play in your fantasy."

Sydney had miscalculated her relationship with Ehndale but was still dumbfounded by his callousness. Perhaps it didn't suit his purposes to do so until now, but she didn't understand why he had not shared his true intentions with her. Obviously, he was not invested in a meaningful relationship with her, and that realization hurt Sydney like a gut punch.

Sydney felt betrayed, which was familiar to her, but it hurt just as much, nonetheless. She recounted her failings in past relationships and lamented this recurring misfortune, which she considered a curse. She wanted to avoid giving Ehndale the satisfaction of seeing her upset, so she decided to swallow her pride and enjoy the evening for what it was, then simply leave with what was left of her dignity the following day.

"I'd like to go say hello to my sisters, Ehndale; you'll excuse me?"

"But of course, my dear…" he courteously replied, "…by all means. Enjoy yourself. After all, this is all for you!"

Sydney had convinced herself that she had a future with Ehndale, but it was clear that he had no interest in her beyond a fleeting affair to satiate his appetite, which made her feel cheap and ashamed. She anticipated some chiding from Lynda, but she was exasperated by her recurring misfortune and left to see if she could find solace in her sisters.

~

Thomas was enjoying his time with his new friend Jack and had all but forgotten his puzzling interaction with Mona. Neither was particularly interested in wearing a costume but were reminded by an attendant that it was required.

Jack picked up a pirate hat with a long, braided wig and pulled it onto his head. He then removed a tricorne hat from a continental soldier's outfit and placed it on Thomas's head. They looked at each other and laughed at how ridiculous they looked, then made their way to the bar.

After the two men had secured what they expected to be their first of many drinks for the evening, Jack remarked, "I imagine Lynn will be busily avoiding Sydney…".

"Why do you say that, Jack?" Thomas asked.

"They don't like each other…." Jack began, "…Sydney is selfish and mean. Always mad about something. She thinks her life is unfair like she's been cheated or cursed. Lynn told me about her failures with men, and believe me, there have been some whoppers!"

Thomas had always made it a point not to delve into the personal affairs of anyone unless it was directly related to his police work. Still, Jack didn't need any prompting, and Thomas believed he was building to something funny, so Thomas smiled and said nothing to dissuade his friend from continuing.

"Says she's a 'committed non-practicing agnostic,' whatever that means!" Jack joked, "She's got a problem with everything, especially men."

"How so?' Thomas innocently asked.

"Been married three times? Maybe it's four. I lost track."

Jack was getting a little too personal for Thomas, who thought he ought to change the subject, but he was curious and allowed Jack to continue, "First husband left her on their honeymoon. She married him in Vegas, and he left her the next day. Took her bank account with him and left her with nothing!"

"That's terrible!" Thomas remarked.

"Yeah, well, Lynn was with her and told her the guy was no good, but Syd thought Lynn was jealous. Said she married the guy to keep Lynn from stealing him from her, then blamed Lynn for forcing her to do it."

"That's crazy! Did they look for the guy?"

"Yup. Lynn found him in jail a few months afterward, penniless."

Thomas became intrigued by the malady that was Sydney's life and asked,

"What's the story with the other husbands?"

"To tell you the truth, I get them confused…" Jack replied, "…the order and number, anyway. But it's always the same thing. Rushed to marry, and then it broke up. One guy was a pilot, and another was just a kid. Probably 10 years younger than her."

"Did she ever have any kids?"

"Nope. And for that, she blames God. Says she's been cursed."

"That's a shame," Thomas remarked.

"Yeah, well, Lynn's tired of being blamed for Sydney's mistakes and has given up trying to help her. Wants nothing to do with Sydney, so she avoids her, and I can't say as I blame her for feeling that way."

Jack finished his drink and asked Thomas if he wanted another.

~

Thurmond had no trouble finding his way to 'Beechwood Downs' and arrived over an hour after the party had started, just as he had planned. As he drove through the estate, vivid memories of his time there ran through his mind, including the night Ehndale had asked him to sign away his soul. He wondered how to approach Monica without enraging her and how to deal with Ehndale, should that become necessary.

When he emerged into the courtyard from under the alley of trees, a handful of anxious valets scurried out to meet him, but he waved them off and parked his truck beside the garage. Thurmond wanted to ensure that he had a swift departure when he decided to leave, should one be required, and put the keys in his pocket so he wouldn't have to wait for someone to retrieve them.

Posted signs directed guests to a costume station, and although Thurmond had no intention of staying there long, he believed wearing a costume may make his detection less likely. There was a limited selection remaining, with a choice between a handful of masks or two full body costumes, a confederate soldier, and a clown. He slipped on the clown outfit and joined the party.

~

After glancing at his watch, Thomas realized he had lost track of the time. He had been enjoying Jack's company tremendously but needed to spend time alone with Hunter before he left. Thomas didn't want to leave Jack alone and looked through the crowd for his wife Lynn and was surprised when he saw her with Sydney and Mona.

Considering the descriptions Thomas had heard about the relationship between the sisters, he believed there was likely a problem. His first inclination was to investigate, but he had a task to accomplish and directed Jack's attention to them instead. When Jack saw what was happening, he excused himself, and Thomas took advantage of the opportunity and left to find Hunter.

As he wandered through the crowd, Thomas spotted a man wearing a clown suit who seemed to be acting strangely. The man was alone and never stopped to engage in conversation. He carried no food or drink and wandered in the shadows, scanning the crowd from the party's fringes as if looking for someone.

Curious about the clown's identity, Thomas wanted to be sure it wasn't Hunter and approached him to find out, but the man moved rather swiftly, so Thomas had to pursue him hurriedly. As Thomas rushed past the other guests with his eyes fixed on his target, he unceremoniously bumped into a woman dressed as Cleopatra, spilling the two drinks she had been carrying. Redirecting his attention from the clown to the woman at hand, Thomas said apologetically, "I'm so terribly sorry! Did you spill anything on yourself?"

"I'm afraid my outfit is ruined…" she calmly replied.

"I'm so sorry…" he repeated, "…I was looking the other way and didn't see you."

Thomas did not recognize the woman but was struck by her gentle manner and continued apologizing. Suddenly a man's voice came from behind Thomas and said, "A policeman should be more aware of his surroundings."

Thomas turned and saw Hunter in a bowler hat and bow tie, grinning from ear to ear.

"I see you've met my date, Officer?" Hunter joked.

Thomas was embarrassed, but neither Hunter nor the young lady seemed terribly bothered.

"I'm so very sorry…." Thomas repeated.

"Will you stop…" The young woman replied.

She handed Hunter what was left of what she had been carrying and used a napkin to clean up what she could. Hunter took the items from Naomi and used the opportunity to introduce her.

"This beautiful but slightly soiled young lady is my girlfriend, Naomi, but don't tell her father I said that. He is unaware that she has any interest other than her economics study at the university."

Thomas had known Hunter since he was a little boy and had always liked him. Kate had been a tremendous example for her son, who seemed to have grown into a thoughtful young man.

"Pleasure Naomi…" Thomas replied. "…very nice to make your acquaintance."

"Pleasure's all mine…" Naomi returned as she offered her hand.

This was his opportunity to speak with Hunter, and although Thomas had imagined they would converse in private, Naomi's being there actually made it less conspicuous. Thomas began their discussion using comments instead of questions to extract information without raising suspicions. Their interaction was brief, but Thomas learned some essential things.

Hunter's familiarity with Ehndale's estate was the result of his having been invited there multiple times, staying overnight on occasion. Ehndale had also asked him to stay at the guest cottage indefinitely, which Naomi disapproved of, but Hunter said he was still considering. Hunter also commented on how excited he was about standing in for Thurmond during his absence and explained that it was his fervent hope that it could lead to a permanent position at the Foundry. Hunter suggested he was considering selling his mother's Diner so that he might dedicate all his efforts to his new job to prove himself, which Vikki had already mentioned to Thomas, confirming Hunter's honesty and truthfulness.

"So, you see, Officer, I fully intend to make the most of this opportunity, and with this young lady here helping me, I don't see how I can fail."

"I have every confidence you'll be up to the task…." Thomas replied.

"Let's hope so…" Hunter returned, "…Thank you."

"You're very welcome, Hunter."

Although Hunter was volunteering a good deal of information, Thomas felt his mission wouldn't be completed until he learned why Ehndale was so interested in Hunter occupying Thurmond's position at the Foundry, so he continued, "I'm sure you'll prove your worth in time. And if you decide to stay here at the cottage, you'll probably want to take full advantage of your relationship with Mr. Ehndale, as I'm sure he will of you."

The insinuation that Ehndale was interested in taking advantage of him made Hunter uncomfortable, and the conversation suddenly fell into a momentary sullenness. Thomas realized he'd made a mistake but couldn't take it back without raising suspicion about why he had said it in the first place. After a lengthy pause, Hunter replied.

"I'd rather not discuss the details of my relationship with Mr. Ehndale if you don't mind, but I can tell you that I am excited about the prospects and am certain I can assist with both Vikki and Ehndale's interests."

Hunter's comment was very telling, but Thomas knew if he probed further, Hunter may be inclined to mention it to Ehndale, which Thomas wanted to avoid. He had learned what he had come to discover; that Hunter was ambitious and reluctant to discuss his close association with Ehndale, so Thomas decided to leave it there.

"I suppose I should be on my way…" Thomas continued, "…I was looking for a friend when I accidentally ran over Cleopatra."

"Cleopatra's name is Naomi…" she reminded him, "…and you didn't run over me. You just made a mess of things."

"Yes, well, I'm sorry I made a mess, Naomi…." Thomas said with a smile, "…my apologies. I'll leave you to enjoy the party…."

Thomas took off his tricorne hat, held it at his waist, and bowed.

"Thank you, officer. Enjoy the party." Naomi replied as she took Hunter by the arm, saying, "All this talk is making me thirsty! Let's go refresh our drinks."

The couple politely took their leave of him as Thomas considered what he would do next. Everything he had come to do had been done, so it was time to find Jack and enjoy the rest of his evening.

~

While searching for Jack, Thomas heard some distant shouting from a balcony, looked towards the source of the disturbance, and heard it again louder still. He looked up and saw Monica arguing with the clown he had been following earlier.

Thomas listened to the clown's voice, hoping it could help him identify the man, but his voice never elevated to an audible level, unlike Monica, who had been the one shouting.

The disturbance was loud enough to attract a fair amount of attention from the other guests, and after a few minutes, the band suddenly stopped playing. Everyone looked to the stage to see what had happened, and Thomas saw Ehndale take a microphone from one of the performers and begin to make an announcement, which instantly quieted the crowd.

"It is so very nice that you should all have come to help us celebrate our good friend, Sydney Berber-Johnston, whose imminent departure is celebrated on this occasion. We honor her with this show of appreciation for her qualities and charms! We shall miss her and look forward to the next time she feels compelled to honor us with her presence!"

After the announcement, the crowd began cheering, but Sydney believed it was because of the person saying it and not for what had been said. She considered it an insult and began to cry, then suddenly ran inside the house. Lynn ran after her in the futile hope that she could console her troubled sister.

~

Kate's funeral, Bella's wake, and now, Sydney's going away party. Monica was furious. This was the third time Thurmond had shown up and cornered her looking for redemption. Monica considered it highly inappropriate and called Thurmond an opportunist who took advantage of situations to break his promise of giving her some space.

Thurmond was not concerned about being ridiculed but implored Monica not to make a scene for her own sake. Monica refused his supplications and, to humiliate him, intentionally raised her voice to attract people's attention. The band began playing again, and the party resumed, so they could no longer be heard by anyone else.

"Please, Mona," Thurmond implored, "... don't make a scene. I only wanted you to know that I love you. Nothing else."

"You did the same thing at Kate's funeral and Bella's wake!" Monica screamed, "You use tragic events or joyous occasions as an excuse to break your promise! You plead your case and profess your love, but why should I believe you? I can't trust you! You're a liar!"

"No, Mona. That's not true at all. I've stayed away and honored your request."

"You have?" she asked sardonically, "...and what is this then? Once again, you are at an event you know I will be attending to plead your case."

Thurmond knew there was no use in arguing with her. He trusted that his friend Emerson had been right, and Mona's memory would be generous in time. She could say or think whatever she wanted, but he needed to express his feelings before he left town.

"I know you're trying to embarrass me, Mona...." Thurmond began, "...and to be honest, I would rather it didn't happen this way, but I don't care. I'm not ashamed of how I feel, and I don't care who knows it...".

Thurmond took off his clown wig and nose and spoke tenderly, "I love you, Mona, and I came here to tell you so before I leave. There is no one else for me but you, and although I have given you cause to doubt me, I'm here to tell you that I will do whatever it takes to win you back."

Thurmond then tried to kiss her, but Mona rejected him by turning away. She wanted to believe him, but her doubts about him brought back the pain she had felt when Vikki first told her about his indiscretions.

Grateful that he at least had the opportunity to say his piece, even if it wasn't well received, Thurmond was also relieved that Ehndale's involvement had not been required to do so. He said goodbye and left Monica alone on the balcony.

Leaning on the railing to keep herself steady, Monica sobbed as she looked out over the crowd and saw Ehndale smiling up at her. She decided it was time to leave and quickly exited the balcony. As she descended the stairs, Mona saw Lynn in the main foyer sitting beside a fireplace with Sydney and a suitcase.

"Let's all go home." Monica called out, "… I've had all the drama I can handle for a while."

Lynn picked up the suitcase, Monica put her arm around Sydney to show her support, and the sisters made their way out the door. When they exited the house, Lynn handed her ticket to the valet, and the three sisters waited for their car to be brought around.

Ehndale had followed Monica and was close behind. When he saw them waiting at the valet station, he called out.

"It's terribly disappointing to see three such beautiful ladies so disconsolate…" he began, "It's far too promising an evening for that. Makes me ashamed to think I could have been so derelict in my duties as a host to have allowed such a thing to have happened."

As he approached, Sydney tried to ignore him, but she could feel her blood beginning to boil. She hugged Monica tighter as Lynn addressed him, hoping she could get him to leave them alone.

"I can't say with any certainty, sir, that you haven't contributed to our discontent…" she began, "…but I can certainly say that we do not require any concessions from you. Thank you very much!"

The virulent look on Ehndale's face made Sydney seethe with scorn. As her sisters stood by quietly listening, Sydney screamed, "You have most certainly contributed to my discontent!"

Sydney released Monica's arm and stepped forward to confront him, and continued, "On more than one occasion, you have complimented me and insulted my character in the same sentence! That's a skill I've not experienced before, probably because of my poor choice of men, but you are mistaken if you think I don't know what you meant! You think you're better than me? Better than all of us? Well, you're not! You're just in a position that makes people think you are! You're conceited and smug, and I never want to see you again!"

Ehndale shook his head and replied, "Your words trouble me deeply, my dear, and I am ashamed to think that you feel my intention was to insult you, as indeed it was not. I was merely trying to help."

"Help what?" Sydney screamed in reply, "…help me feel cheap and stupid or unworthy?"

Monica and Lynn questioned the sincerity of Ehndale's contrition, but it was also nothing new for Sydney to fly into a rage and accuse someone unjustly. They knew how volatile their sister could be and were embarrassed for her, but they said nothing for fear of making matters worse.

Ehndale replied, "I was merely trying to explain the anatomy of a gratifying relationship, my dear. From what I understand, that is something you have had trouble with in the past. I was under the impression you wanted to end that string of disappointments?"

"There you go again!" Sydney screamed, "You pretend to help, but then you insult!"

"You misunderstand, my dear…." Ehndale continued, "…my counsel has always been that self-interest is paramount. You must take responsibility for your life and create something that makes you happy. If you choose, you can share it with another, but it must emanate from within. It's not something people give you, or you get from them. You create it yourself; as such, it is not contingent upon having a relationship with me or anyone else. I advise you to examine your soul, find what fuels your joy, and make it so."

Sydney scoffed at his words, but they profoundly affected Monica. Ehndale had inadvertently described her inner conflict as if he knew what she was thinking, and with all the confusion she had been feeling recently, it seemed to be the only clear thought in her head.

The valet brought their car around, and Lynn helped Sydney into the rear seat before getting behind the wheel. Monica slowly got into the back seat with Sydney as she considered what Ehndale had said, wondering if she hadn't figured out how to end the malaise she had been experiencing.

Ehndale could tell that he had struck a chord with Monica and smiled at her as she looked at him. Before the car drove away, he stepped towards it to address her directly.

"Might I suggest, my dear, that you consider examining your soul to find whatever fuels your joy? I humbly offer my assistance if you ever have any difficulty doing so. Just let me know, and I can help you make it so. You know where to find me."

He stepped back away from the car, smiling as Lynn pulled away.

His words resonated with Monica, and she couldn't stop thinking about what he had said. She repeated them in her mind, wondering if she had been wrong about Ehndale all along.

39

Lavishment

Thurmond had returned to Taipei along with the last of the foundry personnel reassigned there and was very optimistic in his assessment of their progress. With the transfer now complete, Vikki was encouraged by Thurmond's report. Still, because Thomas had confirmed the connection between Hunter and Ehndale, Vikki remained concerned about the foundry operation at home during Thurmond's absence.

Hunter seemed to have settled into the routine that Thurmond set up for him and, by all accounts, was progressing quite nicely. He appeared to embrace his new role as foundry foreman pro tem with tenacity, which was encouraging to see. Still, Vikki remained diligent and monitored his activities closely, looking for signs of Ehndale's influence or interference, but saw no unusual activity.

~

Monica's sisters had both gone, but the consequences of their visit lingered long after their departure. One of these was the friendship between Thomas and Jack, who managed to keep in close contact. They frequently spoke and arranged short weekend adventures together when their schedules permitted, which Vikki saw as a welcome distraction for Thomas. It was also an opportunity for Vikki to focus on the foundry during a critical time in the company's history without affecting her relationship with Thomas.

Another was Sydney's remarkable transformation. Humbled by her sisters' concern for her welfare, Sydney regretted her obnoxious behavior and expressed profuse gratitude for their charity. Sydney acknowledged her shortcomings and abandoned her conceit in a sincere effort toward reconciliation. Monica's reaction was strangely tepid, but Lynn was moved by her sister's humility and happily re-engaged in Sydney's life.

The most striking development was probably Monica's sudden interest in Ehndale, a man for whom she had held nothing but contempt in the past but whose words strangely resonated with her. Ehndale seemed to recognize the emptiness of her life and understood how suffocating her tenuous relationship with Thurmond had become. His empathy for her made her wonder if he might have a remedy for that affliction.

Monica resigned herself to the probability that Thurmond may never return, which she debated was even something she desired. She knew he would disapprove of her consorting with Ehndale, but his opinion didn't seem to matter anymore, and now that he was gone, what she did while he was away was no longer any of his concern.

Sydney's disappointing experience made Monica wary of her sisters' opinions, so she avoided sharing her thoughts about Ehndale with either of them. She longed for insight on how to end her malaise and sought counsel from her friend Ronnie, whom Monica believed would be impartial. However, when Ronnie advised her to be cautious of Ehndale, it became apparent to Monica that to engage in what she referred to as her 'pursuit of happiness,' she needed to withdraw from her friends and family and do it on her own.

Consequently, against her better judgment, and the counsel of her friend, Monica decided to explore a relationship with Ehndale. She met with him frequently and listened attentively to his counsel, and the more she heard, the more Ehndale made sense. She slowly embraced his philosophy, which gave Ehndale the power of persuasion over her, and he used that power to convince Monica that she was better off without Thurmond.

"My dear, for some time now, Mr. Joseph has been setting the pace of your life to suit his own purposes ...." Ehndale reasoned, "...and now he wants you to wait for his return? Can't you see he is preventing you from living the life you deserve?"

"If he's important to me, why wouldn't I want to wait for him?" Monica asked, "... it's not like I'm sitting around doing nothing. I'm living my life while he's away."

"True, but what kind of life is that my dear? What do you have to look forward to? Have you considered that Mr. Joseph may see you as a form of security? A backup plan in case he doesn't find anything better while exploring his options in Asia? Have you considered what will happen if Mr. Joseph finds a more suitable companion? If he does, you will transform from an asset into a liability for him and become expendable. Aren't you afraid he may just discard you?"

Ehndale's suggestion shocked Monica since it wasn't in Thurmond's nature to be so cruel. However, she knew that even if it wasn't probable, it was possible, and the idea made her wonder; Why take that chance? Why wait?

"You need something to shake up your everyday life, my dear...." Ehndale told her, "...something exciting, something adventurous! Stop torturing yourself and begin enjoying your life!"

"I'm not sure what you mean?" Monica replied, "...are you telling me to take a vacation or quit my job? What else would I do?"

"Dearest, is there a place you've never been but always wanted to visit?" he asked, "...A place you've dreamed of? Well, I'm saying, go ahead, pull the trigger, and take the trip! What have you got to lose? It may put things in perspective and help you to think! It may even be the very thing that determines the course of your life! Why not? Experience something new and exciting! Take a break from the mundane and live a little!"

It took tremendous convincing to overcome her trepidation, but Monica eventually agreed. When she mentioned she had always wanted to see Paris, Ehndale said he visited Europe frequently for business and invited her to accompany him on his next trip abroad.

"You will absolutely adore Europe, my dear…" he extolled, "…I have business in London and Geneva, where you are welcome to accompany me, but there is no reason why you can't visit Paris while I'm working. If you want, I can arrange for someone to accompany you, then we can meet in your chosen city. Amsterdam, Prague, Budapest, Vienna, Monte Carlo, Venice, Firenze? There are so many options. We should spend a month, at least. It will take that long to experience Barcelona alone!"

Excited but apprehensive, Monica worried about Ehndale's expectations of her being his 'companion.' It was difficult enough to change every aspect of her working life, but she wasn't prepared to abandon her spiritual one. Monica had been raised in a faith that discouraged promiscuity and remained devout in her convictions, so she made it clear to him that their travel arrangements needed to be for separate accommodation in every respect. Ehndale found her orthodoxy amusing and scoffed at her for being old-fashioned but agreed.

Monica had not been away for some time and had no idea where this adventure would lead her, but she wanted to ensure she gave herself enough time to enjoy it. Consequently, she immediately requested all her vacation, which fueled speculation amongst her colleagues about the reason. To avoid gossip, Monica shared nothing of her travel plans and was on a plane headed for Europe before anyone knew it.

~

Monica had only been on a plane once to attend a conference and was awestruck by the first-class arrangements Ehndale had made. When they arrived at Heathrow airport, Ehndale reminded her that he had some business to attend to in London and suggested that rather than waiting for him to finish, she should go with an associate he had arranged to take her anywhere she wished.

As they waited in the lounge for their luggage to be delivered, Ehndale explained.

"My associate is named 'Ganneau,' my dear. A dashing gentleman that knows our plans and will take you wherever you should like."

Monica was excited to see all the places she had only dreamed of, but she was uncomfortable doing it with a man she'd never met. She appreciated Ehndale's attentiveness and replied.

"That is thoughtful of you, Ehndale, but I don't mind waiting. I don't know your associate and am a little uncomfortable being alone with him in a strange place where I don't know anybody. Besides, there's plenty for me to see here in London. I'll be fine on my own until you've finished your business, and then I'll come with you to Geneva and do the same there. I've always wondered what Geneva was like anyway, and now I'll have the opportunity to see for myself. We can go to Paris together afterward."

"Nonsense, my dear…." Ehndale proclaimed, "…Ganneau is a perfect gentleman, whom I'm sure you will come to appreciate once making his acquaintance. He'll be here momentarily with our luggage. Shall I tell him simply to go home? That you refuse his hospitality? He shall be heartbroken, I fear."

"Stop it, Ehndale, he will not…." Monica replied sheepishly, "… he's probably only doing this because you asked him."

"That is most certainly true, my dear, but happily so. Ganneau enjoys being hospitable. It's his 'Thing'".

Just then, the doors to the lounge swung open, and a tall, svelte, handsome man in his early thirties with straight shoulder-length brown hair came in carrying their suitcases. Monica couldn't help but gawk.

"Ganneau, my dear chap! I'm so glad to see you!" Ehndale exclaimed as he stood to welcome his friend.

Although Monica was struck by Ganneau's dashing appearance, she was still against going with him alone through Europe and had to convince herself it was the right thing to do.

"This is the young woman I told you about…." Ehndale explained as he greeted Ganneau.

"Pleasure Ma'am," Ganneau said as he took Monica's hand and kissed it.

"Pleasure's mine...." Monica returned, feeling awkward and unsure of what she should say.

Ganneau held her hand as Monica studied his face, and a brief non-verbal connection ensued between them. Ehndale gave it a few seconds before breaking the silence.

"Excellent!" he began, "...now, why don't we catch a taxi to the hotel, and we can all get acquainted over dinner there after we settle in? I'll join you after I've unpacked and made a few phone calls."

"I took the liberty of reserving the hotel limo...." Ganneau replied, "...I thought you'd prefer it to a cab ride. It's waiting out front to take us back to the hotel. I checked in last night in anticipation of your arrival."

'Splendid, my boy! Splendid indeed!" Ehndale exclaimed and offered Monica his arm as Ganneau picked up their luggage.

It had been a long trip, and Monica was tired, but meeting Ganneau made her more alert. She took Ehndale's arm and walked beside him as Ganneau led them out of the terminal. After a short walk, they spotted a chauffeur waiting beside an elegant, meticulously maintained Rolls Royce. When the chauffeur saw Ganneau, he popped the trunk and helped with their luggage, and the three travelers sat side by side in the back seat.

Monica found her attention divided between the beautiful scenery out her window and the handsome escort accompanying her on her adventure. Ganneau pointed out landmarks along the way and smiled at Monica when he noticed her staring at him.

As they drove, Ehndale suggested a few cities they should consider visiting while he conducted his business in London. He mentioned to Monica that he had residences throughout Europe but insisted that accommodation would be made wherever she wanted. After rattling off half a dozen places Monica had always dreamed of visiting,

Ehndale suggested they start in Paris since she had mentioned it as a place she had always wanted to see.

"I have an apartment off the Champs-Élysées…." Ehndale suggested, "…it overlooks the Arc de Triomphe. You'll love it. You've been there, Ganneau, no? Do you agree that it will be adequate?"

"Certainement!" Ganneau replied gleefully.

Conflicted about what she would do next, Monica ultimately decided that the best thing for her was to go along with the plans Ehndale had arranged for her and trust that he had her best interest at heart. Once Monica agreed, it all became settled. They would stay overnight in London with Ehndale and leave for Paris the following morning.

~

When they arrived at the hotel, a valet opened Monica's door and held her hand to help her out of the limo. Ganneau assisted the bellhop with the luggage, and Ehndale offered his arm to Monica. A concierge greeted Ehndale as if he had seen him only the day before, and they strolled up to the front desk to check into their suite, which Monica was assured was equipped with separate bedrooms for each of them. Ganneau told Ehndale he had made reservations at the restaurant, and the three retired to their separate bedrooms to unpack and prepare themselves for dinner.

The topics of conversation at dinner were varied, but the general theme was the romance of Paris. As the two men elaborated on their experiences, Monica began fantasizing about the kind of man she would marry. She began to imagine what it would be like if Thurmond had been her companion instead of Ganneau or Ehndale. It was her first thought of him since leaving for London, and she wondered if there were any scenarios where he wouldn't be her choice.

When they finished dinner, Ehndale explained his business was scheduled for early the following day and excused himself to retire for the evening.

Ganneau told Monica he was heading to the bar for some aperitifs and invited her to join him. Initially reluctant, she eventually agreed because of his insistence.

"So, with this being your first European experience, would you say thus far that you are impressed?"

"I really couldn't say…." Monica replied, "…with the opulence Mr. Ehndale has shown us, I would say that it was fantastic, even if we were visiting a coal mining town."

Ganneau was amused by her comment, and the two continued to enjoy each other's company as they discussed and joked about their expectations and disappointments. People began retiring for the evening until Monica and Ganneau were the only customers remaining at the bar.

Suddenly, they heard a commotion coming from the main lobby, and Ganneau excused himself to see what was happening. He returned moments later amidst an entourage of exuberant revelers, with his arm around an attractive man that the crowd treated as if he were royalty.

The rowdy group stumbled up to the bar and began shouting random drink orders unruly. Ganneau approached Monica with the gentleman who had been the center of attention for what Monica assumed to be an introduction. He exuded confidence in every way and was obviously a celebrity, but Monica had no idea how to react or what to say and sat wondering what would happen next.

"My sweet…" Ganneau began, "…I would like to introduce you to the world's best formula-one driver, Esteban Sambrosa! Fresh off a victory at le Grand Prix d'Endurance, LeMans!"

Monica was ignorant of formula one racing and had never heard of the man, but she didn't want to embarrass him or herself by saying something inappropriate or insensitive. She thought for a moment while Ganneau espoused the man's accolades and then replied.

"I am honored to meet such an accomplished person such as yourself, but I must admit I've never heard of you."

There ensued a deadening silence as people who had heard Monica's comment waited to see what Estaban's reaction would be, and after a moment that seemed to last for an hour, he began to laugh.

"Maravillosa! ¡Tienes el encanto de una niña querida y la belleza de un ángel!"

Monica had no idea what the man had said, but he seemed unperturbed, even elated by her comment, which was an incredible relief for her. Esteban turned his attention away suddenly to wave to his fans, who erupted in applause after a toast was offered for his victory at LeMans. Monica used this distraction to ask Ganneau if he knew what the man had just said.

"He said you have a child's charm and an angel's beauty."

Esteban turned back to Monica and kissed her hand tenderly, and said, "It is refreshing to meet someone who sees me as a person instead of a celebrity! Makes me feel like a man and not a trophy! Muchas gracias cara bella!"

Esteban then excused himself to join his fans, who summoned him to the other side of the bar. Ganneau sat again beside Monica and began telling stories of the man's accomplishments. As Ganneau spoke, Monica watched Esteban interact with his fans, and she marveled at his poise with such an unruly and obviously intoxicated crowd.

After a few minutes of excitement, Ganneau suggested that the long day ahead required them to retire for the evening. He bid Esteban a good night with a wave and escorted Monica back to their suite. Before she retired to her bedroom, Ganneau tenderly kissed Monica goodnight, which she neither expected nor resisted.

Every aspect of her experience thus far seemed surreal. The plane trip, the limo ride, the lavish hotel, Ganneau, and Esteban. It had been a whirlwind of excitement beyond anything Monica could have imagined, and she went to bed without a thought of home or of Thurmond.

~

Monica was awakened by the morning sun, which dashed through openings in the low but quick clouds running across the English sky. It took a minute for Monica to get her bearings as the beams of light flashed and danced about the unfamiliar room.

She threw on a bathrobe she found draped across the back of a chair beside her bed and walked into the main living room of the suite. The doors to Ehndale and Ganneau's bedrooms were wide open, and they were nowhere to be seen. Monica noticed their beds were both made, so she assumed they had already left the suite.

She returned to her room, showered, dressed, and packed her suitcase before following a porter down to the main lobby, where she saw Ehndale chatting with Ganneau.

Ganneau noticed her and shifted his attention to watching her approach, which alerted Ehndale to her presence. Ehndale said something to Ganneau that caused him to quickly scurry off on some errand and then turned his attention toward Monica. When she was close enough to hear, Ehndale remarked.

"How are we this gorgeous morning, my dear? Are we ready for Paris?"

Monica cheerily replied, "I am well, and I can't wait, thank you!"

"I understand you met Esteban Sambrosa last night, and I was led to believe that he was impressed with you."

Ganneau had obviously told Ehndale of their experience at the bar, and his comment embarrassed Monica enough to prevent her from responding, so when she delayed, Ehndale continued.

"No need to explain yourself, my dear. The man is exquisite in every conceivable way but one, which is why I would like to offer you a word of caution…."

Ehndale smiled as he explained how extraordinarily successful Esteban had been as a Formula-One racer and how he had become decidedly wealthy and powerful. He also explained that although Esteban was wildly popular, he tended to exhibit poor judgment by keeping the company of some nefarious characters, a dangerous remnant of his life before celebrity.

"I tell you this not to dissuade you from keeping his company but to advise you to be wary of doing so without an escort. I can assure you that Ganneau is fully aware of Esteban's tendencies and is equipped to handle any occasion. He will help you steer clear of trouble. Keep him close."

The description of Esteban surprised Monica, as did Ehndale's concern for her welfare. She appreciated his concern and gratefully replied, "Now that I know, I will be sure to keep on my toes; thank you."

Ganneau returned and reminded Monica of their schedule. Ehndale put his hand on Ganneau's shoulder to thank him and said something about keeping his eye on Monica. Ehndale then kissed Monica and said, "Enjoy your time in Paris, my dear!"

The chauffeur held the door for Monica as she and Ganneau got into the dark limousine. Ehndale stood watching them go as they were whisked away on their adventure.

40

Transgression

Ganneau had arranged a private charter for their short flight to Paris, and although he appreciated the level of service they experienced, he treated it as if it were as it should be. Conversely, Monica had never experienced that level of accommodation before and delighted in the comfort and attention her traveling companion had come to expect. It was an incredible experience that Monica knew she would never forget.

They landed just north of Paris at Le Bourget Airport and were accompanied by the pilots to the terminal. After being whisked through customs, a porter had already retrieved their luggage from the plane and escorted them to a nearby taxi stand. The cab driver helped the porter load their bags into the trunk as Ganneau joined Monica in the rear seat.

Monica hadn't eaten since leaving the hotel in London and had mentioned it in passing to Ganneau, who was also famished. Ganneau relayed the urgency of a quick ride to the driver as he gave him the address where they would be staying. With skillful efficiency and alarming speeds, the driver delivered them in short order to their lodgings along the Champs-Élysées.

When they arrived, Monica's heartbeat furiously from the excitement of the drive while Ganneau joked about the driver's navigational aptitude and apparent affinity for speed. The driver unloaded their luggage from the trunk as Monica gathered herself from the harrowing drive.

When Monica managed to calm herself down, she exited the cab and stood motionless in front of what she considered a stunning example of Beaux-Arts architecture. Ganneau sent the driver on his way and noticed Monica gawking at the building. To assure her that this was where they would be staying, he announced, 'Bienvenue chez Ehndale!'

Ganneau gathered their luggage and carried it toward the canopied entrance, with Monica following closely behind, staring at the exquisite structure as she intently studied every magnificent detail.

Numerous cantilevered limestone balconies protruded from the elaborate façade, which boasted ornate and meticulously crafted iron railings. The façade was adorned with pediments, pilasters, cornices, columns, and scrolled brackets, all carved in smooth, neutral-colored limestone.

When they stepped through the threshold into the entry foyer, Monica looked up to see a mosaic-domed ceiling. As they made their way further into the building, Monica noticed a spectacular crystal chandelier hung from a much higher coffered ceiling inside the main hall.

The decoration was elaborate and ubiquitous, and all the interior spaces were separated by graceful, keyed archways. Sculptures of Greek deities on marble pedestals were displayed in stone niches surrounded by swags, medallions, flowers, and shields, all meticulously carved into the limestone walls.

A grand marble stair with a beautiful iron railing floated majestically to the side of the lobby and wrapped back gracefully over the domed foyer. Highly polished black and white marble squares were arranged in a diagonal checkerboard pattern on the floor. Opposite the stairs in the hall was an obscured passenger lift whose only visible sections were shrouded with beautifully ornate ironwork depicting swirling flora and fauna to match the main stair railing.

Their apartment was on the third level of the building. It boasted half a dozen ornate iron-railed balconies that all provided spectacular views of the Arc de Triomphe and the Champs-Élysées. It was airy, full of natural light, and beyond Monica's wildest imagination.

After securing their belongings in the apartment, they walked a short distance to a sidewalk cafe within sight of the Arc de Triomphe. They ate, drank, and talked for hours about everything and nothing at all. Monica rattled off a list of things she wanted to do and places she had wanted to see, and Ganneau told her he would make all the arrangements.

Ganneau was familiar with the language, the city, and the people and was always greeted warmly whenever they stopped to chat with someone. He was a consummate gentleman and a delightful traveling companion who never compromised Monica's confidence in him or made her feel uncomfortable. Still, when he flirted with her in jest, Monica wondered if she would ever have been able to resist him had they been in earnest. The thought was both exciting and frightening.

They spent their days visiting every attraction the city had to offer and their evenings in the Latin quarter enjoying the music and the food. Monica embraced the local Joie de vivre and appreciated each moment she spent there. She had come to Paris to escape the things that distressed her at home, and with each passing day, 'home' faded further from her consciousness. Monica became consumed with the romance that was Paris, with little thought of anything else. She allowed herself to imagine what her life would be like without Thurmond, who now seldom crossed her mind.

The two had been in Paris for about a week when Ehndale called as expected and invited them to join him in Switzerland. When Ehndale had first mentioned Geneva to Monica, she had thought it would be an exciting place to visit, but now that she had become so enthralled with Paris, she had no interest in leaving, at least not just yet.

Ganneau told her she was not compelled to leave and could stay for as long as she liked, but he insisted he must go, which meant she would have to get along without him. It was a difficult choice, but when she considered that she might never have this opportunity again, Monica decided to stay. Ganneau relayed her decision to Ehndale and left that same evening to join him in Switzerland.

Monica initially missed her escort's company, but the fear of being alone quickly waned. She found comfort and confidence in the routine she had established with Ganneau and toured the city during the day before enjoying dinner and drinks in the Latin quarter afterward.

A few evenings after Ganneau's departure, Monica stopped to eat at a restaurant on the Rue Mouffetard, close to some lively nightclubs. She had been there with Ganneau but had always been measured in her enjoyment of the place. That night Monica decided to throw caution to the wind and allow herself to surrender to the moment, as was the 'Joie de Vivre' way.

Sitting at a sidewalk table outside the restaurant, she listened to the music that washed down the street from the nearby club as she watched dozens of bold young lovers pausing to kiss as they flitted in and out of establishments up and down the road. Watching them, her thoughts turned to wild fantasies which included Ganneau, or someone like him.

Monica consumed two bottles of wine before she had finished supper and became tipsy. She thought about ordering a third bottle but reconsidered the wisdom of that decision. After taking a deep breath, Monica closed her eyes and contemplated embracing this as her new way of life.

Listening to the sounds around her, Monica wondered if she could ever return to the pathetic life she had settled for back home. She began drifting off into sleep when she was suddenly awakened by someone violently bumping into her chair. She quickly opened her eyes and saw several young men running away, laughing as they held what looked like her purse.

She checked the back of her chair to find her purse missing, and her euphoria turned to panic as she realized her passport, money, phone, and apartment key were all in that purse. Now that Ganneau had gone, she was lost without it and had no one to help her or any way of getting in touch with anyone who could.

Not knowing what to do next, Monica began to panic and started looking around to ask someone to help her. Seeing no one familiar, she began to chase after the young men when a young woman tapped her on the shoulder.

"Excusez-moi madame, s'il te plait mais nous connaissons-nous?"

Monica was embarrassed by her lack of comprehension and replied, "English, please?"

"Ah, Oui, yes. I was only asking if I knew you. I believe we met in London… I was with Esteban?"

The consumption of alcohol obscured her recollection, and Monica strained to remember. She recalled the evening she had met Estaban, and after a few seconds, the incident at the hotel bar in London clearly popped into her head.

"You were with the crowd of people who came to the bar with Esteban?" Monica asked in a way that made it seem as if she had known him her entire life.

"Oui !" The woman replied excitedly, "…je le connais assez bien et il est là ! Viens avec moi et je te montrerai!"

Monica's face betrayed the fact that she did not understand the young woman who excitedly continued, but in English, "Yes, I was with Estaban, and he is here! Come, I will show you!"

Monica didn't know whether to trust the young Frenchwoman, but she had no other option. She was alone and needed help and would take whatever help she could get. She took the woman's hand and walked down the street to a dark club that blasted music loud enough to make speech difficult, if not impossible.

When they entered the club, Monica could see that the music was being performed by a young group on a stage at the far end of the establishment. The musicians were blurred by the heavy smoke that wafted through the restaurant air, but the sound was amplified loud enough to be felt pulsing in her chest.

Monica was disoriented and still frantic about the theft of her belongings but had no idea what to do next. The young Frenchwoman introduced herself as Layla and took Monica up to a table beside the bar, ordered something from a waiter who was passing by, then said, "I will go find Estaban. He will be happy to see you again…"

The woman quickly disappeared into the crowd, and a bartender delivered a bottle of wine and two glasses to Monica's table moments later. Monica knew she had had too much to drink but sat wondering what else she would do. At that point, it seemed there was nothing else to do but drink while she waited for the Frenchwoman to return.

Monica poured herself a glass of wine, which she drank as she waited for the woman to return with Estaban, a man Monica had only met briefly and knew almost nothing about.

~

Ehndale met Ganneau at a Chateau outside of Geneva and wanted to know about everything that had happened since they had seen each other in London. He was particularly interested in what Monica had been up to in Paris.

As they enjoyed a few drinks in a lounge with an incredible view of the Alps, Ganneau relayed stories of his time together with Monica.

"She loves Paris…." he began, "…the apartment, the ambiance, the sights. We visited every attraction and enjoyed every day, and I was sure to spend our evenings in the Latin Quarter, where we dined at the restaurants you recommended."

"Splendid!" Ehndale remarked, then asked, "Have you heard back from Layla then?"

"I have not, but I left strict instructions with her and expect to hear from her any time now. I am confident in her capabilities; she has never let me down!"

"Well done, my good man! And Layla knows not to mention anything about us, correct?"

"That is correct...." Ganneau replied, "...I spoke with her in London at the hotel bar you recommended. She brought Estaban, as you suggested."

"How did that go?" Ehndale asked with a smile.

"I introduced him to Monica, as you instructed, and she seemed intrigued by him. Actually, if I'm not mistaken, he was also genuinely interested in her...."

"Splendid!" Ehndale remarked as he delighted in the effectiveness of his strategy.

Ganneau continued:

"Layla's been busy babysitting him, and from what I understand, she had no trouble enticing Esteban to stay with her in Paris. They're lodging at the Luxembourg Gardens apartment."

"Well done, my good man! Keep me apprised of the situation. Now that we've come this far, we can't let the fish off the hook. We must keep her engaged, even if I must pay Esteban extra to do it."

~

A gentle breeze carried the smell of coffee and croissants through open windows draped with delicate curtains glowing white from the early morning sun. The billowing fabric muffled the softer sounds of the coming day, but a sudden blast from a passing vehicle abruptly disturbed Monica's pleasant slumber and rudely awakened her.

Monica rubbed her eyes to help open them and looked slowly around the room. As the dullness of her faculties sharpened, Monica sat up suddenly and didn't recognize her surroundings. She strained through a throbbing headache to remember what she had done and where she could be. As she tried to remember the events from the previous evening, a knock came at the bedroom door, which confirmed that she wasn't alone.

"I'll be there in a minute, thank you…" she replied politely as she inspected the nightgown she wore, without any memory of putting any of it on.

She hopped out of bed, pulled the billowing curtains aside to get an idea of where she could be, and recognized the expansive garden surrounded by magnificent buildings as the Luxembourg Gardens she remembered visiting with Ganneau.

An unfamiliar voice rang out from behind the door in a language she didn't understand.

"Hermosa mañana mujer encantadora!"

She glanced around the room in search of her clothing but found none. The knock came again at the door, and she feared whomever it was would not just go away. She adjusted her nightgown and opened the door.

"Buenos días mi amor!"

It was Esteban Sambrosa, the decidedly handsome celebrity she had met in London, and he was standing in front of her in nothing but a pair of undershorts.

"Good morning…" was all Monica could say as she desperately tried to reconstruct the events of the previous evening to help her understand the predicament she now found herself in.

"¿Tienes hambre? Si… Would you like something to eat?" the handsome Spaniard asked. He stepped up to her, put his hand around her waist, pulled her tight to himself with one hand, and gently kissed her lips as he caressed her face.

Monica could feel her heartbeat accelerating and began to panic. She wanted to scream or run away, but she had no idea what had happened or how she had come to be in the situation she presently found herself in. When she didn't answer his question, he asked her again, and she nervously answered.

"I am hungry, yes."

"Ciertamente!" Estaban replied as he pulled Monica tight, kissed her again quickly, and released her. He whirled across the room as he continued, "...your clothes are in the armoire, Mon Cheri. I will throw something on, and we can follow our noses to a boulangerie for some croissants. ¿Suena Bien?"

Before she could even answer him, he was gone. The door closed behind him, and she ran to the armoire to retrieve her clothes. She quickly changed and threw the nightgown on the bed as she desperately tried to remember the events of the previous evening. She looked around for her purse and remembered that it had been stolen. Then she remembered the young Frenchwoman who had taken her to the nightclub to meet Esteban, but everything else was a blur. She speculated about what could have happened to cause her to be where she presently found herself. She wondered if anything had happened between them, and worried she had done something she couldn't undo. She sat on the edge of the bed searching for an answer, and Esteban returned fully dressed moments later.

"Where shall we go?" he began, "...follow our noses to a boulangerie or follow our fancy somewhere else?"

Monica felt his question had a sinister intention, and she immediately became uncomfortable. She desperately wanted to leave but needed to know what had happened. She decided to prolong their interaction in the hopes that she could derive the events of the previous evening from their continued conversation.

"Boulangerie sounds nice..." she replied, "... let's just follow our noses."

"Bon choix!" he replied with a noticeable Spanish accent and held out his hand to take hers as he held the door open for them to leave.

Although Esteban was the kind of man she had always dreamed of, Monica feared she had made a terrible mistake. It was not in her nature to throw caution to the wind and live with the consequences. She had always been measured in her decisions, but she suddenly found herself in a strange place with a strange man, with no money, no passport, and no keys to her apartment. She had no friends nearby and no way to get home.

Feeling abandoned, vulnerable, and afraid, Monica had no idea what she had done or what this man expected. The city that had so enthralled her suddenly lost all its charm. As she walked through the beautiful gardens with Esteban, she wished she was home. She would give anything to have her sisters with her or for Ronnie to be waiting for her at the boulangerie. She wanted the lonesomeness she felt to go away, but most of all, she wished Thurmond was there.

About the Author

Since childhood, Denis has been interested in the creative arts. As a youth, he was engaged in the performing arts at his parents' insistence but preferred exploring his creativity visually. He studied Architecture and Art and was rewarded with a nomination as an Outstanding Emerging Artist. After receiving numerous commissions as a Fine Artist, he ventured into Architecture as an occupation, where he worked in various capacities on distinctive and exciting projects in the US and abroad.

Denis has also been fortunate enough to have had the opportunity to travel and be actively involved in some notable historical events. These experiences exposed him to intelligent, engaging, and influential people with diverse ideologies, some of whom he disagreed with but respected.

Following his creative instincts, Denis ventured into the written word as a vehicle for artistic expression after creating a bedtime story for his daughters. Once he developed an affinity for it, he began writing the Lost to Heaven trilogy to continue to express himself creatively.